In Plain Sight

MARION TODD

In plain sight

CANELO

First published in the United Kingdom in 2020 by Canelo

This edition published in the United Kingdom in 2020 by

Canelo Digital Publishing Limited
Third Floor, 20 Mortimer Street
London W1T 3JW
United Kingdom

A CIP catalogue record for this book is available from the British Library.

Print ISBN 978 1 78863 819 7
Ebook ISBN 978 1 78863 748 0

Look for more great books at www.canelo.co

Printed and bound in Great Britain by Clays Ltd, Elcograf S.p.A.

For Graeme,
who would have spotted all the mistakes

Sunday, 22 September

Chapter 1

'It's like this, Detective Sergeant West: either you take your trousers off now or I'll take them off for you.'

Chris West glanced at his boss. 'I think you'll find you can't order me around, Clare. We're not on duty now.'

'And I think you'll find I can put you on the traffic rota for the next month.'

Chris scowled at a Lycra-clad runner who elbowed her way past him to the start line.

Clare waited. 'Well?'

'You wouldn't…'

'Try me.'

Reluctantly, Chris West unzipped a pair of navy-blue Adidas trousers, pulling them off over his feet with some difficulty.

Clare appraised her DS's white legs. 'Flipping heck, Chris. When did those legs last see some sun?'

Chris did his best to look offended. 'We can't all go jetting off to the south of France on fat inspector's salaries, you know.'

'You calling me fat?'

Chris handed his trousers to a young girl seated at a desk with dozens of plastic boxes behind. 'Seventy-three,' the girl said. She handed him a numbered token and put his trousers in the corresponding box.

Chris took the token and zipped it into a pocket in his shorts.

Clare observed this, noting the shorts were straining at the waist. 'You really need to lose some weight, Chris. When was the last time you went for a run?'

He pulled his T-shirt out of his shorts to cover his gut. 'I'll get back to the gym. I just haven't had time lately.'

'Yeah, right.'

'So, how was the holiday? Good time?' Chris said, deflecting the conversation away from his bulging waist-line.

Clare tried not to smile but she couldn't help it. 'I've had worse.'

'You and the sculptor still on, then?'

'I am still seeing Geoffrey, yes.'

The crowd of runners began moving slowly along the West Sands towards the start line. Ahead of them lay a stretch of silver sand, almost two miles long, the freezing waters of the North Sea to the east. The midday sun glinted off the waves, which were dancing in the gentle breeze. Clare was glad to see the tide was well out. It would be far easier running on the hard sand. As they fell into step with the other runners she looked over the dunes to the west, where the famous Old Course lay. The dunes obscured her view of the fairway but, on a Sunday, she knew the golfers, with their gaudy sweaters and oversized golf bags, would be absent. It was the one day of the week when the course was open for tourists to wander and explore.

The runners in front came to a halt. Clare craned her neck and estimated there were fifty or sixty ahead of her. She wondered if she could work her way up to the front.

Something caught her eye and she turned, squinting into the sun. A uniformed PC was waving at them from the sand dunes. 'Oh, there's Sara,' she said.

Chris turned to see PC Sara Stapleton and a smile spread across his face.

Clare saw this and nudged him with her elbow. 'You two still an item, I take it?'

'Mm–hm.'

Clare gave Sara a wave and thought how happy she looked. She glanced back at Chris. She was fond of him but was he really was right for Sara? 'You see you don't break that girl's heart,' she said, 'or you'll have me to answer to.'

Chris was prevented from answering by a garbled announcement over a megaphone.

'It's about to start,' Clare said. 'Come on. Let's get up to the front.'

Chris stepped to the side to allow a clutch of pink-shirted men to pass him. 'My lace is loose. I'll just…'

Clare scowled back at him as she was carried along with the pink shirts. 'You'd better not duck out,' she shouted.

He responded by cupping a hand to his ear as if he hadn't heard, before the crowd swallowed him.

Typical. Clare knew he hadn't done any training.

Looking along the dunes, she saw Jim, her uniformed sergeant, smiling and waving from the side. He wasn't in uniform today, of course. Still signed off work. He was shouting something but it was lost on the wind. She shook her head to indicate she hadn't heard.

'Good luck, Clare,' he shouted again. 'And thanks.'

Clare gave him a thumbs-up. 'Is Mary with you?'

Jim shook his head. 'A bit tired today, you know. But she's so grateful to you all for the sponsorship money. Means a lot.'

A klaxon sounded, disturbing the herring gulls. They soared upwards and out towards the sea, screeching in protest. Clare gave Jim another thumbs-up and moved back into the sea of runners. She glanced over her shoulder and saw them snaking along the beach behind her. There must be two hundred of them, at least. The dunes were lined with spectators and she suddenly felt outstandingly happy.

The queue had stopped again now and she became aware of some movement among the spectators, a bit beyond the start line. 'They'll be knocked over if they're not careful,' she said to her neighbour, a girl of about eighteen who was jumping up and down on the spot, clearly impatient to be off.

And then they were shifting forward again, funnelling towards the start line, as the overhead digital clock came to life. But almost as soon as they started to move, they came to an abrupt halt. Clare bumped into a tall man in front of her but managed to steady herself. There were shouts and some swearing, and she strained to make out the instructions being given via the megaphone. She looked over to Jim who was walking quickly along the grassy bank to the start line. Clare ducked out of the queue of runners, jogging up and onto the bank.

'What's going on, Jim?'

'Bloody protesters. Must be thirty of them at least. Lying down right across the beach.'

The race forgotten, Clare scanned the beach for Chris but he was nowhere in sight. From her vantage point on the bank she could see the start line. The runners' progress was blocked by around thirty men and women in green T-shirts, lying down on the sand. They were chatting amiably among themselves, with the odd apologetic gesture to the organisers. The runners, now stuck in a bottleneck beneath the overhead clock, were remonstrating with them, to little effect. Clare looked back along the dunes and could just make out Sara, talking to someone, probably Chris. Putting two fingers in her mouth, she gave a piercing whistle. Sara put up a hand up to shield her eyes from the sun and Clare waved her arm. When Sara began running towards her, Clare ran back down onto the sand and forced her way through to the head of the race. The organisers were arguing with the protesters who wore T-shirts, emblazoned with a tree logo and the letters NEFEW.

'What the hell's NEFEW?' Clare called to Jim, but his answer was lost in the clamour. She saw two uniformed officers approaching and ran across to them. 'Get onto whoever's manning the station. Tell them we need another six bodies and a couple of vans, just in case. We'll get this lot shifted so the race can carry on.'

Sara arrived; Clare motioned to her and the other officers to follow. She moved to the start line and commandeered the megaphone. She introduced herself in the hope that the presence of a Detective Inspector would carry some weight. 'Would you all please move to the side to allow the race to proceed?'

The protesters laughed at this and there was more swearing from the runners, impatient to be off. The clock was showing two minutes now, and counting.

An elderly man with a shock of white hair eased himself up to his feet, wiping sand from his hands, and approached Clare. She saw that, as well as his green T-shirt, he wore faded brown corduroy trousers and a pair of well-used trail shoes.

'Detective Inspector,' he began. 'We represent NEFEW—'

Clare cut across him. 'I can see that, sir. What's this all about?'

'McIntosh Water. You've doubtless heard they plan to build a bottled water plant on Priory Marsh. Are you familiar with the area?'

The name didn't immediately ring a bell. 'No, sir, I'm not. But I do know that you're—'

'Priory Marsh is home to several rare examples of lichens, and provides a haven for wildlife. To threaten this in the name of plastics production is something we cannot allow.'

There was a ripple of applause from the protesters, some offering '*hear hears*'.

Clare regarded them, unimpressed. 'I appreciate that but you're disrupting a charitable event here.'

'An event which is sponsored – unsurprisingly – by McIntosh Water,' the man continued. 'Call me cynical, Detective Inspector, but it wouldn't be the first time a business tried to buy goodwill through philanthropy. They think if they donate a few hundred bottles of water and a box of medals, people will forget the damage they do.'

Across the dunes, Clare could see the first of the police cars approaching. Then she saw the photographer from the Fife Newsday website. He recognised Clare and pointed his camera.

'Don't you dare!' she warned him. 'We've enough to do here without you splashing us all over the Internet.'

The cars were coming closer now and she could see a police van a short distance behind. She turned back to the man. 'I'm guessing you don't have a permit for this protest.'

The cars drew to a halt on the other side of the dunes. Doors slammed and a small group of uniformed officers began making their way towards the protest. Clare glared at him. 'Do you?'

'I'm sure you are aware, Inspector, that the right to peaceful protest is enshrined in law.' He smiled and Clare felt her patience evaporating.

'Very well. My officers will shortly assist your group across the sands, away from the start of the race, where you can continue your protest.'

The white-haired man opened his mouth to speak, but was forestalled by an ear-piercing scream. It came from somewhere behind Clare, further down the queue of runners and spectators. She turned to see a woman a short distance away, one hand on a pram handle. She was in her early thirties, Clare thought. Her hair, dark with blonde highlights, was scraped back in a doughnut bun, accentuating her heavily tinted eyebrows. Her head jerked back and forth as she looked all round. Her magenta lips were opening and closing but no words were coming out. And then, finally, she found her voice, the words a strangled cry.

'My baby. Someone's taken my baby.'

Chapter 2

They stood, huddled together, the woman joined by a man now – the baby's father, Clare assumed. Were they married? The woman's hand was still on the pram and Clare's eye went to a platinum band on her ring finger. She noticed they had matching tattoos on their arms. A name – beginning with A, she thought – with a collection of little hearts surrounding it. The woman seemed frozen while the man's eyes flicked left and right, as though struggling to take in the events unfolding around them.

They mumbled in response to Clare's gentle prompts for information. The baby was a girl. Six months old. When Clare asked what the baby was wearing, they looked at each other for a moment, confusion in their eyes. Then:

'Pink,' the man said. 'Pink sleepsuit.'

'Red rosebuds on it,' the woman said.

'Any distinguishing features?'

The man's face clouded. 'Eh?'

'Hair, teeth. That sort of thing,' Clare said.

The woman said, 'Tooth. She has one tooth. In the front. Just through.'

'And her neck,' the man said. 'Small birthmark. Sort of purple.'

'This is really helpful,' Clare said, writing in a notebook borrowed from Sara. 'Erm, which side of her neck?'

'Left,' the woman said and she lifted her hand, indicating the spot on her own neck.

The sun had gone behind a cloud and the woman began to shiver. The man lifted a blanket from the pram and put it round her shoulders. She looked at him then down at the blanket and clutched it round her front.

Another police van came to a halt on the road close to the start of the race, and disgorged four uniformed officers. Clare waved at them and they ran across.

'More on the way,' one of them said. 'Want this lot shifted?' He indicated the green-shirted protesters, now on their feet, looking shamefaced.

'Hold them here for now and keep an eye on them. I want every last one of them spoken to,' Clare said. 'Meantime, we've a missing baby.' She held out her hand. 'Your radio, please.'

The officer handed over his radio and Clare was soon issuing instructions to the control rooms in Glenrothes and Dundee. 'We're probably too late now but I want every car leaving town searched. We're looking for a six-month-old female baby, pink sleepsuit with red rosebuds, a single bottom tooth and small birthmark on the left side of her neck.'

A second van drew up and Clare set about directing the officers. 'Interview everyone; I don't care if they saw anything or not. Names and addresses. Ask if they saw anyone hanging around who didn't look like a runner or a spectator. Anyone who didn't fit in.' Clare turned to Sara, whose face was chalk white. 'Sara, I want the parents taken home. Stick to them like glue. Keep the pram here. SOCO will need to process it.'

Sara didn't respond, her hand over her mouth, as if she might be sick.

'Sara! Missing baby – do your job.'

She shivered involuntarily. 'Sorry boss. It's just – well, a baby – who would do this?'

'Detach, Sara, and quickly. Get the parents home and I'll join you as soon as I can.'

Clare watched the young PC lead the parents to a waiting car and hoped she was up to the job of dealing with them. Chris jogged up, having retrieved his trousers.

'Chris, can you arrange for a Family Liaison Officer? As soon as I'm done here you and I will follow Sara to the parents' house. And, when you've done that, get onto the Dog Unit. See how many dogs we can get out within the hour.' She pointed in the direction of the town, south of the beach. 'I want dogs all over this part of the beach. Start them at the rocks and work north, along the dunes and west to the hotel.'

'Even the golf course?'

'It's a missing baby, Chris. I want every inch combed, so get as many dogs and cops as you can lay your hands on. Any problems, refer them to me.'

The grey-haired protester was standing, waiting to speak to her. 'Inspector,' he began, 'my volunteers are at your disposal. If we can help at all...'

Clare looked at him. His face was lined with worry and his concern seemed genuine. But she simply didn't have time to direct a group of amateurs, especially with the disruption they had just caused. 'Does it occur to you, sir,' she began, 'that by disrupting the race, you made it easier for this baby to be abducted?'

The man swallowed and moistened his lips. 'Oh, but…'

Clare felt a stab of guilt. 'Look, sir, I know you mean well, but unless you saw the abductor, I doubt you can help.'

Chris appeared at her side. 'Dog Unit alerted. More cops coming from Dundee and Cupar.' He checked his watch. 'Cupar lot should be here in about twenty minutes. Dundee probably another ten minutes behind them.'

Clare nodded. 'Thanks, Chris.'

The runners were becoming restive, some rubbing their arms to keep warm. Others were queueing at a burger van which was parked on the road behind the dunes.

Chris nodded towards them. 'Please tell me you don't want all the runners interviewed?' He indicated the crowd. 'We don't have the manpower.'

He was right. There were hundreds of runners, thirty-odd protesters, the distraught parents to support and a baby to find.

'Fair enough, Chris. Just names and addresses for now – unless they saw anything.'

Jim appeared, his face creased with worry. 'Is it right, Clare? A baby's been taken?'

'Afraid so, Jim.'

'Right,' he said, 'tell me what you want done.'

'You're still on compassionate leave. Go home and look after Mary.'

Jim shook his head. 'How do you think she'd feel, knowing I wasn't out helping find the wee soul? You can count me back to work, as of now.'

12

Clare smiled at him. 'Oh, Jim. I'd love to turn you down, I really would. But the truth is I could do with your help.'

'Right. I'll take the uniforms from the vans and start with the runners. They'll be getting cold, hanging about.'

Another group of uniformed officers appeared. Clare scanned them, assessing their numbers, and decided she had enough to begin interviewing the protesters. 'You six,' she said, 'take the protesters. Don't waste time, though. Names, addresses and, unless they saw something, get them out of here.'

'Is it likely they were part of a diversion?' one of the uniforms said. 'Make it easier to snatch the kid?'

'Highly unlikely. But if anyone does strike you as odd, give me a shout.'

The six officers headed off to begin interviews and Clare turned to the remaining cops. 'I want a search of the dunes, the road, the car park and the golf course beyond. The Dog Unit will be here shortly. Start up at the rocks and fan out across the road, covering the golf course.' She glanced at Chris. 'Golf course sorted?'

He nodded. 'This end's clear now and they've taped it off to prevent more tourists wandering over. It'll take a bit longer to clear the far end, though.'

Clare looked along the beach to the point where the North Sea became the Eden Estuary and the golf course ended. 'It's unlikely anyone out that way would have seen anything. And someone snatching a baby would be too visible out on the course.'

Chris followed her gaze, along the dunes. He seemed lost in thought for a moment, then he nodded. 'What next?'

Clare fished a numbered token out of the pocket of her shorts. 'Come on. Let's get my stuff back then we'll speak to the parents.'

Chapter 3

Kevin and Lisa Mitchell lived in a modern, detached villa on the outskirts of St Andrews. From the outside it seemed to be one of the larger properties with a well-kept garden to the front, laid out with grass and shrubs. The Mitchells had the corner site, giving their house more ground than the others on the street. A red Audi A3 and a black Volkswagen Arteon sat on a hardstanding at the front of the house.

'Whatever they do, it obviously pays well,' Chris said as he climbed out of the car.

Clare took in the rest of the street. 'Is this anywhere near the protesters' camp?'

'Not far. It's about a mile north of here. The group have said they'll stay until the council change their minds about the development.'

'When did all this happen?'

'About ten days ago, I think. Not long after you went off to France.'

'Can't turn my bloody back for a second,' Clare said. She started walking up the drive, then stopped. 'That protest, Chris…'

'Yeah?'

'Convenient for whoever snatched the baby, wasn't it?'

'I suppose. But it couldn't have been planned as a diversion. Surely you don't think that? All these people – in league with a baby snatcher?'

Clare's brow creased for a few seconds. 'No, I doubt it very much. But it was a gift to whoever took the baby, wasn't it? Put yourself in the abductor's shoes: you see a pram, wonder if you might have the opportunity and suddenly the protest kicks off and it's all confusion. It must have been the perfect diversion. Everyone's looking at the protesters and he – or she – takes their chance.'

'You think it was a spur of the moment thing?' Chris asked.

Clare hesitated. 'I'm not sure. If we're talking about someone who desperately wants a baby, then maybe. They see a baby and they're overcome with the need to hold it and it goes too far. I can only hope it's someone like that who's taken her.'

'And you're thinking...'

'Chris, you don't need me to tell you why babies are taken. People – abusers – they hang around family events. They're experts at finding places where children gather.' She shivered involuntarily and shook her head. The prospect of a baby being taken to be abused was chilling. She looked at the house and thought of the couple inside, almost certainly distraught. Her chest felt as if there was a lead weight pressing on it. The worst part of the job by miles. She took a couple of breaths to steady her nerves, then said, 'Come on. Let's get on with it. See what they can tell us.'

Sara met them at the door. Clare was glad to see the colour was back in her cheeks.

'How are they?' Clare asked, her voice low.

'As you'd expect. Frantic.'

Clare followed Sara into a large sitting room. It was comfortably furnished without being cluttered. On one wall there was a large TV screen, while the other walls were hung with photos, many of a smiling baby, the latest ones showing a single tooth in an otherwise gummy smile. The baby's presence was everywhere – toys, a changing mat, an open pack of nappies, a baby gym. Clare took it all in with a practised eye. There was money here, too. Not super rich, but the ornaments were expensive, the sofas large, real leather, and the carpets soft underfoot.

The baby's parents sat together on one of the sofas. Clare scrutinised them. She decided her earlier assessment was correct. Late twenties or early thirties at most. They both wore jeans but none of your Primark bargains. Lisa's top was Fred Perry and Kevin's Hugo Boss. Yes, there was money here, all right. Lisa's eyes were swollen and she was shaking. Kevin had his arms around her.

'I've called their GP,' Sara whispered.

Clare nodded. 'Hot sweet tea,' she said.

Sara left the room in search of the kitchen.

Clare sat down opposite the couple. 'Mr and Mrs Mitchell, I'm Detective Inspector Clare Mackay and this is Detective Sergeant Chris West. Let me say, first of all, we have every available officer out looking for your baby…'

'Abigail. We call her Abi.' Lisa dabbed her eyes with a crumpled tissue.

'Abi. We have alerted our colleagues in Dundee and across Fife and they've put everything on hold to search for her.'

'You'll find her though, won't you?' Kevin this time, his eyes pleading.

Clare avoided the question. 'I just want to go over what you told me earlier. At the beach.' She offered what she hoped was a reassuring smile then checked her notebook. 'Now, you said Abi is six months old?'

'That's right. Six months last Thursday.' Lisa fished in her pocket and produced a rose-gold iPhone. 'I'll get a photo.'

'She's wee though, isn't she, Lisa?' Kevin said.

'Oh yeah. Quite small for her age. Dinky, my sister says.' Lisa swiped the screen then held it out for Clare to see, her hand shaking. A tiny face swathed in frothy pink beamed back at her.

Clare studied the pair and concluded Kevin was coping better than his wife. She wrote a phone number on the back of a business card and handed it to him. 'Could you forward maybe three or four good photos to this number please, Kevin? We'll get them circulated and on the news.'

Kevin stared.

'Now please, Kevin,' Clare said, her tone still gentle, but insistent. 'Every minute counts.'

Kevin took Lisa's phone from her. Clare saw that Lisa was still shivering and she glanced round the room. Her eyes fell on a red chenille throw draped over an easy chair and she rose from her seat to fetch it. She put it round Lisa's shoulders but she barely seemed to notice.

'Tell Sara to hurry up with that tea,' she said quietly to Chris, and he left the room. Then she sat back down opposite the pair and continued. 'Now, you said Abi was wearing a pink sleepsuit with red rosebuds. Is that correct?'

'Present from one of the neighbours,' Kevin said, his voice flat.

'And under the sleepsuit?'

'White top. Hello Kitty.'

'Hat at all?'

'Yeah, same as the T-shirt. Hello Kitty.'

'Eyes?'

'Blue. Like Lisa's.'

'Hair?'

'Not much. A bit of blonde on top. Bald patch at the back. Where she sleeps, you know?'

Clare scribbled this down, nodding.

'She had a bib on too,' Lisa said suddenly. 'A green one, I think.'

'Over the sleepsuit?'

Lisa nodded. 'She's teething, you see. Dribbles a lot so the suit gets wet. Makes her chin sore.' She said, 'Will they know that? Whoever's got her?'

'That's the photos sent,' Kevin said. 'Lisa took one of her this morning when we were getting ready to go out – the fun run, you know. I've sent you that one. Shows the sleepsuit.' A spasm of pain crossed his face at the mention of the run. He put Lisa's phone down on a glass-topped coffee table and rose suddenly from the sofa. 'I can't sit here waiting. I'm away out to look for her.'

Sara opened the door and held it for Chris, who walked in carrying a tray of mugs and a packet of biscuits. Clare stood too and put a hand on Kevin's arm, gentle but firm. 'You need to leave that to us, sir. You're needed here.'

Kevin put his head in his hands. 'I'm her dad. If anyone finds her it should be me.'

Clare led him gently back to his seat. 'As soon as we find Abi, you'll have her back. I promise. But for now, Lisa needs you here. She needs you to be strong.'

Kevin sat down reluctantly and took his wife's hand.

Chris cleared his throat. 'Is there – is there someone we could call? To be with you both? Parents, maybe? You shouldn't be here alone.'

Lisa shook her head.

Kevin said, 'Lisa's mum – they don't get on. Haven't spoken for years.'

'You don't think maybe…?' Clare began.

'No!' Lisa pulled the chenille throw tightly round herself. 'I don't want them here.'

Clare glanced at Chris. 'Okay, that's fine.'

'There's Ashley,' Kevin said.

'Ashley?'

'Lisa's sister. Ashley McCann. Lives in the town.'

Clare looked at Lisa.

Lisa avoided her eyes. 'No. She's – busy. We'll manage.'

Clare and Chris exchanged glances.

'Maybe just tell us where she lives then, Lisa. We can call in for a quick word.'

Lisa reeled off the address then said, 'But she won't know anything.'

Clare watched Lisa carefully, wondering what she had meant. Was there some problem between the sisters? 'That's okay, Lisa. We'll just let her know what we're doing. That sort of thing.'

Kevin cleared his throat. 'Ashley – well, she sometimes takes stuff. Pills and that. She's not always with it, you know?'

Clare glanced at Chris again, then turned back to Kevin. 'Okay, Kevin. Thanks for that. Is there anyone we can call for you?'

He shook his head. 'My mum died a few years ago. Dunno where my dad is.'

Clare thought of her own family. Her doting parents. Too doting, most of the time. Her sister Jude – they were so close. She couldn't imagine facing something like this without their support. Poor Lisa and Kevin. She wondered if the estrangement was connected to Abi's abduction. Grandparents prevented from seeing their granddaughter. She hoped that would turn out to be the case. Far more straightforward than an unknown abductor. 'If you could just give me their names,' she said. 'We won't approach them unless it's absolutely necessary.'

Lisa scowled and said nothing. Kevin glanced at her then reeled off the names, which Chris wrote down.

Clare waited while he did this then said, 'And I'll need both your mobile numbers too, please. I have to make you aware that we'll be listening in to any calls you make and receive.'

Kevin gaped. 'You're – you're going to bug our calls?'

Clare nodded. 'The chances are Abi's been taken by someone who just wants a baby. Maybe a mum who's lost one of her own. Usually, in these cases, the baby is returned within a few days. It's highly unlikely this is a ransom situation but, if a call does come in, we'll hear everything that's said.'

Kevin and Lisa looked at each other but said nothing.

'We won't be interested in anything personal,' Clare went on. 'I can assure you both of that. But we do need to monitor all calls, in and out.' She paused to let that sink in then went on. 'Our techy guys will arrange to send you a piece of software to install.'

Kevin was still frowning. 'Then what?'

'The software alerts us when a call is made and it immediately places a call to a phone at our end, activating the microphone. We can then listen in to the conversation. It's not the most sophisticated solution but it's something we can do quickly.' She gave what she hoped was an encouraging smile. 'Is that okay?'

They nodded. 'Suppose,' Lisa said. 'But will they know? I mean, if the person who has Abi calls us, will they know you're listening? They might hurt her – if they hear…'

Clare shook her head. 'They won't know unless you say something to give it away. So, if a call does come in, act as naturally as you can. Pretty difficult, I know. Just tell them you want Abi back and see what they say.'

Clare paused to let this sink in. Then she said, 'Are you both up to answering a few more questions?'

Lisa looked at Kevin. He took her hand and said, 'Yeah.'

'Okay.' Clare pressed on. 'What time did you arrive at the fun run?'

'Just before the start,' Lisa said. 'Maybe ten minutes before, I think.'

'So, about ten to twelve,' Clare said, scribbling in her notebook.

'Yeah, I think so. About that.'

'Thanks, Lisa. That's great. Now think back, see if you can remember. Who was standing beside you?'

Lisa turned to Kevin again. 'I can't think. Can you?'

'Some teenagers, I think.'

'Boys or girls?'

Kevin thought. 'Girls mainly. Might have been a few boys. I – I can't remember.'

'Okay. Anyone behind you?'

He looked blank. 'Not sure. Don't think I noticed.'

Clare went on. 'Can you recall how you were standing? Side by side? Or one behind the other?'

Lisa closed her eyes. Then she said, 'I was on the left, Kevin a little behind me. It was a bit of a squeeze.'

'And the pram?'

Lisa's head lowered and she started to sob. She dabbed her eyes again with the tissue, then raised her head. 'I was afraid she'd get squashed or the pram bumped by the runners so I put it over to the side, away from the crowd. Just by the dunes. I mean, I could still see it but I wasn't beside it. She had just fallen asleep, you see, so I didn't want to lift her.'

'And when was the last time you saw her in the pram?'

Lisa thought. 'Maybe five to twelve – I think. Yeah, about then. She was girning a bit. Unsettled, you know. I jiggled the pram, and when she started to fall asleep, I moved away. Sometimes she sleeps better when I'm not close by.'

'And when did you realise she was gone?'

'Just after the race started. I heard that horn. A few of the spectators were going back and forward to the burger van and I said to Kevin we should have one.'

'And then I said we should have ordered a pizza,' Kevin added.

'Ordered a pizza?' Chris repeated. 'At midday?'

'Yeah,' Kevin said. 'There was a pizza delivery bike heading away, towards the main road. Next to the golf links, you know? Somebody must have phoned for a pizza.'

The doctor arrived and administered a sedative to Lisa Mitchell. Kevin waved away the offer of something to help him sleep.

'She needs me,' he told the doctor. 'Abi. I need to be ready for her – when you find her.'

'You need to leave it to us, Kevin,' Clare said. 'I understand you want to go out there and look for Abi yourself, but we know what we're doing.'

Kevin looked at Clare. 'Have you had your baby stolen, Inspector?'

Clare said nothing.

'Thought not. Then, with respect, you don't have a fucking clue.'

'All the same. Please, will you leave it to us?'

The doctor said, 'There is something else. Lisa, did you give Abi her medicine this morning?'

The colour drained from Lisa's face and she leapt to her feet. 'Her medicine! Oh my God. Her medicine!'

Kevin was on his feet too. 'We have to find her. We *have* to!'

Clare looked at the doctor. 'Medicine?'

'Lisa, Kevin,' he began, 'please don't panic. Now think: did you give her a dose this morning?'

Lisa was crying again now. 'I don't know. I can't think…'

The doctor took hold of Lisa's hands. 'Focus, Lisa. Close your eyes and think back. When do you usually give Abi her morning dose?'

Lisa bent her head to think. Then she said, 'Yes! Yes I did. Same as usual, with her morning feed.'

'So she isn't due another dose until tonight?'

Lisa looked at Kevin and he nodded.

'Now, she can miss tonight's dose,' the doctor went on, 'and probably tomorrow as well without any lasting damage.'

Clare could stand it no longer. 'What medicine? What does Abi need medicine for?'

Lisa was sobbing loudly now, her head buried in Kevin's chest.

'Abi has a congenital heart defect,' the doctor explained. 'She needs digoxin twice a day.'

Clare's mind was a whirl. Baby abductions were rare these days, but more often than not the abductor was someone who would love and take care of the baby. This changed everything. It meant little Abi could be in real danger, even if she had been taken by someone who would look after her. They had to find her in time. 'We'll put out a press release. Suggest the baby is brought to a hospital.'

They were prevented from further discussion by the arrival of the Family Liaison Officer, a blonde PC in her early forties.

'This is Wendy,' Clare said to the couple. 'She'll stay with you for as long as you need her and she'll keep in regular touch. You can call Wendy any time, day or night. And we'll station someone at the front door. Make sure you're not bothered.'

With Wendy installed, Clare, Chris and Sara left the room, closing the door quietly behind them.

'Get round the neighbours, Sara,' Clare said. 'See if there's been anything untoward over the past few weeks. See what they think of the Mitchells.'

'Will do, boss.'

Sara headed out to speak to neighbours while Clare and Chris went upstairs for a look round.

'If necessary, we'll come back with a few more bodies and do a thorough search,' she said. 'But, for now, just look for anything unusual; or something that might give us a clue as to why Abi was taken.'

Lisa and Kevin's bedroom was painted dove-grey with dark red curtains and bedding. There was an assortment of cushions on the bed and two tall table lamps stood like sentries on low bedside cabinets. On the wall opposite the bed was a cot, the wooden spars painted in different pastel hues. The covers were folded back and a small toy giraffe was tucked into the corner. Along the wall opposite the window were mirrored wardrobes. Clare pushed gently on one of the doors and it slid back noiselessly to reveal neat rails and shelves of clothes and shoes.

'We'll leave these for now,' she said. 'Just go through bedside drawers, the dressing table – that sort of thing.' She put a hand on the wardrobe door to close it then stopped. Something had caught her eye. She bent down and retrieved a small parcel of pink tissue paper which she unfolded carefully. A tiny gold heart on a chain. She held it out for Chris to see. 'What do you make of this?'

'Nice. Where was it?'

'Tucked inside one of her shoes.'

'Bit odd.'

'Isn't it? Especially as there's a jewellery case on the dressing table.'

'So why hide it?'

Clare folded the tissue paper up and replaced it in the shoe. 'So Kevin doesn't find it.'

'Want to ask her about it?'

Clare considered. 'Not just now. It's probably nothing to do with Abi's abduction and it might just add to their distress.'

'Okay.'

They carried on working through the bedroom but found nothing that seemed significant. Clare rose from looking under the bed. 'Come on. Let's investigate the other rooms.'

The room next to the Mitchells' bedroom was sparsely furnished. There were two single beds with pale blue duvets, a bedside table between them.

'Spare room,' Clare said, and Chris nodded his agreement.

The next door led to a smaller room, furnished only with an exercise bike and an elliptical trainer.

'They like their fitness,' Chris observed, closing the door behind them. 'The best of stuff, too.' He followed Clare towards a door at the end of the upstairs hall. A wooden carved hot-air balloon brightly painted with the name *ABIGAIL* hung on the outside of the door. Clare turned the handle and switched on the light. The room was a sea of pink and lilac. Fairy lights were draped along one wall with a baby changing unit below. The other walls were decorated with bright acrylic paintings of circus performers, and a matching mobile hung from the ceiling. A chest of drawers stood next to the changing unit and four tell-tale indentations in the carpet showed this was where the cot had stood before Abi's arrival must have prompted the Mitchells to move it into their bedroom.

'Right. The sooner we get started...' Clare moved to the chest of drawers and began sifting through tiny vests, sleepsuits and cardigans while Chris investigated the changing unit.

It didn't take long to complete the search.

'Come on,' Clare said. 'There's nothing here. Let's see if Sara's had any luck with the neighbours.'

As she moved to the door, she saw a bottle of digoxin on a small shelf and she was suddenly aware of how little time they had to find Abi.

–

The doctor was closing his case as Clare put her head round the door.

'We'll be back to see you again,' she told the Mitchells. 'Meantime, if you think of anything – anything at all – just let Wendy know.'

They emerged into the quiet street. The police car parked outside the Mitchells' house had drawn a few neighbours to their windows but there was no sign of Sara. As they stood, taking in the surroundings, the doctor came out of the house. Clare approached him as he made for his car. 'Realistically, Doctor, how long do we have to find the baby?'

The doctor's expression was grave. 'It could be as little as forty-eight hours,' he said. 'Longer if we're lucky, but without digoxin in the correct dose she could suffer heart failure, slip into a coma and die. I suggest you throw everything at this, Inspector. And soon.'

Chapter 4

Ashley McCann lived in the ground-floor flat of a 1960s-built block, just off Albany Park near the East Sands Leisure Centre. Chris drove slowly along while Clare looked for house numbers. The nearby car park at the leisure centre was busy with swimmers arriving and leaving while small groups of students, some in their traditional red gowns, were walking to and from a block of flats. Beyond the leisure centre lay the North Sea and round the coast on an elevated site the Kinkell Braes caravan park.

'Take a right here,' Clare said suddenly, 'then left.'

Chris crawled along until they were outside Ashley's flat and he drew into the kerb to park.

'She's landed lucky with a flat here,' Clare said, taking in the street as they walked up the path. 'Nice outlook.'

'Suppose.'

Clare rang the bell. When there was no response she knocked on the door and rattled the letterbox. 'Check the back,' she said to Chris, and he strode off round the side of the block.

He returned, shaking his head. 'No sign of life. I reckon she's out.'

'Okay. Let's try the neighbours. You take left, I'll go right.'

Clare knocked on a fairly new glass-fronted door and, after a few minutes, a young lad of about fifteen appeared in boxers and a T-shirt, yawning widely. Clare showed him her badge and asked about Ashley.

The lad rubbed his eyes. 'No idea. Don't see her around much.'

'Is anyone else at home?'

He shook his head. 'Gone shopping.'

Clare asked when they would be back and he shrugged.

She saw Chris waiting and she thanked the lad for his time.

'Any luck?'

'Nope. No one at home.'

'Or they're not answering.'

'Yeah, could be.'

'Get on the radio,' Clare said, clicking to unlock the car. 'I want a check run on Ashley McCann. See if she has any pre-cons and post someone outside her flat.' She put the key in the ignition. 'I want to know the minute she gets back.'

–

The police station car park to the side of the low red-brick building was mercifully quiet when Clare and Chris drew in. But she knew if they didn't find Abi within the next twenty-four hours, the car park would be overflowing, the station swollen by reinforcements from neighbouring stations, to say nothing of the inevitable press pack. The magnitude of the task facing her was not lost on Clare. A missing person was bad enough but a missing baby – and one with a heart defect – was something else altogether.

She could only hope someone would spot the baby before the night was out.

'Nothing from the road blocks,' Jim said, as Clare and Chris entered the station. She thought how odd it was to see Jim behind the public enquiry desk, out of uniform. She should send him home, really. Home to his sick wife Mary. But at that moment, Clare knew she needed every officer she could lay her hands on. Experience told her if they didn't find Abi within the first twenty-four hours, the chances of returning her to her parents safe and well would be greatly reduced.

'They're still checking,' Jim went on, 'but the baby's probably well away by now.'

'What about the dogs?'

Jim shook his head. 'The search team's still out on the golf course but it's not looking hopeful. Been through the bins as well.'

'Any luck with the burger van, Jim?'

'Interviewed the couple who own it. They didn't see anything.'

'Okay, Jim. Thanks.' Clare suddenly remembered what the Mitchells had said about a pizza delivery bike. 'Jim – could you check if any pizza companies were at the West Sands on Sunday?'

'Pizza? At the fun run?'

'Yes. You didn't see them?'

'No. Just the burger van. But I can phone round if you want?'

'If you could. It was probably just one of the drivers on his way to work. Stopped in to watch the start of the race.'

'I'll check it anyway.'

Clare smiled at her sergeant. Nothing was ever too much trouble for Jim. 'Just a couple more things, Jim – could you get me the press officer on the phone? I need to put something out urgently. And when you've done that, can you trace Kevin Mitchell's dad? His mum died a few years ago. He says he doesn't know where his dad is.'

'Aye, no problem, Clare. What about the baby's mum?'

'Yes, her parents too, please. She was very definite she didn't want her mum contacted and that makes me suspicious.'

'Okay, Clare. Any pointers as to where they are?'

'None. But Chris has a note of their names. So let's check our own records first. If they've not come to our attention, go through the usual channels – voter's role, phone book etc. Worst case, we can try the Registrar General in the morning but ideally we need to get onto it quicker than that.'

Jim noted this down then picked up the phone.

Clare turned to Chris. 'Can you call Tech Support, please? Get that bit of spyware sent to Kevin and Lisa's phones. Let them know it's two iPhones – in case it matters. And warn Wendy when it's being sent so she can make sure they install it properly.'

As Chris went to call Tech Support, Clare saw Jim signalling. She took the phone from him and began to explain the situation to the press officer. 'The baby needs prescription medication – digoxin. It's not available over the counter so it's vital the abductor leaves the baby at a hospital where she can be cared for properly. The usual stuff about treating the abductor with compassion and so on.'

The phone call done, Clare sought out Jim again. 'Any joy with the interviews?'

'Nothing so far. The cops in the incident room are running names through the Police National Computer just now so we'll soon know if any of them have pre-cons.'

'Has anyone spoken to our eco-warrior? I'd like to see to him myself, as soon as possible. Make absolutely sure he's not linked to Abi's abduction.'

'He's come in, voluntarily. Wants to do whatever he can to help. Seems like a genuine enough guy.'

'Yeah, they always do, Jim.'

Jim made no reply to this.

'Where is he?' Clare asked.

'Interview room.'

'Okay. And the camp? What's the deal with that?'

'I think Sara attended about a week ago. Spoke to them all. She said they seemed nice enough but determined not to shift.'

'Who owns the land?'

'It's McIntosh Water now. They bought it from the farmer about six months ago. They have planning permission for a bottled water plant. From what I can gather, the protesters are an environmental group, opposed to the development of the land. Plus they're not happy about the idea of more plastic bottles.'

Clare's lips tightened. 'Is that so?'

'It's a fair point,' Jim said. 'Plastic pollution is a huge problem now.'

'Doesn't give them the right to occupy private land without permission. What's more, without their diversion and the confusion it caused, that baby might not have been taken. We need to be absolutely sure the two incidents aren't connected.' She nodded to Chris. 'Come on. Let's see what he has to say for himself.'

–

Nicholas Stewart was quite different from the protesters Clare had dealt with on marches and demonstrations. He was sixty at least and she had the impression, from the way he spoke, that he came from an academic background. He seemed to weigh her questions and gave his answers willingly, admitting his part in disrupting the fun run.

'Sometimes you have to take action if the cause justifies it,' he said. 'But I am sorry that the runners were disappointed today.'

'It's a little more than that,' Clare said, levelly, trying to hold on to her temper. 'Quite apart from the funds this race would have raised for a most deserving charity, you created a diversion that facilitated the abduction of a baby. A baby which, if it does not receive the correct medication within the next two days, could die. So tell me, Mr Stewart, how the cause justifies that.'

He stared and seemed momentarily lost for words. He ran a hand through his hair then said, 'But I had no idea. How could I have known? No one could have known.'

Clare returned his gaze. 'No. That's quite correct. You couldn't have known. But it does mean it's vital we find the baby without delay.'

'Then ask me anything you wish, Inspector.'

Clare gave a curt nod then said, 'Tell me about the protest.'

'Of course. My wife and I planned it when we learned McIntosh Water were to sponsor the race.'

'Who else knew?'

'No one, until this morning. I told the others to be ready for something on Sunday morning, but that's all. If news of the protest had leaked out, McIntosh would have had security guards at the race, so secrecy was vital. I told the others to wear their NEFEW T-shirts under their sports tops. We didn't want to reveal who we were until the last minute.'

'NEFEW?'

'Ah, my apologies. North-East Fife Environment Watch.'

Clare wrote this down. 'And how did they know where to come?'

'We met at the aquarium, just round from the West Sands, about an hour before the race. I explained the plan and told them to make their way to the start line and to jog about as if they were runners. A few minutes before the race started, we pulled off the sports tops to show our T-shirts and, as the klaxon sounded, we lay down in the path of the runners.'

'And no one else knew of your plans? Did your wife tell anyone?'

'No. Like me, she knows the importance of keeping our plans secret until the last minute. I gather she's given a statement to your colleagues. I can give you her mobile number if that would help.'

Clare waved the offer away and asked instead if he had seen anyone acting suspiciously. He spread his hands in response.

'I wish I could say I had, Inspector. But I was entirely focused on making the protest as effective as possible.'

'How well do you know the other protesters?' Chris asked.

Nicholas Stewart considered this. 'Some, I've known for most of my life. Others I met through work or friends of friends.'

'Do any of them strike you as different?' Chris continued.

'In what way?'

'Maybe not as committed as the others; or too committed.'

He sat back in his seat, pressing his hands together as he considered this. And then he said, 'You are thinking, Sergeant, that one of our group may be connected to the abduction?'

'Probably not,' Chris conceded. 'But we do need to consider all possibilities.'

'I understand. But I fear I can't help. There is no one who particularly stands out, as you suggest.'

This was getting them nowhere. Clare scraped her chair back. 'Thank you for your time, Mr Stewart. We'll be in touch if there's anything further.'

He took the cue and rose from his seat. 'I am truly sorry about the baby and I hope you find her soon. My heart goes out to the parents.'

Clare forced a smile. 'Thank you, Mr Stewart. We appreciate your co-operation.'

He stood, pulling on his jacket, and seemed keen to linger. Clare started for the door but, when he spoke again, she paused.

'May I ask, Inspector, if you are the officer who so bravely tackled the gunman over at Mortaine Castle a few months back?'

Clare was momentarily disarmed. Then she gave a brief nod and moved to the door, reaching for the handle.

He followed her, saying, 'Then I must commend you for your bravery. I think also, if what I read in the newspaper is correct, that you must know my good friend, Geoffrey Dark? He's a sculpture expert. I gather he assisted you in identifying Mortaine Castle from photographs of the interior?'

Clare stopped in her tracks again. 'You know Mr Dark?'

'Oh, yes. Very well. I used to lecture in Fine Art, you see, before I retired. Geoff was one of my most promising students. I knew he'd do well. You were fortunate to have his assistance.'

'We were.' She smiled again. 'Thank you for your time, Mr Stewart. We'll be in touch if we need anything else.'

–

Jim motioned to Clare as she left the room. 'Press Office been on the phone. They want you to do a TV interview and they're sending an outside broadcast crew over to the West Sands now.'

Clare groaned inwardly. She loathed being on camera. But it had to be done. They needed maximum publicity if they were to have any chance of finding Abi. 'Okay, Jim. I'll call them now.'

The press officer talked Clare through her script before she set off for the beach. She parked just outside the search area and spoke to a uniformed cop manning the cordon. 'TV crew?'

'Down on the beach, boss,' he said, indicating the nearest footpath across the dunes.

Clare made her way over the wooden boards and down onto the soft sand. The tide had turned and was creeping up the beach now. The wind, which had been a welcome breeze earlier in the day, had become blustery and cold. She saw the TV crew and made her way across the beach towards them. As the wind whipped round her face, Clare searched in her pocket for a hair-tie which she used to scrape her hair back into a ponytail. She introduced herself to the crew. They were just four – a reporter, cameraman and a couple of technicians. She discussed what she wanted to say with the reporter and, after a few tests runs, the recording began. She described the sleepsuit Abi had been wearing that morning, holding up a print of the photo Kevin had given her to illustrate this. She went on to mention Abi's solitary front tooth, her eyes and the birthmark on her neck. And then the reporter prompted Clare about Abi's medical condition.

Clare looked directly at the camera. 'Whoever took Abi is probably a very caring person. If you are that person I want to appeal to you now to take her to the nearest hospital and leave her with staff. You don't need to say anything or tell the staff who you are. Abi has a congenital heart defect and needs medicine called digoxin twice a day. You cannot buy this medicine over the counter. It is only available on prescription. Abi may look healthy enough just now but, without this medicine, her condition will deteriorate quickly. Please, whoever you are, return Abi to us so we can make sure she gets the medication she needs.'

The reporter then concluded the piece, giving a number to call with any information. When the filming was done, she thanked Clare.

'How quickly can you have it out?'

'Within a couple of hours, hopefully. Three at the most. We'll run it on all our news bulletins.'

Clare thanked the crew and headed back over the dunes to her car. The search team was packing up now, the cops climbing into a fleet of minibuses, the dogs back in their vans. Clare was glad to get into the car and turned on the heater. She executed a quick three-point turn and headed back to the station where she found the press camped out. As she opened the car door they clamoured round, and she did her best to push through them.

'Have you found the baby, Inspector?' one of them called.

'How are the parents holding up?' another asked.

She turned as she reached the station door. 'Rest assured, ladies and gents, as soon as we have any information, we'll let you know.' And, with that, she escaped indoors.

'Any news?' she asked Sara, who was manning the desk.

'Nothing concrete,' she said. 'A few false alarms.'

'But you're checking them all out?'

'Yep. Mostly crying babies neighbours hadn't noticed before.'

'Cheers for that, Sara. I'm just going to check my emails then I'll catch up with you on the Mitchells' neighbours. Briefing in the big room, ten minutes. Pass the word around.'

Clare went to her office and powered up her computer. As she waited for it to come to life she took out her mobile phone and checked for messages. Two. Both from Geoffrey. She swiped to read:

Fancy an end of holiday dinner tonight?

My treat?

The second message read:

> I'm guessing you're knee-deep in holiday washing.
> Message if you can make dinner. I miss you already x
> PS How was the fun run? Personal best time?

The fun run! It seemed so long ago now. She sighed. Dinner with Geoffrey would have been lovely. She sent back a quick message saying something had come up. She added a line of X's at the end and put her phone back in her pocket.

The computer came to life and she clicked to open her email, groaning as her inbox loaded. One hundred and twelve. Most of them rubbish, probably. She scrolled quickly down, looking for anything of interest. One marked *Urgent* caught her eye – a drugs death while she was away. She opened the email and scanned it quickly. Another youngster. A schoolgirl this time. Just sixteen. What a waste. She jotted this down on her notepad to check with the drugs team. See if there were any new suppliers in town.

There was another message that stuck out. From the Assistant Chief Constable. Something about improving relations between police and the media.

'That'll be the day,' she muttered, highlighting the email to read later.

Chapter 5

The incident room, normally home to no more than five or six cops at a time, was more crowded than Clare had ever seen it. Phone calls had gone out to anyone on a day off and, to a man, they had come in prepared to work as long as necessary. In spite of the seriousness of Abi Mitchell's plight, Clare felt a rush of pride at this response. They might be a set of moaning buggers at times but, when they were really needed, there was no finer bunch than the cops squeezed into this packed room.

Half a dozen extra desks had been unearthed from the store and were occupied now by officers sitting back-to-back, some in uniform, others in plain clothes. Suit jackets had been cast aside in the stuffy atmosphere, and the air hung with the combined odour of sweaty bodies and Pot Noodles. There was a low-level hum from the computers and laptops, punctuated by conversations on mobile phones and across desks. The window blinds had been closed against prying eyes and the room was bathed in the glare of artificial light. Clare took it all in and, for a moment, was transported back to her days in the busy Maryhill Road station in Glasgow. And then she saw the photo. Pinned on the wall, next to the whiteboard. A smiling, single-toothed baby – Abigail Mitchell. A stark reminder of why they were here.

She stood by the photo of Abigail, waiting for the hubbub to die down, the phone calls to end. They were an assorted bunch. Male, mostly; maybe a third of them female; all ages, stages, shapes and sizes. The chatter subsided and they turned to face her.

'Thanks, everyone. I won't keep you long. For those of you who don't know me, I'm DI Clare Mackay. I'll be heading up this enquiry, until we're allocated a DCI.'

There were a few polite smiles and Clare pressed on.

'First of all, I'd like to welcome our colleagues from other stations. I realise it's a bit more cramped here than you're used to but we're so close to the parents' house, it makes sense to be here.'

There were nods and murmurs of agreement.

She turned to the wall and indicated the photo of Abi. 'Abigail Mitchell. Six months old. Has one front tooth and a birthmark on the left side of her neck.' She paused for a moment then went on. 'Complicating factor is she needs a medication called digoxin twice a day to correct a heart defect. Without it, she will die.'

'How soon?' Jim asked.

'Not sure, but the doctor thought anything more than forty-eight hours could be dangerous. So it goes without saying that we throw everything we have at this. A baby's life is in danger.'

Heads shook and someone said, 'Chrissake.'

'Quite. Now, we don't know if Abi has been taken for ransom or if there's another motive for her abduction. So we'll be following the standard Child Rescue Alert procedure in the first instance. Any questions?'

No one spoke and Clare continued. 'Runners and protesters. Where are we with those?'

A stocky detective in his early forties raised a hand and Clare averted her eyes from the damp patch under his arm.

'All been interviewed, boss. Janey and I' – he indicated a blonde officer across the desk – 'we're running names through the PNC. Nothing yet.'

'And you are?'

'Bill, boss. From Dundee Bell Street.' He nodded again at the blonde. 'That's Janey.'

'Thanks, both.' Clare scanned the room again. 'Who's updating HOLMES?'

A dark-haired woman in a grey suit raised her hand to indicate she was updating the Home Office database. 'Nita,' she said. 'From Cupar.'

'Right, Nita – thanks.' Clare nodded at her then went on. 'Anyone on social media?'

Two female uniformed officers raised their hands. 'Erin and Liv, boss,' one of them said. 'From Glenrothes.'

Clare smiled. 'Okay, guys. Make sure you have COSAIN installed on your laptops.' She saw a few blank faces around the room. 'Software for monitoring social media platforms,' she explained. 'It'll save you hours trawling through nonsense so, if you don't have it, get it installed ASAP. Any problems, get onto Diane down at Tech Support and she'll give you the download key.'

Bill raised his hand again. 'What about registered sex offenders?'

'Definitely.' Clare hesitated, then carried on. 'We can't ignore the possibility that Abigail Mitchell may have been taken to be abused.' She paused to let this sink in. A few heads were shaking.

'Jesus,' someone said. 'Six months.'

'I know,' Clare said. 'It doesn't bear thinking about – only, we have to think about it. So, volunteers to check up on registered offenders?'

Three hands shot up and Clare nodded in acknowledgement.

'Strictly by the book, mind,' she added. 'We're all desperate to find that baby but I don't want any complaints of heavy-handedness and I especially don't want any evidence ending up inadmissible because we haven't followed procedures. Okay?'

The cops who had volunteered nodded and she added, 'Ten-mile radius for starters.'

Janey's hand went up again. 'Boss – could other children be in danger? If the baby has been taken by paedophiles?'

'Sadly, Janey, it's a possibility. But I don't want to cause the Mitchells any more anguish than they're already experiencing. So, we say nothing about possible sex abuse to anyone outside this room. Every parent in the country will be keeping a close eye on their children now. It's a natural response to something like this, so I think we can avoid spelling it out to the press in the meantime. I hope we're all clear on that?' She looked round the room and there were nods and mutters of 'Yes, boss.'

Clare let that sink in then she said, 'Now, the next bit's more sensitive. We need to check anyone who's had a baby die recently. So that means cot deaths, stillbirths, late miscarriages or late terminations. Anyone who might be grieving for the baby they should have had. I need volunteers to contact local GP practices and hospitals.'

Janey raised her hand. 'Bill and I could do that. We're nearly through that list of runners and protesters.'

Clare smiled at them. 'Thanks, both. Now, once we have a list we'll divide them up. It's a sensitive area and ideally I'd like promoted officers to handle these enquiries. Whoever does it, remember we have Standard Operating Procedures for dealing with this type of investigation. The handbook's online. Check the guidelines, and use them.' She hesitated for a moment. 'There's no getting away from the nature of this case. A six-month-old baby has been taken from her pram in broad daylight. She has the potential to become ill very quickly. So we need to get out there and find her. But the people you will interview could be as distressed as Abi's parents. Perhaps more so. And, as unlikely as it might seem, one of them could have Abi. Someone does. So you need to go gently, but firmly. We don't want anyone scared but we do want information. And fast.'

'What sort of information are we after?' one of the uniforms asked.

'Movements on Sunday morning and since. Look round the houses for any signs of a new baby. But bear in mind if they bought baby stuff for a new arrival they may still have it sitting out. It's not toys and cots you're looking for, more used bibs, bottles, a changing mat, an open pack of nappies – that sort of thing. If you have grounds for suspicion, ask to have a general look round. Check the washing line for baby clothes, bins for dirty nappies. But – and I can't stress this enough – go gently.' She looked round to make sure the message had hit home then turned to Janey whose hand was raised again.

'What's the family set-up, boss?'

45

Clare said, 'Kevin and Lisa Mitchell. A married couple in their early thirties. They're distraught, as you can imagine.'

'No indication of an inside job?' Janey asked.

'No, I don't think so. Nice house, quite close to here. They seem to have money but not enough for a kidnap from what Chris and I could see. No sign that they want to involve the press so my gut instinct is to rule them out of it. Either way, we need to look into their background for any clues as to why Abi's been taken.' She scanned the room. 'Who's running the Police National Computer check on the Mitchells?'

Nita raised her hand. 'Me, boss. They're clean.'

'Okay, thanks Nita. Jim – any luck with Kevin and Lisa's parents?'

Jim shook his head. 'No convictions or cautions. Still looking for addresses.'

'Pass that to Nita then please,' Clare said. 'Give her what you've got so far.'

Nita and Jim exchanged nods and Clare pressed on.

'What about neighbours, Sara?' she asked, scouting the room until she saw her PC.

'Nothing much. Mostly keep themselves to themselves. One said Lisa could be a bit sharp but they all seem to like Kevin.'

'Okay, thanks Sara. Can you give the neighbours' details to Nita as well, please? PNC check, Nita. Anything at all – complaints, noisy parties, disturbances. If anyone so much as raised a voice to the Mitchells, I want to know about it.'

Sara indicated she would and Nita scribbled this down on her notepad. Clare eyed Sara. Normally so alert and keen, but now she just looked tired. This case seemed to have hit her hard. Best keep her busy. 'Sara, can you go through prison releases for, let's say two months? Especially anyone with child-related convictions.'

'Sure, boss.'

'Any other family we should be looking at?' Bill asked.

'Yes. Lisa has a sister – Ashley McCann. Chris and I called at her house but no one was at home.'

'I'm pretty sure I jailed her,' Liv said. 'Down in Glenrothes. She assaulted her boyfriend's ex. Did time for it, I think.'

'She did,' Erin said. 'I remember it. A bit more than an assault. She stalked and threatened her. Made the girl's life a misery and finally gave her a kicking. I think she got a year, probably served half that.'

Clare glanced at Chris. 'Did you run a check on Ashley? Please tell me you did that while I was doing the TV interview?'

Liv raised a hand. 'Sorry, boss. DS West asked me to do it. I'm on it now.'

Clare's lips tightened and she shot Chris a look. Then she turned back to Liv. 'Quick as you can, please, Liv. Do we have a uniform outside her flat?'

Jim raised his hand. 'Sent young Gary. He called in about half an hour ago. No sign of her yet.'

Nita raised her hand again. 'What about the Family Liaison Officer?'

'Wendy Briggs is acting as FLO to the Mitchells,' Clare said. 'She's experienced and tactful. She also has a sharp pair of eyes so she's a good person to have in the family home. If there's anything going on, she'll spot it. And, if we need to do a full search of the house, she'll keep them occupied.'

Clare went on. 'Chris, do we have monitoring of the parents' phones set up yet?'

Chris eased himself off a desk and took a phone from his pocket. 'Yep, done now. Wendy called half an hour ago to confirm.' He turned to face the room. 'Kevin and Lisa's phones have had a bit of spyware installed. Basically, when the phone is used, it comes through to this handset as well. So we can listen in on any calls, in or out.'

'What sort of calls are we looking for?' Sara asked.

Chris looked at Clare. 'Boss?'

'To be honest, Sara,' Clare said, 'I'm not sure. The Mitchells seem pretty well off for a young couple but not the kind of money a kidnapper might try and extort. On the other hand, if Abi was taken because of something they've said or done, or something they know, we might just get a clue from their calls.' Clare's eye fell on Jim. 'Can you co-ordinate monitoring of the phone, please, Jim? We need someone on it, day and night.'

Jim indicated he would do this. 'What about laptops?' he asked.

Clare looked at Chris. 'Dammit. Forgot to check.'

'It's okay,' he said. 'Wendy's sorted it. Just the one laptop between them. She had a cop call round for it while you were at the beach. Should be at Tech Support by now.'

Clare smiled. She had a good team round her, despite Chris's occasional tendency to offload the more tedious tasks to colleagues. She checked her notepad and saw the word *pizzas*. 'Pizza bikes, Jim – anything?'

'Sorry, Clare, I forgot to say. No pizza delivery company sent an order to the West Sands on Sunday.

Most of them don't start delivering much before two in the afternoon.'

Clare looked round the room. 'Right. So I need someone to phone the pizza companies back. I want the names and addresses of the delivery staff plus the rotas for Sunday, including any last-minute swaps. We need to know why a pizza bike was at the West Sands on Sunday at midday.'

'Could just be someone watching the race,' Sara said. 'Maybe a friend was running.'

'Almost certainly,' Clare said. 'But we can't leave it to chance.'

Jenny, a Detective Sergeant from Dundee, indicated she would look into that.

Clare smiled at Jenny then went on. 'Okay, last thing: I need a couple of bodies to get onto Kevin and Lisa's phone records. Texts and calls in the last four weeks, please.' She looked round the room and nodded at Robbie and Gillian, both uniformed cops, who had raised their hands. 'Okay,' she said. 'That's it. Let's reconvene at six tonight. Good luck, guys. Keep in touch.' The room began to hum with chatter again, as the cops went about their duties. Clare watched Chris follow Sara towards a vacant desk; but before Sara could sit, he put a hand on her shoulder. Sara turned and they stood talking. Then she sat down at the desk, pulling a computer keyboard towards her. Chris ambled back.

'Ready, boss?'

She raised an eyebrow.

'What?'

'Nothing. It'll keep. Come on – let's see how the parents are now.'

Wendy met them at the door. She stepped outside, pulling the front door closed behind her. 'They've had a visitor.'

'Who?'

'The sister.'

'Ashley?'

'Yeah, that's her.'

'We've been trying to get hold of her. Is she still here?'

'No. Left about half an hour ago.'

'Stay long?'

'About twenty minutes.'

Clare hovered on the doorstep. 'Chris,' she said, lowering her voice, 'check with young Gary to see if Ashley's come back home. Let me know right away if she has.'

Chris went back to the car to make the call while Clare and Wendy went into the front room. Kevin was still sitting on the sofa, twisting a tiny pink Babygro suit in his hands. There was an ashtray full of dog-ends on the coffee table and the smell of tobacco smoke hung in the air, catching in Clare's throat. There was no sign of Lisa. Clare looked at Wendy, who jerked her head upwards. Clare looked towards the stairs and Wendy took her cue. 'I'll just...' And she left the room in search of Lisa.

Clare sat down. 'Hello, Kevin. How are you holding up?'

He glanced at her, his face blotchy, eyes pink. 'Dunno. Okay, I suppose. No news?'

Clare shook her head. 'You'll be the first to know, I promise. We've circulated Abi's photo to all the newspapers, and her abduction will be on the national news tonight.'

Lisa trudged back in. She looked faintly annoyed. 'Can't even have a pee in peace,' she said, throwing Wendy a look.

'Actually,' Wendy said, 'I might just go myself. All these cups of tea… Do you mind?'

Lisa flicked her hand in assent and Wendy left the room. Chris appeared and joined Clare on the sofa. She glanced at him and he gave a slight shake of his head.

Clare turned back to Lisa. 'I was just telling Kevin that we'll have Abi's photo on the front page of every newspaper tomorrow morning and she'll be on the national news tonight.'

'Right.'

'I'd like to get some background information on you both,' Clare went on. 'It's possible that someone you know might have taken Abi, either to get back at you for something or simply because they wanted a baby.'

'Get back at us for what?' Lisa snapped. 'You saying we've done something to deserve this? Like it's our fault?'

'Of course not, Lisa. But you never know; there's a chance you might be working with someone who's involved with Abi's abductors. Maybe you mentioned you were going to the fun run and they saw an opportunity. You can't tell who you're mixing with these days. So the sooner we can rule out your own contacts, the sooner we'll find the real culprit.'

Lisa picked up her cigarettes and lit one. She held the pack out to Kevin, but he waved it away.

'You know I don't like you smoking with Abi in the house.'

'She's not in the fucking house, in case you hadn't noticed.' She drew on the cigarette then scowled at Kevin. 'Dipshit!'

Kevin started to cry again. Clare wondered at the change in Lisa, so broken and bereft just a few hours ago and now fighting mad. Was this a mother's instinct kicking in? Perhaps it was worth speaking to the doctor again.

'Listen,' she said, 'I understand this is a dreadful time for you both. But the sooner we have the information we need, the quicker we can give you some space.'

Lisa drew deeply on her cigarette again and exhaled. She seemed calmer now. 'Sorry,' she said. 'It's just…'

'I know. No need to apologise. Maybe you could start by telling me where you work, Lisa? Or are you a stay-at-home mum?'

'Tanning salon. Woodburn Place. Bronzalite, it's called.'

'I know it. I reckon Chris here could do with a few sessions.'

Chris took his cue. 'Yeah, you're not wrong. Worked there long, Lisa?'

'About three years. Just afternoons through the week. Sometimes do the odd evening or weekend. Just depends.'

'Who looks after Abi when you're there?'

'My sister sometimes. Mostly she goes to Wee Tots Daycare just along the road.'

Chris noted this down.

'Get on okay with the others in the salon?' Clare asked.

'Yeah. I'm usually there by myself, though,' she said. 'It doesn't take a lot to run a tanning salon. Just get them to sign in, take the money, that sort of thing.'

'Lonely?'

'Not really. I have the radio and my magazines.'

Clare said, 'If you give me the manager's name and number we'll let them know you'll not be in tomorrow.'

Lisa picked up her phone from the coffee table and swiped until she found the details. 'Her name's Sacha.' She held the phone out for Clare to see, adding, 'She's the owner.'

Clare noted down the number then turned to Kevin. 'And you, Kevin? Do you work?'

'Groundsman at Melville College. Private school, a mile or so out of town.'

'Been there long?'

'About a year.'

'Nice place to work?'

'Aye, sometimes. Some of the kids can be a bit snobby. Staff too, but the other gardeners are all right.'

'What did you do before that?' Chris asked.

'On the rigs. Lost my job when the oil prices dropped. Then Abi was on the way and I didn't want to be away from her for weeks at a time.' Kevin drew a hand across his eyes and Lisa threw him a look. She stubbed out her cigarette and went to take another from the pack.

'Again, if you let us know who to contact we'll tell them you won't be in tomorrow.'

'Aye, sure.' Kevin reeled off the name and number from memory and Clare noted them down.

'Is there anyone you noticed recently – anyone taking a particular interest in Abi? Hanging about the street, looking in the pram, that sort of thing?'

Lisa shrugged. 'Don't think so. Maybe worth asking the Wee Tots staff but I don't remember anything like that.'

'Anyone you've fallen out with recently? Neighbours, anyone at work?'

'Nope.'

Clare looked at Kevin. He glanced at his wife then shook his head.

'I don't know why you're asking us all these questions anyway,' Lisa said. 'Should you not be out there finding Abi?'

'Rest assured, Lisa, we have every available officer working on this. We just need to be thorough. Sometimes a bit of background information can point us in the right direction.'

'Sorry.' She raised her eyes to meet Clare's. 'I'm not normally like this.'

Clare rose. 'No need to apologise. I think you're holding up remarkably well. Both of you.' She smiled at them and Kevin attempted a watery smile in return. 'And if there's anything else you remember, let Wendy know. She'll stay with you until this evening and she'll be back in the morning. I'll leave an officer outside your door overnight. Keep the press away.'

'Thanks,' Lisa muttered. She stood up. 'I'll see you out.'

'I'll do it,' Wendy said to her. 'You sit tight.'

Wendy came out into the garden with Clare and Chris. 'She's got another mobile,' she told them. 'An Alcatel. Looks like a pay-as-you-go. I reckon Ashley must have brought it round. The two of them disappeared upstairs together then Ashley came down and left the house.'

'Has she used it?'

'Yep. She was in the bathroom for a while before you came and I was sure I could hear her voice. She'd put the radio on in the bedroom, though, so it was hard to be sure.

I had a look for it while you were speaking to them just now. She's stashed it in the bathroom. It's at the bottom of a laundry basket under a pile of washing. I put it back so she wouldn't know I'd found it.'

'Who did she call?' Clare asked.

'Got the number here.' Wendy took out a notebook and tore off a page. 'Probably a pay-as-you-go, but still worth a check.'

'Cheers, Wendy. I'll get onto it. In the meantime, could you keep an eye on that phone, please? There must be a reason Lisa's using it.'

'Will do.'

Wendy returned to the house. Clare and Chris climbed into the car.

'Any thoughts?' she asked Chris.

'What do you reckon a groundsman earns?'

Clare regarded the house. It wasn't exactly a starter home. 'Not enough for that place, anyway, even with Lisa's afternoons at the tanning salon.'

'A couple of expensive cars in the drive, too.'

'He was on the rigs until a year ago, though. That's good money. They could have been stashing it away. Put it towards the house, or paid cash for the cars.'

'Sure. But they're a young couple. They must have twenty years of their mortgage left. Even if he'd been saving up over the years, I can't see they'd have enough to keep up payments on a house that size.'

'Good point.' Clare started the engine. 'But there could be a perfectly reasonable explanation. Meantime, we have a baby to find.'

Sunday Evening

Chapter 6

It was almost ten o'clock when Clare finally climbed into her car. The evening had grown cold and it took a few minutes to clear the windscreen of condensation. She sat while the heater blew cool air and watched until it was clear enough to pull out of the car park. She left the town behind at the Bogward Road roundabout, driving through farmland towards Daisy Cottage, her home for the past six weeks. It was dark now, of course, but she could see the distant lights of two combine harvesters, working late into the night to bring in the crops before the weather changed.

Clare had grown tired of renting in St Andrews and decided it was time to put down roots. The detached Victorian cottage on the country lane, known to locals as the Craigtoun Road, had piqued her interest when she had been investigating a series of hit-and-run murders in the area.

She drove on, blinking away fatigue as the fields bordering the road gave way to dense woods. It wasn't so long since she had raced through these same woods, trying to escape a shotgun-toting killer. She shook her head. That, along with so much else, was in the past and Daisy Cottage was the future. Or at least it would be once the builders had finished with it.

The woods cleared and she slowed for the entrance to her cottage. She swung the car off the road and up the short drive, the headlights picking up the wooden portico and red-brick walls. A security light blazed, dazzling Clare, and she wondered if it could be adjusted so it didn't shine right in her face every time she approached the house. She killed the engine and climbed out of the car. Inside the house, Benjy, her English Bull Terrier, heard her approach and began to bark. She fished in her pocket for the house key and opened the front door. Benjy flung himself against her legs and she led him out to the garden to pee. While he sniffed under the privet hedge, Clare picked up a note on the mat and moved about the house, lighting lamps. She stepped carefully over a series of gaps where the floorboards had been lifted by the plumber.

Benjy returned from his night-time wanderings and followed Clare into the kitchen. She was reading the note from Moira, her nearest neighbour, half a mile further along the road.

> *Saw you weren't back so walked Benjy this after-noon.*
> *Let him out again about six. Hope all ok,*
> *M*

God bless Moira. She was the perfect neighbour and so fond of Benjy. Clare opened a cupboard and took out a bag of dog food. She poured some into a bowl and Benjy made a beeline for it.

'Benjy,' she said in what she hoped was a warning tone. He looked at her.

'We've talked about this,' she went on, trying to look stern. 'Wait until you're told!'

He looked at her again with puppy-dog eyes and she relented. 'Go on then,' she said, and he fell on the bowl, devouring the food in less than a minute.

She unearthed an M&S chilli meal from the back of the freezer and put it in the microwave to defrost. As the microwave hummed, the fatigue she'd felt in the car washed over her once more. Travelling back from France last night, up this morning for the fun run and then Abi's kidnapping. It had all caught up with her. She pointed the remote at the kitchen TV. It flickered into life and she saw herself being interviewed on the West Sands. Great coverage, but would it help? She stared at the close-up of Abi's photo on the TV.

'Where are you?' she wondered aloud.

–

Clare ate her chilli on a tray in front of the coal fire. It was cosy but smoking a bit and she added *find a sweep* to the to-do list on her phone. There might even be an old bird's nest up there. As the fire sparked and spitted she wondered about replacing it with a woodburning stove. *If* the central heating was ever sorted out!

Her phone buzzed from the arm of the chair. She picked it up. Geoffrey:

> Just checking you're okay.
> Saw the news – dreadful. Poor things.
> Hope you're not too exhausted,
> Love G xxx
> PS still ok for dinner on Tuesday?

Dammit. She'd forgotten Geoff's sister had invited them to dinner. The invitation had come before their holiday, a holiday that was fast becoming a distant memory. Tuesday was just two days away, about as long as they had to find Abi Mitchell. Benjy wandered through and stretched out in front of the fire. The sight of him made Clare yawn. It had been one hell of a day. She rose from the sofa, carried her tray into the kitchen and loaded her plate in the dishwasher. She whistled to Benjy and opened the door for him to have one last pee in the garden. Then she switched out the lights, stepped carefully across the missing floorboards and went upstairs to bed.

Monday, 23 September

Chapter 7

Further reinforcements from Glenrothes, Cupar and Dundee packed into the station the next morning. The incident room was bathed in autumn sunshine, raising the temperature until someone thought to close the blinds. As Clare entered the room, it seemed to be a sea of bodies but gradually, as they became aware of her, they found desks and chairs to perch on and the chatter subsided.

'Right,' she said. 'First of all, any sign of Ashley McCann?'

Jim raised his hand. 'Nothing at all. She's not turned up at her house yet.'

'So where has she been?' Clare asked. 'She was round at the Mitchells yesterday but she's not been home since. Any thoughts?'

'Probably kipping up with someone,' Chris suggested.

'Or getting a hit,' Bill said. 'Could have gone somewhere to score and crashed out.'

Clare sighed. 'Not permanently, I hope. Anyone checked her previous convictions? Liv, was that you?'

Liv began shifting papers on her desk until she found the one she wanted. 'Yep. Pre-cons for possession and supply of Class A. She's a minor player, though, judging by the sentences. And she served six months for serious assault.'

'The minute she surfaces,' Clare said, 'I want to speak to her. She's the victim's nearest relative. And there's something else. Ashley gave Lisa another mobile phone. An Alcatel, and Lisa has chosen to conceal this from us. Wendy found it hidden in the bathroom. The question is why? Why did Ashley give it to Lisa, and why is Lisa hiding it?'

'Boss, why not just ask her?' Liv said.

'It's a fair point. My concern is, if she does have something to hide and we go steaming in, she'll clam up and we'll lose any intel we might get from that phone. So, for now, we monitor the activity – calls and texts – and see what we can learn. Who knows, it might give us a pointer to what's going on here – to who's taken Abi, and why.'

Liv nodded and Clare pressed on. 'So, Kevin and Lisa's iPhone records up to midday on Sunday – who was on that?'

Robbie raised his hand. 'Lisa called her sister, Ashley McCann.'

'Time?'

Robbie checked his notebook. 'Just before ten in the morning. Call wasn't answered.'

'Okay, any other calls?'

He scanned his notebook again. 'One inbound, to Kevin's mobile. One of those have-you-been-in-an-accident calls.'

'And anything after the time Abi was snatched?'

Robbie shook his head. 'Just a text message from Lisa's phone – about half twelve.'

'To?'

'Ashley again.'

Clare nodded. 'Figures. Probably sent from the car when Sara was driving them home. Is that it, Robbie? No other calls?'

Robbie shook his head. 'I'm checking her contacts now, boss, but nothing of interest so far.'

Clare mulled this over. 'So, certainly no ransom or other demands for Abi's safe return, on their iPhones at least.'

'What about the other phone? The one Wendy found in the bathroom?' Chris asked.

Robbie flicked over a page in his notebook. 'Wendy texted about half an hour ago, boss. She checked the phone this morning. According to the call log there was one outgoing call yesterday afternoon, about half-three, then another last night at ten thirty. Both around two or three minutes long.'

'So the second call was after Wendy left?' Clare said.

'Looks like it.'

'Same number?'

'Yeah. Untraceable. Must be a pay-as-you-go.'

Clare looked round the room. 'So Lisa Mitchell has made two calls on a phone she doesn't want us to know about. Why?'

Chris sat forward and loosened his tie. 'I'm starting to think she might have another bloke. Remember we found that gold necklace hidden in the wardrobe? And she was downright fidgety when we went back the second time yesterday. If she has someone else on the go, she'll be frustrated at not being able to see him. Could be that's who she's been calling.'

'I think any mum would be fidgety if their baby had been taken,' Nita said.

'Think about this, then,' Chris went on. 'What if the baby's not Kevin's? He was away on the rigs, remember.'

'Yes, that's a good point,' Clare conceded. 'And, if the baby isn't his, do we have a lead? Could Abi's real father have snatched her? Maybe Lisa wanted to break it off and he's trying to hold on to her. And Abi.'

'Bit of a stretch, boss,' one of the uniforms said.

'Yeah, I know. But it's worth bearing in mind. Most kids are snatched by someone known to the family. There's Kevin, too, of course. He could have a girlfriend.' She moved to the whiteboard, picked up a pen and wrote *sexual partners?* Then she looked back round the room again. 'Any other thoughts?'

'Social media,' Chris said.

'Thanks, Chris. Who's on that?'

Erin raised a hand. 'That's me, boss. Not much for Kevin. Lisa's had a few spats on Facebook but definitely nothing that would make someone snatch her baby.'

Clare nodded at this but, before she could go on, the station phone began to ring out in the main office. Sara rose to answer it. Again, Clare saw Chris's eyes following her out of the room, and he wasn't smiling. She wondered for a moment if they'd had a fight. And then she recalled herself. Finding Abi Mitchell was all that mattered for now.

'If that's Lisa Mitchell's GP,' she called after Sara, 'I want to speak to him. The surgery said they'd get him to call me.'

As Sara left the room, Jim entered, dressed in his sergeant's uniform. For a moment, despite all the worry over Abi, Clare's heart softened. God bless him. Signed off to nurse his wife after her debilitating stroke, and yet here he was in full uniform, ready to pitch in. She thought his trousers looked loose around the waist and wondered if he was so focused on caring for his wife that he was neglecting himself. She mouthed, 'We need to speak,' and Jim nodded.

She turned back to the room and continued. 'Any luck with known sex offenders?'

A bearded officer raised his hand. 'Not so far, boss. There's a fair number in Fife and Dundee. We're working our way through them but no luck so far.'

'You're checking the houses, yeah?'

'Yes, boss. And they're mostly happy to let us do it.'

'Okay, keep on it until you've checked them all.' Clare scanned the room. 'Who was doing hospitals and GPs for bereaved parents?'

Bill and Janey raised their hands.

'Anything?'

Bill shook his head. 'Ninewells in Dundee have given us a list of recent miscarriages and we're working through it. The nurse we spoke to said there are probably more that never come to hospital.'

'Stillbirths?'

'Ten in the last month. Most of the parents devastated, as you'd expect. But the nurse said one particular mum had caused them concern. Two weeks ago.'

'Concern? How?'

'The way she was. Wouldn't hold the baby, didn't want any photos, footprints.'

'And that's unusual?'

'So the nurse says.'

'How was Dad?'

'More as they'd expect, apparently. He asked the nurses to take the photos and so on when the mum was having her shower.'

'Did she see a psychologist? Or a grief counsellor, even?'

The officer shook his head. 'Refused. Discharged herself the next day.'

Clare wondered about this. What was the normal reaction to such a tragic event? How on earth would a mother start to get over it? Her mind went, momentarily, to her sister Jude and her nephew James. What joy he had brought them. She couldn't imagine her sister enduring such pain. But this woman – with her reaction – the hospital staff said she *caused them concern*. Was there something here? Had this woman been disturbed enough to see a baby in a pram and, in a moment of madness, to take her? It sounded unlikely, but someone had. And how would she react if she was questioned about it? Clare didn't want to add to her pain but she couldn't ignore it. She sighed. This case was filled with sadness.

'Okay,' she said. 'Give me the details and I'll follow that one up myself. For the others, remember I want promoted officers doing this in the first instance. And steer clear of the parents if you can. Speak to midwives and GPs first. We don't want to distress anyone if we can avoid it.' She let this sink in, then went on. 'What about Fife hospitals?'

'No stillbirths in the past month but a pretty long list of miscarriages.'

'GP surgeries, Janey?'

'Still checking them, boss. Spoken to about half of them so far. But Dundee and Glenrothes are pitching in so we should finish the rest this morning.'

'Make it a priority,' Clare said. 'They all need following up. Who was checking on prison releases?'

'That was Sara,' Chris said.

'Right, we'll see what she says when she comes off the phone. Talking of which, did anything come in after the appeal was broadcast last night?'

'Fifty-odd calls. Glenrothes have been helping follow them up. Reckon they should get through the last of them today.'

'Okay, Chris. Keep me informed. Now...' Clare broke off when Sara came back in. Something in the girl's expression stopped her in mid-flow. 'Sara?'

'Pharmacy in Dundee broken into last night.'

Clare frowned. 'That's Dundee's problem, Sara. We've enough on here.'

Sara stood her ground. 'It's what they took...'

'Which was...?'

'The usual – methadone, tramadol, diazepam – but there's something else. They stole two bottles of digoxin. The pharmacist said it comes in three strengths and they took the right one for a child of Abi's age. Whoever took it knew what they were doing.'

Clare pondered this. 'Is that likely to be on an addict's shopping list?'

A plain-clothes officer from Glenrothes raised his hand. 'Definitely not, boss. I mean, they'll try anything to get a hit, but it's not the sort of drug they could sell easily.'

Clare's head was buzzing with this new information. What did it mean for Abi? Was it good news, if her abductors had stolen the digoxin? She began pacing back and forth, processing this development. 'I particularly mentioned digoxin on the news report,' she said. 'Now, it went out about teatime on Sunday. And the pharmacy was broken into that same night.'

'So, the abductors saw your appeal and realised they needed the medicine,' Sara said. 'It's good news, isn't it, boss? It means they're looking after Abi.'

Clare frowned. 'I'm not so sure, Sara. It could just be a coincidence. Pharmacies are a regular target and other drugs were stolen. Could the pharmacist have made a mistake? Misplaced the digoxin? Get onto them and ask them to check again.'

'Whoever did it would have to be quick,' one of the Dundee officers said. 'Pharmacy alarms are linked to our systems. The Bell Street lads would have a car there within minutes. It wouldn't give the thieves long and the local dealers would know that.'

Clare stood thinking for a few moments, her head bowed. There was so much information here to process. So many possible leads. She could feel every eye in the room on her. She had to get things clear in her head. This operation, finding Abi, all these officers. She couldn't afford to blow it. Her mouth was dry and she licked her lips. Then she took a deep breath in and turned back to the whiteboard. 'Right, let's concentrate on what we do know.'

'Abi's been taken,' Chris said.

Clare jotted down *Abi snatched twelve p.m. Sunday*. Then she said, 'I put out an appeal to the media, naming digoxin.' She added *digoxin info released six p.m. Sunday* to the board.

'Dundee pharmacy broken into that night,' Bill said, and Clare jotted this down too.

'Digoxin is taken, along with the usual meth and so on,' Clare said, her pen squeaking as she wrote. 'Why?'

'Could be they were after stuff to sell on the street – took the digoxin by mistake,' Chris said.

Clare wrote this on the board then said, 'Or they were after the digoxin and took the other drugs as a cover?'

Nita raised her hand. 'They took the right dose, boss. Maybe too much of a coincidence?'

Clare stopped writing. 'Yes they did. According to the pharmacist there are three strengths. So it's a one-in-three chance.'

'Are we treating the burglary as part of the abduction then?' Chris asked.

'For now – yes. Until it's ruled out. So let's think. Who would know which strength to steal?'

The officers began calling out and Clare wrote steadily.

'The parents.'

'The GP and other staff at the surgery.'

'The sister – Ashley.'

'If Kevin isn't Abi's father, the real dad might know.'

Clare stopped writing at that suggestion. 'At this point, we've no reason to believe that is the case. Even if Lisa does have another bloke, it doesn't mean he's Abi's father.' She turned back to the board. 'But I'll bear it in mind.'

'Staff at Ninewells Hospital? If they were treating Abi,' someone said.

'Abi's daycare,' Chris added. 'Wee Tots. Staff there might know.'

Clare wrote this on the board. 'Yes, they would have to know.'

Erin raised her hand. 'Boss, any of us could find that out on the Internet.' She indicated her phone. 'I've just googled digoxin and it's all there. How much to give, how often and so on. Anyone who knew Abi needed it could find that out.'

'That's true, Erin, although it might vary, depending on the illness; and we've not released specific details of her condition.'

'Is it worth checking if any doctors or nurses have had the sack lately? If they were dipping into the drugs cabinet?' Sara asked.

Clare considered this. 'Possibly. But what are the chances of someone like that being connected to our abductors?'

No response.

'Well? Anyone else have any theories?'

Silence.

'Fine. Then we'll work on the basis that Abi's abduction wasn't a random act. Whoever took her is educated enough to know what she needs and ballsy enough to break into a pharmacy to get it.' She stood thinking for a moment then said, 'I'm starting to think this isn't a child abuse case. Can't rule it out, of course. But if the abductor did see our broadcast they'd have realised her life would soon be in danger. I reckon a potential abuser would have dumped her somewhere. Hospital car park or somewhere she could be found quickly. Either way, they wouldn't want her death on their hands.'

'Yeah, I agree,' Chris said. 'They'd get rid of her as fast as possible.'

'So, our abductor is someone who wants Abi to live,' Clare said. She looked round the room. 'Thoughts?'

'Has to be family,' Bill said.

'Or someone known to the family,' Janey added.

'So, let's prioritise friends and family.' Clare looked at Nita. 'Get a few more bodies to help you, Nita. I want that done this morning.'

Hands went up and Clare nodded her thanks. 'Now, we can't be sure the burglary is linked to Abi's abduction but, if it is, it buys us some time. So let's get cracking. I want the CCTV from the pharmacy and any surrounding streets. I want the car registration and photos of the burglar. Anything we can get our hands on.'

The phone began to ring again.

Jim rose. 'I'll get it.'

Clare nodded her thanks then turned to the whiteboard. She wrote *prison releases.*

Sara raised her hand. 'Following up three, boss. Two men and one woman. One of the men took his son from his ex's house. Tried to take him to Spain.'

'Unlikely he's our man,' Clare said. 'Go on.'

'The second man did six months for paedo porn on his phone.'

Clare's eyes narrowed. 'Quick as you can with that one. Remind him he's out on licence. Anything at all, he goes right back inside. The woman?'

'Susan Clancy. Addict, chaotic lifestyle, had her baby taken away by social services. Apparently, she got clean in prison and now she wants the baby back. But the prison welfare officer I spoke to said that's unlikely, given her history.'

Clare's eyes lit up. 'We need to get onto that one straight away. Give me the details Sara, and I'll look into that myself.'

Clare turned back to the board and wrote *workplaces.* 'Now,' she said, 'let's check if the Mitchells have upset anyone or had any problems at work. So visits to both workplaces. Also the daycare facility. I want to know if any of the staff have noticed anything, or if there's anybody working there with experience of sick babies.'

Jim came back into the room. He stood, his hand still on the door jamb. Something in his manner made Clare stop.

'Problem?' she asked.

'Could I have five minutes in private?'

Clare followed him out of the room and into her office.

Jim closed the door. 'The DCI's on his way, Clare. Should be here by lunchtime at the latest.'

Clare scrutinised Jim's face. 'Who is it?'

'Apparently they're short of DCIs just now. Two on annual leave and another three off sick.'

Clare sank down in a chair. 'It's Tony McAvettie, isn't it?'

Jim sighed. ''Fraid so. And he said he's particularly looking forward to renewing his acquaintance with DS West.'

'Dammit,' she said. 'Dammit to hell.' She sat for a moment, taking this in, then rose and moved to the door. 'I'd better go tell Chris.' She stopped in the doorway. 'Jim, it's good of you to come in but I'm not sure you should be here. How is Mary?'

'She's probably as good now as she's going to be. Her right side is affected, and she struggles with speaking. But she's doing her exercises and the therapists are pleased with her. This morning I took her a cup of tea and she said thanks. Not too clearly, but she said it.'

Clare squeezed his arm. 'I'm glad. But are you sure about being back? You know you can have as much time as you need.'

'I'm fine, thanks, Clare. Mary's sister lives a few streets away, so she'll keep an eye on her while I'm here.' He rubbed his chin. 'To be honest, it does me good to have something else to focus on.'

'I suppose so. But see you take proper breaks, and go home on time, okay?'

Jim smiled. 'I will. And thanks, Clare. I appreciate it.'

The phone in the main office began ringing again. Jim moved to answer it. Clare went to find Chris but Jim called her back. He held out the phone. 'Lisa Mitchell's GP.'

Clare took the phone.

'I gather you wanted to speak to me,' the GP said. 'Is there any sign of Abi?'

Clare related the news of the pharmacy break-in.

There was an audible sigh of relief from the GP. 'At least someone's taking care of her. Was that what you wanted to tell me? Or was there something else, Inspector?'

'There is, actually. About Lisa. Her reaction. Yesterday when you saw her she was crying, shaking – as if she was in shock. She couldn't seem to get warm.'

'Unsurprising,' the GP said. 'Fairly typical reaction.'

'But when we went back later, her mood had completely flipped. She was chain-smoking and snapping at Kevin if he so much as looked at her. I couldn't believe it was the same person.'

'And you're wondering if that's unusual?'

'Exactly. Whether we should read anything into it.'

'Hard to say. What Lisa's experiencing is a bit like a bereavement. Something like this takes folk in different ways. Given the circumstances, it wouldn't be unusual for her to seem frustrated.'

'She didn't seem frustrated to me. She was angry.'

'My experience of this kind of thing is limited, Inspector,' the GP said. 'I've dealt with mothers whose babies have died or been stillborn, but they at least have a body to deal with – a funeral to arrange. These things give them focus and a sense of closure. Lisa and Kevin don't have that. They can do nothing but wait. So, no, I wouldn't say her reaction was unusual. Another mum might not react that way, but everyone is different.'

Clare thought back to the gold necklace. 'You've known the family a while. Do they seem a happy enough couple to you?'

'I don't tend to meet happy people, Inspector. Usually they're unwell and worried about it.'

Clare thanked the GP and rang off. She handed the phone back to Jim and returned to the incident room.

'Okay, is there anything we've forgotten?'

'Is it worth going up to the protest camp for a look around?' someone suggested.

'Good idea,' Clare said. 'I doubt there's a connection but we need to cover everything. Could two of you go up and check it over, please? Are they in tents?'

'Caravans and campervans.'

'No slumming it for them,' Clare said. 'Make sure you search all the vans. Any sign of a baby, insist on seeing it. Remember Abi's birthmark and her single tooth. Right, that's it. Keep in touch.'

They began to file out of the room. Clare saw Chris talking to Sara, his hand on her arm. She wondered if this case was going to be too much for Sara. She hadn't struck Clare as over-sensitive before but there was definitely something up with her. And, as willing as Jim was, it wouldn't be fair to rely too heavily on him. Clare really needed Sara pulling her weight. Maybe Chris could shed some light on it. She checked her watch. There was a hell of a lot to do but a baby's life depended on it.

She caught Chris's eye as she passed. 'Come on, let's see what Susan Clancy has to say for herself.'

Chapter 8

Susan Clancy lived in a flat in Alderwood, a housing scheme in the north of Dundee. The gardens in front of the flats were mostly knee-high with grass, which was littered with old washing machines and the like. A grey velour sofa, now rain-soaked, was piled high with black bin bags which had been torn open by rats or seagulls. Across the road a car with no tyres was up on bricks. A couple of toddlers were playing on the pavement while an older boy threw stones at the gulls who swooped and screamed in response.

They climbed up two floors until they saw Flat 6, the address the Dundee officers had given them for Susan. The orange paint on the front door was peeling and someone had scratched a swastika into it. There was no sound from the bell when pressed, so Clare rapped on the door.

'I'm no' in,' a voice said behind them. They hadn't heard Susan climbing the steps.

Clare turned to take her in as she approached. She was thirty, maybe. Pencil thin, her faded jeans hanging from her waist. The sleeves of her lightweight hoodie were pulled up and Clare could see the tell-tale scars going up her left arm where she had cut herself repeatedly. None of the scars looked recent, though. There were small round scars too. Cigarette burns, Clare thought. Had Susan done this to herself or had it been someone else? Her hair had been dip-dyed in the past but the ends were dry now, the roots dark. She wore no make-up but her cheeks were flushed with the effort of carrying her shopping.

She fished in her pocket and took out a key. ''Scuse me,' she said, elbowing Chris out of the way. She shoved the key in the lock and opened the door. 'Polis, I'm guessing?'

Clare reached for her warrant card but Susan waved it away.

'Come in. I've nothing to hide.'

If Clare had expected the inside of the flat to match the dinginess of the outside, she was to be surprised. There was a smell of new paint and the flat was clean and tidy. Susan dumped her shopping bags on a small kitchen table and started to unpack. 'You'll be wanting a coffee or something?' she said, her back to them as she put her shopping away.

'Just a quick word, Susan, and maybe a look around if that's okay?'

'Depends.' Susan turned, hands on the sink behind her. 'What's it about, like?'

Clare decided there was no point in beating about the bush. 'We're investigating the abduction of a young baby.'

Susan stared. 'And you think I took it?'

'She has a heart problem and if we don't find her very soon, she could die.'

'I hope you do find her,' Susan said, her expression mulish. 'But I still don't see what it's got to do with me.'

'All right if my colleague has a quick look round?' Clare said.

'Suppose.'

Chris took the hint and went off to investigate the rest of the flat. Left alone, Clare said, 'Susan, I know you had your own baby taken into care.'

'And I'm getting her back.'

'Have they said as much?'

Susan shrugged. 'Not yet, but they will. I'm clean now. Search the place if you like. Check the cupboards.' She made a show of opening cupboard doors. 'Fresh fruit and veg, proper food.'

'All the same…'

Susan folded her arms. 'You think I'm not going to get Paige back so I've taken someone else's baby, don't you?'

Clare was about to reply when Chris reappeared. He shook his head, indicating there was no sign of Abi.

'Follow me,' Susan said. She led Clare and Chris out of the kitchen into a small sitting room. The furniture was old, but serviceable enough. The curtains were clean and there wasn't a speck of dust to be seen. Susan's face beamed out of a series of photos taken with her baby. Then she led them into the bathroom. A plastic tub of bath toys sat in one corner. 'Even got the right bath stuff,' Susan said, showing Clare a bottle of Johnson's bath liquid. 'Across the hall,' she said, ushering the pair out of the bathroom.

Clare and Chris walked into a room decorated in pale pink. Susan's bed was against the window and, next to it, was a cot, old but freshly painted. A mobile hung above the cot and a pink teddy was tucked inside the covers.

'I'm not going to mess it up this time,' she told Clare. 'I want Paige back with me, where she belongs, not some other baby. Got it?'

–

As they walked back to the car, Clare saw that Susan was watching them from the window. 'You know, she might just get her baby back. She's making a real effort.'

'Once an addict, always an addict.'

Clare glanced back at the window. 'You could be right. I hope not, though.'

They got into the car and pulled their belts on. Clare started the engine.

'What next?' Chris asked.

'Next, we're going to check on the woman whose baby died. The one the hospital staff were worried about.'

'Oh God…'

―

Clare and Chris's next call couldn't have been more different from their visit to Susan Clancy's flat. Clare swung the car into a driveway at the end of a quiet street in Broughty Ferry, a suburb of Dundee to the east of the city. She came to a halt in front of a high, wrought-iron gate. To the side was an intercom; she pressed the buzzer.

A woman's voice: 'Yes, who is it?'

'Detective Inspector Clare Mackay and Detective Sergeant Chris West to see Mr or Mrs Mistry.'

There was no reply but, within a few seconds, the gate began to slide open. Clare drove slowly through and up a circular drive, arriving in front of a substantial two-storey Edwardian house. It had been built in sandstone, Clare thought, but in a warmer, almost pink tone, in contrast to the grey sandstone she was used to seeing in St Andrews. The moulded stone windows were high, the dressed stone matching the decorative quoins up either side of the frontage. On the upper storey the tall eaves were finished with ornamental soffits picked out in a soft blue. It would not have looked out of place on the cover of an exclusive properties brochure.

'Money here, right enough,' Chris said.

They walked across the gravel, which crunched beneath their feet. As they approached the front entrance, the door opened and they were met by a woman in her late thirties. Clare thought she might be Indian. Like Susan Clancy, she wore no make-up but, with her dark eyes and her glossy hair, wound up with a clasp, she was quite stunning.

She held out a hand. 'I'm Gita Mistry. Come in, please.'

Gita showed them into a sunny room with long sash and case windows, hung with rich curtains. Clare took in the room. It was beautifully decorated and furnished, as though it was ready for a magazine shoot. An enormous Bang & Olufsen TV sat on an oak stand and a copy of *Country Life* lay on the coffee table. Clare noticed it was open at an article on Norland Nannies. On the wall opposite the window were French windows leading to another room. Clare could see the end of a grand piano and, to the side of it, a cello resting on a stand. It was opulent, studied and tasteful.

Gita indicated a cream sofa. 'Please, sit.' Her voice was little more than a whisper and she twisted an embroidered handkerchief between her hands. She waited for them to sit then took a seat opposite. Clare couldn't help noticing she still had a bit of a baby bump from her recent pregnancy.

'I'm afraid, Mrs Mistry…'

'Gita, please.'

'Gita, I'm afraid we've come on rather a delicate matter.'

Gita continued to twist the handkerchief.

Clare pressed on. 'You may have heard in the news that a baby was taken from her pram on Sunday morning.'

Gita's eyes were bright, but she didn't speak.

'It was a little girl,' Clare said, watching her carefully. 'Abigail. And we need to find her quickly. She has a heart condition which has to be medicated and monitored carefully.'

Gita swallowed. 'I had a little girl, you know.'

Clare gave what she hoped was a sympathetic smile. Chris shifted in his seat, his eyes anywhere but on Gita.

'She was perfect,' Gita went on. 'Almost seven pounds.' She raised her eyes, now brimming with tears, to meet Clare's. 'A problem with the umbilical cord. It took them five minutes with forceps. She was blue when she finally came out. They tried for twenty minutes but it was no use.'

There was an unbearable silence, then Clare mustered her strength. 'I'm so sorry, Gita. You must be devastated.'

Gita dabbed her eyes with the handkerchief. 'My husband, you know, he's so angry. I can't see the point…'

Clare asked, 'Have you anyone to help you, Gita? Give you support?'

Gita's lips tightened. 'Oh yes. I'm lucky. *Lots* of family. Coming and going all day.' She finally gave up on the handkerchief and put it down. 'I think they want to make sure I'm not going to *do* something to myself.'

'Might you?' Gita seemed so fragile that Clare felt she couldn't leave the possibility hanging in the air.

'No. I won't do anything,' Gita said, her voice flat. 'We're Hindus, you see. It would be sinful.'

'I understand.'

Chris shifted in his seat again and Clare took the cue. 'Gita, I'm afraid I must ask you something.'

Gita saved her the trouble. 'You think I have taken that baby because I couldn't have my own little girl.'

'I'm so sorry, but we have to ask.'

Gita shook her head. 'I don't know how you can think that.' Her voice was barely audible now. 'If you knew...' She took up the handkerchief again. 'If you knew the pain, you would understand I could never...' She shook her head. 'I think I would like you to leave now.'

Clare stood. 'Before we go, Gita, I wonder if we could have a look round the house. Please?'

Gita didn't answer.

They waited and Clare became aware of the ticking of a clock, cutting through the tension. In another room, perhaps. Had they passed one in the hall?

Gita stood, stiff, as though trying to decide what to do. Then the fight seemed to go out of her. 'Do whatever you wish, officers.' And she left them standing in the hall.

'Come on,' Clare said to Chris, her voice low. 'Before she changes her mind.'

They made their way through the French windows into what appeared to be a music room.

'No sign of a baby here,' Chris said, and they moved on. A small study also gave no hint of a baby in the house. Through the window Clare could see Gita in the garden, standing with her back to them, smoking a cigarette. Their searches of the kitchen and dining room were also unsuccessful.

'Upstairs,' Clare said, and they made their way back into the hall and up the wide staircase, the carpet soft beneath their feet. The bedrooms were tastefully furnished with light oak furniture and pristine white linen. They moved through the rooms, looking for evidence of a baby in the house, but there was nothing.

And then they found the nursery.

The pale lemon walls were decorated with a frieze of merry-go-rounds while the ceiling had been hand-painted to look like the sky with fluffy white clouds on a cornflower-blue background. In the centre of the room was a Moses basket on a stand, with a quilt to match the frieze. There was a miniature wardrobe and a chest of drawers on which sat a large Steiff teddy bear. Next to the chest of drawers was a nappy-changing station, with a pack of infant nappies, unopened. A neat stack of picture books sat on a mantelpiece over a fireplace, which had been boarded up.

Chris let out a low whistle. 'It's like Mothercare in here. She's got everything.'

'Everything but the baby,' Clare said. 'Come on, Chris. Let's get out of here.'

Clare started the car and followed the gravel drive back round, approaching the gate once more. This time it slid back automatically. She emerged onto the main road and turned back towards St Andrews.

Chris looked out of the window while Clare drove. The houses built along the edge of the River Tay gave onto a long strip of grass with a view across the mile-wide river to Fife. A woman in a pink tracksuit was throwing a ball for a springer spaniel, the dog racing after it. The sun sparkled on the river, and in the distance they could see the tall derricks of two oil rigs, berthed on the river. It was all so completely normal and seemed a million miles away from the horror of Abi Mitchell's abduction.

As they approached the Tay Road Bridge, Chris exhaled audibly then said, 'That was fucking horrible, Clare. That poor woman...'

'Not one of the better bits of the job,' Clare agreed.

'Tell me you don't suspect her.'

Clare eased the car up the slipway and onto the bridge. 'No. Whatever's happened to Abi, Gita Mistry isn't involved.'

'Thank Christ for that.'

The radio buzzed, and Chris clicked to listen. It was one of the detectives from Glenrothes.

'Been to the daycare place and the tanning salon, boss,' the voice said.

They were approaching the end of the bridge now. Clare slowed for the roundabout, taking the St Andrews road. 'And?'

'Nothing at the salon. Everyone got on with Lisa. No problems with customers. Daycare staff devastated. The other mums too. All shocked by what's happened. Hanging onto their own kids for dear life.'

'Any of the daycare staff trained nurses?' Chris asked.

'No. They all have the usual qualifications – first aid, childcare – but none of them are actually qualified nurses.'

Clare thanked the disembodied voice and said they'd be back in fifteen minutes or so. She fell silent, thinking for a few minutes, then said, 'The daycare staff – they might not be trained nurses but they would have some experience of medicating children.'

'Yeah, maybe.'

They lapsed into silence, Clare driving, Chris looking out of the window. She slowed down as they entered Leuchars village. They would be back at the station soon. She glanced at Chris then and decided to go for it. 'Chris, everything okay with you and Sara?'

There was a pause. Just long enough to tell Clare that her suspicions were justified. Chris continued looking out of the window. 'Yeah, all fine. Why?'

'She doesn't seem herself just now. If there's anything worrying her...'

'She's fine.'

'Sure?'

'Yep.'

'You two cooling off a bit?'

Chris sighed heavily. 'Clare, you're my boss, not my mother. For the record, Sara and I are absolutely fine and it's really none of your business.'

'As long as it doesn't affect your work,' Clare said.

'It won't.'

Ten minutes later, Clare pulled into the station car park and stopped dead.

'Shit,' she muttered.

Chris looked at the dark blue Lexus, then back at Clare. Finally, he said, 'Did you know?'

'That Tony's the DCI they've sent? I only heard this morning, Chris.'

'And you didn't think to tell me?' he said. 'You didn't think to mention that the DCI whose nose I bust last year after I caught him sleeping with my girlfriend is taking over this case? You didn't think maybe that was something I should know?'

Clare backed the car into the only remaining space and killed the engine. 'Chris, I meant to, I really did. But what with going to see Susan Clancy and then Mrs Mistry… It just went right out of my head.'

'He'll finish me,' Chris said. 'You do know that?'

'No he won't.' Clare's expression was grim. 'He'll have to get past me first.'

'I don't need a fucking minder, Clare.' Chris got out of the car and slammed the door behind him.

Clare hurried after him and they entered the station together.

Tony McAvettie was sitting on a chair, his long legs splayed out. He was lean, in his early forties with an easy smile he had employed to great effect over the years. His elevation to DCI, Clare reckoned, owed more to his ability to charm an interview panel than his dedication to the job.

He was flicking through a newspaper while Sara made him a coffee.

'Tony,' Clare said smoothly. 'Good to have you on board. You remember Chris?'

Tony's mouth formed itself into a smile, but his eyes didn't follow suit. 'Ah, Christopher. How's that right hook of yours?'

'Chris, why don't you see if all the miscarriages have been checked, eh?' Clare said quickly. 'I'll take the DCI into my office and bring him up to speed.'

Chris hesitated, his face puce. Clare put an arm on his back and directed him towards the incident room door.

Then she turned back to Tony. 'My office?'

Tony, as she expected, took Clare's seat and waited for her to take one of the other chairs. 'So, Clare, what's been happening? Any sign of the baby?'

'Not so far. But we do think she's been taken by someone who'll look after her.'

'Explain, please.'

Clare told him about the break-in at the pharmacy and the stolen digoxin.

'Where was this?'

'North end of Dundee.' As she said it, she realised it could only be half a mile from Susan Clancy's flat. Was that something? She hoped not. Desperate as she was to find Abi, she didn't want it to be Susan who had taken her. Still, she made a mental note to find out if Susan had worked as a nurse or in a pharmacy.

'CCTV?' Tony asked.

'The team are looking at it but I've not had a chance to catch up with them yet.'

'Chrissake, Clare, get a move on.'

'I've been checking on possible suspects,' she said.

'The CCTV is your next priority. I want the photos on my desk pronto. What about the parents?'

'Young couple in their thirties. Detached house, two expensive cars but he's a groundsman and she works part-time in a tanning salon.'

'You're thinking they're into something illegal?'

'Could be.'

'How do they seem?'

'Up and down. The dad's shell-shocked. Mum too, at first; then she changed. Just like that. Laying into us for not doing enough.'

'Spoken to the GP?'

'Yes. He said mood swings are not unexpected in the circumstances.'

'Who's the FLO?'

'Wendy Briggs.'

'Talked to her today?'

'Not yet.'

'Then get onto that. Maybe pop out and see the parents again.'

Clare didn't say anything. There were so many things she needed to do, so many interviews she didn't want to leave to the other detectives. 'Actually, Tony, I think my time would be better spent chasing up leads.'

'Ah well,' he said. 'Sometimes life isn't fair. Got to be seen to be doing the right thing. And don't forget that CCTV. Okay, is that it?'

Clare shook her head. 'We have a protest camp.'

Tony laughed. 'Really? And what are the good folk of St Andrews protesting about? Not enough quail eggs in the shops?'

'Actually,' Clare said, 'there may be a connection.' And she related the events at the fun run, leading up to Abi's abduction.

'Anyone been up to turn the camp over?'

'We've got officers up there now, but…'

'But?'

'I don't think the protesters are involved. Not sure why. Just my gut reaction.'

'Get it turned over properly,' Tony said. 'We can't afford to tiptoe round their middle-class sensibilities.'

'I won't go upsetting them,' Clare said. 'We can be effective without being heavy-handed. This is a sensitive case, Tony. We need the community onside.'

Tony leaned back in his chair and began drumming on the table with a biro. 'I'll tell you what this is, Clare. This is my ticket to Regional Superintendent. That's what it is.'

Clare gaped.

'Oh yes. Your good buddy Superintendent Campbell – surely you remember asking him to reassign Chris to you after he so kindly decked me? Yeah? Well he's retiring.'

'I didn't know.'

'I bet you didn't. I'm guessing you'll miss having him to run to. But if this case goes well, then I'll be hard to beat. So, if I were you, Detective Inspector, I'd keep in with me.'

Chapter 9

Clare found Chris in the incident room, staring at a computer screen.

'Come on,' she said. 'We've to go and check on the Mitchells again.'

'Seriously?'

'Tony's orders.' She noticed Chris's fists were balled. 'Look, take it easy. He's a lazy bugger so if we keep busy you'll not see much of him.'

'I really hate him, Clare. Arrogant bastard.'

'I know,' she said, slapping him on the back. 'I know.' They walked out of the station and made for the car park.

'He dumped Emily, you know,' Chris went on. 'Only a couple of months after I found out about them. He didn't even want her. Just wanted to prove he could.'

They climbed into the car. Clare thought it wise to change the subject. 'Any of the miscarriages look likely?'

'Nope. They've checked out all but two. One's still in hospital, the other's on holiday.'

'Abroad?'

'England, I think. Supposedly headed off on Saturday, which would rule them out. But I'll check that. I've got the car registration so I'll notify all forces and see if we can track them down.'

'Okay. Let's see how the Mitchells are today.'

They found Lisa Mitchell glued to the TV, watching Judge Judy lose patience with two neighbours who were arguing over a broken fence.

'Kevin's clearing out the garden shed,' Wendy told them. 'Said he's better doing something.'

'I'll see him in a few minutes.' Clare sat down opposite Lisa. 'How are things, Lisa?'

The girl turned to her with a glazed expression. 'You found Abi yet?'

'Not yet. But we're following up a number of different leads.'

'Leads?' Lisa slurred. Clare thought she didn't seem quite right. She shot a glance at Wendy, who mimed swallowing pills.

'The doctor's given Lisa a sedative,' Wendy said aloud.

'Have you had any phone calls, Lisa? Letters? Anyone been in touch?'

'Reporters,' Lisa said. 'Lotsa reporters.' She looked towards the window. 'See them in the street.'

'I'm sorry about that. We'll have them pushed back.'

'Good.' Lisa closed her eyes and sank back into the sofa. On the TV, one neighbour was accusing the other of deliberately knocking down two fence panels. The other neighbour was yelling back. Judy bore it for a minute or two then told the first neighbour he was a moron. Clare left Lisa watching the proceedings and motioned to Wendy to follow her into the kitchen.

'Anything?' she asked.

'Not much,' Wendy said. 'She's called that same number again. Another three calls.'

'Was she on for long?'

'Two minutes or less. The last one was only thirty seconds.'

'How does she seem?'

'So-so. I think she's mixed up her tablets and taken the ones for night, but if it gets her through the day, what's the harm?'

'And Kevin?'

'He's quiet for a bit, then he cries, then he goes quiet again. He won't take any tablets. Says he needs to be alert for Abi.'

'Okay, Wendy. Look, I'd like to speak to Lisa again but not while she's like this. If you could let me know when she's a bit more lucid?'

'Will do.'

Clare and Chris walked down the garden to find Kevin sitting on a stool in the shed. He didn't move as they approached and Clare tapped on the open door. 'Hi Kevin.'

He looked up, his face expressionless. 'Hi.'

'Mind if we come in?'

Kevin stood to let them come in. 'Nowhere to sit. Unless you'd like…' And he indicated the stool.

'That's okay. Listen, Kevin, I have a very difficult question to ask you. I'm sorry, but it's important we consider absolutely everything. It might help us find Abi. Is that all right?'

Kevin looked at them, a spark of interest in his eyes. 'Of course. Anything.'

Clare swallowed. But there was no putting it off. 'Kevin, have either you or Lisa been involved with someone else?'

He stared.

'Kevin, have you had a girlfriend? Since your marriage, I mean?'

Kevin looked from Clare to Chris then back at Clare. 'What? Why are you saying this? Of course not!'

'And Lisa? Could she have been seeing someone else? Another man?'

Kevin's brow furrowed and his eyes darted around, as though trying to make sense of this. And then he said, 'My Lisa?' His voice was hoarse. 'My Lisa with another bloke? You serious?'

'I'm so sorry, Kevin. We have to ask.'

He shook his head. 'I don't believe you people. First I lose my baby and now you're trying to tell me I've lost my wife as well?'

Chris put a hand on his arm. 'Kevin, mate...'

Kevin shrugged Chris's hand off. 'I'm not your mate!'

Chris stepped back with his palms raised. 'Sorry, Kevin. Look, we know it's probably not true. But look at it from our point of view. We're trying to find Abi. That's it. Our only priority. Now if Lisa had been knocking about with someone else, maybe he wanted to get back at her by snatching her baby. Maybe whoever it was even thought Abi might be his. Now, none of this is pretty. We know that. But sometimes we have to think these things and say them too. So, we're sorry about that but we need to know everything – and I mean everything – if we're to stand a chance of finding Abi. See what I mean?'

Clare shot Chris a warning glance but he ignored her.

'Kevin?' he said again.

Kevin sank back down onto his stool. He put his head in his hands and his shoulders began to shake. Clare

94

opened her mouth but Chris forestalled her with a look. He let Kevin sob for a few minutes then spoke again.

'Okay, Kevin. We need a name. Address too, if you have it.'

Kevin raised his head and drew a hand across his eyes. 'She thinks I don't know.'

They waited. Then Chris said again, 'A name, Kevin.'

He looked at Chris. 'You really think he could have our Abi?'

Chris's expression didn't alter. 'Almost certainly not. But we have to check every single thing. It's thorough checking that'll bring Abi back. So – name, please?'

–

Back in the car, Clare said, 'That was bloody amazing, Chris. Well done.'

He smiled. 'Sometimes, with blokes, the gentle approach doesn't work. Bit of straight talking's more effective. Cruel to be kind and all that.'

Clare started the engine with a new respect for her DS. 'So what's the address?'

Chris checked his notebook. 'He actually lives in Cupar but I reckon we should head to his work. Catch him there.'

–

The last time Clare had driven through the gates of the Kenlybank Hotel was to investigate a series of hit-and-run murders. As the car crunched up the gravel drive towards the car park at the rear, she thought back to that case and the tangle of crimes at the heart of it. She shivered involuntarily, a gesture that didn't escape Chris.

'Back here again, eh?' he said.

'Yep.' She killed the engine. 'Come on then. Let's see if we can track him down.'

By coincidence, the duty manager, Pawel Nowicki, had also been at the reception desk on the night of that hit–and–run, all those months ago. As usual, he was as neat as a pin, in a plain grey suit and white shirt with a dark red tie. He smiled as they approached, although there was a hint of concern in his eyes.

'Inspector,' he said. 'How lovely to see you again. Not on business, I hope?'

'It's good to see you too, Pawel,' she said. 'But I'm afraid it is an official matter.'

'Then you must tell me how I can help.'

'We'd like to speak to a member of your staff, please. I gather he's one of the chefs.'

'His name?'

Chris checked his notebook again. 'It's Philip Patrick.'

Pawel frowned. 'Oh yes, Phil. He's our pastry chef. I'm afraid he'll be rather busy, preparing for the afternoon teas. All our pastries are handmade in the kitchen, you see. I don't suppose it could wait?'

Clare shook her head. 'Sorry Pawel, I'm afraid not. It's a matter of some urgency.'

Pawel gave Clare a little bow. 'Of course, Inspector.' He pressed a bell on the desk and a girl appeared from a door behind him. 'Could you go to the kitchen please, Maria, and ask Phil Patrick to come to reception?'

The girl made to move but Clare stopped her. If Phil was involved with Abi's abduction, she didn't want him alerted.

'If you don't mind,' she said to Pawel, 'I think we'll go with Maria. Save time.'

Pawel hesitated then gave Maria a brief nod.

The girl led Chris and Clare along a corridor to a pair of doors marked *In* and *Out*. 'This way,' she said, opening the *In* door. They followed her into a large room, with huge cooking ranges around the edge and stainless steel workstations in the centre. A man dressed in pale blue from head to toe was loading an enormous dishwasher while others in white uniforms and aprons chopped and sautéed as if their lives depended on it. A woman dressed in chef's whites was barking instructions in all directions and Clare wondered how any of them knew what they were doing.

Maria steered them over to the side, out of the way of the double doors, which swung to and fro with a steady stream of waiting staff. She approached a man dressed in blue and white striped trousers and a white tunic. He wore a tall chef's hat and was bent over a tray of delicate tarts, a piping gun in his hand. Clare heard nothing over the clamour, but could see Maria speaking to him and guessed he was answering as he piped. At one point he straightened up and glanced across at them. He said something else, then bent over his tarts again. Clare was ready to go over and march him straight outside, but Chris put a warning hand on her arm.

Maria came back over. 'He says can you wait two minutes while he finishes piping some tarts, then he'll be right with you.'

Clare thanked Maria and she left them to wait.

–

A young lad in a pale blue uniform was sitting at a plastic-topped table, reading a newspaper and eating a cheese roll when Phil Patrick led Clare and Chris into the small staff room. The table was cluttered with dirty mugs and plates which the lad had used to prop up his paper. On the wall opposite the door there was a vending machine with an *Out of Order* notice sellotaped across the middle. Someone had added *Owes me 50p!* to the notice.

The lad looked up as they entered. Phil gestured at the door and the lad left without a word, eyeing Clare as he went. Phil closed the door behind him, then turned to face them.

'So?'

Clare said, 'Mr Patrick…'

'Phil's fine.'

'Phil, then. Do you know Lisa Mitchell?'

He looked at Clare for a moment then said, 'I'm guessing you know I do. Otherwise you wouldn't be here.'

'Can you tell us how you know Lisa?'

'Again, I think you already know.'

'All the same, I'd like to hear it from you.'

He sighed. 'All right, then. Lisa and I had a relationship.'

'Had?'

'Had.'

'Can you tell me when it ended?'

'Just over a week ago, as it happens. Saturday before last.'

'And was that your decision? Or Lisa's?'

He avoided Clare's eyes. 'Hers.'

'Did she give a reason?'

Phil shook his head. 'Said it was a mistake. She felt guilty. It wasn't fair to Kevin or Abi.' He raised his eyes to Clare's again. 'She was bored with me, Inspector. She'd had her fun. Wanted to go back to playing happy families.' He swallowed and cleared his throat. 'Can I ask… I mean, is there any sign of Abi?'

Clare ignored the question. 'How long had the relationship been going on?'

'About four or five weeks.'

She counted back in her head. 'So you started seeing Lisa Mitchell, let's say, sometime in August?'

He avoided her eye. 'Yeah, about then.'

Clare studied his expression. Was he telling the truth? Something didn't feel right about what he was saying. 'How did you and Lisa meet?'

His shoulders sagged. 'Okay. I've actually known Lisa for a few years. Met at college. We had a bit of a thing back then. But it fizzled out – you know, ran its course. Anyway…'

They waited.

'It's one of those things. Now and then, one of us will get a bit… fidgety, like. Call the other up, a few drinks, sometimes it leads to something, sometimes it doesn't.'

Chris folded his arms. 'You're fuck buddies?'

Phil had the grace to look abashed. 'I wouldn't put it quite like that.'

'How would you put it?'

'We like each other. We're attracted to each other. But it wouldn't last. That's what she said anyway.'

Clare took over. 'How did you feel when she broke it off, Phil?'

A stud had come undone on his tunic. He fiddled with it, popping it back into place. 'Dunno. To be honest, it wasn't the same this time. Lisa — she seemed more distracted, like. Plus Kevin not being away on the rigs — well, he's around more, isn't he? Didn't make it easy — to see each other, you know.'

Clare said, 'Any idea what was distracting her?'

Phil shrugged. 'Don't ask me. I mean, we were okay for a couple of weeks. Then she never seemed to have the time. Not for me anyway. Always busy, you know?'

'Busy with what?'

'Dunno. Abi, I suppose. Hospital appointments and that.' He looked up at Clare. 'Having the baby — it made a difference.'

Clare did a quick mental calculation. 'Were you seeing her last summer? Around about June, say?'

He looked up, surprised. 'I've no idea. Probably not. Why?' And then his face cleared. 'Oh, I get it. You think Abi's mine, don't you?'

Clare watched him carefully. 'Is she?'

He snorted. 'No chance. I'm not the type. Too careful.'

'What about Lisa? Is she careful too?'

Phil shook his head. 'Inspector, if that baby's mine, it's the first I've heard of it.' He glanced at the clock on the wall. 'Now, if you don't mind...'

Clare stood up. 'I'd like you to accompany us to your house just now, Phil. And we'd like your permission to search it. You can of course refuse but that refusal would be noted and we will apply for a warrant anyway.'

He shook his head. 'You do know this is my busiest time? I've a hundred more pastries to make for this afternoon.'

'Too busy to help us rule you out as a suspect in the abduction of a baby?'

He slapped a hand on his forehead. 'A baby I know nothing about.' His voice rose. 'How many times do I have to tell you? I'm not baby material. Why would a single guy like me want to take her?'

'No need to get angry, sir,' Chris said. 'The quicker we go, the quicker you'll be back.'

Phil thought for a minute. Then he said, 'No, I won't go. I'll come with you if you'll wait a couple of hours but I can't leave the kitchen just now. You'll have to arrest me if you want me now.'

Clare looked at him, unsmiling. 'As you wish. We'll just motor over to your house ourselves, then. And, of course, if we have any suspicions that there is evidence of a crime being committed we'll be duty bound to break in.'

'Duty bound,' Chris repeated.

Phil regarded them. 'Jesus, you guys just do what the hell you like, don't you?'

'We do when there's a child's life on the line,' Chris said.

Phil sighed and stared at the floor. 'Give me five minutes.'

–

Phil Patrick lived in a small, terraced house on a side street behind the shopping centre in nearby Cupar. 'You'll have to excuse the mess,' he said, as he put his key in the door.

He led them through a small, dark hallway into a sitting room. The sofa was strewn with an assortment of clothes, the coffee table in front of it bearing the remains of his last meal.

'Look wherever you like,' he said, perching on the end of the sofa. 'I've nothing to hide.'

The kitchen was little better than the sitting room, the sink full of unwashed dishes.

'He obviously doesn't bring his work home with him,' Chris whispered, taking in the mess. 'Even I'm tidier than this.'

They checked the cupboards for evidence of baby formula, went through the bins for nappies, but there was no sign that a baby had been anywhere near Phil's house.

A thorough search of the bathroom and bedroom followed. After almost an hour, Clare was satisfied that Abi hadn't been in the house.

'Come on,' she said, 'we'll run you back.'

'An apology would be nice,' Phil said, climbing into the back of the car.

Chris nodded. 'I imagine so.'

Chapter 10

Clare stopped the car at the edge of the road, just outside the hotel. They watched as Phil strode up the drive towards the kitchen at the back.

'I wouldn't fancy being one of his juniors this afternoon,' Chris said.

Clare checked over her shoulder and pulled the car back out into the road. 'Fancy a trip to the protest camp?'

'Suppose. Better than going back to the station anyway.'

She came up to a fork in the road and took a right, back towards the town. It was busy with tourists, and students going between lectures. As she passed the Byre Theatre her eye was caught by a group of toddlers in yellow fluorescent tabards. They were ambling along, hand-in-hand under the watchful eye of half a dozen uniformed adults. She thought they were about two or three years older than Abi Mitchell and it occurred to her that the group might be from Wee Tots.

Wee Tots, where Abi would have been this afternoon if she hadn't been snatched from her pram just yesterday. Was it only yesterday? It seemed so much longer.

At the top of Abbey Street Clare swung the car to the right, past St Rule's Tower. 'Miss out all these damn zebra crossings,' she muttered. She continued down North Street, past the West Sands and the iconic Old Course

Hotel until the town was behind them and the country-side ahead.

As they approached a narrow road to the left, Clare slowed down and took the turning.

After a short distance, Chris said, 'Just in here.'

Clare pulled the car into the side of the road beside a farm gate.

They climbed out of the car and leaned against the gate which was padlocked shut. A collection of campervans was parked towards the far end of the field in a semi-circle. Closer to the gate, a few protesters were gathered around a brazier, clutching coffee mugs. One of them recognised Clare and gave her a cheery wave. An elderly lady, wrapped up in a knee-length padded jacket and a Barbour hat, stood painting in front of an easel.

'It's not your typical protest camp,' Clare said.

'Want a look?'

'Might as well.'

Chris examined the padlock and stout chain, both considerably newer than the gate. 'Okay to climb over?' he said.

Before Clare could answer, a familiar figure began walking towards them.

'Good afternoon, officers,' Nicholas Stewart called.

'Hello again, Mr Stewart. Would you open the gate, please, so we can have a look round?' Clare asked.

Nicholas Stewart fished in his pocket for a key and released the padlock, pulling the chain away from the post. The gate swung open and Clare and Chris walked into the field.

'Mind your feet,' he told them. 'It's muddy. If you'd like to follow me.' As they approached the brazier he turned and said, 'Coffee?'

'No thanks,' Clare said. 'We'll just check the vans then be on our way.'

'Of course. But your colleagues have already been here today. Uniformed officers.'

'I know,' Clare said. 'But I'd like to see for myself. All the vans, please.'

He stared at her for a minute then said, 'I presume you're still looking for that poor child.'

Clare made no response and, after a moment's hesitation, he led her to the first of the campervans.

'Wait outside, Chris,' she said. 'Keep an eye on things while I'm in the van.'

The campervans were surprisingly well appointed. She lifted bench cushions, opened doors and checked the overhead storage. No sign of a baby. The next van was the same. By the time she approached the sixth van she was starting to think it was an exercise in futility. And then she heard it. A baby crying. Following the sound, Clare wrenched open the van door and stepped inside. A woman with long dark wavy hair glared back at her but Clare's eyes were fixed on the baby at her breast.

'Most people knock,' the woman said, detaching the baby and lifting it up. She began gently rubbing the infant's back as it nuzzled against her shoulder.

Clare whipped out her warrant card but the woman waved it away.

'This isn't her, you know,' she said. 'Abigail. This is my son. You can check in his nappy if you don't believe me.'

Clare looked at the baby. 'Would you mind turning him please, so I can see his face?'

The woman lifted the baby under his arms and settled him on her lap, facing Clare. He was nothing like Abi, his round, moon-like face a contrast to her tiny features. Clare checked anyway for the birthmark that was on Abi's neck but she knew it wouldn't be there. The baby, alarmed by seeing this stranger, opened his mouth to bawl, showing only gums. No teeth.

'Sorry to have troubled you,' Clare said.

'Was that a baby?' Chris asked when she emerged from the van.

'Yep, but not Abi. Come on. Let's get the rest of them checked out then we'll get back to the station.'

As Clare emerged from the last of the vans, she saw Nicholas Stewart approaching her again. 'All fine, I presume, Inspector?'

'Yes, thank you, Mr Stewart.' She looked round at the camp. 'How long are you planning to stay here?'

'Until they bring the bulldozers,' he said. 'We will do what we can and then, I know, we'll be forced to withdraw. But I still hope that sense will prevail. Scotland does not need another bottled water plant.'

Clare thanked him. 'We'll just have a walk round the field, then we'll be out of your way.'

As soon as they were out of earshot, Clare said, 'Those trees – at the far end. Behind the fence.'

Chris looked to where she indicated. 'Yeah – what you thinking?'

'Just wondering how deep they are.'

'Not very. Couple of hundred yards at the most.'

'And on the other side?'

'Open farmland.'

'So, no cottages or other places a baby could be hidden from the road then?'

'I doubt it.'

Clare stood looking over at the trees for a minute then said, 'Sorry, Chris. Waste of time. I just thought there might be something.' She saw that Nicholas was still watching them and she waved to indicate they were leaving. 'Come on. Let's get back to the station.'

As she closed the gate behind them Clare saw Nicholas striding across to replace the padlock. She started the engine and pulled away. Her phone began to ring and Chris picked it up. Sara. He switched it to speaker. 'Go ahead Sara. Clare's driving but you're on speaker.'

'Boss, there's a journalist here asking for you.'

'Direct him to the press officer. We won't be giving another statement today unless things change.'

'No,' Sara said, 'he's not here for that. He says it's some scheme the Assistant Chief Constable came up with. He said something about shadowing you.'

'What?' Clare swerved to avoid a dog walker and her collie. 'Sara, I've honestly no idea what you're talking about. Can he come back tomorrow?' But, in the back of her mind, she was remembering an email. Something to do with fostering good relationships between police and press.

'He says he's happy to wait.'

They had reached a farm steading now and Clare executed a turn in the yard. 'I'm on my way back, Sara. Ten minutes.'

'Thanks boss. I'll tell him.'

As she drove back, Clare contemplated the problem of Tony and Chris. She had no doubt Tony would try to goad Chris into losing his temper and, with so many extra staff around to witness an outburst, it would be hard to defend Chris a second time.

She drew in at the far end of the car park, away from Tony's car, and entered by the side door. She sensed Chris tense up and decided to forestall trouble. 'If you could check on that miscarriage couple who've gone on holiday, Chris, I'll update Tony.'

Chris headed off to the incident room and Clare went to hang up her jacket.

'Detective Inspector Mackay?'

She turned to see a beaming figure in a Donegal tweed suit, tortoiseshell-rimmed glasses perched on his nose. He was clutching a tablet computer and looked improbably young.

'Yes?'

He held out a hand. 'Lyall McGill. I've been nominated by The Press Association to be your POMED Link.'

Clare stared at him. 'My what?'

'POMED. Police and Media. Didn't your ACC tell you to expect me?'

This must be the journalist Sara phoned about. Clare studied him and decided he looked more like the head boy at a private school than the world-weary hacks she was used to dealing with. Was he even twenty, she wondered?

She forced a smile. 'Look, Mr – er...'

He smiled back. 'McGill. Lyall McGill.'

'Mr McGill. I'm sorry – it's really not a good time just now. I'm right in the middle of a difficult case. I'm not even sure what this is all about. Could you possibly come back next week? Or the week after?'

He continued to smile. 'But that's perfect! I don't want to shadow you when everything's going well. I'm here to see things from your point of view. The trials and the tribulations, so to speak. And maybe educate you about the pressures we face. A bit of mutual understanding, you know.'

Clare thought that a little of Lyall McGill would go a very long way this week and she considered briefly if it was worth appealing to Tony. Or maybe she could palm him off on someone else. 'Mr McGill…'

'Lyall, please.'

'Lyall. A lot of what I do is very tedious. Sitting at a desk, trawling through data. And some of it will be too sensitive for me to share with you anyway.' She was racking her brains. Who could he shadow instead of her? There had to be someone…

'But that's the point, Inspector. We in the press want to know about your job: the highs and the lows, the exciting bits and the tedium. Don't they say that detection is ninety-nine per cent perspiration and one per cent inspiration?' He inclined his head and peered at her over the top of his glasses.

Clare groaned inwardly. It was going to be a very long afternoon. 'Get yourself a coffee then.' She went into her office, closing the door firmly behind her.

Tony looked up as she entered. 'Ah Clare – what news from the front?'

She sat down heavily. 'Did you know about that man-child out there?'

Tony grinned. 'I see you've met our journalist friend. I thought you'd like him. Just keep him sweet and send him out the room if anything sensitive comes up.'

'I suppose...'

'Any progress with the baby?'

'I saw the parents again. Mother's out of her head on tranquilisers. Dad keeping himself busy. I don't think they're doing very well. Wendy says there's a phone hidden in a laundry basket. She thinks the mum's been making regular calls to the same number.'

'Checked it out?'

'Yeah. Pay-as-you-go. Can't trace it.'

'Any texts?'

'Nope. Just calls. All outgoing.'

'Okay. Anything else?'

'Dad admitted that Mum had a boyfriend.'

Tony's eyebrows shot up. 'Checked him out?'

Clare nodded. 'Spoke to him and he agreed to his house being searched. None too happy about it, but he came with us. Nothing, though. I doubt he's involved.'

'Right. That it?'

'We visited the protest camp on the way back. Searched all the vans. There's a baby there but it's not Abi.'

'Sure?'

'Yes. Looked for the birthmark and tooth. Definitely not her.'

'What about the pharmacy? Checked on the CCTV?'

'Just about to do it.'

'Make sure you keep that reporter away from it then. We don't want him leaking anything sensitive.'

'Honestly, Tony, I've no idea what to do with him. I'm too busy to babysit a journalist.'

'Give him a guest login. It'll let him get on to Google without being able to access our systems. Get him to research psychological profiles of baby abductors. Tell him it's a lead you're following up. Ought to keep him busy for a while.'

'Good idea, Tony. Thanks.'

'I have my uses. Don't suppose you'd make me a coffee as a thank you?'

Clare rose. 'No, I don't suppose I would.'

She found Lyall in the main office, reading the notice-board. 'I've a job for you, Lyall, if you're up for it.'

He positively beamed. 'You bet!'

Clare installed him in front of a computer and said how important it was that they understood the mindset of the abductors. He seemed to swallow this and began tapping in search terms. Clare moved to another computer and called up the CCTV footage which had been put on the network for her to access. The alarm had been triggered in the control room at about two in the morning. She scrolled forward to just before two and set the footage to run.

Chris wandered over and stood behind her, looking at the screen.

'Any luck with that couple's car?' she asked.

'The ones who've gone down to England? Yeah, I think so. They pinged an ANPR camera on the A623 on Sunday but didn't register on the next one along so they've left the road somewhere between the two.'

Clare furrowed her brow. 'Where's that?'

'England. The Peak District.'

'Crikey. Needle in a haystack then?'

'Could be. I've spoken to the local police. They'll check all the hotels and B&Bs in the area. Hopefully get them soon.'

'What time did they pass the camera?'

'Sunday teatime.'

Clare paused the footage to consider this. 'Is it possible? Could they still have been here on Sunday? Would they have had enough time to snatch Abi at midday and make it down to the Peaks?'

'Possible, but unlikely, I'd say.'

She restarted the footage and focused on the screen. The pharmacy was in darkness and, while the images were in colour, it was hard to make out anything other than rows of fully stocked shelves. And then the screen brightened as the emergency lighting came on and the coloured boxes and tubs of medicines could be seen more clearly. Clare and Chris watched as two figures wearing dark clothing and balaclavas appeared behind the counter, one quite tall, the other shorter. She paused the footage.

'Chris, see if there's anyone from Dundee in the incident room. They might recognise something about this pair.'

Chris returned with three PCs from Dundee and Clare restarted the footage. They watched as the shorter one went to the middle of a shelf and picked through bottles, examining and discarding each one in turn. Then he signalled to the other, who seemed to be grabbing bottles at random. As they made for the door, stashing bottles in their pockets, the taller one glanced briefly in the direction of the camera.

'Stop,' one of the Dundee PCs said.

Clare froze the frame and zoomed in. 'Any ideas?'

'Could be. I've seen that jacket before. See the badge on the sleeve?' he said to the other two.

'Yep,' one of them said. 'I've definitely seen that. Or one like it.'

The third PC said to Clare, 'Mind if I check something?'

She moved aside and he sat at the computer. He shook the mouse then navigated to the force intranet and clicked to open a database. He typed in the search box then began scrolling through the list of names that appeared. After a few minutes' peering at the screen, he stopped and jabbed it with a finger. 'Could be Paul Sinclair.'

Clare said, 'Go back to the pharmacy.'

The PC returned to the frozen image of the burglar's face and the other two nodded.

'Yeah, I think that's him.'

'You sure?' Clare asked.

'Not absolutely, but if it's not him it's someone pretty like him. I've arrested him often enough,' the PC said. 'Same build too.'

'What about the other one?' Chris asked.

They all peered at the screen. The other one was a good few inches shorter than Paul Sinclair. Clare pointed. 'That's hair, isn't it? Coming out from under the balaclava?'

Chris peered at the figure on the screen and the hank of red hair. 'A woman?'

'Could be. Looking at the build, the shape from behind, and the longer hair, I'd say so.' She turned to the Dundee lads. 'Any idea who she is? Is Sinclair married?'

They shook their heads. 'We'll ask around,' one said. 'Might ring a bell with someone.'

'Can you get onto Dundee, please?' Clare said. 'Get them to pick up Paul Sinclair and bring him over?'

The Dundee PCs left and Clare sat, staring at the footage.

'This could be it,' Chris said. 'The break we need.'

Clare wondered. Was this going to be it? Had they found their abductor? 'Yes, could be,' she said. But, in the back of her mind, she was asking herself *Why?* Why would a small-time offender like Paul Sinclair steal a baby? What could he possibly want with her?

Chris wandered off but Clare continued staring at the screen. What if Paul Sinclair wasn't stealing digoxin for Abi? What if there was no connection? It was more than twenty-four hours now since Abi had been taken. What had that doctor said – forty-eight hours? She dragged the scroll bar back to the start of the pharmacy footage, at ten that morning when it had opened. She flicked idly through, not even sure what she was looking for. She was about to give up when something caught her eye. 'Chris?'

He came over and stood behind her again. Clare zoomed in on the figure of a woman in a blue denim jacket. 'Recognise her?'

Chris moved closer and peered at the screen. 'Is that who I think it is?'

'It certainly is. Come on; get your coat. We've a call to pay.'

Chapter 11

From his seat in the back of Clare's car, Lyall regarded the flats without enthusiasm.

'I'm afraid you'll have to wait here,' Clare said. 'This has to be confidential.'

He looked out of the window. Two young boys were standing outside the car, peering in at him.

Chris laughed. 'Don't worry, we'll lock you in. Protect you from the locals.'

Lyall didn't smile.

As they walked away, Clare and Chris heard one of the boys say, 'What have you done, mister?'

'You goin' to the jail?' the other asked.

'I almost feel sorry for him,' Clare said as they climbed the steps.

'Let's see if you're still saying that by the end of the week,' Chris said.

'Oh God! He's not staying all week, is he?'

The door opened and Susan Clancy's face fell. 'Not you two again.'

'Afraid so,' Clare said. 'Can we come in?'

Susan stepped back to admit them. 'What is it this time? I've still not stolen any babies.' She led them into the sitting room and motioned to them to sit. Clare and

Chris sat on the edge of the sofa while Susan remained standing, her arms folded. 'Well?'

'It's like this,' Clare began. 'I don't believe in coincidences, Susan.'

Susan stuck out her chin. 'So?'

'So this: last night a pharmacy two streets away was broken into.'

'And you think I did it?'

'No,' Clare said, 'but we think you visited it earlier the same day.' She reached into her bag and produced a print of the CCTV image from Sunday morning. 'This is you, isn't it?'

Susan studied the photo. 'So? What if it is me?'

'Mind if I ask why you were there?'

'Bit nosey, Inspector. I had a prescription to pick up.'

'For?'

'I don't think I have to tell you that. In fact, I'd like you both to get out now. *If* you don't mind.'

'Look, Susan,' Clare said, 'we're up against it here. We're no nearer to finding that baby and, with every hour that passes, she's in more danger.'

Susan exhaled. 'Yeah, okay.' She walked over to a wooden dresser and reached into one of the drawers. 'It was this,' she said, holding out a blue inhaler. 'I'm asthmatic.'

'Still got the box?' Chris asked.

'Hold on...' Susan left the room and they heard the bathroom door open. A minute later, she returned with the inhaler box and handed it to Chris. 'Happy?'

He checked the date and nodded to Clare. 'Thanks, Susan. That's fine.'

But Clare wasn't done. 'Are you in the pharmacy a lot?'

'Depends. Why?'

Clare ignored the question. 'How often?'

'I dunno. Maybe every couple of weeks.'

'Did you see anyone particular when you were there on Sunday?'

'Like who?'

Clare reached into her bag and withdrew a printout of the pharmacy burglars. 'Recognise either of these two?'

Susan gave the photo a cursory glance. 'Nope.'

'Look more carefully, Susan. Please. We need to find that baby.'

Susan sighed audibly and looked again at the photo.

'We think this one is a woman,' Clare said, indicating the figure with the hank of red hair.

Susan stared at the figure for a few seconds. Then she handed back the photo. 'Sorry.'

'Sure?'

She didn't meet their eyes. 'Yeah, sure.' She stood and walked to the door. 'Now, if you don't mind, I've things to be getting on with.'

They followed her to the door. Clare took out a card and handed it to her. 'If you do think you know either of the figures, please contact me.'

As Susan moved to open the door, Chris said, 'Did you hear anything about the break-in? I mean from friends or neighbours?'

Susan glared at him. 'I'm no' a grass.'

'A baby's life, Susan.'

She shook her head. 'You've seen it round here. Not exactly Mayfair, is it? Could be any one of fifty.'

'The thieves knew what the baby needed,' Chris went on. 'Do you know anyone round here with medical knowledge?'

'Nope. And now, if you don't mind...'

Susan held the door open, waiting for them to leave, but Clare stopped on the threshold. 'Susan, can I ask what you do? For a job, I mean?'

She folded her arms. 'What do you think? You reckon they're queueing up to give ex-cons jobs, Inspector?'

'So you're not working just now?'

'Nope.'

'And before?'

'Bit of this, bit of that.'

Clare waited.

'Christ, you do not give up! Right. Left school at sixteen and worked in a shop. Kept that till I was eighteen then started doing bar work. Oh, and I had a paper round when I was twelve. Okay?'

'What kind of shop?'

'Eh?'

'When you left school. What kind of shop was it?'

Susan stared at them. 'Like it matters? If you must know, it was a newsagent's.'

'You've never worked in a pharmacy? Or any kind of medical role?'

'Pfft. I wish. Not brainy enough, Inspector.'

'Okay, thanks Susan. We'll leave you in peace.'

The door slammed behind them and they began walking down the steps. Chris said, 'Believe her?'

'Yes, I think so.'

They emerged into the sunshine. Clare said, 'I think she has an idea about the woman in the photo but she's either not sure or too scared to tell us.'

'We could take her in. Lean on her a bit.'

'I doubt it would make much difference. She's a tough cookie, that one.'

They found the car surrounded by kids with Lyall still in the back, pretending not to notice them.

'Beat it,' Chris said to the kids and they began to drift off, the entertainment over.

'Any luck?' Lyall asked.

'No,' Clare said, 'but it's as important to rule things out as in.'

Lyall typed this into his tablet.

Clare checked her watch. 'Chris, get onto the station while I drive. Get them to chase up any medical staff sacked in the last six months. Tayside and Fife.'

As they drove on through the streets, Lyall continued tapping away at his tablet. 'Will you put the parents on TV?'

Clare had been thinking the same thing. The sight of devastated parents often brought results. And if the Mitchells did know something about Abi's abduction – however unlikely that seemed, given the measure of their distress – it would be an opportunity to see how they reacted on camera. 'We may do,' she said, 'but it won't be my decision.'

'Should I suggest it to that DCI? Tommy, is it?'

'You do that, Lyall.' Clare turned her head so he couldn't see her grin. 'I'm sure *Tommy* would be grateful.'

–

The station was buzzing with activity when they arrived back. Sara was talking on the phone and waved Clare across. 'Human Resources from the hospital.'

Clare took the phone and explained they were looking for any doctors, nurses or other medically trained staff who had lost their jobs recently.

'I'm afraid we can't give that information without a warrant,' a female voice said.

Clare was about to protest when the voice carried on.

'However, I can tell you there's been nothing like that for the past year.'

'Anyone undergoing disciplinary proceedings just now?'

There was a pause then the voice said, 'Nothing that would result in being struck off or even sacked. Minor stuff, mostly – timekeeping, complaints from difficult patients. All nonsense of course, but we have to investigate. But if you do get a warrant, we will prioritise it.'

Clare thanked her and ended the call. She sat thinking for a minute. Another dead end. And where the hell was Ashley McCann? 'Any news of Ashley?' she called.

Sara's face fell. 'Sorry, boss. I should have said. She rocked up at her flat about half an hour ago.'

Clare called Chris over. 'Can you think of anything for Lyall to do?' she said, her voice low. 'We need to see Ashley now and I do not want him tagging along.'

'Leave it to me.'

–

The street was more congested than it had been on Sunday, thanks to a cable company whose vans were parked nose to tail. Tall orange cones had been placed on the pavement across from Ashley's flat where a yellow-jacketed man was breaking up the tarmacadam with a powerful Hilti gun. As Clare killed the engine she said, 'Not a word about the phone Lisa's hidden in the bathroom, okay? I don't want Ashley telling her we know about it.'

As they waited for Ashley to answer the door, Clare said, 'What did you give the boy wonder to do?'

'He's entering the data from the traffic survey into the computer.'

'Weren't you supposed to do that when I was on holiday?'

Chris was saved from answering by Ashley opening the door.

Ashley's face was set in a scowl. She'd had one too many spray tans, Clare thought. The mahogany tinge to her skin made her blue eyes look pale and watery. Her eyebrows were plucked into thin lines and her ears pierced with scaffold bars. Her hair was short, cut in a pixie style and needed a wash. She looked from Clare to Chris, one hand on the door, the other planted on her hip. 'Yeah?'

Clare held out her warrant card and introduced herself and Chris. 'Mind if we come in, Ashley?'

Ashley's response was to turn and walk up the hall. Clare and Chris followed her, closing the door behind them. Ashley had resumed her seat on a sofa that had seen better days, a cigarette burning in an ashtray on the arm. The television was on and she was watching a quiz show.

Clearly, she wasn't going to invite them to sit so Clare took a seat anyway. Chris opted to stand.

'We've been trying to get hold of you since yesterday, Ashley,' Clare said.

Ashley continued staring at the television. 'Found Abi yet?'

'Not yet,' Clare said, 'but we're doing everything we can. We hoped you might be able to help.'

Ashley's eyes never left the television. 'Dunno how.'

'Have you seen Lisa today?'

'No. She's out of it. Too many happy pills. Best thing for her, probably.'

Clare tried to tune out the television. 'Ashley, we know you went round to see Lisa on Sunday afternoon. After Abi had been abducted. Can you tell us what the two of you talked about?'

Ashley sighed. She muted the television. 'What do you think? She was crying about Abi. What d'you expect? Fucksake!'

'Must have been a shock,' Chris said.

Ashley scrutinised Chris. 'Seen you before, haven't I? You got a girlfriend?'

Chris ignored this. 'What did you say to Lisa?'

'Asked her who did it and she said she didn't know.'

'And you believed her?'

'Why wouldn't I?'

'And since Sunday? Have you been back to see Lisa? Phoned her?'

'Not really. I pop in, you know. But can't do much.' She glanced back at Clare, her eyes narrowed. 'You'd better get the bastard. I love that wee girl.' Her eyes flicked across to the window. 'Since you're here, why don't you do something useful and get that lot out there to stop their drilling? It's doin' my fuckin' head in.'

Clare threw Chris a glance that said *This is hopeless*, her eyes indicating the door.

Chris tried again. 'Ashley, we know you've done a bit of time...'

'Yeah, so?' She eyed him. 'What are you, twenty-eight, twenty-nine?'

Chris continued, avoiding the question. 'Is it possible you could have upset someone?'

Ashley frowned. 'You think they've taken Abi to get back at me?'

'Is it possible?'

She shook her head. 'Nah. Snatching a kid, you'd do major time for that. If they wanted to get back at me, they'd just set fire to the house. Wouldn't be the first time.' Her eyes strayed once more to the television and she picked up the remote control again, clicking to show subtitles.

'You're sure no one's threatened you recently?'

Ashley shook her head. 'I'd remember.'

Clare swallowed. This next bit was going to be difficult. 'Ashley, I'm sorry to have to ask this, but you've rubbed shoulders with a few dodgy characters in your time. You come across anyone with an unhealthy interest in children?'

Ashley turned from the television and stared. The first real reaction. 'You mean paedos? Jesus! You think it's a paedo that's taken Abi?'

'We can't discount the possibility.'

Ashley shook her head. 'Nope. Not met any. Not round here at least. They tend to stick together, not mix with the rest of us.'

Clare handed her a card. 'If you do remember anything will you give me a call?'

'Yeah sure, whatever.'

As they walked to the door, Ashley called to Chris, 'What time do you get off tonight?'

'You're well in there,' Clare said as they walked back to the car.

'Fuck off.'

'Fuck off, Inspector,' she corrected him.

'Fuck off, Inspector.'

–

Tony was holed up in Clare's office with a *Do Not Disturb* sign on the door.

Clare looked at the door then at Sara, who mouthed, 'Hiding from *him*.'

She jerked her head towards Lyall, still typing traffic data into the computer.

Clare grinned and tapped on her office door. Tony looked relieved to see her.

'Thank Christ it's only you. That boy has been driving me mental. This is the last day I spend with him.'

'And he's here all week,' Clare said.

Tony shook his head. 'Waste of bloody time. Anyway – progress?'

Clare sat down. 'Not much, to be honest. Just back from seeing Susan Clancy again.'

Tony raised an eyebrow.

'She's the ex-offender who had her baby taken away by social services. She popped up on the pharmacy footage on Sunday. Picking up a prescription – all checked out but we took the chance to show her the CCTV photo of the two burglars.'

'Did she recognise them?'

'No, at least I don't think so.'

'She holding out on you?'

'I'm not sure. She might be.'

'Okay. What else?'

'Sara was checking up on ex-offenders but I've not caught up with her yet. There was one who did time for dodgy images on his phone. He's out on licence.'

Tony shook his head. 'No go. Guys have been to his house and turned it over. No sign of any kids, let alone a baby.'

Clare sighed. 'I don't know whether to be glad or not. Oh, and no doctors or nurses have been struck off in the last six months, or are about to be. Have the guys had any luck following up on calls from the public?'

Tony rose. 'They're probably skiving in the incident room. Let's see...'

As they walked through the main office, Tony's eye fell on Chris and Sara who were deep in conversation. 'Check Romeo and Juliet,' he said to Clare, his voice a little too loud.

Chris's face darkened but Clare pulled Tony towards the incident room before Chris could reply.

'Cut it out,' she warned him. 'We've enough on without you provoking one of my officers.'

'But he's my favourite,' Tony said. 'You know that.'

The heat from the extra computers and the radiator, which seemed to be stuck on *High*, hit Clare and Tony as they walked in. Someone had pulled back the blinds to open windows but the room was airless. A few heads looked up as they entered, while others carried on taking phone calls. Bill, whose sweaty armpits were even more apparent on the dark red shirt he was wearing, gave Clare a smile.

'Any luck with the miscarriages?' she asked.

Bill shook his head. 'All checked out okay so far.' He lifted a printout. 'Only a few more then we're done.'

'Another dead end,' Clare said. 'What about Paul Sinclair? Have they tracked him down?'

'The lad that burgled the pharmacy? No, sorry. No one at his flat. They're checking known associates but nothing so far.'

'Okay, thanks Bill. Keep me posted.' She looked round the room and saw Nita, waiting to speak to her. 'Nita? What have you got?'

'Nothing at all with the Mitchells' own parents. Lisa's mum's living through in Paisley with her stepdad. Lisa hasn't been in touch with her and there's certainly no sign of a baby there.'

'And Kevin?'

'His mum died five years ago. Dad's in Aberdeen, out of his head with drink. He can barely look after himself, never mind a baby.'

'Okay, thanks Nita.' She stared at the whiteboard. One by one their leads were drying up. 'I'm thinking we need to put the parents on TV, Tony.'

'Yeah, I agree. I'll get onto the press office.'

'The mother will be a problem, though. She's drugged up to the eyeballs.'

'That's okay. Might melt a few hearts. Stick her up there, but let the dad do the talking.'

Clare checked her watch. 'Could we get that arranged for tomorrow? I really need to get home. Let the dog out.'

'Aye, go on,' he said. 'Plenty of lads out doing house-to-house and the news have stepped up coverage. I'll set up the press conference for tomorrow, hopefully midday. If that doesn't bring anything in, then we'll really start to worry.'

–

Clare's hopes of some progress with the central heating at Daisy Cottage were to be dashed again. Another section of the floor had been taken up and a scribbled note said, as far as she could make out, that the existing pipework wasn't compliant. She surveyed the chaos of her house, with its crumbling plasterwork, single-glazed, draughty windows and now a network of planks across an ever-increasing number of gaps in the floor.

'Remind me why I moved here?' she asked Benjy, who simply wagged his tail in response.

Her phone began to ring. She swiped to take the call. 'Hi, Geoff.'

'You sound tired,' he said. 'I'm guessing the missing baby's taking it out of you.'

'Just a bit.'

'Still okay for dinner tomorrow night?'

Clare sat down on an easy chair and kicked off her shoes. God, her feet hurt. She flexed them back and forward. 'I'm not sure. We're putting the parents on show tomorrow and that usually generates a hell of a lot of calls. It could be a late one. I can't really justify taking time off with a missing baby.'

'Oh, but they're all dying to meet you,' he said. 'Nicola phoned today to ask if you had any dislikes or allergies.'

Clare closed her eyes. She was so tired and the thought of another day of hunting for Abi Mitchell, followed by a dinner party with Geoffrey's sister and her friends was fast losing its appeal. 'Can I let you know?'

'Of course. But do try, Clare. For me.'

Tuesday, 24 September

Chapter 12

'Press conference arranged for twelve midday,' Tony told Clare as she entered the station.

'Does Wendy know?' she asked.

'Don't think so. Give her a call, please. And get the boy wonder to help set up the room. Tell him we need his journalistic abilities to get it properly prepared.'

Clare glanced at Lyall, who was tapping away at his tablet again. 'Good idea, Tony.'

'And that, Inspector, is why I'm going to be the next Superintendent!'

Clare ignored this and walked through to the incident room. 'Anything come in overnight?'

Nita looked up. 'Nothing much, boss. Managed to get a car reg off the CCTV around the pharmacy. Turned out to be stolen. Found it burned out on a bit of waste ground in Dundee.'

'Where was it stolen from?'

'Perth Road.'

'Figures.' The houses at the far end of Dundee's Perth Road were large with leafy gardens. Easy enough to pick up a car without being observed. 'Ah well, another dead end.'

Janey rose from her computer. Clare thought she seemed tired. 'They've found that couple in the Peak

District, boss. Checked out. Absolutely no sign of a baby. No child seat in the car or anything like that.'

Clare sighed. She could only hope that the press conference would yield something. They were all starting to feel the strain.

Sara put her head round the door. 'Boss, could you come out here, please?'

A woman in a raincoat was standing near the front desk. Clare thought she might be in her late forties but somehow she had the world-weary air of someone much older. A young lad who towered over her stood a little behind, his fingers drumming continuously against his legs. The lad had a shock of hair and, beneath a thick fringe, Clare could see that his eyes were flicking left and right.

She approached them with a smile. 'Hello, I'm Detective Inspector Clare Mackay. How can I help?'

The woman hesitated, and the boy continued to look at his surroundings, avoiding Clare's eye.

'Let's go somewhere quieter,' Clare said.

In the interview room, with the door closed, the woman began to relax. 'I'm Marjory Brown,' she said, 'and this is my son Devon.'

'Devon?'

'It's a family name.'

Clare smiled at the lad. He must have been about eighteen, but he lacked the confidence normally found in kids of that age. Maybe the surroundings were making him nervous. 'Nice to meet you, Devon,' she said. Then she turned back to Marjory. 'Was there something you wanted to tell me?'

Marjory glanced at her son. 'Devon, you know, has a learning difficulty. He struggles with social situations, but he does like going out and about by himself.'

Clare was beginning to wonder why Sara hadn't interviewed Marjory and Devon herself. 'I see…'

'He went to the fun run on Sunday,' Marjory was saying. 'Down on the West Sands, where that poor baby was taken.'

'On Sunday?'

'Yes, that's right.' Marjory turned to her son now. 'You were standing quite near the couple and the pram, weren't you, Devon?'

Devon nodded. 'Saw the baby.'

Clare's mouth was dry now. 'Devon, did you see someone take the baby?'

Devon shook his head. 'I saw pizza.'

'Devon loves pizza,' Marjory explained. 'And when he saw the motorbike with the pizza bag on the back, he thought they might have some for sale. So, he went across the dunes to ask if he could buy some.'

Devon nodded again. 'But the man said a swear word and that meant I had to go away.'

'Did you see who bought the pizzas?' Clare asked.

'No pizzas.'

'He didn't have any?'

'No. Didn't have pizzas. Bag was empty. It was a big empty bag.' And he held out his hands to indicate the size of the bag.

'Devon thought it was strange,' Marjory said. 'He'd seen the bike arrive and the driver hadn't taken anything out of the bag.'

Devon was watching Clare, his eyes dark beneath the fringe. 'I really like pizza.'

'Me too, Devon. No mushrooms though.'

He grinned. 'No. No mushrooms.'

'Devon asked the man if he could look inside the bag,' Marjory went on. She gave her son an encouraging smile. 'I don't think you believed him about there being no pizza, did you?'

Devon shook his head. 'But the man unzipped the bag and showed me it was empty. Then he told me to go back and watch the race. In case I missed the start.'

'And is that what you did, Devon?'

He glanced at his mum. Marjory took her cue. 'Tell the Inspector what you saw next, Devon.'

'The man came over to watch the race. But then he moved away a bit. I think he wanted to look after his bike. In case it was stolen. I watched the runners like he said and the next time I looked he was back at his bike. He zipped up the bag and rode away.'

Clare waited.

'But the bag was full,' Devon went on. 'It wasn't flat any more. It was really full so he must have been picking up pizzas, not delivering them.'

Clare stared at Marjory then back at Devon. A picture of the incident room, buzzing with activity just minutes before, flashed across her mind. She thought of the TV appeals, the officers out knocking on doors, the hours spent trawling through phone records, interviewing possible suspects. They were ploughing a colossal amount of resources into this investigation. And here she sat, isolated from it all, in this tiny interview room, with this socially awkward lad and his mother. Was it possible that they held the key to Abi's abduction?

She was suddenly aware of her heart pounding away in her chest. 'There was something in the bag, Devon? As the man rode away?'

'I thought it was pizzas,' Devon said, 'but pizzas don't move and the bag was moving. Maybe it was the man's cat. Cats move, don't they? They make a noise, too.'

Clare said, 'So, the man arrived with an empty pizza bag, and when he left, there was something moving inside the bag? Is that right, Devon?'

The lad nodded again.

'Devon, did you notice which pizza company it was?'

'Railway Pizzas,' he said, then he reeled off the phone number of the company. 'In Leuchars.'

Clare snatched up a pen and jotted it down.

'He knows the registration number too,' Marjory said. 'Go on, Devon, tell the Inspector.'

Devon gave Clare the registration number. Clare wrote this down and rose from the table. 'Excuse me a moment, please.'

Out in the main office she motioned to Chris.

'What is it?' he asked.

'The baby was carried off in one of those pizza delivery bags.'

'What – on the back of a motorbike?'

'Yes, I think so. Here's the registration and the phone number of the company. It's in Leuchars. According to the young lad, you go through Guardbridge, head right for Leuchars and it's shortly after the railway station. Take a couple of lads and head over there now. It's only six miles. Blue light it until you're within a mile then kill the siren.

Do nothing to put them on their guard. Just say you're checking up on untaxed bikes.'

Chris picked up a set of car keys and made for the door.

Clare returned to the interview room. 'Sorry about that – I just wanted to let my colleagues know what Devon has told us.' She smiled at him. 'Thank you, Devon. You've been really helpful.'

Marjory frowned. 'I'm sorry it's taken us so long to come forward. It was only when Devon mentioned the man might have a cat in the bag that I realised what it could be…'

'Please don't apologise. You've helped us enormously.'

'There's something else, too, isn't there, Devon?'

The lad nodded. 'The pram,' he said.

'The baby's pram?'

'Yeah. I heard the lady screaming. Dead loud. So I looked at her.'

'Yes?'

'She was looking in the pram and she screamed. Then she picked up a piece of paper and she read it. And then she screamed again. Really loud. And she said about her baby being gone.'

'What sort of paper, Devon?'

'Like from a notepad. With lines.'

'Could you see what was written on it?'

'No. But she looked at it like she was reading. And she screamed.'

Clare's mind was racing. 'Did you see what the lady did with the paper, Devon?'

'Put it in her pocket.'

'You're sure about that?'

He nodded his head vigorously.

Clare said, 'Devon, can you describe the pizza man?'

Devon nodded. 'He had a helmet on when he arrived but he took it off and rubbed his hair. Then he put it back on again.'

'Was this when he was watching the race?'

Devon shook his head. 'No. When he stopped the bike he took his helmet off. But then he put it on again to come and watch the race.'

'Would you like to give a description to another officer? Maybe help make up a photo on the computer?'

Devon brightened. 'I like computers.'

Clare rose and gave the lad a smile. 'You've been really helpful, Devon. If you wait here, I'll find someone to take you to one of the computers. See if we can come up with a photo of the man.'

Clare found Janey in the incident room. 'Got a minute?'

Janey followed her to a spare computer in the corner of the room and Clare explained the situation.

'Can you work on an E-FIT with the young lad, please? See if we can get a clear image of the abductor.'

'Will do.'

Clare took Devon and his mum into the incident room. A few heads looked up then went back to their enquiries. Janey greeted them with a smile, pulling out chairs for the pair, and Clare left them to it.

'Boss,' Sara called as she appeared. 'Chris on the phone.'

'Bloody hell. That was quick.' Clare took the phone from Sara. 'Chris?'

'Spoke to the owner of the pizza shop. Bike was stolen sometime between Saturday night and Sunday morning.'

'You had a good look around?'

'Yeah. Nothing here. We've got the names and addresses of all their riders so we'll get them checked out. Could you get one of the uniforms to see if any of them have pre-cons?'

'Sure, give me the names. Oh, and Chris…'

'Yeah?'

'Back here for midday, please. I want you in with the reporters, watching the reaction of the Mitchells when the cameras are on them.'

Clare hung up and stood thinking for a minute. The bike could have gone past ANPR cameras, depending on which direction the rider took.

'Sara?' she called across the office. 'Job for you.'

While Sara checked the ANPR database, Clare's thoughts returned to Lisa Mitchell. Until now, she had no reason to think Lisa was anything other than a distraught parent. A victim of a random abduction. But now – that note – why would she conceal it? And that phone too. Who was Lisa calling that she didn't want them to know about? She thought again about the Mitchells' finances. A large house and two expensive cars and they were, what, a groundsman and a tanning salon assistant? It didn't add up, even if he had earned a packet working on the rigs.

She opened her office door to find Tony bent over a copy of the force Mission Statement. He scooped the papers up and put them in a drawer as she entered.

'The Mitchells' finances,' she said, 'I'd like to look into them.'

'Reason?'

Clare related Devon's tale about Lisa finding a note in the pram and putting it in her pocket.

'Ask her about it.'

Clare frowned. 'I'm not keen. With the press conference coming up, I want to see how she is in front of the cameras. If she is holding something back, I don't want to put her on her guard. I'd rather wait to see if she trips herself up.'

'That the only reason?'

'No,' Clare said. 'They seem to have a lifestyle beyond their means.'

'So you want a court order?'

'Yes please. I'd like a credit check, bank account balances, direct debits, mortgage payments, insurance, car loans plus monthly income.'

'You sure about this, Clare? There'll be hell to pay if they're clean and it gets out we investigated them.'

'Can't take the chance, Tony. We have to find out why Abi was taken.'

'What about the E-FIT photo? Are you planning to hand copies out to the press?'

'No. I want everyone here to see it first. Someone might know him. But, if we release the photo, he might leg it before we can pick him up.'

'Okay, Clare. Let's hope one of the lads recognises him, then.'

'Amen to that.'

–

Clare found an empty interview room and sat down to think. She was starting to believe there was more to the Mitchells than she had first thought; Lisa's affair with Phil Patrick for a start, and now this. She wondered what the court order would turn up. Surely Kevin's salary would be above board, but the tanning salon… It was an easy business if they wanted to avoid money going through the books. Perhaps they didn't even record the number of clients they saw in a day. Maybe Lisa offered a discount for cash in hand. Maybe the owner didn't even know.

Clare checked her watch. Two hours until the press conference began and she wanted a good hour to run through statements with Tony. Wendy was bringing the Mitchells in about half an hour before.

She had time. She snatched up her car keys and told Sara she'd be back by eleven.

Chapter 13

Bronzalite was on Woodburn Place, a small street which led to the harbour. Clare found a parking space opposite the salon and killed the engine. Despite the warm September sunshine, she felt a cold blast of wind straight off the North Sea as she stepped out of the car. She pulled her jacket round her and walked across the road. The salon had been a house at one time but now the downstairs windows were bricked up and a sign above the front door proclaimed it to be *St Andrews foremost tanning salon*. Looking at the outside, Clare doubted that, somehow. She pushed open the front door and a bell rang, alerting staff to her presence. Inside, she found the walls lined with yellow pine, reminiscent of a 1970s sauna. A young girl with jet-black hair and an expression to match greeted Clare without enthusiasm.

Clare showed her card and asked if the owner was in.

'Suppose this is about Lisa's baby,' the girl said.

Clare neither confirmed nor denied this. 'The owner?'

'Hold on.' She disappeared through a door behind the counter and a few minutes later, an older woman emerged. She was impeccably made-up and clearly a sunbed addict herself.

'I'm Sacha,' the woman said. 'You've come about Lisa, poor lamb. How is she?'

'Oh – you know,' Clare said, avoiding the question. 'Actually, I've just come to say that we don't want Lisa and Kevin bothered with phone calls and visits. So if you do need to get in touch with her, maybe you could go through us?'

Sacha seemed to swallow that. 'Of course,' she said. 'Anything to help. Anything at all.'

'You must be missing her,' Clare said.

Sacha shrugged. 'We're not busy just now so I'm managing.'

Clare strolled round the salon, stopping to look at the products in a glass case and the price list behind the counter. 'I've never had a tan.'

Sacha studied her. 'You look pretty tanned to me.'

'Just back from France.'

'Nice. Soon fades, though, doesn't it? I could book you in for a top-up. Do you a good price.'

'Maybe another time. I'm guessing you don't get many police coming in.'

'You'd be surprised,' Sacha said. 'They like a tan, the polis. But it's mainly older kids and students. Especially when they're having dances and that. Then just before the summer we get busier. Nobody wants to go on the beach chalk white, do they?'

'As long as you can make a living at it, eh?'

'Not as much as I'd like,' Sacha said. 'I'm thinking of hiring someone to do nails as well. Bring in a few more customers.'

Clare thought it wouldn't do any harm to keep Sacha onside. 'I can hand out a few cards at the station for you, if you like. Spread the word.'

Sacha lifted a handful of business cards from the counter and gave them to Clare. 'Tell your colleagues I'll see them right. You lads find Lisa's baby and it's half price for you all.'

Clare thanked Sacha and, clutching the business cards, left the salon, the door ringing again as she went. She checked her watch. There was still plenty of time before the press conference and she strolled the short distance to the harbour. A small bascule bridge, which formed part of the Fife Coastal Path, was in the process of lifting, to allow a motorboat to putter its way through. She stood, watching the bridge for a few minutes. A queue of walkers were waiting to cross.

'You look hungry, hen.'

Clare turned to see a woman of around sixty carrying a blackboard on a metal stand. She was dressed in a long, striped apron, tied round her middle, and Clare guessed she was from the tiny harbour cafe, little more than a portacabin but a hit with locals and visitors alike. She glanced at the board and read:

Today's Specials:
Leek & Potato Soup
Salmon Quiche
Caramac Cake

'Polis?' the woman said.

Clare smiled. 'That obvious?'

'Doesn't take a genius, hen. I'm guessing you've been along at the tanning salon. Suppose there's no sign of the wee baby?'

Clare hesitated but the woman waved this away.

'Don't mind me. Too nosey for my own good. But we're all keeping our eyes open.' She indicated a sheet of paper stuck on one of the windows. It showed the same photo of Abi that Kevin had shown them on his phone. Beneath the photo were the words:

Have You Seen This Baby?
Taken from the West Sands
Phone 999

Clare smiled at the photo. 'Appreciate it.'

The woman spread her hands. 'Not much else we can do, eh?'

Clare made to leave, then the woman said, 'Do you a quick bacon roll if you like?'

She was about to refuse then realised how hungry she was. 'As long as it's quick.'

'Two shakes,' the woman said. She disappeared indoors and seconds later the aroma of bacon grilling reached Clare's nose. 'Ketchup?' the woman shouted.

'Please.'

Two minutes later, she was tucking into the best bacon roll she'd tasted in a long time. She fished in her pocket for some coins but the woman waved it away.

'You find wee Abi. That'll be payment enough for me, hen.'

Clare tried again to pay but the woman was insistent. 'You're very kind,' she said to the woman. 'Thank you.'

The woman returned to her pot of leek and potato soup and Clare strolled back to the car, trying not to let bacon grease drip on her shirt. As she passed Bronzalite she thought about how quiet the salon had been, and Sacha's comment about bringing someone in to do nails.

She doubted there was enough custom for Lisa to slip a few quid in her pocket when Sacha wasn't there. So how were the Mitchells living?

Her phone buzzed. She fished in her pocket for a tissue to wipe her hands then swiped to answer the call. 'Jim?'

'Hi Clare. Just had a phone call from an irate farmer.'

'Not the protest camp?'

'No. Same direction but a bit further on, nearer Guard-bridge. His tractor was ploughing a field when it ran over a motorbike. Looks like it was driven into the field and abandoned. Done a load of damage to the tractor but...'

'Is it our pizza bike, Jim?'

'Think so. Sara's on her way there now to check the registration.'

'Okay, I'm heading back now.'

–

'Bike found, I hear,' Tony said as Clare entered the station.

'Yeah, hopefully. Sara should confirm soon.'

'Which means they've almost certainly transferred the baby to a car and it could be any-bloody-where by now.'

'She.'

'Eh?'

'She. The baby is a girl. Abigail.'

Tony rolled his eyes. 'Aye, whatever. Any point in checking ANPR footage for cars instead?'

'Probably not. Needle in a haystack, Tony. There must have been thousands of cars out on Sunday. The only thing we can say for sure is he's left St Andrews, heading towards Guardbridge.'

Tony took out his phone and called up a map. 'So Guardbridge is where, from here?'

Clare indicated the road out of St Andrews, past the Old Course Hotel. 'It's about five miles west of the town.'

'And beyond Guardbridge?'

She used two fingers to zoom in on the map. 'There's a roundabout, as soon as you enter the village. Only two options: straight ahead takes you to Cupar, going right would take him through Leuchars towards Dundee.'

Tony sat back and pressed his fingers together. 'Given the pharmacy break-in was in Dundee...'

'I agree. It seems likely he would head that way, although just because the burglary was in Dundee doesn't mean our abductor lives there. And,' she added, 'there's every chance the car they transferred to was also stolen. With the resources we have, it would be a waste of manpower.'

He considered this for a moment then said, 'Okay, fair enough. Any news on the pizza drivers?'

Clare was about to say that Chris was out checking them but she stopped herself in time. The less Tony and Chris had to do with each other, the better. 'I've a couple of lads out checking that now. Told them to be back for the press conference, though.'

'All right. Come into my office,' he said, ignoring the fact that it was actually *her* office he was using. 'We need to run through your statement before the hacks get here.'

Chapter 14

The press began gathering from eleven o'clock onwards. Clare, having worked in a busy Glasgow station, was used to the scale of it but Sara, still early in her service, was amazed by the number of reporters and photographers queueing for a seat. As well as the newspaper journalists who had been hanging round the station since Sunday, TV and radio reporters had crammed into the room and an array of cameras stood behind the chairs. Lyall flapped round, trying unsuccessfully to place them in the journalistic equivalent of a pecking order.

'I'd like you and Tony in with the press,' Clare told Chris. She saw his face darken. 'Yes, I know,' she said. 'I know. But this is too important, Chris. You'll just have to put your differences behind you – for today at least. Okay?'

Chris exhaled. 'Yeah, sure. Whatever you say.'

'Okay. So, I'll be on one side of the Mitchells with Wendy on the other. Your job is to watch them like a hawk for any sign of abnormal behaviour, unusual reactions – that sort of thing.'

'It's called duping delight, you know,' Chris said.

Clare stared at him. 'You what?'

'Duping delight,' he repeated. 'It's where the guilty party enjoys the attention from the situation they've created. They're so pleased with themselves for getting away with whatever they've done that they give off small signals. A sudden flash of a smile, or an inappropriate comment. Making light of a serious situation – that sort of thing.'

'Detective Sergeant West, you never cease to amaze me. Where the hell did you learn that?'

He shrugged. 'I dunno. Some TV programme.'

'Okay, then. You and Tony are on *duping delight* duty.'

'Joking aside, Clare,' Chris said, 'you don't really think they've got anything to do with it, do you?'

'I'm ruling nothing out,' Clare said. 'It's clear they're going through hell. But that doesn't mean it isn't a hell of their own making.'

The Mitchells arrived with Wendy just after half-past eleven. She took them in a side door so they wouldn't have to face the clamour of reporters. They seemed composed, if a little in awe of their surroundings. Kevin was hollow-eyed and Clare wondered if he had slept at all since Abi's abduction.

'This will help find Abi, won't it?' he said to Clare.

She patted his arm. 'It certainly won't do any harm, Kevin. Seeing the parents can be enough to prick someone's conscience.' She looked at Lisa. Her mouth was set, her lips tight. She seemed dead behind the eyes. 'Are you okay to do this, Lisa?'

Lisa regarded Clare with contempt. 'I want my fucking baby back.'

'Lise…' Kevin started.

She turned on him. 'What have you done to find her, eh? Clearing out the garden shed when you should be out

147

there looking!' Her eyes burned. 'You should *all* be out looking for her, instead of this bloody circus.'

Wendy moved towards Lisa but Clare stopped her.

'Lisa,' she said, 'listen carefully to me. You can't go out there angry. The whole point of putting you and Kevin in front of the cameras is to elicit maximum sympathy from the public. If somebody out there knows or even suspects something, we want them to come forward. We want every mother in the country to put herself in your shoes. It's the only way. But if you go out there angry – well, folk can be funny. They might see you as hot-headed and maybe not a good mother.'

'She's a fantastic mother,' Kevin said. 'Don't you say that!'

'I know that,' Clare said. 'You're both great parents. Everyone here knows that. But we need everyone else to know it too. It might just help.'

'What if it doesn't?' Lisa's expression was still sullen.

'It will,' Clare assured them with more confidence than she felt. She took a deep breath. 'Before I talk you through what will happen at the press conference, there's something I need to tell you.'

The Mitchells looked at her, their faces drawn. Kevin stiffened. 'What?' he asked.

'On Sunday, we believe Abi was put into a large bag on the back of a motorbike and ridden away towards Guardbridge.'

Lisa's hand went to her mouth. 'My baby?' Her voice rose. 'On a motorbike?'

Clare nodded. 'We think it was the pizza delivery bike that you saw.'

Kevin's expression clouded as he processed this. 'You mean that bike? When I said we should have a pizza? Our Abi – was in there? Zipped up in a stinking pizza bag?'

Clare nodded. 'I'm sure whoever took her made sure she was safe inside the bag.'

'You don't know that!' Lisa spat. 'You don't know how she felt – if she was crying for me – you don't even know where she is!'

Kevin put a hand on Lisa's arm but she shrugged it off.

'The bike was found abandoned in a field, just outside Guardbridge,' Clare went on. 'There was no sign of Abi or the rider so we think she must have been transferred to a car.'

Kevin's head was in his hands now and he sniffed audibly.

Lisa said, 'How long have you known this?'

'We only found out a couple of hours ago. A witness came forward this morning,' Clare said.

'Who?' Lisa said. 'I want to see this witness. Who was it?'

Clare shook her head. 'He's not here any longer. It was a young lad. He's been helping us put together an E-FIT photo of the rider.'

'Can I see it?' Lisa asked.

'As soon as the press conference is over.'

Kevin frowned. 'You're not showing it to the press?'

Clare shook her head. 'Not yet. I want the local cops to have sight of it first. If someone does recognise him we'll pick him up before the press get wind of it. We don't want him forewarned and making a run for it.' She hesitated. 'I'm sorry to spring the motorbike on you but I'm going to mention it in the press conference and I wanted to let you know first. The more publicity we have, the better.' She smiled at them. 'Is that okay?'

The Mitchells exchanged glances, then nodded.

'Right then,' Clare said. 'Let me tell you what to expect when you meet the press.'

—

At two minutes to twelve, Clare entered the room to speak to the assembled journalists. Lyall, she noticed, had taken a seat facing the throng, rather than joining their ranks.

He rushed up as she came in. 'All ready for you, Inspector. Just as you asked.'

'Thanks, Lyall. I'm going to make a brief announcement before we bring the parents in.'

Clare cleared her throat and the room fell silent. 'Good morning, ladies and gentlemen,' she began. 'Thank you for your attendance today. The format is as follows: I will give a short summary of where we are in the investigation which will be followed by the opportunity to ask questions. As usual, nothing of an operational nature will be revealed. Following around five or ten minutes of questions, Mr Kevin Mitchell, Abigail's father, will make an appeal. I would ask that you do not shout out or interrupt Kevin. The Mitchells are understandably shattered by the abduction of their daughter…'

'Rebecca Wilson, *Fife News*,' a young blonde reporter said. 'Will Mrs Mitchell be speaking?'

'No,' Clare said. 'Kevin will speak for both of them. Please don't address any questions directly to Mrs Mitchell. She's trying very hard to remain positive.' Clare scanned the room before going on. 'There is one further thing. I will again give details of Abi's medical condition and the medication she needs in my statement. This is life-saving treatment and the more you can do to emphasise that in your reports, the better. We need to make this absolutely clear to her abductors. But – and this is vitally important – I do not want Mr and Mrs Mitchell questioned on the subject. They've been through enough already and they do not need reminding of the danger to Abi's life.' Clare checked round the room again to assure herself they were taking this in. 'I hope that's clear to everyone?'

There were murmurs of assent and she left the room to fetch the Mitchells.

As they prepared to enter, Clare warned Lisa and Kevin to expect some flashes from the cameras, but even she was taken aback by the noise and light that filled the room for the next two minutes. Clare took a seat next to Lisa, who was clutching a baby blanket. Wendy flanked Kevin at the other end of the row.

'All right?' Clare whispered to them. They looked at her but made no reply.

She rose to her feet and recapped briefly the events of Sunday morning. She held up a sleepsuit identical to the one Abi had been wearing and a photo of Abi flashed up on a screen to the side. 'We believe that Abi was removed from the West Sands, hidden in a zipped bag on the back of a motorbike – the kind used to deliver pizzas. We have recovered the bike in a field near Guardbridge and believe Abi was then transferred to a car.'

'Which pizza company was it?' a reporter asked.

'The bike was stolen from Railway Pizzas in Leuchars,' Clare said, 'about six miles north-west of St Andrews. So we want to know if anyone saw a pizza bike between late

Saturday night and midday on Sunday, particularly if it was somewhere you wouldn't normally see one.'

Clare went on to speak about the medication Abi needed and the image of Abi on the screen was replaced by a digoxin bottle. Then she looked over the heads towards the cameras behind. 'I'm appealing now to whoever has Abi. You may have taken her because you desperately want a baby of your own. You might be unhappy now and feeling panicky. I want to assure you that, if you bring Abi into the nearest police station, you will be treated with compassion and understanding. Abduction of a baby is a serious charge, but if you need medical care then we will ensure you receive it. And if that seems too difficult, then please take her to a hospital or doctor's surgery and leave her where she can be found. We all want Abi safe, but she needs her mum and dad. They miss her dreadfully and she must be missing them. Please bring her back to them.'

The questions came thick and fast. Rebecca Wilson was the first to catch Clare's eye. 'What is being done to find Abi?'

Clare gave the stock response about following a number of leads.

'Charlie McAinsh, *North News*,' said an older man in an open-necked shirt. 'How hopeful are you that Abi will be returned home safely?'

Clare responded by saying they were linking Abi's abduction with the pharmacy burglary and, as such, they believed Abi was being well cared for. 'We hope to have her back with Kevin and Lisa very soon.'

The next to speak was a veteran national reporter Clare had met many times while on the Glasgow force. He raised his hand.

'Sandy?'

'Have you examined the CCTV from the pharmacy and, if so, has the culprit been identified? Is he or she known to police?'

Clare kept her counsel on that last question. She didn't want Paul Sinclair to be panicked into fleeing the area. She gave what she hoped was a noncommittal answer then turned to Kevin. 'Mr Mitchell – Kevin – would now like to say a few words.'

The atmosphere in the room was electric. Cameras flashed again for a few minutes then stopped and the room fell silent.

Kevin cleared his throat. 'Abi…' His voice cracked and he stopped. Wendy pushed a glass of water towards him and he took a drink. Then he tried again. 'Abi is such a lovely little girl. And so good. From the day she was born she was content. She loves to be out in her pram in the garden, watching the washing blow on the line.' Kevin's face lit up at the memory and he stopped again. Wendy gently touched his elbow and he went on. 'She likes the mobile over her cot and her musical toys, doesn't she?' He smiled at Lisa who nodded, her head turned to the side, to avoid the gaze of the cameras. 'She watches our every move and we love her more than we can say.' He put his hand in Lisa's and gripped it tightly. 'On Sunday, we were having a day out, like any other family.'

Lisa began to cry quietly and Clare passed her a tissue.

Kevin seemed almost in a trance now. He was looking beyond the cameras, his mind back at the West Sands. 'And, in that second – the split second we took our eyes off Abi's pram – someone took her. They took her away from us. Away from her mum and dad. But she needs us and we need her too. She's our baby and we want her back.'

Without warning, Lisa lifted the blanket to her face, holding it against her cheek. 'I miss holding her so much,' she blurted out, her voice quavering. She held the blanket to her nose and inhaled deeply. 'I miss her smell. That wonderful baby smell.' She breathed in the scent from the blanket again then lowered it from her face, still clutching it in both hands. 'But every day it's there a little bit less. And I'm afraid – I'm really, really afraid that if we don't get Abi back soon, there won't be any smell left.'

Kevin put his arm around his wife. Lisa buried her head in his neck and began to sob loudly.

Clare rose from her seat and cleared her throat. 'I think that's everything now, ladies and gentlemen.' She glanced over to Wendy who took the cue, leading Kevin and Lisa out of the room. Clare held back for a minute, watching the journalists gathering up their things and rushing outside to phone in their reports. When the last one had left she asked two uniformed officers to help Lyall put the room back to rights. Then she joined Wendy and the Mitchells in her office.

'You both did so well. Thank you for being so brave.'

Lisa flicked a glance at Clare then looked away again. Kevin said, 'As long as it helps.'

'Wendy will take you both home shortly,' Clare said, 'but I'd like to show you that E-FIT photo now.'

Lisa sat forward. 'Go on, then.'

Clare reached into her desk drawer and withdrew the photo. She pushed it across the desk towards the couple.

Kevin picked it up. 'Is this him? The man who took our Abi?'

'It's possible,' Clare said. 'Our witness has a good memory so we're hopeful it's a decent likeness. Do you recognise him? Either of you?'

Kevin stared at the photo, as if trying to make sense of what he was seeing. Lisa began to cry again.

'Does he look familiar? Anything about him?' Clare asked again.

Kevin shook his head. Lisa wiped the tears away and studied the photo.

'Lisa?' Clare said, her voice gentle.

Lisa stared intently at it.

Clare waited. Was this it? Was Lisa remembering something? She held her breath. Then Lisa shook her head.

'No, sorry. I don't know him.'

Chapter 15

When Wendy had taken Kevin and Lisa back home, Clare called Tony and Chris into her office. 'How did they seem?'

Chris shook his head. 'If they're acting then they're bloody good at it.'

Tony glanced at Chris then back at Clare. 'I agree. Genuine grief, the pair of them.'

'I think we'll give it a couple of hours to see if anything comes of the press conference, then I'd like to go back and confront Lisa about the piece of paper she took from the pram.'

Tony frowned. 'Should have done that right after the press conference, Clare.'

'You saw how they were,' Clare said. 'We wouldn't have got any sense out of Lisa. And, to be honest, it might be better if I ask her about it when Kevin's not there. I'm not sure what's going on with her but I reckon there's something up; and I don't just mean her fling with the pastry chef.'

The phone on Clare's desk started to ring.

Tony snatched it up. 'DCI McAvettie… Okay.' He handed the phone to Clare. 'Head gardener at that posh school.'

Clare took the phone and introduced herself.

'Sorry to bother you, Inspector,' the gardener said. 'I spoke to two of your officers yesterday and then I remembered something. It's probably not important, but they did say if there was anything at all…'

'Yes, of course. What was it you remembered?'

'Well it was young Kevin. His car. Don't know if you've seen it but it's a rather nice Volkswagen Arteon.'

'I have seen it.'

'He was going to sell it, you see. The baby was due soon and he said he could do with the money. I said I might know someone who would be interested, so he gave me all the details. Mileage and so on.'

'When was this?'

'Oh, let's see – about eight or nine months ago, I think. To be honest, Inspector, I think the lad was a bit short of cash.'

'But he didn't sell?'

'No. My friend was coming to see the car then Kevin changed his mind. Said he wasn't selling it after all.'

'Did he say why?'

'No, he didn't.'

'Did he seem short of cash after that? As if he was tightening his belt?'

'Not that I noticed. I don't pay much attention, Inspector. As long as the work gets done. But I thought you might want to know.'

Clare put down the phone and relayed the conversation to Tony and Chris. 'What do you make of that?'

'Could be innocent enough,' Chris said. 'Might have had a win on the horses.'

'Doubt it,' said Tony. 'More likely he paid off a car loan with money from working on the rigs.'

'That would run out eventually, though,' Chris said.

'Yeah, suppose. We'll dig into their finances as soon as the court order's through.'

'I called in to the tanning salon,' Clare said. 'Normally I'd say it was the ideal business for Lisa putting the odd payment in her pocket, but it wasn't exactly busy. I can't see her being able to cream off enough to fund their current lifestyle.'

'We might just have to ask them,' Tony said.

Clare sighed. 'I know. But let's see if anything comes of the press conference first.'

Clare and Chris left Tony and went to speak to Janey, who had helped Devon with the E-FIT photo.

'I've put it up on the Force portal,' she said. 'Hopefully someone will recognise him.'

Clare looked at the image. It showed a man somewhere between thirty and fifty, hair starting to recede on top, clean shaven. His eyes were blue, his complexion pale.

'Bill?' she called through to the incident room. 'Got a minute?'

Bill came wandering through and peered at the image. 'I've seen him somewhere before,' he said. 'What do you reckon, Janey?'

Sara was hovering. 'Boss, it's DCI McAvettie.'

'What about him?'

Sara swallowed, then said, 'He says he's going to fucking kill you.'

Clare sighed. 'I'd better come and see him.'

Chris made a move to join her but she held a hand out. 'You stay put. I don't want blood on that nice new shirt.'

She found him standing in the doorway of her office, hands on his hips, his face livid with rage.

'You stupid bloody woman,' he said, and he stood back to admit her, slamming the door behind her.

Clare tried to keep her voice steady. 'Problem?'

'Depends, Inspector. If you think it's absolutely fine to blunder in, completely unannounced, to the home of a woman who has recently buried her newborn baby and ask her if she's stolen somebody else's, then no. We do not have a problem.'

'Ah,' Clare said. 'Mrs Mistry been on the phone?'

'No, Inspector.' Tony's eyes were flashing now. 'Mrs Mistry is too fucking upset to come to the phone. Mr Mistry, on the other hand, was able to express his displeasure most eloquently. And after he expressed it to me, he planned to express it again to the Chief Constable. That's his *friend*, the Chief Constable.'

Clare looked at him wordlessly.

'You remember the Chief Constable, Inspector? He's the man who could put us all out of a job.'

Clare took a deep breath. 'Tony…'

'Don't even start. Don't even try to justify it. You go clodhopping in, accusing this man's wife of stealing a baby, for God's sake. Did you even look round at the house? Even you must have spotted how wealthy they are.'

'You think being rich precludes you from committing crime?'

Tony sighed heavily. 'No, of course it doesn't. But it does mean you can buy the best legal help available. Not that our Mr Mistry needs to do that because he's the senior partner in Mistry & McLeod. Offices in Dundee, Perth and Edinburgh, in case you didn't know. Mr Mistry himself defended that scabby wee gangster from Cramond last year. We should have nailed him but Mistry got him off on a technicality. And this is who you choose to upset in the middle of a busy investigation. Well played, Inspector!'

Clare sank down on a chair. 'Tony, I had to check her out. You know that something as dreadful as losing a baby can disturb the balance of your mind. And the hospital staff thought her reaction was worrying. I *had* to.'

'All right. You had to. But you could have been a bit more subtle.'

Clare shrugged at this but Tony went on.

'Ask the neighbours, her GP, the midwife – anyone but Mrs fucking Mistry herself.'

'Sorry, but we're up against it here. I'd rather put Abi's life ahead of Mr Mistry's feelings.'

This seemed to calm him down. He sat back in his chair. 'So would I, Clare, but there are ways of doing these things.'

She looked at him. 'What's happened to you, Tony? You were never known for your subtlety. I seem to recall you ruffling a few feathers in your time.'

'Ah,' he said, 'you're thinking of the old Tony.'

'You've gone corporate! You've sold out. All because you're in line for promotion.'

He eased back in his chair and crossed one long leg over the other. 'Do you know the difference between a Chief Inspector and a Superintendent, Clare?'

'I've a feeling you're going to tell me.'

'About ten grand a year, actually. Think about it.'

'It still needed checking out.'

He exhaled deeply. 'Of course it did. It just needed someone with a lighter touch than you to do it. Now fuck off and do something useful – preferably without upsetting anyone rich and powerful.'

Chris was waiting outside the door for Clare. 'Okay?'

'Yeah, I suppose. That woman we went to see – the one who lost her baby?'

'Mrs Mistry?'

'Turns out her husband's a mega-powerful solicitor and a personal friend of the Chief Constable.'

Chris began to laugh.

'Shut up. Or I'll tell Tony it was your idea.'

As they wandered into the incident room, Janey glanced up from her computer. 'That E-FIT of the motorbike man, boss. I think we've got him.'

'Name?'

'Paul Sinclair. Dundee lad.'

Clare stared. 'Paul Sinclair? You sure, Janey? He's the bloke the Dundee lads identified from the pharmacy. You sure it's him?'

'Pretty sure.' Janey turned her monitor round to show Clare. 'Have a look.' She jabbed the screen with a finger. 'This is the E-FIT that lad Devon helped us with.'

Clare looked at it. 'Okay...'

Janey clicked the mouse and another photo appeared. 'Now this is Sinclair's photo from the files.' She turned to look at Clare. 'See the similarity?'

Clare nodded then said, 'Can you call up the pharmacy photos, Janey?'

Janey took the mouse and located the stills taken from the pharmacy CCTV. She waited while Clare peered at them then said, 'What do you think, boss?'

'I think you're right, Janey. Same guy.' She stood thinking for a minute, then said, 'Pre-cons?'

'The usual. Housebreaking, drugs, assault.'

'Done time?'

'A couple of spells in Perth. Been out a few years now, though. Kept his nose clean. Until this.'

'That's definite then. There is a connection between the abduction and the break-in at the pharmacy. Get his photo circulated across the Force. Scotland wide, in case he's out of the area now.'

'Will do, boss. I'll give Bell Street a call too. See if he's turned up yet. Want it out to the press?'

Clare shook her head. 'Not yet. If he is still around Dundee we don't want him legging it. Let's see if we can pick him up first. If not, we'll go public.'

Clare noticed Jim hovering in the doorway. 'Jim?'

'Sorry, Clare. I know you're snowed under with this baby search but I'm trying to clear a backlog of paperwork here.'

'That's fine, Jim. What's the problem?'

'It's that drugs death that came in when you were on holiday.'

Drugs death. Clare searched her memory. It rang a vague bell. And then she remembered an email she had seen on Sunday, after Abi's disappearance. It seemed light years ago now. 'I did see the email, Jim. I'm afraid I've not had a chance to look at it.'

'If you're happy to leave it with me, I'll finish off the paperwork. Let the parents and the school know we're closing it off.'

'School? Was it a youngster, Jim?'

'Sixteen-year-old girl. Yvette Jackson. Bloody waste of a life.'

'Local?'

'Yes, parents lived towards Dunino, about five miles south of the town. But she was at school here. Well, I say here, but on the outskirts really.'

'You don't mean Melville College?'

'I think so. Want me to check?'

'Please, Jim. And let me have a look at the file.'

Five minutes later, Clare and Chris were on their way to Melville College.

—

The school was set about a mile out of town.

'Slow down,' Chris said. 'It's just along here.'

Clare dropped her speed then she saw the sign: dark blue with the words *Melville College* in gold lettering. She turned the car off the road and drove up a tree-lined avenue to the front entrance. The school was a substantial building with playing fields behind. Unusually for this part of Fife, it was built in red brick, not unlike the brickwork at her own Daisy Cottage. For a brief moment, her mind wandered to her plumber and the seemingly endless job of installing a new central heating system. She hoped fervently that she'd see some progress when she went home that evening.

The receptionist asked them to take a seat while she telephoned the headteacher's office. As they waited, Clare contemplated the opulence a private education could buy. A substantial mahogany trophy cabinet was full of cups and shields while a wooden honours board had the names of the head girls over the years inscribed in gold lettering. There were fresh flowers on the reception desk and the carpet had been designed to include the school crest.

Chris rolled his eyes and Clare administered a warning kick to his ankle.

A door opened and the headteacher greeted them, her black gown flying behind her. She was in her late forties and the epitome of efficiency. Her blonde hair, showing the first signs of silver, was short but immaculately cut and beneath her gown she wore a plain grey blouse and darker skirt. She led them along a wood-lined corridor and showed them into her office.

'Tea?' she asked, her smile fixed.

Clare suddenly found she would love a cup of tea and so the headteacher's secretary was dispatched to make a pot.

'You are here, no doubt, because of the Mitchell baby's abduction.' She removed her glasses and met their eyes. 'It goes without saying that my thoughts are with the family, as are those of all our staff.' She formed her lips into a smile but her eyes did not follow suit.

Clare thought the head probably didn't appreciate unscheduled visits. But that was the least of her worries. She decided not to mention Yvette Jackson's death at this point. If the head was happy to talk about Kevin, they might learn something the uniformed guys had missed.

Somewhere outside the room, a bell began to ring. The head clasped her hands together and waited until it had stopped. 'Afternoon break,' she told them when the ringing had ceased. Then she put her glasses back on and opened a desk drawer. 'I spoke to your colleagues about Mr Mitchell yesterday and gave them details of his employment – dates, duties and colleagues. But I have another copy here if it would be helpful?' She withdrew a sheet of paper from the drawer and offered it to Clare.

Clare thanked her and took the sheet of paper. 'Do you find Mr Mitchell to be a satisfactory employee?'

'As far as I am aware. But my contact with him was limited. The head gardener is the chap you need to speak to. I'll ask my secretary to show you to his office once you've had your tea.'

Clare asked a few more questions but there was little more forthcoming so they drank their tea. 'As we're here,' she said, taking a second shortbread finger, 'can I ask about one of your pupils, please? The young girl who died recently – Yvette Jackson.'

The headteacher's smile froze and her lips tightened. 'It's very sad, of course. But I rather thought we had dealt with that. It's so unsettling for the girls, you see.'

My God, Clare thought. *She cares more about the school's reputation than the life of one of her pupils.* She watched the headteacher carefully for any sign of emotion – regret, even. But there was only the mask of professionalism. Clare decided not to spare her. 'Is there a problem with drugs in the school?'

The headteacher looked askance. 'Certainly not. This was an isolated incident which occurred well away from the premises. Most unfortunate and sad, of course, for the family. But I assure you, Inspector, that Yvette's untimely death is nothing whatsoever to do with Melville College.'

Clare took a last sip of tea and replaced her cup on the saucer. 'I'd like to speak to Yvette's friends, please. Those she was closest to.'

The lips tightened again. 'Is that really necessary? As I said, it's unsettling.'

'I'm afraid so. If you wouldn't mind?'

The headteacher rose and excused herself. A few minutes later she returned. 'I've spoken to the form mistress and she's sending up two girls: Rachel and Ebony. Please don't keep them long. This is an important year for them.' She stood, her hands clasped in front of her, eyes on the door.

'If we could see them alone, please?' Clare said.

The headteacher gave Clare a withering glance. 'I should make you aware that these girls are just sixteen, Inspector. I am, therefore, in loco parentis.' She looked at Chris. 'I am acting as their parents, you see.'

For the second time, Clare tapped Chris's ankle with her foot and he remained obediently silent. She fixed her smile and said, 'Of course. We understand your duties towards the girls completely. We do have the right to interview them without parental consent but we always prefer to have the parents onside. Perhaps if your secretary could telephone the parents, I could reassure them before talking with the girls?'

The headteacher's eyes narrowed and she regarded Clare without speaking for a moment. Then she turned on her heel and left the room. A minute later she returned and resumed her seat. The telephone on her desk rang and, after speaking a few words, she passed the receiver to Clare. Clare spoke to the mother of the first girl to reassure her about their enquiries and consent was duly given. When the second phone call had been completed the headteacher rose.

'I'll ask the girls to come straight in. Please send them back to class when you have finished.'

And, with that, she swept from the room, closing the door behind her, a little louder than was strictly necessary.

'You've made a friend for life there,' Chris said.

A few minutes later there was a gentle tap at the door and it opened slowly. Two girls dressed in white blouses and checked pinafores stood in the doorway.

Clare rose to meet them. 'Come in, girls. Nothing to worry about.'

Ebony, unlike her name, had an unruly mane of Titian curls and a face full of freckles. She seemed more confident than Rachel, who hung back, twisting a strand of blonde hair in her fingers. Clare pulled out two seats. Ebony sat, then motioned with her head to Rachel who came slowly forward and perched on the edge of the other seat, smoothing her pinafore down over her legs.

Clare smiled at the pair. 'We won't keep you long. I'd just like a bit of background on your classmate – Yvette, wasn't it?'

Ebony and Rachel exchanged glances.

Then Ebony said, 'But we told all this to the other policemen.'

Clare spread her hands. 'I know. Just one of those things. And I'd rather hear it from you girls. I gather you were Yvette's closest friends?'

Rachel bit her lip. 'We really miss her.'

'Tell me what happened. Yvette had taken some drugs, yeah?'

The girls nodded.

'Some pills she had. She showed us,' Rachel said.

'They were really pretty,' Ebony added. 'Little pink ones.'

'Did she offer them to you?'

The girls glanced at each other again but didn't speak.

'It doesn't matter to us if she did,' Clare said. 'We're more concerned with what happened to Yvette and who gave her the drugs.'

Rachel nudged Ebony, who took the cue. 'She said she got them in town. But she wouldn't tell us where.'

'Did she tell you when she bought them?' Chris asked.

Ebony shook her head. 'No, but I think it was maybe the Wednesday before – in the afternoon.'

Chris said, 'That's really helpful, Ebony. What makes you think it was Wednesday?'

Ebony smiled at Chris and sat back, crossing her legs. 'We have games on a Wednesday afternoon. Only, Yvette said she had a stomach ache and Miss Samson – she's the games mistress – she said Yvette could go and get changed and sit quietly in the changing room. But I saw her...'

Chris sat forward in his seat. Clare decided it was sometimes useful to have a young, good-looking male colleague.

'Go on,' he said.

Ebony had relaxed now and was clearly enjoying the attention. 'She winked at me, as she went away, you see. And when she was out of Miss Samson's view, I saw her heading for the main gate.'

'So she went home early?' Clare asked.

'Home, or to town.'

'What makes you think she was going to town?' Chris said.

'Next day, she showed us the pills. So she must have gone into town to get them, don't you think?'

Clare didn't answer this. 'And do you know when she took them?'

'She said she was saving them for Saturday night, didn't she, Rach?'

Rachel nodded. 'She was going to a party. Said we could come too if we wanted.'

'And did you go?'

The girls shook their heads.

'Rach was going away with her mum and dad for the weekend and I had cousins come to visit,' Ebony told them. 'We went ice skating in Dundee. Then, next day, we heard...'

'About Yvette?'

The girls nodded.

'It was all over Facebook,' Ebony said.

'So you think she went to the party, took the drugs there, then collapsed?'

More nodding.

'Obviously, if we'd known...' Rachel began.

'Girls, has anyone at school ever offered you drugs?' asked Chris. 'Any of the staff?'

Rachel stared.

'No way,' Ebony said. 'They're dead strict here.'

'What about other pupils?' Chris asked.

The girls looked at each other.

'Not me,' Ebony said. 'Rach?'

Rachel shook her head.

Clare looked at Chris. There was nothing here. 'Okay, girls, thanks for your time.'

Ebony eyed Chris and parted her lips. 'Don't suppose we could stay a bit longer? Ten more minutes and our class will be finished. It's hardly worth going back...'

'Beat it!' he said, laughing. 'Or your headmistress will be chasing me.'

'Not if we get you first, eh Rach?' Ebony said, elbowing Rachel, and they left the room, giggling.

They sat for a minute, after the girls had left. Then Chris broke the silence. 'What do you reckon? Coincidence?'

'Yvette being a pupil at the same school Kevin Mitchell works at? Yes, I think it probably is. Odd though.'

Chris rose from his seat. 'Not really. St Andrews isn't a huge town. We're bound to come up against this kind of thing, now and then.'

Clare followed him to the door, lost in thought. 'Suppose.'

Chris said, 'Want to see the head gardener?'

'Nah. We have his statement and the info about Kevin's car. Let's get back.'

As they walked along the wood-lined corridors back to the reception area, Clare said, 'Do me a favour, Chris – when you have a minute could you check the tox report on Yvette, please?'

'Sure. Any reason?'

'Just curious.'

They walked past the reception desk and pushed open the front door, emerging into the fresh air. The sun was out and Clare was suddenly glad to be out of the rarefied atmosphere of Melville College. She threw the car keys to Chris. 'You can drive us back. Just for a treat.'

Chapter 16

The press were camped outside the station when Clare and Chris arrived back.

'Any news following the press conference, Inspector?' one of them called.

'How long before Abi's life is in danger?' another asked.

'What are you doing to find her?' a third called out.

They squeezed past the pack, Clare saying something noncommittal about a statement in due course.

In the main office, Tony was speaking to Bill and Janey.

'Any news?' Clare asked.

Janey shook her head. 'The Dundee lads haven't seen Paul Sinclair for a good few months.'

'He's not on licence any more,' Bill added. 'Rumour is he's moved to Glasgow, but he's not been seen there either.'

'Dammit.' She stood thinking for a moment, the words of the reporter ringing in her head.

How long before Abi's life is in danger?

How long, indeed. She thought momentarily of Abi's face in those photos. It was more than forty-eight hours now since she had been taken from her pram. Was she slipping into a coma now, as the doctor had warned? Or was she being cared for by whoever had stolen the digoxin?

Clare found there was a lump in her throat making it difficult to swallow. Her mouth was bone dry.

She glanced at Tony, hoping he'd forgotten their earlier exchange about the Mistrys. 'We can't wait any longer. We have to find Abi and we need to find her fast. I'll call the press office now. Get his name and a proper photo out there, okay?'

Tony appeared distracted. 'Yeah, okay. Keep me informed.' And he turned and walked back into Clare's office, closing the door behind him. Clare stared at the door for a moment, then went to make the phone call.

'I reckon he's working on his application for the Super's post,' she told Chris when she came off the phone from the press office. 'Given we have a missing baby on our hands, he seemed pretty uninterested.'

'Short attention span,' Chris said.

'You okay with him being here?'

'Yeah, I suppose. I mean, me and Emily – him and Emily – well, it's all in the past now.'

'And you have Sara?'

A smile spread across Chris's face. 'Yeah, I have Sara.'

In her pocket, Clare felt her phone buzz. Her own mobile. She took it out and looked at the display. Her sister. It wasn't like her to call when she knew Clare was working. She swiped to answer the call. 'Hi Jude. How's things?'

Her sister sounded distracted, as if she hadn't expected Clare to answer so quickly. 'Oh, Clare, hi. Sorry to call. You're busy, I expect. That poor baby…'

Clare was about to agree but something in her sister's voice stopped her. 'Never too busy for my wee sister. Are you okay, Jude?'

'Yes, I'm fine thanks.'

'And Mum and Dad?'

'Oh yes. Busy as ever. Still going to their lunch club and that sort of thing. Just had their flu jabs too…'

'Jude, are you sure you're okay?'

'It's just that…'

'Is James okay? There's nothing wrong with him?'

'He's fine, really. I've had the health visitor here this morning – for his assessment, you know.'

'Is he not doing what he should? What do they call it – reaching his milestones?'

'Oh no,' Jude said quickly. 'He's doing everything he should. More, in fact.'

'That's my nephew,' Clare said, smiling. 'I must come and visit soon.'

'But she said…' Jude broke off again.

'What? What did she say?'

'He doesn't make eye contact. Won't look at her.'

'He doesn't know her.'

'She said most toddlers, by this stage, they respond when you play with them, talk to them. James doesn't really do that. She said it was as if she wasn't there.'

Clare was at a loss. 'Jude, are you sure she's not just—'

'She gave him some bricks to check his motor control. He was supposed to stack them, one on top of the other.'

'But they all develop at their own speed, Jude. Godsake – I was as clumsy as hell, remember? The number of times I fell off my bike.'

'Oh no, Clare. He stacked them no problem. But then…'

Clare waited.

'...he began to arrange them – by himself. First, he grouped them by colours – all the blues, all the reds.'

'I told you he was clever.'

Jude carried on as if Clare hadn't spoken. 'And then he grouped them again by shape – all the cubes, then the cylinders...'

'So he's a bit brighter than average. I'm not surprised, Jude. You and Frank are both bright sparks. And you read to him all the time. It's not like you stick him in front of the telly.'

'Clare,' Jude interrupted, a note of exasperation creeping into her voice. 'She said that kind of sorting wasn't just way above his stage. It's not the kind of thing children of his age even think of.'

Clare waited.

'Oh Clare.' Jude's voice cracked. 'She thinks James is autistic.'

Chapter 17

The afternoon wore on, a succession of phone calls following the press conference. The Dundee uniforms were chasing up reports of Paul Sinclair in the north of the city, mostly in the same housing scheme as Susan Clancy's flat.

'It can't be a coincidence,' Chris said. 'Susan, the pharmacy and Paul Sinclair all in the same estate.'

'It might be,' Clare said. 'It's a huge estate with a long-standing drug problem.'

'Suppose. Tell you something else, though, Clare...'

Clare was scrolling down a computer screen full of possible sightings of Paul Sinclair. 'Mm-hm?'

'Those girls at the school. Did you notice their skin?'

'Not really. Typical spotty teens, I suppose.'

'Not that. The colour of their skin. Like they'd been to the tanning salon.'

'They're too young, surely,' Clare said.

'Not necessarily. Sunbed – yes. But there's no minimum for spray tans. Most salons would expect an adult to accompany a sixteen-year-old but not always. Was the salon busy when you were there?'

Clare shook her head. 'Not really.'

'And the owner – Sacha is it? Did she seem like the kind of person who might not always ask for proof of age?

Those girls could easily pass for eighteen. You know they could.'

Clare considered this. 'You're thinking there's some connection between Yvette and the tanning salon?'

Chris shrugged. 'I don't know. I mean maybe we should get the drugs cops to check it out.'

'Yeah, and wait till Christmas when they can spare someone.' She clicked to lock her computer. 'It'll be quicker if we go ourselves. Grab a photo of Yvette. It's time to pay Bronzalite another visit.'

—

Sacha didn't hide her dismay at the sight of Clare and Chris. She indicated a couple of customers waiting at the counter. 'I'm pretty busy, if you don't mind.'

'If we could just see your appointment book,' Clare said.

Sacha looked at them for a minute as though weighing up whether to object, then said, 'Oh, what the hell. Here!' She shoved a black desk diary at them and went to deal with her customers.

Chris flicked back through the pages. 'So you went off to France on the Friday. It must have been the Wednesday before that. Let's have a look.'

They scanned the pages, flicking back and forward.

'Nothing for Yvette,' Chris said.

'Found what you're looking for?' Sacha said over Clare's shoulder.

Clare held up the photo of Yvette. 'Recognise this girl?'

'Yeah, that's the girl that died, isn't it?'

'Was she a customer?'

Sacha turned the desk diary round so she could read it and began leafing through pages. 'She was, but I didn't recognise her at first. From the paper, I mean. She called herself something different.' She continued flicking back and forth until she stopped. 'Here you are – Evie Jack. She was in for a session on the Sunday. Before she was found, I mean.'

Clare took out her phone and snapped a photograph of the diary entry. 'You know she was just sixteen, right?'

Sacha shrugged. 'That's not what her ID said.'

Clare raised an eyebrow.

'Look, Inspector, you should know how easy it is for kids to get a fake ID these days. And there's no way we can check them all out.'

Clare tapped the appointment book with a finger. 'You're not exactly snowed under.'

Sacha folded her arms. 'Like I said. Her ID showed she was eighteen.'

Clare decided there was little to be gained from pressing the point. She needed Sacha onside. She smiled at her. 'Sorry – I do know it's difficult. You can't always be sure.'

Sacha shrugged but said nothing more.

Clare went on. 'Was she a regular customer? Evie, I mean?'

'I'd have to look back. I wasn't always here when she came in. Does it matter?'

'Probably not.'

'Do the names Ebony and Rachel ring a bell?' Chris asked.

Sacha spread her hands. 'Honestly, I've no idea. I'd have to look. Why do you want to know?'

Chris shook his head. 'Doesn't matter. Thanks for your time.'

Outside, they walked towards the harbour and stood looking at the boats bobbing on their moorings. There was a small queue at the Harbour Cafe now, and Clare thought longingly of her bacon roll. 'Nice food there,' she said, nodding towards it.

'I'm pretty hungry.'

A bitter wind was blowing across the harbour, causing the boats to creak as they tugged at the strong ropes tethering them to the wall. The sun was low now and the mercury falling.

Clare looked at the queue. 'Another time. Come on – let's get back.'

They turned away from the harbour and headed back to the car.

'What do you think, then?' Chris said, as they walked.

'About Bronzalite? Well, I reckon Yvette was probably a regular but she's certainly not in the book for a tan that Wednesday. I can't see anything connecting the salon to the drugs she took. My guess is she slipped away from school that afternoon and went to meet a lad. Boyfriend, or a dealer, even. Could be anywhere in the town.'

They reached the car. 'Come on,' Clare said. 'We can flag this up to the drug squad. Meantime, we've a baby to find.'

–

The office was a hive of activity when they returned. 'Dundee lads chasing up three positive sightings of Paul Sinclair,' Sara told Clare. 'The lab have confirmed his DNA on the bike so if we find him…'

'Good stuff. Anything more following the press conference?'

'Calls still coming in. Lots of people reporting babies they hadn't heard before.'

'They all have to be checked,' Clare said.

'Any chance of a few more bodies?'

'I'll see what I can do.'

Tony was poring over a sheaf of papers when Clare entered her office. He looked up. 'Any progress?'

'Not much. A few sightings of Paul Sinclair in Dundee. Following those up now. Baby reports, too, but all legit so far. We're a bit pushed, actually...'

'Aren't we all, Clare?'

'Don't suppose you could rustle up a few more bodies?'

'Doubtful.'

'It is a baby we're talking about, Tony. One with a life-threatening heart condition.'

Tony sighed and pushed his papers to one side. 'I'll see what I can do, but we've already drafted in every available cop.'

'If you could try...'

'No promises.'

'Thanks. I appreciate it.'

He studied her for a moment, then said, 'Sit.'

Clare looked at him. 'Why?'

'Just sit, for God's sake.'

She pulled out a chair and sank down in it, wondering what he was playing at. 'What's up?' she asked, when he didn't speak.

'You look done in,' he said.

'Well thank you very much! You're not looking so hot yourself.'

'I'm serious, Clare. Since Sunday you've been running this investigation, single-handed, and I've not exactly been a help. I've been...' He indicated the papers in front of him. 'Well, I've been distracted.'

'It's fine, Tony. We're managing. A few extra bodies would help though, and now we've gone public on Paul Sinclair, it should only be a matter of time—'

He cut across her. 'Take the night off.'

She stared. 'In the middle of an investigation? You're not serious?'

'I mean it, Clare. I looked at your diary on the portal. You've blocked tonight out. Something on?'

She had almost forgotten about it. Dinner with Geoffrey's sister. 'No, it's okay. I'll cancel it. Abi Mitchell takes priority.'

Tony rose to his feet. 'I'm not asking you, Clare. I'm telling you. You're way over your hours, even for a major investigation. Chrissake – you were supposed to be on holiday on Sunday and you were here till God knows when. And back again early the next morning. Take the night off to do whatever it was you had planned and be back in the morning. You'll be all the better for a break.'

Clare left her office, deep in thought. What the hell was Tony playing at? Since when had he cared about anyone except himself? She saw Chris looking at her and walked across.

'You okay?' he asked.

'Tony's just given me the night off.'

'Eh? He had a bump on the head?'

'Don't ask me. Look, Chris, there's something I should be doing tonight. I wasn't going to but since he's making a fuss about me being over my hours, I might as well.'

'He wouldn't have to ask me twice.'

'Yeah, I know. But if I do go home, will you promise me you'll keep in touch? Let me know if anything happens? Anything at all?'

'Sure. Anyway, we need to give it a few hours. Someone will know where Paul Sinclair is. We just have to sit it out.'

—

Clare had dressed quickly, erring on the side of caution with her choice of a navy woollen dress from Boden. She was so used to spending her working days in trouser suits then coming home to change into dog-walking clothes that she felt strange – unlike herself. She sat down at her dressing table and inspected her hair. There was no time to do anything with it so it would just have to do. She pulled a hairbrush through it quickly and gave it a shake. Then she peered in the mirror and applied a quick coat of mascara and some lipstick. A distant *peeping* announced Geoffrey's arrival. She pulled on a pair of high-heeled boots, grabbed her coat and handbag, and stepped out into the night. She opened the car door then turned back.

'Hold on,' she called, feeling in her bag for the front door key. 'Forgotten something.'

She ran back into the cottage, to Benjy's misplaced delight, and scooped up a bunch of chrysanthemums from the bathroom sink. Giving Benjy a last quick rub behind the ears, she locked the door behind her and climbed into the car.

Geoffrey leaned over and kissed her on the lips. He waited while she fastened her seat belt then reversed out of her drive. He glanced at the flowers. 'You shouldn't have bothered, Clare. It's only dinner.'

He was right. It *was* only dinner. Should she really be out for a meal when Abi was God knows where? It had been a rush, too. A detour via the florist, abandoning the car on double yellow lines because she couldn't find a space; then home to give Benjy a ten-minute walk. A cold shower because her boiler, while now in situ, still wasn't connected and she didn't have time to wait for the immersion to heat the water. And now she was sitting in Geoffrey's car in these unfamiliar clothes, fretting about a missing baby. And for what? Some dinner she could have rearranged?

'I can't come empty-handed,' she said.

Geoffrey took one hand off the steering wheel to squeeze hers. 'It's only Nicola and another couple of friends.' He turned the car away from St Andrews and drove in the direction of Strathkinness, a small village to the west of the town.

'Remind me of her husband's name again,' Clare said.

'Ollie. You'll like Ollie. He's a good chap.'

'And the others? You said another couple of friends?'

'I think Nicola said she'd invited the Daventrys. Nice couple.'

They were approaching the crossroads now and he turned right, slowing as he reached the twenty-miles-per-hour sign at Strathkinness. He drove slowly up the hill, navigating the speed bumps, and crested the rise at the top of the village. Beneath them lay the Eden Estuary and to the west the busy village of Guardbridge. Clare couldn't help thinking of Abi Mitchell, being bundled from a pizza delivery bag into a car by Paul Sinclair – to be taken God knows where. She wondered if the Dundee cops had found him yet.

'Clare?' Geoffrey was saying.

She turned to look at him. 'Sorry – I was just… What did you say?'

He took her hand again and squeezed it. 'I was asking how you managed to get the night off.'

'Oh, my boss. He said to go.'

'Really? The one you said was bone idle?'

She nodded. 'Yeah, that's him. Something about checking my hours and noticing I was over the maximum.'

'That's good, then. He's obviously looking after your welfare.'

'Pfft. That'll be a first,' she said. 'He's never bothered before. Lately, he's been more interested in the promotion he's applying for than finding our missing baby.'

'Ah, that explains it.' They were in Guardbridge now and Geoffrey indicated right at the roundabout.

Clare wondered if this was the route Abi had been taken on, after being transferred from the motorbike. 'Explains what?'

'If he's up for promotion. Obviously I don't know how the police do things but, these days, there's a drive to consult staff when someone is considered for promotion. See how well respected they are. Your Tony's probably covering his backside. Making sure you'll say nice things about him.'

Clare turned to Geoffrey and stared. 'Seriously? Is that what they do now?'

He shrugged. 'Maybe.'

She nodded. 'That explains it. He'd looked in my diary. I reckon he was looking for an opportunity to send me home. I had blocked tonight out so…'

'Well, I'm not complaining. I can't wait for you to meet Nicola and Ollie.'

They were passing Railway Pizzas now. Clare looked at it as they drove by. It was busy with early evening customers. One of the motorbikes was being revved by a rider, a full bag of pizzas on the back. Clare felt sick at the thought of Abi being zipped into one of these bags. She opened her mouth to tell Geoffrey to turn back and then closed it again.

As they approached the bridge that would take them across the River Tay and into Dundee, he said, 'We're out for the night now, Clare. You might as well relax.'

Clare looked at him. 'Geoff, I've a missing baby to find. One that could be seriously ill by now.' She swallowed, then said, 'Sorry. It's just this baby case. It's hard to switch off from it.'

He sighed. 'Do you want me to take you back?'

They were crossing the bridge now. The sun was setting over the river, casting an orange glow across the clouds which had begun to gather. Ahead, to the north, lay the city of Dundee, set out on the slopes of the iconic Law Hill. It was dark to the north and she could see the street lamps beginning to come to life across the city. On the bridge the lamp posts on the central walkway flicked past like fireflies. And just off to the left she could see the distinctive shape of the V&A Gallery looming up, the multicoloured lights of Slessor Gardens drawing nearer.

'No, it's fine. We're nearly there now.' The tension in the car was palpable and she thought she'd better make an effort. 'So, tell me about everyone. What do they all do?'

The car came to a halt at traffic lights and he turned, giving her a smile. 'Well, Nicola, as you know, is a journalist. Travel writing, mainly. Does bits for the local press and the odd bit in the *Guardian*.'

'And Ollie?'

'He's a careers officer at the university. His office is quite close to mine so we often have lunch together.'

'Sounds like a nice job.'

'Yeah, he's been doing it for years. Keeps saying he wants a change but he never shows any real signs of shifting.'

'And the others – what did you say their names were?'

They were driving along the Perth Road now, passing restaurants, the university tower building on the right. The street became narrower, with tall tenement buildings close to the road on either side. The ground-floor properties were mainly given over to takeaways and small shops. Clare took it all in with a studied eye as they drove along. They reached a junction and Geoffrey turned right, away from the shops, and began weaving through a maze of residential streets.

'The Daventrys,' he was saying. 'Beth and Leo. Beth's a psychologist at the university here and Leo's a graphic designer.'

Clare's palms were starting to feel damp. Why did they all have to be so bloody marvellous? She wiped her hands on her coat. 'Goodness. They do sound a clever bunch.'

'Don't be daft,' Geoffrey said. 'They're just people. And not half as clever as you.'

Clare's thoughts drifted back to Abi and she did a quick calculation. It was fifty-five hours now since she had been taken and they were no further forward with the investigation. 'I wouldn't bet on it.'

–

Nicola and Ollie Steedman lived in a semi-detached Victorian house just off Dundee's Perth Road. A wrought-iron gate opened onto a tiled path, bordered on either side by small shrubs and herbs, spilling over onto the tiles. A light behind the stained glass in the front door cast a warm and inviting glow. Geoffrey rang the bell and immediately opened the door, walking in ahead of Clare.

'Hello?' he called.

'Don't they lock the door?' Clare whispered, and he just laughed.

A tall, slender woman, hair cut into a sleek dark bob, appeared from a door, smiling broadly.

'Geoff,' she said, embracing him warmly. 'Great to see you.' Then she looked at Clare. 'And you must be Clare. Lovely to meet you at last. Come in and I'll introduce you to everyone.'

Clare held out the chrysanthemums and realised immediately they were wrong. They had been the best of a poor selection in the florist's and now she saw that the bright purple daisies were out of place. Gaudy and vulgar. Nicola took them, saying how lovely they were, and ushered Clare into a large dining kitchen. It was a colourful room with an assortment of kitchen units, painted in a deep blue, set off with oak worktops. A collection of black and white photos of Nicola and what Clare presumed were celebs decorated one wall, with prints by the Scottish

Colourists on another. A long green trug filled with pots of herbs sat on a recessed windowsill and, next to it, was a gaily painted jug filled with sunflowers. At the far end of the room was a conservatory extension with a collection of easy chairs facing out to the garden. In the centre of the room three people sat at a scrubbed refectory table, chatting and laughing. The hubbub died down as Clare entered and three pairs of eyes turned to take her in.

A man with sandy hair rose to greet them. 'Hi, Geoff. And this must be Clare. I'm Ollie.'

'Pleased to meet you,' Clare said, turning her cheek to allow him to kiss her. She was surprised when he kissed the other cheek too. It was a clumsy exchange and she felt her face redden.

'Come and sit down.'

The other couple waved at Clare but didn't rise from their seats. Geoffrey introduced Beth and Leo and Clare smiled. Ollie relieved her of her coat and instantly she became aware that she was overdressed. Nicola was in jeans and a black T-shirt, a pair of Birkenstocks on her otherwise bare feet. Beth was even more casually dressed in a pair of dark green harem pants, a faded sweatshirt and what seemed to be very holey trainers.

Ollie pressed a glass of wine into Clare's hand.

'Oh no,' she said. 'I can't.'

'Geoff,' Nicola said, her tone reproving, 'I thought you were going to drive tonight?'

'It's not that,' Clare said. 'Work. I may have to go back.'

'Clare's a police officer,' Geoffrey said. 'Detective Inspector.'

There was a short pause, then Beth Daventry said, 'Goodness. How peculiar.'

Clare settled herself on a chair with Leo on one side and Geoffrey on the other.

The wine was flowing and there seemed to be little happening in the way of food. Eventually, Nicola produced a dish of flatbreads and a bowl of dip.

'Baba ganoush,' she said. 'Aubergines, you know.' Her comment was directed at Clare.

Clare pressed her lips together. She did know but she wasn't about to rise to the bait.

'So tell us, Clare,' Leo said. 'Is it *fun* being a police officer?'

Clare had the distinct impression that she was the entertainment for the evening. 'It can be at times. Other times less so. Like any job, I suppose.'

'Clare's working on the missing baby case,' Geoffrey said.

She flashed him a look.

Nicola picked up a bottle of red and topped up glasses around the table. 'Oh, how awful, Clare. Have you not found her yet?'

Were they genuinely curious or were they just taking the piss? She decided to give them the benefit of the doubt. 'I'm afraid I can't discuss it.'

'Oh,' Beth said. 'What, not at all?'

'Sorry.'

'Top secret, then.' The corners of Beth's mouth were turned up. Just a bit. Clare decided she really *was* taking the piss.

'Confidential,' she said.

Beth took a slug of her wine but said no more.

The empty dip bowl was removed, and an assortment of odd plates and cutlery handed out. Ollie opened another bottle of red and Nicola bore a large casserole dish to the table.

'Watch, it's hot,' she warned them.

'Fish cobbler?' Geoffrey asked.

'Yup.'

'Mm. My favourite.' He gave Clare an encouraging smile. 'Can I serve you?'

Clare held out her plate and Geoffrey loaded it with fish and a savoury scone.

'Veggies,' Nicola announced, putting a dish of mixed greens down on the table.

The conversation turned to Beth's latest project at work. 'I'm researching Seasonal Affective Disorder and whether it afflicts babies under twelve months.'

Babies. Clare's thoughts drifted back to Abi. She wondered if the Dundee officers had tracked down Paul Sinclair yet. Or would he be lying low, knowing he'd been identified?

'…before you joined the police?'

Clare looked up. 'Sorry?'

Geoffrey touched her hand, lightly. 'Leo was asking—'

'I wondered what you had done before joining the police. What's your degree in?'

Clare stared at him. Was it compulsory to have a university degree these days? 'I didn't go to university.'

Leo looked surprised. 'Oh.'

'What, not at all?' Beth said.

'No.'

'So, what did you do after school?'

'I joined the police.'

Even Nicola, doing her best to be a good hostess, couldn't contain herself. 'You joined the police straight from school?'

'Uh-huh.'

'But why?' Beth blurted out. 'Did you not want to see a bit of the world first? Have some fun?'

'What would be the point? If I already knew what I wanted to do?'

Geoffrey squeezed her knee under the table. 'What you lot can't understand is that Clare is a square peg in a square hole.'

Clare wasn't sure about that. Did she want to be a square peg?

'She knew what she wanted and she went for it,' he continued. 'Isn't that better than farting around for years at university?'

Beth raised an eyebrow. 'If you say so, darling.'

Clare rose. 'Could I just…'

Nicola smiled. 'Down the hall – the door facing you at the end.'

In the peace of the small downstairs loo, Clare sat on the seat and took out her phone. She swiped to Messages and sent a quick text to Jude.

> I'm at the dinner party from hell.
> Could you phone in half an hour and pretend
> to be work?
> I need an excuse to leave.

She sent the message and a few minutes later Jude replied with a thumbs-up. Clare flushed the loo, washed her hands and returned to the party.

Nicola greeted her with a broad smile. 'I've been telling them off for being such a bunch of bastards. The trouble with us is we're not used to meeting people who are not like us.'

Clare knew Nicola's words were kindly meant but what the fuck did *not like us* mean?

'Not at all,' she said, smiling. 'Of course, it doesn't help that our thoughts are controlled by microchips in our brains. They do it at police college, you know.'

The joke fell flat but Clare was prevented from further embarrassment by her phone ringing. Jude was a bit quick off the mark. It was barely five minutes since she'd texted.

'Excuse me,' she said, taking the phone out of her bag. She glanced at the display: Chris. An uneasy feeling began to form in the pit of her stomach. She rose and moved to the corner of the room.

The others watched, Beth still glugging on her wine.

'Chris. What's going on?'

'Sorry, Clare,' Chris said. 'We need you out.'

Chapter 18

They drove back in near silence, the roads quieter now.

As they approached St Andrews, Geoffrey said, 'Shall I drop you at home so you can pick up your car?'

'No, station please. I'll get a lift home later.'

'Want me to let Benjy out for a pee?'

'If you would. I'd – well, I'd be grateful. I'm sorry about tonight…'

He stared straight ahead, focusing on the road, which was wet from a recent shower of rain. 'It's fine. Can't be helped.'

They fell silent again.

Clare said, 'Nicola's nice.'

'Yes, she is. They all are. You just need to give them a chance.'

Clare wanted to say that they hadn't given her much of a chance but now wasn't the time. 'I'm sorry.'

At the station, she climbed out of the car. 'Spare key's in the box at the front door.'

'Combination?'

'8175.'

'Right. Night.' And with that, he reached over to close the door then roared away. She watched until she could see the car no more then turned, walked across the car park and into the station. For a few seconds the room fell quiet, the silence broken finally by someone giving a soft wolf whistle. Bugger. She was still in the dress and heels. But it was too late to do anything about it now.

'Incident room everyone,' she said, making for the door. When they had gathered, she looked round. 'Tony?'

'Not coming out yet, Clare,' Chris said. 'He asked to be kept informed.'

Clare rolled her eyes. His concern for her wellbeing hadn't lasted long. But, in truth, she was relieved not to have him around. She knew now that she should have spoken to Lisa about the note in Abi's pram. She should have done it straight after the press conference but it was too late for that now. And she knew as well that there was no chance Tony would back her on that. He wouldn't want any mud sticking to him with his upcoming interview. No. Tony McAvettie would hang her out to dry. But that wasn't her immediate concern. 'Okay, fill me in, please.'

'Wendy called in about an hour ago,' Chris began. 'She took Lisa and Kevin home after the press conference. Said they seemed fine. A bit subdued. They ordered a takeaway and it arrived about six. After they'd eaten it Lisa said she was going for a bath. Wendy heard the taps running. When she hadn't come back downstairs an hour or so later, Wendy went to look and she was gone.'

Clare ran a hand through her hair. How the hell could this happen? 'Did Wendy not hear her go?'

Chris shook his head. 'She thinks it was probably when she was in the kitchen making a cup of tea. Reckons Lisa waited until she heard her ask Kevin if he wanted a cup and she took her chance.'

'Did Kevin know?'

'No, Wendy thinks he didn't. He looked shell-shocked.'

'Tried the sister?'

'Bringing her in now. Should be here soon.'

'And the phone? The one Lisa had hidden in the bathroom?'

'Gone too.'

'Dammit. What about her iPhone? The one we're monitoring?'

'She left it behind. On the coffee table.'

'Okay, Chris. Get hold of the phone company for that bathroom phone. See if she's made any calls – pinging any masts, assuming it's switched on. What about friends? Other family? Sacha at the tanning salon?'

Chris shook his head. 'Kevin's tried everyone he can think of. No one's seen her.'

Clare looked round the room. 'Is Nita here?'

'On her way in.'

'Good. She knows where Kevin and Lisa's parents are. Get her to check on them. I know they're estranged but desperation might just have driven Lisa to her mum.' Clare checked her watch. Half-past nine. 'So Wendy's best guess is – what time?'

'She reckons between half-seven and eight.'

'What about the Mitchells' cars?'

'The Audi's gone. Keys gone too, according to Kevin. They always keep them in a bowl near the door.'

Clare turned to look at a map. 'So realistically she could be a hundred miles away by now. Maybe even more.'

'You reckon she knew anything? Someone contacted her?'

'Wendy checked the phone before the takeaway arrived. No outgoing or incoming calls. After that, she doesn't know, but we'll find out, assuming it's switched on.'

Clare leaned against a desk, facing them all. 'Right. That Audi's bound to have pinged an ANPR camera somewhere.'

Erin raised her hand. 'I'll do that, boss.'

'Thanks, Erin,' Clare said. 'Find the last camera she passed and take a thirty-mile radius from there. I want as many cars as possible out looking for that Audi.'

Clare scanned the room again. 'I need two of you to get onto Tech Support to go through her social media accounts – Facebook and Instagram. With luck she'll be logged on. She could have another laptop or a tablet we don't know about. If she does, she'll be using that to access emails and social media, so check everything. All her accounts. Get hold of Diane if you can. Tell her we need anything that's been deleted. Go back a couple of months. If that doesn't throw up anything, start going through her friends for anyone with pre-cons. When you've done that, get into her emails. Kevin should know the address.'

Clare turned to Chris. 'I want Lisa's photo on the Force portal as soon as possible – do it now, please. Then you and I are going to pay Kevin a visit.'

'Shouldn't we contact the press?' Chris asked.

'On what grounds? She's only been gone a couple of hours at most. Hardly makes her a missing person.'

'Yeah, but given the circumstances...'

Clare stood thinking. Then she said, 'Let's see what we can find out in the next couple of hours. If she doesn't turn up soon, we'll go public.'

'What about Ashley?' another officer asked. 'She'll be here any minute.'

'Stick her in an interview room when she arrives and let her stew. I'll bet my pension she knows more about this than she's letting on.'

The assembled officers began to move.

'One more thing,' Clare said. 'We can't discount the possibility that the balance of Lisa's mind is disturbed.'

'You thinking she's topped herself, boss?' one of them asked.

Clare winced at the expression. 'It's possible. Check car parks beside bridges, rivers, beaches, Tentsmuir Forest – any known suicide spots. And if you find the car, call it in as an emergency. Get an ambulance and a negotiator. But no sirens, mind. If she is teetering on the edge of whatever, we don't want her frightened.'

'Could she be in danger from the kidnapper?' Chris asked.

Clare considered this. 'If she has some idea who's taken Abi, then it's possible. Remember that lad Devon saw her take a note from inside the pram. She might well have gone after them herself. Things could be very serious for her so let's throw everything at this.'

–

Kevin Mitchell looked haunted. His face was ashen, his eyes bloodshot. He sat on the edge of a dining chair, his hands gripping the sides. He rose when Wendy led Clare and Chris into the room. 'You found her?'

Clare shook her head. 'Kevin, we have every available officer out searching and we're checking traffic cameras for the Audi. We'll find her.'

'You said that about Abi.'

Clare pulled out a couple of chairs and they sat down. 'Kevin, I know this is a dreadful time for you…'

'With respect, DI Mackay, you know fuck all.'

'Kevin, if we're to find Lisa we really need to know what's been going on in her head. If we can work out *why* she's gone, we'll have a better chance of knowing *where*.'

Kevin forced a smile. 'Sorry. I know you're only doing your job.' Then he brightened. 'Maybe she's just gone out for a bit of air, you know. Clear her head. I've been driving her mad. That's it. She probably just needs a break.'

Clare smiled at this. She didn't share his optimism but there was nothing to be gained by saying so. Instead, she asked, 'How was Lisa after the press conference?'

Kevin thought for a moment then said, 'Quiet. Not like herself.'

'Did she say anything? Share any thoughts with you about what might have happened to Abi?'

He shook his head. 'No, nothing.'

'You watched the press conference on the news, didn't you, Kevin?' Wendy said.

'Yeah. We watched it on iPlayer. Lisa kept watching it. Again and again. Like she thought it would help, I suppose.'

Clare and Chris exchanged glances. Was there something there? Had watching the press conference over and over stirred some memory for Lisa? Something that had made her take her car keys when Wendy wasn't looking and go off to find Abi herself?

'And then there was another news flash,' Kevin went on. 'Said you were looking for someone called Paul Sinclair.' He raised his bleary eyes to meet Clare's. 'Was that the same man you showed us in that picture? The motorbike man? Is this Paul Sinclair – is he the one who took Abi?'

'We think so. We have men out looking for him. And we'll find him, Kevin. I promise you that.' She paused. They couldn't wait any longer. 'Kevin, I'm sorry to ask, but did you and Lisa have any money worries?'

He stared. 'Eh? What sort of worries? Why are you asking that?'

'It might be important. So – did you?'

'Important how?' He shook his head. 'I don't know why you're asking me.'

They waited.

'But no. We don't. Lisa – she's really good with money. Makes a little go a long way.' He shook his head. 'I still don't know why you're asking.'

Clare continued. 'Kevin, did you know Lisa had another mobile phone? One she didn't tell us about?'

He stared. 'What phone? What's going on? I don't understand this.'

Clare glanced at Wendy, who gave a slight nod. 'Wendy happened to see it in the bathroom. We think Lisa's been making phone calls from it since Abi was taken.'

Kevin shook his head. 'We don't have any old phones. Lisa sells them on eBay. Maybe she kept one. I don't know.' He frowned. 'Is it important?'

'Do you know who she might have phoned?'

'Dunno. Ashley, probably.'

'Anyone else?'

He spread his hands. 'Her work? I really don't know.'

Clare smiled. 'Okay, Kevin. Don't worry. It's probably not important.' She glanced across at Chris and Wendy. 'Kevin, there's something else I need to ask…'

'Okay.'

'On Sunday, after Abi was taken, we have a witness who says that Lisa took a piece of paper from the pram. He thinks there was something written on it and that Lisa read it.'

'Paper? What sort of paper? You mean like a ransom note? Why didn't you tell me this before?'

'We don't know what was on the paper. Only that Lisa read it, then she stuffed it in her pocket.'

Kevin was on his feet now, pacing the room. 'But she'd have told me! If it had been a ransom or something like that. She'd have told me. And we don't have that sort of money! Not like kidnappers want.'

'Are you sure? Could Lisa have been keeping something from you?' She hesitated, thinking of Lisa's on-off affair with Phil Patrick. 'You know we talked about Lisa having a relationship with another man.' She softened her tone. 'Could there be some other things? Maybe some things she didn't always tell you about?'

Kevin clutched his head. 'No, no-no-no-no!' His voice was high and unnatural. 'It can't be anything to do with Lisa. Must have been a Tesco receipt or something like that. It couldn't have been a note. She'd have said…'

Wendy had an arm round Kevin's back, guiding him to a chair. 'It's okay.'

Clare motioned to Chris. 'Hot sweet tea – now, Chris. Then call his GP.' She moved to sit next to Kevin. 'Chris is going to bring you a cup of tea and then, if you don't mind, we'd like to look through Lisa's things. Her clothes, bedside drawer – that sort of thing. Anywhere she might have put that piece of paper.'

He looked at her. The energy seemed to have drained out of him. 'You really think it has something to do with Abi?'

'We simply don't know, Kevin. But we can't discount the possibility.'

He waved a hand. 'Look where you like.'

–

They pulled on disposable gloves and began in the bathroom, checking the laundry basket. The phone was gone, of course, but Clare removed every item of clothing and checked carefully in the pockets. Then she moved to the bin, emptying the contents bit by bit onto a mat. Nothing. The cabinet on the wall held only medicines, contact lens cleaner and the like. Clare checked behind the curtain, feeling in the lining in case the note had been concealed there. Chris prised off the bath panel and even lifted the linoleum. Satisfied that the bathroom held nothing of interest, they moved on to Lisa and Kevin's bedroom.

The room was much as it had been on Sunday. The only difference was the baby blanket Lisa had clutched at the press conference. It hung now over the cot bars, a forlorn reminder of Abi's plight. Clare checked the cot, lifting the blankets and mattress, then she tipped it up to check the underside. Nothing.

Chris moved to the wardrobe and slid the door to the side. He stooped to look at the shoes and saw that the pink tissue paper holding the gold necklace was still there. Then he stood up and ran a hand through the dresses and tops that hung there. 'She has a lot of clothes.'

'Check everything.'

'I know. Just saying.'

It took them a full hour to go through all the clothes, the bed linen, the curtains, to look under the bed, empty cupboards and replace the contents.

Chris stood and brushed some carpet fluff off his trousers. 'There's nothing here, Clare.'

'On to Abi's room then.'

Again, the room was almost unchanged from their last visit. With little furniture, the search didn't take long.

The other rooms yielded nothing and Clare peeled off her gloves. 'Come on,' she said, and Chris followed her downstairs. 'We'd better get back to the station. See what Ashley has to say for herself.'

Wendy met them in the hall. 'The doctor's with Kevin now,' she said.

'I'll send someone over to relieve you, Wendy,' Clare said, giving her arm a squeeze. 'You must be exhausted.'

'Thanks, Clare. I must admit, my bed is calling me.'

–

Ashley McCann was strutting round the interview room when Clare and Chris entered. 'What the fuck time do you call this? Two hours I've been stuck here. Two hours while my sister's Christ knows where!'

'Sit down, Ashley,' Clare said.

Ashley scowled at her.

'Please?' Chris said, pulling out a chair.

She regarded Chris for a moment and the scowl disappeared. 'Since you asked so nicely...'

'Right,' Clare said. 'Let's not waste any more time. Ashley, do you know where Lisa is?'

She shook her head. 'No, I fucking don't. You think I'd be sitting here if I knew?'

'We know that Lisa had a mobile phone she didn't tell us about. Did you give her that?'

Ashley began examining her fingernails.

'Ashley, it's not a crime to give your sister a phone. We just need to know where she got it.'

Ashley glanced at Clare then away again. 'Yeah, what if I did?'

'Did she ask you to get the phone or was it your idea?'

Ashley bit her lip and flashed them a look. 'My idea. It was just a cheap one.'

'Why did you think she needed another phone?'

Ashley shrugged.

Chris took over. 'Come on, Ashley. We can't find Lisa if we don't know what's been going on in her head this week. So why did you give her the phone?'

Ashley gave an exaggerated sigh. 'You lot. You haven't a clue.'

'Okay,' Chris said. 'Tell us.'

Ashley met his gaze. 'Okay. It's like this. Soon as you guys get involved with anything, you take over. You take away anything you damn well like. Evidence, you'll say, and to hell with whether we need it or not.'

'But we didn't take Lisa's phone,' Chris said. 'Or Kevin's.'

'No, but you're bugging it, aren't you? I knew you'd probably take the phones or do something like that. Lisa's the victim here but you lot are treating her like a criminal.' She broke off to nibble at a broken nail, then said, 'I just thought she might want a bit of privacy, you know? Make a few calls without the world and his dog listening in.' She looked from Chris to Clare. 'I mean, put yourself in Lisa and Kevin's shoes. They've had their baby taken. No idea where she is – how she is – and they can't even make a phone call without it being overheard.'

Chris smiled. 'Yeah, I get that, Ashley. I really do. I'm sure Lisa appreciated it.'

'Fuckin' right,' Ashley mumbled.

'Do you know who she might have been calling?' Chris asked. 'There's one number in particular...'

'Is it not on her other phone? In her contacts, like?'

Chris shook his head. 'The number's there but it's unlisted. Pay-as-you-go phone.'

Ashley shrugged again. 'No idea.'

Clare decided they had exhausted that topic. 'Okay, Ashley,' she said. 'Let's try something else. On Sunday, when Lisa discovered Abi was missing, she was seen taking a piece of paper out of the pram and reading it. She then stuffed the paper into her pocket.'

Ashley picked up her mobile phone and began tapping at it, avoiding Clare's eye. 'Paper? What paper?'

'That's what we're trying to find out,' Clare said. 'Now, we know you went round to see Lisa on Sunday. After Abi was taken. Did she mention the note?'

Ashley swiped to read a text message and she started typing a reply.

Clare's lips tightened. 'Could you put the phone down for a minute? Please?'

Ashley gave an exaggerated sigh and slammed the phone down on the table. 'Yeah, what?'

'On Sunday – Lisa texted you, didn't she?'

'Yeah, so? What do you expect when her baby's been taken?'

'She asked you to come round?'

Ashley nodded. 'I was in Dundee for the night. Got the next bus over.'

Clare watched her carefully. 'When you saw Lisa – on Sunday afternoon – did she mention finding a note in Abi's pram?'

Ashley's eyes strayed back to her phone again. 'Don't think so. She was in a right state but she didn't say anything about a bit of paper.'

Clare rose. 'Okay, Ashley, we'll take a break for now. Can I get you a cup of tea? Or a coffee?'

'I'd rather have a drink.'

'Me too,' Clare said, and left the room.

In the main office, waiting for the kettle to boil, Clare said, 'She knows more than she's letting on.'

Chris said, 'I agree. Maybe let her stew for a bit.'

The main office door opened and a figure appeared. Clare looked and took a moment to register who it was. Lyall had forsaken his tweed suit for jeans and a dark green rugby shirt. She thought how much better he looked out of his formal suit and she wondered briefly why he felt the need to dress as he did. He strode up to her, his face creased with worry. 'I heard about the Audi on the news. It's the mother's car, isn't it? I wondered if something had happened. Thought maybe you'd appreciate an extra pair of hands.'

Clare looked at him. Was this just journalistic opportunism? His face was creased with worry and his concern seemed genuine. But she didn't have time for him, just now. 'I don't think so, Lyall, but thank you—'

'Boss?' Sara called, phone in hand.

Clare left Chris to fend off Lyall and went to the phone.

'Got the phone company on,' said Sara. 'Looks like Lisa made another call tonight – same number as before.'

'Dammit. We can't trace that number. Can they at least give us a time? Location?'

'Yep. 8:24 p.m. Call lasted just under four minutes. Best location is St Andrews.'

'So chances are she made the call either from the house or she drove a couple of streets away to do it.'

'News is on,' someone called across the office.

They gathered round the television and watched as a photo of Abi flashed on the screen. The report also showed Paul Sinclair's photo and said that police were anxious to trace a red Audi A3.

As the report finished, Clare called, 'I want you all ready to take calls from the control room. Every possible sighting of the Audi is to be followed up.'

Lyall approached, nervously. 'Is there anything I can do, Inspector?'

What *could* she ask him to do? She couldn't deny an extra pair of hands would be useful. And then she remembered Yvette Jackson. 'There is something, actually, Lyall. Could you trawl back through press reports, please? I'm looking for anything to do with drugs in Fife over the past six months.'

'Delighted.' He hurried off to find a spare computer. He really did remind her of Benjy. The real Benjy was probably tearing into one of her cushions right now. Geoff, having walked Benjy, would be on his way home. Or maybe he'd gone back to his sister's. Back to that dreadful dinner party. Maybe they were all sitting at the scrubbed wooden table right now, lingering over the cheese, Ollie handing out whiskies. Talking about Clare, likely as not.

'Ach, to hell with the lot of them,' she said to herself, and went to look for Chris. She found him deep in conversation with Sara. There was definitely something up with these two. But there was no time for that now. 'Chris, I want a record of Ashley's mobile calls and texts for the past two weeks. Can you get onto the phone company right now, please? If there's nothing significant, we'll let her go for tonight. But we keep tabs on her phone, yeah? She phones or texts someone after she leaves here, I want to know about it straight away. Until further notice, okay?'

'Yeah, will do.'

Chris went off to contact the phone company. Clare noticed Sara watching him as he went. 'Sara, do me a favour and keep an eye on Lyall. He's researching drug-related incidents in the past six months. Just keep checking to see what he's turned up.'

'Will do.'

Clare glanced again at Sara. She looked tired. They all were, actually. But they had a missing baby and now a missing mother too. What the hell had been on that note in Abi Mitchell's pram?

–

At two in the morning Clare sent them all home. The night shifts in both Dundee and Fife were out on patrol looking for Lisa's car, and the phone calls following the news broadcast had dried up.

Chris approached her. 'Give you a lift, boss?'

'Can you drop me at the cottage?'

'Sure. Just let me get my jacket.'

Clare noticed Lyall was still tapping away at a computer. At least it had kept him out of her hair. 'Call it a night, Lyall. You've done enough. Thanks for your help.'

'Is there a printer connected to this computer?' he asked. 'I've found a few incidents and typed them up.'

Clare took the mouse and clicked the printer icon. Lyall stood, massaged the back of his neck for a minute then went to collect his prints.

'Here you are,' he said. 'I hope it's what you're looking for.'

She thanked him and suggested he start a bit later in the morning. Chris was waiting at the door, jingling the keys in his hand. Clare followed him out to the car.

At Daisy Cottage she saw Geoffrey had put on a couple of lamps and she was glad of the welcoming glow as she walked towards the front door. Benjy, surprised at her late-night return, greeted her enthusiastically. She took a treat from the cupboard and used it to lure him back to his bed. Then she put out the lamps and climbed the stairs. It was cool in the bedroom and she clicked on the electric blanket. She undressed quickly, letting her dress fall to the floor, and climbed into bed, pulling the duvet up around her neck.

The printout from Lyall lay on her bedside table. She wondered idly if there was anything of interest.

She picked it up and began to read.

And then she was wide awake.

Wednesday, 25 September

Chapter 19

A vicious wind had blown up overnight, unsettling Benjy, who had barked intermittently outside Clare's bedroom door. She had fared little better, sleeping fitfully, as her mind ran over the contents of Lyall's printouts. It seemed she had only just fallen asleep when the alarm buzzed at six thirty. Outside, the rain drummed against the bedroom window and she lay there, reluctant to leave the warmth of her bed. Reaching over to turn on the bedside lamp, her hand knocked something to the floor — Lyall's printout. She picked up her phone to call Tony. Straight to voice-mail. She thought about leaving a message but didn't quite know what to say. How to explain. Instead she texted Chris asking him to be in early.

In the kitchen she flicked on the immersion switch and filled the kettle. Shivering, she pulled her dressing gown round her and took a box of granola from the cupboard. Benjy trotted after her and she opened the back door to let him out into the garden. A gust of cold wind rushed in, making the door to the hall slam behind her with a bang. Summer was most definitely over. Clare closed the back door and waited until she heard Benjy's bark a few minutes later then opened the door just wide enough for him to squeeze in. He shook himself, spraying her with rain, and sat expectantly at her feet, waiting to be fed.

In the bedroom she dressed quickly and pulled a brush through her hair. Her blue woollen dress from the night before lay on the floor, where she had stepped out of it, and her thoughts returned to the dinner party and that miserable journey back to St Andrews with Geoffrey. Her phone buzzed. Chris. She swiped to read:

> What's up?

She typed back:

> Ashley McCann, that's what!
> See you soon.

Then she added:

> BTW, did you get those tox results for Yvette Jackson?

The phone buzzed a minute later.

> Yes. Bit odd. Not the usual stuff.
> Maybe worth running past the drugs guys.

She sent back a thumbs-up in reply and put her phone down to make a pot of coffee. Then an impulse seized her and she sent a quick text to Geoffrey.

> So sorry about last night, G.
> This case is just awful.
> Fancy coming over tonight about 7?
> I should be finished by then.
> Nothing fancy. Pasta maybe?
> C xxx

Minutes later her phone buzzed. A thumbs-up reply. He was coming. He was coming and she would make it up to him. Her heart soared. Maybe today would be a better day.

At the station she found Jim at the front desk with a few of the Dundee lads milling about. There were a couple she didn't recognise but, frankly, she was glad of the extra help.

'Any sign of Lisa?' she asked.

They shook their heads.

'What about her phone?'

'Sorry, boss,' one said. 'Must be switched off. No sign of the car either,' he added. 'It crossed the Tay Road Bridge into Dundee but it's not pinged any cameras on the main routes out of the city so we think it's still there.'

'Check petrol stations, supermarket car parks – anywhere with CCTV,' she told them. She turned to Jim. 'Any sign of Chris or Tony?'

He glanced at the wall clock. 'It's early for Tony yet. Chris phoned to say he'll be in shortly. Sara's going to be late though.'

'Oh, is she now?'

'Toothache, I think she said. Managed to get an emergency appointment with the dentist.'

Clare said nothing further but made a mental note to catch up with Sara come hell or high water.

'Did anyone manage to get hold of Diane at Tech Support last night?' she asked.

A plain-clothes officer jumped up from the desk he'd been sitting on. 'Yes, boss. Nothing much, though. Loads of private conversations on Facebook Messenger, all friends asking if they can help. Nothing much in her emails either.'

'Okay, thanks.'

Another dead end. The front door swung open and Tony strode in.

'Morning comrades,' he said, walking straight through and into Clare's office.

Clare followed him in.

'This looks serious,' he said.

'Any contacts in the drug squad?' she asked.

Tony took off his outdoor coat and threw it across an empty chair, sending a shower of raindrops over the desk. '*Por qué?*'

'This,' Clare said, and thrust Lyall's printout at him.

He scanned it briefly. 'What am I looking at?'

'Here.' Clare jabbed the paper with her finger. 'Ashley McCann. Lisa's sister.'

Tony read. 'So she did some time for possession and dealing. Not exactly news.'

'Keep reading – see the co-accused?'

'Ah. Big Val Docherty.'

'The very same.'

'And you think that's relevant?'

Clare spread her hands. 'I don't know, Tony, but there are connections in this case. Connections that bother me. They might just be coincidences but hear me out.'

'Okay...'

'So, first of all, we had a drugs death. Two or three weeks back, while I was on holiday. Schoolgirl from Melville College. Chris and I talked to her friends who think she bought the pills somewhere in the town.'

'Nothing new there.'

'True, but then the tox results came in and it's different stuff. Not the usual gear the students and locals pass around.'

'You think someone's bringing it in from outside Fife?'

'Has to be. Now, we know Val's down in Edinburgh these days. Could be she's trying to branch out. Move north into Fife, possibly even as far up as Dundee.'

'And you're thinking it's Ashley who's selling? For Val?'

Clare pulled out a seat and sat down opposite Tony. 'I've been turning it over all night. Try this: Val supplies Ashley, who starts selling in St Andrews. Our schoolgirl...'

'Yvette?'

'Yeah, that's her. Yvette buys from Ashley, somewhere in town and, for whatever reason, reacts badly and dies.'

Tony sat back in his chair, crossing one leg over the other. 'I still don't see what Yvette's death has to do with the baby abduction.'

'Think, Tony! Where does Kevin Mitchell work?'

'You think he's the link?'

Clare shrugged. 'He could be. And if he's connected somehow to the supply of drugs around the town, and he's stepped on someone's toes, maybe Abi's been taken to warn him off.'

'So you think Val supplies Ashley and Ashley supplies Kevin?'

Clare frowned. 'Not exactly. The girls we spoke to – Yvette's friends – they said she bought the drugs some-where in town. They swore blind there are no drugs at the school.'

'They could be lying...'

'Yeah, they could, but I didn't get that impression. It's maybe more tenuous than that. Could be Kevin gets chatting to some of the girls, drops a hint, tells them where to find Ashley. And she gives him a few quid for his trouble.'

'That would explain where the Mitchells' extra cash was coming from.'

'Exactly,' Clare said. 'Now, if Ashley is muscling in on someone else's patch, maybe Abi's been taken to scare Ashley off? Stop her dealing in the area.'

'You tried leaning on Ashley?'

'Not about the drugs.' Clare hesitated. She didn't want to bring up the note Lisa had found in Abi's pram. No point in reminding Tony she'd slipped up. 'But we'll bring her in again. Meantime, there's something else…'

'Go on.'

'The girl who died, Yvette. Not only was she a pupil at Kevin's school, she was a customer at the tanning salon as well.'

'The one Lisa Mitchell worked at?'

'Yep.'

Tony lifted the phone. 'I'll get someone from drugs to come over.'

—

In the outer office, Sara had arrived and was chatting with Chris. Clare watched them for a minute. Chris had put his hand on Sara's arm but she shrugged it off. They weren't arguing exactly, but they didn't look happy either. And, in the middle of a major investigation, Clare couldn't afford to have two of her team with their minds elsewhere.

'How are your teeth?'

Sara seemed distracted for a minute, then she said, 'I had a filling.'

'Too many sweets, eh?' Clare said.

'Yeah, probably.'

Chris shifted on his feet and glanced at Clare. Obviously waiting for her to go. To hell with that.

She said to Sara, 'Spare me a minute?'

Clare turned on her heel and motioned for Sara to follow her. She flicked on the light in one of the small interview rooms and held open the door, closing it behind Sara. She indicated a seat and, when Sara hesitated, she smiled and softened her tone. 'Please sit, Sara. I think we should talk.'

Sara did as she was told and began fiddling with a strand of hair that had come loose from her normally tight bun.

Clare pulled out a chair and sat opposite. 'Sara – I think there's something wrong. I have an idea what it might be but, before I go any further, I want you to know that, whatever it is, I'm here to help and support you.' She smiled then said, 'I'm your boss, Sara, but I hope we're friends too.'

Sara made no reply and continued fiddling with her hair.

'Okay,' Clare went on. 'How about this – I'll tell you what I think and you can let me know if I'm wrong.' She paused for a moment. 'I think maybe you were at the doctor's this morning. Would I be right?'

Sara's eyes were brimming with tears.

Clare put a hand over Sara's. 'I'm so sorry to pry but I do have a duty of care towards you. This case is putting a strain on everyone. But – if you are pregnant – there are some things I need to make clear to you. Things that are important, that you should know... if you are.'

The tears were coursing down her face now. Clare pulled a tissue from a box on the table and handed it to her. Sara blew her nose and dabbed her eyes.

'Sara, if you are expecting a baby, it's lovely news. But I do need to take heed of that and ensure your duties are adjusted accordingly.'

Sara gave Clare a tearful smile. 'It wasn't meant to happen. I don't know how it did…'

'I'd imagine it was the usual way!' Clare squeezed her arm and gave her what she hoped was a reassuring smile. 'And it can be the best news in the world. If you want it. There are other options, of course, and it's not for me to comment…'

Sara shook her head vehemently. 'I couldn't.'

'And Chris?' Clare asked. 'How does he feel about it?'

The girl's head dropped. She opened her mouth to speak but nothing came out.

'I'm guessing he's not so keen,' Clare said.

Sara shook her head. 'He thinks it's bad timing. But that's not the baby's fault, is it?'

Clare didn't answer this. Instead, she said, 'How far along are you?'

'Almost eight weeks.'

'And feeling pretty grotty, I'm guessing, from the look of you over the past few days?'

'I have been a bit rough. Sick a few times. Tired, you know. It's this case. I can't stop crying…'

Clare sat back and sighed. 'Sara, I wish I could take you off it but I simply haven't the manpower. You'll stay behind a desk, though. No more street work for you.'

'That's not fair, Clare. Not when we're so busy.'

'No choice. We need to keep you – both of you – in good health. I'll put you in touch with the force welfare officer.'

Sara rolled her eyes. 'Elaine Carter! That's all I need.'

'You and me both, Sara. But it has to be done.' She passed the box of tissues across the desk and rose from her chair. 'I need to get back out there. You take a few moments to compose yourself. Once you feel a bit calmer, could you make a start on checking any CCTV around Dundee, please? Last night, from eight onwards. We need to find that car.'

Sara dabbed her eyes again. 'Will do, boss.'

Outside, Chris was hovering and made to go into the interview room.

'Give her a few minutes, Chris,' said Clare.

'She's told you, then?'

'She has.'

'Suppose you think I'm a right bastard.'

Clare sighed. 'Chris, it's not my opinion that matters. But right now that girl needs your support. Whatever she chooses to do, it has to be her decision. And you need to stand by her.'

Chris's hand went to his face. 'It's such a big thing, Clare. Life-changing.'

'For both of you, yes. But far more so for Sara.' As she spoke, Clare's mind went back to her phone conversation with her sister Jude. Sara and Chris could have no earthly idea what the future would hold for them as parents. Chris was right. It would be life-changing. She hoped her smile was hiding her real thoughts. She slapped him on the back. 'Don't worry,' she said, hoping she sounded more cheerful than she felt. 'It'll be the making of you.'

'If you say so.'

'Tell you what, after this one's born, I'll make you an appointment with Doctor Knackeroff. Sort you out.'

'Very funny, Inspector.'

—

Lyall appeared shortly after, back in his Donegal tweeds, and made a beeline for Clare. 'Any news?'

Clare shook her head. 'Not yet. But that list you did last night was very helpful.'

His face lit up. 'Want me to look back at any more cases?'

Clare looked at him. He was so eager to help. 'Actually, yes, if you don't mind.'

He was beaming now. 'Anything you like, Inspector. Just tell me what you want done.'

'Can you go through press archives for anything in the last couple of years on Valerie Isobel Docherty? Anything at all.'

Lyall gaped. 'Big Val?'

'The very same.'

'Saw her a couple of times at drugs trials. Not the kind of woman you mess with.'

'Indeed.'

'Can I use that PC on the desk?'

'Yes, help yourself before someone else grabs it.'

Lyall moved the mouse to bring the computer to life. 'What sort of information are you after?'

Clare shook her head. 'I'm not sure. Anything drugs related for a kick-off. Trials, accusations, co-accused, witnesses.'

'Just crimes? Or other stuff?'

'I'll take anything you can lay your hands on,' Clare said, and left him to it. Her phone buzzed and she took it out of her pocket. Tom, her ex, from her days in Glasgow. She stared at the screen. Why on earth was Tom messaging her? Surely he wasn't still trying to revive their relationship? Her sister Jude had mentioned something about Tom putting himself out there again. Had his attempts at dating been unsuccessful?

She thought back to earlier in the year when she had started seeing Geoffrey. Tom's weekly messages had continued. She knew he was struggling to accept that Clare had moved on – that he still hoped Clare would take him back. And she hadn't minded the messages, really. They were chatty, friendly, always with a *still here for you* at the end. She told herself the sensible thing was to stop replying. But if she had stopped replying, maybe Tom would have stopped sending the messages. And she had avoided facing the obvious conclusion. The unpalatable truth that, while she did not want Tom any longer, she didn't want him to stop wanting her.

And then Geoffrey had happened. She had told Tom, of course, and he had messaged to say he was glad for her but that he would always *be here for you*.

And then the messages had become shorter. The single X at the end was missing. And the *here for you* comments had stopped. And, in the end, they had tailed off. Clare was glad, of course. Glad to see Tom moving on. At least, that's what she told herself. And when the messages stopped coming, she found she checked her phone more than ever, especially in the evenings when she knew he would be settled down with a glass of wine or a pot of coffee.

'Everything okay?' Geoffrey would ask, as she checked her phone for the third time in an hour.

'Just work,' she would say. 'Just work.'

Finally, she had given up. Accepted that Tom had moved on and that he no longer needed her. She had started to look to her own future. A future with Geoffrey Dark.

And now this. What on earth could Tom want, so many months down the line? Had his new relationship foundered and he was trying to win Clare back? If she replied, maybe it would all start again. And how would she feel about that? She looked round the room. There were other priorities for now. Whatever Tom wanted, it would have to wait.

Sara had emerged from the interview room. Clare thought she looked a bit better. Cheerier. There was no sign of Chris, and Clare decided it wouldn't be a bad thing to keep the two of them apart for a few days.

At that moment he emerged from the loo.

'Chris, do you have a minute?'

He lumbered across, with a sidelong glance at Sara. Clare wasn't quite sure what she was going to say but, as he approached, a call went up from one of the Dundee uniforms.

'Found the car.'

Clare turned to stare at the cop who had shouted.

'The Audi,' he said. 'We've got it.'

Chapter 20

Bingham Terrace was a quiet side street near the Eastern Cemetery in Dundee, fourteen miles to the north of St Andrews. Behind its broad, leafy pavements sat large houses dating from the late nineteenth and early twentieth centuries, the older ones on the north side of the street.

'Some nice properties here,' Chris said, as they drove slowly along, checking left and right for Lisa's Audi. The street was a dead end to the west, a set of Victorian wrought-iron gates leading to the sweeping lawns of Baxter Park.

'Nice park, that,' Chris went on, indicating the gates in the distance. 'Lots of grass and trees. And there's a weird sort of Italian pavilion in the middle.'

As they neared the park gates, they saw the Audi. Clare pulled into the side of the road and the two cars following her did likewise. The officers emerged from their vehicles and gathered beside Clare's car to await instructions.

'You two,' she said to a pair of uniformed officers. 'Take the northern half of the park, beyond that pavilion thing. You three, take the southern bit. Stick to the edges but keep an eye on the open grass area in the middle. Anything suspicious, get on the radio.'

The officers went off on their mission and Clare turned to Chris and the others. 'House-to-house, guys. Show

Lisa's photo, ask if they've seen anything suspicious – the usual. You lot start across the road; Chris and I will take the bigger houses behind.' She scanned the street. 'Get these car registrations checked out as well. And ask Sara to check the voters' roll for this street and any streets running off. Cross-check with PNC records. Anyone with a conviction, I want to know about it.'

While Chris photographed the car registrations and phoned them in to Sara, Clare took a walk along to Lisa's car. The rain had stopped now but pools of raindrops sat on the polished bonnet and roof. She tried the driver's door but it was locked. There was condensation on the windows and the bonnet felt cold. Clare peered through the glass where she could, but there seemed to be nothing unusual inside the car.

She glanced over at Chris, who was still on the phone. 'I'm going to start on house-to-house,' she called, indicating the first of the large Victorian villas.

Chris responded with a thumbs-up. Clare began walking up the garden of the first house. It was a substantial property, built in local sandstone and, from the look of a stone staircase, which had been added to the side wall, the house had been divided in two at some point. The front room bay windows had blinds drawn and there seemed to be no sign of life. The nameplate said *Carstairs*. Clare rang the doorbell but there was no sound from within. She rang again and, after a few minutes, she stepped back and took in the front of the house. No curtains twitching. It looked as if no one was at home. She moved round the side of the house and mounted the stone steps that led to a door on the upper storey. The illuminated doorbell had a white card for the owner's name but the sun had bleached it blank. She rang the bell but, again, there was no response.

As she descended the steps, Chris appeared.

'Should hear back from Sara shortly,' he said. 'Anything here?'

'Nope. Let's try next door.'

The next three houses yielded nothing. This was obviously a street where everyone went out to work. But the nameplate on the fifth house rang a vague bell with Clare.

'Does the name Tennant mean anything to you?' she asked Chris.

'As in the lager?'

'Different spelling – A, N, T.'

Chris shook his head. 'Should it?'

Clare noted the house number. 'I'm not sure. I'll check it later. Come on. Lots more houses to check.'

They moved along the street, speaking to the few householders who were at home. It was the same story each time. No, they hadn't seen anyone unusual. No, they hadn't seen Lisa in the street, but their hearts went out to her, of course. Yes, it was generally a quiet street, nice folk, mostly out to work.

They carried on along the street without success until every house had been checked. As they wandered back to the car the officers searching the park emerged through the open gates. Clare was disappointed but not entirely surprised to hear they had found nothing, other than the usual discarded needles and condoms.

'There's a maze of streets going off the park though,' one of them told Clare. 'Mostly tenement flats. We could be all day knocking on doors.'

Clare considered this. With the manpower she had, it wasn't feasible. Maybe Tony could wave a magic wand and conjure up some extra bodies but she doubted it. 'We'll leave it for now. But I'd like two plain-clothes guys in an unmarked car keeping an eye on that Audi. If you two could stay here for now, I'll get another couple to relieve you in a few hours.' She took out her phone and dialled Tony's number.

He answered with a curt, 'Yep?'

'It's time to go public on Lisa Mitchell,' she said. 'I want her photo on every news bulletin within the hour. I'm treating her as a missing person.'

Chris drove back to St Andrews while Clare phoned Wendy to check on Kevin.

'Pretty much as you'd expect,' Wendy said. 'Quiet, worried. Keeps going to the window to look for Lisa's car.'

'Can you ask him if Lisa has any friends in Dundee?' Clare said. 'Particularly around the Baxter Park area?'

There was a short pause. Clare could hear Wendy and Kevin talking. A few minutes later Wendy was back. 'He doesn't recall anyone, but he's going to have a think and let me know.'

'See if he has something like an address book,' Clare said. 'Maybe a list for Christmas cards – that sort of thing. If he finds anything at all, get straight back to me.'

When they arrived back at the station, Clare saw that Tony was talking to a tall girl in faded skinny jeans. Her tatty grey sweatshirt was too big, and she had rolled up the cuffs. Her long, blonde hair was scraped back in a high ponytail. Tony was perched on the corner of a desk, his legs splayed out, a smile playing at the corners of his mouth. The girl, with her back to Clare, tossed her head and laughed, making her ponytail swish. Tony caught Clare's eye and the girl followed his gaze. She wasn't wearing a scrap of make-up but there was no mistaking how attractive she was.

'DI Mackay,' Tony said. 'Meet DI Donovan. Drug squad.'

The girl looked Clare up and down, and Clare was suddenly conscious of her rather dull work uniform of a black trouser suit from Next.

'Amy,' the girl said.

Clare held out a hand. 'Clare Mackay.'

There was a just a suggestion of a smile on Amy's lips. 'Erm, okay.' She held her hand out, adding, 'We don't usually go in for polite handshakes in the drug squad.'

Clare took Amy's hand briefly then let it drop. 'Has Tony filled you in?'

'Sort of. But it's probably best I hear it from you, Clare.'

'Good idea, ladies,' Tony said. 'My office...' And he turned on his heel.

'Want me to get the sign on the door changed?' Clare snapped, then, seeing his smirk, instantly regretted it. They followed Tony into Clare's office and pulled chairs out.

There was a tap on the door and Sara appeared. 'Got that info for you, boss.'

Clare opened her mouth to reply but Tony cut across her.

'Give us five, pet.'

Sara raised an eyebrow and glanced at Clare, who gave a nod, and the door closed again.

'Honest to God, Tony,' Clare said. 'Don't be so bloody patronising. Have you never heard of dignity in the work-place?'

'Aye, all right,' Tony said, sinking down on Clare's seat. 'Let's get on with it.'

Clare shook her head but the gesture was lost on Tony. She turned instead to Amy. 'I'm after some information on one of the Edinburgh dealers.'

'Okay. Name?'

'Docherty. Val Docherty.'

'Yeah, our paths have crossed once or twice,' Amy said. 'I put her away for two years at one point, but it was reduced to nine months on appeal. It was better than nothing at the time. She's kept her nose clean since then, though. Or rather, we've not been able to pin anything on her. What's your interest?'

Clare frowned. 'To be honest, Amy, I'm not entirely sure. We have a missing baby…'

'Yeah, I know. I've been following it. Pretty grim. Still no news, right?'

Clare shook her head. 'We also had a drugs death recently. Schoolgirl. And something tells me there could be a link.'

'What sort of link?'

Clare sat back. 'Do you think Val could be operating in Fife?'

'Wouldn't surprise me. You got a tox report for the kid?'

Clare reached over and angled the computer monitor so Amy could see it. Tony grabbed the mouse, but not before Clare saw that he was working on a statement in support of his application for the Superintendent post.

'That's not how you spell liaison,' she said.

He glared at her. 'Just get on with it.'

Clare called up the tox report on Yvette Jackson.

Amy read a few lines, then said, 'Can you copy that to me?'

'Sure.'

Amy scrolled down the report. 'Could be wrong, but I'd say that looks very much like one we had a few weeks ago in Edinburgh. And possibly another in Leven. Is Leven your patch, Clare?'

Clare shook her head. 'Just outside my area. Probably about fifteen or sixteen miles south-west of here. And Edinburgh's definitely not my patch. It's a good thirty-five miles on from Leven.'

'Well, I'd say you've got a new supplier working their way north.'

'So Val could be moving into Fife?'

'Yeah, could be.' Amy rose. 'If you can give me ten minutes or so, I'll check them out.'

Clare followed her to the door. 'I'll be out in the main office.'

Sara was fielding phone calls, following the news that Lisa Mitchell was now missing. She handed Clare a sheaf of papers as she spoke, and Clare smiled her thanks. She found a spare desk and sat down to scrutinise the papers. The top sheet was a list of everyone on the electoral roll in Bingham Terrace and the surrounding streets. Clare saw that Sara had highlighted four entries – those with criminal records. The other sheets detailed their convictions. One was for drink-driving, another for non-payment of council tax and the others were assaults. None were within the last two years and it seemed that the residents were largely law-abiding. The name Tennant came back into her head. Clare scanned the list of names and addresses again. And there they were. Ronald John Tennant and Margo Elizabeth Tennant. But no convictions.

So why did they sound familiar?

She looked up from the papers to see Jim at her side. There was something in his manner. 'Jim?'

'It's a body, Clare. The cops in Dundee. They've found a body.'

Chapter 21

Dunsinane Avenue was a long road running east to west through a small industrial estate in the north of Dundee. Its network of right-angled junctions made it popular with learner drivers but today it was deserted, closed off at either end by police cars parked broadside. Employees in the factories that peppered the road had been allowed to remain at work but deliveries to and from the estate had been halted. About halfway along the road, Clare could see a patch of ground where a building had recently been demolished. Most of the debris had been removed but, to the rear of the site, there were four high-sided skips, their yellow paint scored and rusted in places. Three police cars were parked on the road bordering the site and the familiar blue-and-white tape had been strung across the entrance. A uniformed officer waved Clare and Chris through the cordon towards a parking space. They jumped out of the car and took forensic suits and overshoes from the boot.

As they approached one of the skips, they could see Raymond Curtice, the SOCO, standing on a ladder peering into it, directing a photographer, who was standing beside him on another ladder.

'I'm guessing that's where our body is,' Clare said.

Beneath the skip other white-suited SOCOs were carrying out a fingertip search of the ground. When the photographer had finished, Clare approached Raymond. 'Any chance of a look?' she said, indicating the photographer's ladder.

'Sure, Clare. Just don't touch anything.'

Clare mounted the ladder and, holding onto the sides, peered over and into the skip. The body of a male lay, partially obscured by debris which, she presumed, had been thrown in to conceal him. She peered at the clothing and a knot began to form in her stomach. The jacket looked similar to the one worn by the pharmacy burglar. Could she really be looking at the body of Paul Sinclair? And if it was him, had their only chance of finding Abi Mitchell gone with him?

'Reckon it's him?' Chris called.

Clare dismounted. 'Have a look for yourself,' she said. 'And mind you don't touch the skip.'

Chris leaned over and studied the body. 'Looks like him, I'd say. Any local cops around who know him?'

'Let's just wait till the pathologist gets here. We don't want half the cops in Dundee clambering up for a look.' As she spoke, another car drew up and Neil Grant the pathologist stepped out.

'Afternoon, Clare. What do you have for me?'

'Body of a male,' Clare said. 'I'm concerned he might be the man who abducted our missing baby so keen to have him ID'd as soon as possible. Cause of death too, but the ID is the important thing just now.'

Neil regarded the ladders. 'And I'm guessing he's in the skip?'

'Afraid so.'

He shook his head. 'I'm getting too old for this lark.' He smiled at Raymond. 'Am I okay to get in there?'

Raymond indicated one side of the skip. 'By my reckoning, he's been thrown in from this side. So, if you can approach him from the other side, we should avoid cross-contamination.'

Neil began putting on a white suit and moved the photographer's ladder round to the far side.

'Come on,' Clare said to Chris. 'Let's get out of their way and work this out.'

'There's a restaurant round the corner,' Chris said, more in hope than expectation. 'And we did miss lunch...'

'Okay, let's go and find some food. We can talk it over while we eat.'

The lunchtime rush was over and the early evening diners hadn't started to arrive so they had their pick of the tables. Clare chose a table in the corner to avoid being overheard and she sank down onto a bench seat, glad of the rest. A smiling waitress in a maroon blouse and dark trousers approached to take their order. Chris, with scant regard for his cholesterol, ordered a fry-up. Clare shook her head at this and chose the haddock quiche. 'You won't see forty at this rate,' she told him, handing her menu back to the waitress.

'But I'll die happy.'

She looked round. There was no one within earshot but she kept her voice low. 'So – our body...'

'Okay,' Chris said. 'You're thinking it's Paul Sinclair?'

Clare opened her mouth to reply, then she saw their waitress approaching with a tray bearing cutlery and condiments. They fell silent as the waitress set their table. Clare waited until she was out of earshot then said, 'It could be Sinclair. I mean, we've only seen photos of him but, from the pharmacy footage, I'd say the body could be him. Same build and probably about the same age.'

Chris nodded. 'That jacket too. Pretty similar to the one worn by the pharmacy burglar.'

'With a bit of luck they'll have him out of there soon and we can find someone to identify him.'

The waitress approached again carrying two plates, which she set down before them. Clare smiled her thanks.

'Better eat up and get back,' Clare said.

Chris tore the corner off a sachet of ketchup and squeezed it onto his plate. Then he speared a sausage with a fork and dipped it into the sauce. 'Mind you, Clare,' he said, between mouthfuls, 'if it is him in the skip, and he was killed and dumped there, it doesn't necessarily mean his death is anything to do with Abi's abduction, does it?'

Clare considered this. 'No, that's true, but it would be quite a coincidence. Think about it, Chris. He takes Abi on Sunday, dumps the bike in the field just outside Guard-bridge and hands her over to someone else. Someone with a car.'

'Okay, with you so far,' Chris said.

'He heads back to Dundee and then whoever ordered the kidnap sees our broadcast and realises Abi needs digoxin.'

'Sinclair gets another call,' Chris said, picking up the thread, 'and heads to the pharmacy that night to steal the drug.'

'Sinclair and someone else, don't forget,' Clare added.

'Yeah. No idea who though.'

Clare started to speak then broke off as the waitress approached again to ask if everything was all right with their meal. When she had moved away, Clare said, 'Then yesterday Sinclair is splashed all over the news. Whoever has ordered the abduction knows it's only a matter of time till we pick him up. He's become a liability.'

'And he needs to be silenced. Permanently.'

'Wouldn't be the first time it's happened. Hire someone to do your dirty work then get rid of them.' She looked at Chris. 'What do you reckon?'

Chris munched on a piece of hash brown. 'Yeah, you could be right, Clare. Guys like Sinclair are ten a penny. If you're the kind of bloke who pays for babies to be kidnapped, getting rid of a scumbag like him, well, it's all in a day's work. Assuming it is Paul Sinclair.'

Clare's phone began to buzz. Neil Grant.

'He's out of the skip now, Clare, if you want a look. The ambulance is here but I can get them to hold on, if you're nearby.'

'Come on,' she said to Chris, rising from the table and tucking a twenty-pound note under the salt. 'The body's out of the skip.'

Chris grabbed a rasher of bacon and followed Clare out of the restaurant.

The body lay on an ambulance trolley, the face white and waxy. There were marks on his head but Clare found it impossible to tell if it was bruising or just grime from the skip. They stood, scrutinising it for anything that might help with his identity. The jacket certainly looked familiar but Clare couldn't be sure.

'I suppose it's too early for a cause of death?' she asked Neil Grant.

'Probably the knife wounds in his back. From the blood loss, he was alive when the knife went in. But I'll give you more details once I've done the post-mortem.'

It was left to one of the Dundee uniforms manning the cordon to confirm what Clare feared.

'It's Paul Sinclair.'

'You sure?' Clare said. 'According to the pathologist there's no ID on the body.'

'Definitely. He tried to stab me with a needle once when I was arresting him. You don't forget that, Inspector. And that tattoo on his hand – the serpent one. I recognise that. Jailed him a few times. Another scumbag off the street.'

Clare didn't share his sentiment. Paul Sinclair had been their link with Abi and now they were further away than ever from finding her. 'Next of kin?'

'Mother used to live in Dundee. Housing estate in the north of the city. Not sure if she's still alive, though. She was getting on a bit.'

'Alderwood?' Clare asked.

'Yeah, you know it?'

'Susan Clancy lives there,' Clare said. 'And we keep coming back to her.'

Chapter 22

Eventually, Paul Sinclair's body was borne off to the mortuary to await the post-mortem exam. Reinforcements had arrived and were now combing the area for a weapon. Employees in the adjacent buildings were being interviewed, although Clare doubted any of them would have seen anything. SOCO had completed their initial investigations and were now packing up their equipment.

Clare decided to leave Chris in charge of the search for a weapon and head back to the station. She found Amy Donovan bent over a computer, her low-cut jeans showing the top of a pink lacy thong. Clare wondered how the hell she could work in one of those things, recalling one endlessly uncomfortable wedding when Tom, her ex, had persuaded her to wear the matching underwear he'd bought for Valentine's Day.

Tom.

She remembered his text message that she'd left unopened and was about to take out her phone when she saw Tony approaching. His eyes, too, were focused on Amy's thong. He put a hand on her shoulder and Clare was nettled to see Amy didn't object. The man was a sexual harassment case waiting to happen.

'Any luck on those drugs?' he asked Amy, before Clare could speak.

'Yep. Looks like the same stuff.'

'So Val Docherty could be operating in Fife?' Clare asked.

Amy turned to face Clare, shrugging off Tony's hand. 'I'd be surprised if she's doing it herself. She'll be at least one person away from it, if not two. She's not daft.'

Clare considered this. 'So Val supplies someone, possibly in St Andrews, and that person deals to users, or even other dealers in the town?'

'Yeah, something like that,' Amy said.

'Would they need a car? That would let Susan Clancy out. Pretty sure she doesn't have one.'

'Not always,' Amy said. 'But it wouldn't be an issue. Cars can be found. Taxis, if the deal's big enough.' She sat back to think, then said, 'If I were you, Clare, I'd bring Val in for a chat.'

Clare frowned. 'Is she likely to talk?'

Amy shook her head. 'No. You'll be very lucky to get anything out of her. But if word gets out that she's in for questioning, it'll stir things up a bit. Then we'll see whose head pops up. My lads will spot any activity.'

Tony yawned. 'I need a coffee.'

Clare watched him go. 'Why do you let him paw you like that? It's completely inappropriate.'

Amy laughed. 'Calm down, Clare! I'm just winding him up. He thinks he's getting somewhere but the truth is he never will. Now, do you want me to get someone in Edinburgh to bring Val in?'

'Please. You got an address for her?'

'Yeah, some quiet street in Barnton. The lads know where it is. Been over the house often enough looking for drugs.'

'Barnton, eh?' Clare's eyes widened at the idea of Big Val Docherty living in one of Edinburgh's more expensive suburbs.

Amy gave a wry smile. 'Yeah, drugs pay. If you're far enough up the line.'

Clare saw Lyall hovering and she went to speak to him. 'Any luck, Lyall?'

'Maybe. I'm not sure.' He picked up a pile of printouts from the desk. 'I've found out Val lives in Edinburgh…'

'Yes, we know that.'

'But she wasn't born there. Originally, she was brought up in Newport-on-Tay. It's about eleven miles from here. On the way to Dundee, just beside the Tay Road Bridge.'

Clare said, 'I know it. Nice place.'

Lyall fished out another sheet of paper and handed it to Clare. 'Now Val has a sister, and from what I can gather, she's down in Ipswich. But this' – he pointed at the paper – 'is their mother's last-known address. The family house in Newport.'

'Is the mother still there?'

Another sheet of paper. 'She died five years ago. But I can't find any record of the house being sold.' He handed Clare another printout with a map of Newport-on-Tay. He had circled a house. 'This one here. Number twenty-six.'

Clare studied the map. 'Are these ex-council houses?'

'Yes, I think so.'

She stared at the map, trying to visualise the street. Had she been to that part of Newport before? She couldn't remember. 'But surely the house has been sold by now?'

'That's just it. I can't find any record of a sale. I think Val and her sister might still own it. She could be renting it out, of course. I'd have to trawl through estate agents records to find that. And they might not be willing to give me the information. But they'd tell you.'

Clare looked at the reporter. 'Lyall, this is excellent work. I'm very grateful.'

His face lit up and she felt a stab of conscience. He meant well. He really did.

'Go and get yourself a coffee,' she said. 'You've earned it.'

—

It was mid-afternoon before Chris returned from Dundee. 'No sign of a weapon,' he told Clare. 'SOCO have taken samples from around the body and the edge of the skip. There's a short blood trail from a few feet away. I reckon he'd arranged to meet someone there and was taken by surprise. Killer knifes him in the back, he falls then he's manhandled into the skip with some rubble thrown in after him.'

Clare leaned back against a desk. 'So, assuming Paul Sinclair snatched Abi and did the pharmacy burglary – he could have been killed to shut him up. Maybe he wanted more money or maybe whoever is behind the abduction wanted to make sure he wouldn't talk – if he was arrested.'

'Yeah, we worked that out in the restaurant.'

'But what we don't know, Chris, is who his accomplice is. Who is the other pharmacy burglar? And, is that person our killer or could he or she also be in danger from whoever killed Sinclair?'

'Good point.'

'We really need to bring in some of Paul Sinclair's known associates and start leaning on them,' Clare said.

'We've lost Sinclair so that other burglar is our only lead now.' She leaned forward, off the desk, and began massaging her neck with her hands. 'God, I hate this case.'

'Would a coffee help, boss?' Sara said.

Clare shook her head. 'We need to find out what was on that note Lisa took from the pram.'

'Ashley,' Chris said. 'Want me to bring her in again?'

'Let's go and see her at her house. I don't want her in the station when Val Docherty arrives. If Ashley's involved with Val's drugs ring, we don't want her seeing Val and being too scared to speak to us.'

Clare's phone began to ring and she snatched it up.

'Boss,' a voice said. There was a lot of background noise and she struggled to hear the caller. Then she realised it was one of the officers she had left in Bingham Terrace, keeping an eye on Lisa Mitchell's Audi.

'Sorry, guys, I meant to get someone—'

'The car, boss. Two guys appeared out of the park. Didn't pay them much attention then suddenly they were in the car, reversing back along the road. They've headed up to the Kingsway. We're after them now.'

Clare's heart began to pound. Two men in the car. They must have had the keys and now they were on the Kingsway, a broad dual carriageway that ran along the north end of Dundee. 'Get onto the traffic boys in Dundee.'

'Already done,' the voice said. Clare could hear the radio crackling in the car, punctuated by the squeal of tyres as they rounded a corner.

'Do not lose that car,' Clare said, into the radio. 'I want those guys in one piece.'

More squealing and prolonged hooting on the horn. 'The way they're driving…'

'Map of Dundee,' Clare called, and Sara ran off to find one.

'Driving like a fuckin' maniac,' the voice said.

The team had gathered behind Clare in the incident room and she switched her phone to speaker.

'Where are you now?' she asked.

'Just passing Caird Park. Jeeeeeeesus – he nearly hit a cyclist on the roundabout.'

'Be careful,' she said. 'I want them alive but not at any cost.'

Sara appeared with a large map of Dundee which she pinned up on the board. Bill, who lived in Dundee, put a pin in the Kingsway. 'That's Caird Park,' he said. 'If they've come from the Baxter Park end, they're heading west.'

'Passing Tesco now,' the voice said. 'Picking up speed. The traffic car's approaching the Coupar Angus round-about from the other end. Should just be in time to cut them off.'

Through the phone, Clare could hear the siren from the traffic car. She held her breath.

'Traffic car sitting broadside over the roundabout now,' the voice said. 'Another car blocking the route south.'

They waited. Surely this was the break they needed.

'Shit!' the voice said. 'The bastard's gone the wrong way on the roundabout. He's heading out the Coupar Angus Road now. We're following him…'

There were more sirens now. Clare found it almost unbearable, listening to the chase from fifteen miles away.

'He's taken a right,' the voice said. 'Heading for Templeton Woods.'

Bill shifted the pin showing the woods. The car was almost off the top of the map now.

'Is there a way of heading them off?' Clare asked.

Bill shook his head. 'Not a chance. There's a network of country lanes out there. No way of knowing which way they'll turn. Best just to stick on their tail.'

The screeching of brakes and sirens drowned out everything else; and then she heard the noise she dreaded more than anything. The ear-splitting sound of metal twisting.

Then silence.

'He's hit a fuckin' tree,' the voice on the radio said.

'Get an extinguisher,' Clare said. 'Do not put yourselves in danger.'

They heard the sound of the car doors opening and the wind buffeting the phone. Then the voice spoke again. 'Driver looks to be unconscious. Passenger struggling with his door. Dammit, he's legged it. Benny's gone after him.'

The wait was agonising. Only a minute or so, but to Clare it seemed endless. The room was silent.

And then the voice again. 'Driver looks pretty bad,' he said. 'Traffic boys have gone up the road after Benny and the passenger.'

'Get an ambulance,' Clare ordered.

'Already called.'

Another pause and then the phone crackled again. 'Benny's got him.'

'Yes!' Clare said, punching the air. 'As soon as the paramedics have checked he's fit to be questioned get the traffic car to bring him over here.'

The distant siren of an ambulance was coming nearer and Clare thought, for the first time, that maybe this was the break they had been waiting for. 'We're coming for you, Abi,' she said, quietly. 'Just hang on.'

Chapter 23

The Dundee officer called a short time later to say the paramedics had examined the car passenger. 'They are insisting the lad needs to go to hospital,' he told Clare.

'Is there no way we can interview him?' Clare said. 'I wouldn't ask if it wasn't important.'

'Sorry, boss. They say he's showing signs of mild concussion and he needs immediate medical care.'

Clare tutted her frustration and thanked the officer. As she put the phone down, Amy shouted across.

'It's Val Docherty,' she said. 'Edinburgh lads say no one at home. Curtains drawn. Neighbours say she's gone away for a few days. Asked them to feed the cat.'

Clare groaned. It was one step forward, two steps back with this case. 'Can you get Tony to authorise putting Val's photo out please? Wanted in connection with enquiries – nothing too specific.'

'Will do. They may find her yet. There's a few places they know to try.'

'Okay, thanks Amy. Keep me posted.' Clare stood for a minute thinking what to do next. She checked her watch. She was running out of day and they still hadn't spoken to Ashley. 'Get a couple of cops to bring Ashley in here,' she said to Chris. 'It's not like she's going to run into Val now. Might as well save our time.'

Ashley McCann arrived in high dudgeon and even the sight of Chris didn't improve her mood.

'This is harassment,' she said, scowling, her arms crossed in front of her. 'You've no right. I'm the victim's sister. You should be treating me properly.'

Clare found she couldn't summon up the energy to argue. 'Yep, you're right, Ashley. We're all about harassing the family.'

This clearly wasn't the reaction Ashley had expected. 'Yeah, well,' she said, then fell silent. She accepted Chris's offer of a coffee. 'Three sugars,' she told him as Clare showed her into an interview room.

Chris put the cup down in front of her. She looked at it then back at him. 'Any biscuits?'

'You think if I had biscuits I'd be handing them out?' he said, hoping to lighten the mood, but Ashley simply glared back.

'So, what is it this time?' she asked.

Clare did not immediately respond. After a fitful night's sleep and a stressful day, she was tired. Her neck ached and she was fed up of dealing with people like Ashley who, she was convinced, knew more than she was letting on. She pulled over a chair, sat down opposite, and picked up her own coffee.

'Take your time, why don't you,' Ashley said.

Clare put down the coffee and folded her hands in front of her. 'We've found Lisa's car.'

Ashley was on her feet. 'When? Was she in it? Where did you find it? Is she okay?'

Clare indicated the chair. 'Sit down, Ashley. There are questions we have to ask you.'

Ashley glared at them.

Clare waited until she had resumed her seat, then said, 'Does Lisa have any friends in Dundee?'

'How the fuck would I know? Is that where her car was?'

'You would know because you are her sister. You told us how concerned you were for Lisa and Abi. Are you telling me you don't know who her friends are?'

Ashley shrugged. 'We don't have the same friends.'

'No one comes to mind?'

'Nope. Where was the car?'

'Near a park, a mile or so from the centre of town.' Clare watched Ashley carefully as she said, 'Baxter Park.'

No reaction.

'Doesn't ring a bell?'

'Nope. Is it still there?'

Clare couldn't face telling Ashley about the car being stolen and crashed into a tree. She didn't feel strong enough for one of Ashley's tantrums. 'That's not important just now. We'll speak to Kevin about the car. But there's something else you need to tell us.'

'Like what?'

'I think you know very well.'

Ashley picked up her coffee cup and slurped a mouthful. She avoided Clare's eye.

Clare went on. 'We asked you before about the note Lisa found in Abi's pram. Right after she was taken.'

Ashley put down her cup and began tracing round the rim with her finger.

'Now, all three of us here know that Lisa told you about that note. She told you what it said. Abi was taken on Sunday and this is Wednesday. The doctor clearly said

245

forty-eight hours was the best Abi could hope for without medication. We have no idea if she is being properly cared for. She could die if we don't find her soon.'

Ashley shifted in her seat and knocked the leg of the table, spilling some of the coffee out of her mug. 'Look what you made me do.'

'The note, Ashley.'

Chris leaned forward in his seat. 'Ashley?' His voice was soft. 'The more you hold back, the worse it could be for Abi.'

Ashley's face had grown pink. A single tear escaped from her eye and she rubbed it away with the side of her hand. 'Don't you say that.'

'I have to say it, Ashley,' Chris went on. 'You know I do. Now, please. If you care for Lisa and Abi at all, tell us what the note said.'

They watched her carefully. Her eyes flicked from side to side. She swallowed and picked up the coffee cup again, sipping from the edge. Then she laid it down on the table and met their gaze.

'Okay,' she said. 'I'll tell you.'

–

'Is that all it said?' Tony asked. 'Just "you were warned"?'

'So she says.'

'And you believe her?'

'Yes, I think I do.'

'Warned about what?'

'She says she doesn't know. And I believe that too.'

Tony sighed. 'You'd better find out then, hadn't you?'

–

'I don't know what else I expected from Tony,' Clare said to Chris in the outer office. 'I don't believe he's done a day's work in his life.'

Sara called them over. 'I've just had Benny on the phone...'

Clare looked at her. 'Benny?'

'The car-chase cop. The one who chased after the passenger. He's at the hospital now.'

'What's the news?'

'The driver's still unconscious. They'll reassess him in the morning.'

'And our passenger?'

'Staying in overnight. Doctor's saying he shouldn't be questioned until tomorrow at the earliest.'

Clare's lips tightened. 'We'll see about that.' She checked her watch. Six o'clock. She'd been on duty for the best part of ten hours. They all had. She'd spoken to Rob, the DI from Dundee who was coming in at seven. Was there really any more she could do tonight?

She put her head round her office door. Tony had shut down the computer and was in the act of putting papers into his briefcase.

'Not much more I can do tonight, Tony,' she said. 'I've handed over to Rob from Dundee until the morning. I'm heading home now, but Rob has my mobile if there are any developments.'

He swept the briefcase off the desk and reached for his jacket, which was hanging on the coat stand in the corner. 'We're running out of time on this one, Clare. I think I'll bring someone else in.'

Clare's eyes narrowed. 'Someone else?'

He didn't look at her. 'Another DI. There's a guy in Edinburgh did a child abduction case a few months back. Had the child back home the same day.'

He began moving towards the door.

Clare squared up to him, stepping between him and the door. 'If you mean the McDonald case, that was a domestic. Mum stopped the dad seeing the boy and the dad grabbed him. It's hardly the same thing.'

'Even so, it's been three days now. It doesn't look good. I'm starting to get pressure from upstairs.'

Clare's eyes flashed. 'Oh, and we can't have that, can we, Tony? Not when you have the Super's job in your sights.'

He put his hand on her arm to move her aside and she swiped it away.

'Don't you dare touch me,' she said. 'I'm not fucking Amy!'

He smirked. 'No, you're not, are you?' He side-stepped her and opened the office door. 'Night, Inspector. Give my love to your joiner.'

–

The rain was spitting when Clare left the office. She stood for a minute, her face turned up to the sky, feeling the cool raindrops on her burning cheeks. Fucking Tony. Fucking sleazy bastard. She unlocked the car and climbed in, throwing her work bag onto the passenger seat. She glanced at her phone. Another two texts from Tom. What the hell was he playing at? It really was about time he got the message. Her finger hovered over the messages. She was tempted to delete them without reading, then decided she would save them for later. After dinner.

She put her phone back in her bag and glanced at the car clock as she drove out of the car park. Quarter to seven. Geoffrey would be there by the time she reached Daisy Cottage.

She drove on, squinting to see clearly in the dark and drizzle. The roads were quiet and she was soon approaching the cottage. As she swung the car into the drive she saw that Geoffrey had let himself in and lit some lamps. She put her key in the door and was met with a delicious aroma. Her spirits lifted. He was cooking. He greeted her with a kiss and a glass of cool white wine. Clare looked at it with real regret.

'I can't,' she said. 'I could be called back out.'

'Not even a sip?'

Clare's thoughts went back to the time she had been sent home for having a glass of wine before going on duty. She had called in Elaine Carter, the force welfare officer, to back her up and paid a heavy price for Elaine's support. Months of regular meetings had followed, with Elaine declaring herself personally responsible for what she termed Clare's *wellbeing*.

Clare looked again at the wine glass, condensation forming on the outside, and decided to play it safe. 'Definitely not. But thanks for the thought.'

She moved into the kitchen. 'It smells amazing. What are you making?'

'It's only vegetable chilli. I'll do some rice and salad to go with it. Fancy a bath first?'

She put her arms round his neck. 'How did I ever manage without you, Geoffrey Dark?'

He kissed her softly. 'Go on. I'll bring you up a cup of tea.'

Upstairs the bathroom was chilly but Geoffrey had switched on the immersion and the room soon filled with steam from the gushing taps. She poured in a generous helping of Jo Malone bath oil, bought from the airport Duty Free shop on the way back from their holiday. A holiday which already seemed like a lifetime ago. Clare stepped into the warm water and let out a satisfied sigh. Minutes later, Geoffrey was at her side, bearing a mug of tea and an almond biscuit. He bent to kiss her and, in that moment, she forgot that Abigail and Lisa Mitchell were missing, that Paul Sinclair was lying in a mortuary fridge and that two young lads who could hold the key to the missing mother and baby were in Ninewells Hospital, one with life-threatening injuries. She luxuriated in the fragrant water and the love of a truly good man.

–

She wandered downstairs in an old tracksuit, velvety with age, running her fingers through her wet hair. The sitting room door was ajar and she could see Geoffrey had lit the coal fire. The radio was on in the background and it smelled as if dinner was ready. Clare thought she could get used to this. And then she realised it wasn't the radio she could hear. They had visitors. She pushed open the sitting room door and saw the dining table was now set for four. And then she saw two figures sitting at the table, chatting as Geoffrey handed out plates. They had their backs to her but, even before she saw their faces, she knew. She recognised the broad shoulders, the faded blue cashmere jersey, starting to go at the elbows.

Tom.

It was Tom.

Tom, her long-standing ex-boyfriend from Glasgow, was sitting at her dining table chatting to her new boyfriend, Geoffrey. Tom, who she had thought was texting her to try to rekindle their relationship. Surely he hadn't come to plead his case again? Surely not in front of Geoff?

But Tom hadn't come alone.

They turned, full of smiles, and Tom rose from his chair. 'Clare,' he said, and he stepped forward to take her in his arms. She saw Geoffrey standing across the room. He too was smiling. She stiffened as Tom embraced her. It was so familiar. The softness of that jersey she knew so well, his Douro cologne and the feel of him. It was all she could do not to clasp him in her arms and pull him in. Instead, she let her arms hang awkwardly. Then she lifted a hand and clapped him gently on the back, before moving away, out of his embrace.

'Tom, what a surprise,' she said, her mouth suddenly dry. 'Why didn't you...?' And then she began to remember.

It must have been July – June, even. Not long after she'd moved into Daisy Cottage. He had sent a card, wishing her well and suggesting they have dinner. And Clare, full of bonhomie with her new house and her new relationship with Geoffrey, had felt generous. *Come to dinner*, she had said. *Come and see the new house.* She had been surprised when he'd accepted. She had the vaguest memory of Tom suggesting dates and her agreeing. September had been mentioned, but had they actually set a date? It was starting to come back to her now. How could she have forgotten?

She looked from Geoff to Tom and spread her hands. 'I'm so sorry. Your texts, Tom. I'm so sorry. I didn't have time...'

'Don't worry, Clare. I remember what it's like, you know. Geoff and I introduced ourselves and he explained you're in the middle of that awful baby case.' His smile faded a little. 'Any news?'

Clare shook her head. 'Afraid not.' Then she became aware that the other person – a woman – was also on her feet. She was slim and fair, with blonde hair curling round her face. Her eyes were baby blue and all at once Clare felt rather old. She managed to smile at the vision of youth, and held out a hand.

'This is Gillian,' Tom said.

'Gilly,' the woman corrected, all smiles. She grasped Clare's hand with both of hers. 'It's so good to meet you, Clare. Tom talks about you such a lot. I mean' – she gulped, clearly nervous – 'I do realise that you and Tom used to be – well, a couple. But Tom says that you're just the best of friends now and I do think that's marvellous. So many couples – well, it turns a bit nasty when they break up, doesn't it? But you two have managed to stay such friends.' She beamed round at them.

Clare shot a glance at Tom to see if he was finding the encounter as awkward as she was but he seemed blissfully unaware, his eyes fixed firmly on his companion. *He's smitten*, Clare thought. *He's absolutely smitten.*

Clare bent in to kiss her on the cheek. 'It's lovely to meet you too.' She turned back to Tom. 'Great to see you, Tom. It's such a nice surprise.'

She thought Tom looked relieved. *He wants my approval. He's decided to move on and he needs to know I'm okay with it.* But was she? She was so used to Tom always being there. Always wanting her, no matter how many times she rejected him. But now, it looked as if she had rejected him for the last time. *He's moved on, and I should be pleased for him. It's the right thing for all of us.* She made an effort and smiled at them again. Behind Tom and Gilly, she could see Geoffrey watching them, faintly amused.

'If that glass of wine's still on offer, I'll have it,' she said.

He raised an eyebrow but Clare ignored him, holding out her hand for the glass. To hell with work. If she was going to spend the evening with Tom and his new girlfriend, she needed a drink. And a large one at that.

She saw Tom glance at Gilly and give her a smile. He took her hand in his.

'Actually, I have some news.' He put his arm round Gilly. 'Or rather *we* have some news.'

Oh God. They're engaged.

'We're engaged!'

Gilly held out her hand to show Clare the ring, an exquisitely cut diamond on a platinum band.

Clare fixed her smile and embraced them both. 'Congratulations. What lovely news.' She saw the relief on Tom's face.

She'd pulled it off. Good. She clinked glasses, toasting their future.

—

Dinner was interminable. Clare's face ached from smiling and she could feel a pressure headache building at the back of her neck. Geoffrey kept the conversation going with his light, easy manner while Tom and Gilly exuded joy, chatting about their plans for the future. Clare knew she should be happy for Tom. And for herself. No more texts from him offering to come through and see how she was. He wouldn't be her problem any longer, not now that he had Gilly. She should be heartily relieved. And Gilly – well, she was perfect for Tom. They made a handsome couple. As they prattled on, Clare hoped she was making the right noises in response. She caught Geoffrey looking at her now and then, and she immediately tried to brighten, but the whole evening was a terrific strain.

'And this is your house?' Tom said, surveying the gaps in the floor. 'Are you having lots of work done?'

'Central heating,' Clare said, thinking that, after five years of abstinence, she would very much like a cigarette. 'Plumber's having some issues with the boiler.'

'You need to get rid of him and get someone else,' Geoffrey said. 'Almost three weeks it's been like this.'

'I know,' Clare said, her tone sharper than she meant. 'I've been a bit preoccupied.'

'My cousin has a heating company,' Gilly said. 'I'd be happy to put you in touch with him. He's busy of course but I'm sure he'd do it if I asked him.'

Christ. She really was perfect. Golden hair, radiant smile and a cousin who could sort the central heating out.

Clare shook her head. 'It's fine, really. I'm sure it'll be working by the end of the week.'

'I wouldn't bet on it,' Geoffrey said, rising from the table and clearing the plates. 'Coffee?'

Clare escaped to the bathroom after coffee while Geoffrey kept the conversation going. She tiptoed through to the bedroom and took her mobile phone from her bag. Thankfully, no work calls. She saw the messages from Tom and cursed herself for not checking earlier. She might have been able to put him off and have avoided this exhausting evening. Lesson learned. Always check messages from Tom; not that there would be many more, now that he was engaged to the blonde vision downstairs.

When she rejoined them, Gilly was telling Geoffrey about her job at a girls' school. 'I'm a PE teacher,' she said. 'Dance is my speciality but I can turn my hand to any field sport.'

'Gilly used to dance with Scottish Ballet,' Tom said.

Clare smiled. Of course she did. Add it to the list of talents.

'What's it like teaching in schools these days?' Geoffrey asked. 'Some of the things you read in the news...'

'Oh, ours isn't so bad,' Gilly said, beaming. 'It's fee-paying so the kids are mostly okay. I coach the hockey team as well,' she added.

'Did you play hockey at school, Clare?' Geoffrey asked.

She shook her head. 'Nope. Zero hand-eye coordination. I ran, though.'

Gilly laughed. 'We have a few girls like that. I always say to them, "Girls, if you can put one foot in front of the other"...'

'Yeah, that's us.' Clare took a slug of wine. 'The dunces.'

'I can't catch a ball either,' Geoffrey said, giving her a smile.

She shot him a grateful look and went to open another bottle of wine.

Finally, they left, Gilly giggling about Tom booking them a suite at the Old Course Hotel.

'He insisted,' she said, ruffling his hair.

'Well, you're worth it,' he said, taking her hand in his.

Clare said good night to them but, as Gilly moved forward to give her a hug, she stepped back, standing a little behind Geoffrey, and the moment passed.

As the tail lights vanished from the garden she closed the door and leaned heavily against it.

'Oh Geoff,' she said. 'I'm so sorry.'

He took her in his arms. 'No need to apologise. Just one of those things.'

Clare surveyed the dining table, piled high with dirty dishes. Geoffrey followed her gaze.

'Up to bed, you,' he said. 'You've had a long day and a dinner party with – well, I'm not quite sure how to describe them.'

'Don't even try,' Clare said. She looked again at the table. 'Let's leave this until morning.'

'If we don't clean up, Benjy will. You go up,' Geoffrey insisted. 'I'll do some and soak the rest.'

Clare climbed the stairs, so thankful that Geoff had been there. She couldn't have imagined dinner with those two on her own. In the bathroom she gave her face a cursory scrub and cleaned her teeth. She drank a glass of water to ward off the effects of the wine then fell into bed. Downstairs, she could hear Geoffrey moving about, clattering dishes and humming to himself. She checked her mobile phone again for messages and suddenly remembered her sister. Poor Jude, worried sick about baby James. She must call her in the morning. Her eyes were closing now and she picked up a paperback to read, determined to stay awake until Geoffrey came up. But she lasted no more than a page before sleep overtook her.

Thursday, 26 September

Chapter 24

'I don't even remember you coming to bed,' Clare said, pouring milk over granola.

'You were sound asleep by the time I came up.'

She surveyed the kitchen, clear of last night's debris. 'You shouldn't have done all these dishes.'

Geoffrey bent and planted a kiss on her head. 'I told you, it wasn't a problem. I'm not working today.'

'Lucky you.' She pressed the cereal into the milk with the back of her spoon and waited for it to soak in.

'So, Clare,' Geoffrey began. 'You and Tom – can I ask how long it's been since...'

'Long enough.'

'But you kept in touch? After you broke up, I mean.'

'We did – or rather Tom did. He thought we could mend it.'

'But you didn't.'

'No.' She rose and flicked the switch on the kettle.

'Coffee's already made,' Geoffrey said.

'I think I'll have tea,' Clare said, although she wasn't quite sure why she said it.

'Sorry, Clare. I know you've never wanted to talk about – well, what happened in Glasgow. But it might help...'

She turned and leaned against the sink, her hands behind her. 'Okay, Geoff. You want to talk about it? Let's talk!'

Benjy, hearing Clare's voice raised, gave a low growl and Clare bent to shush him.

'Clare...' Geoffrey began.

'No. You want to know, so I'll tell you. You want the truth so you're going to get it. The truth is, Geoff, I came here – I came to St Andrews because I shot someone. With a gun. And he died. There was an enquiry and I was cleared. But he still died. Okay? Satisfied?'

'Clare,' he said again, 'you don't have to – I mean, I do know a bit about it.'

'Google me, did you?'

'Well...'

'So you'll know it was a hostage situation. The boy I shot had taken a woman hostage and we had no bloody idea what was going on in that shop. And when he came out, brandishing that weapon – I didn't know. *We* didn't know what he might do. Didn't know if he was off his head on drugs, or what.'

Benjy stretched up to reach her hand and began licking it. Geoffrey was watching her, saying nothing.

'He raised the gun, you know, Geoff. Pointed it straight at me. I thought he was going to shoot so I shot him first.'

The kettle came to the boil with a hiss of steam. Clare picked it up and poured hot water into the teapot. She turned back, her eyes flashing. 'But Google has no doubt told you that the weapon was a replica. A good one, but a replica all the same.'

'You couldn't have known,' Geoffrey said. 'The reports I read said it was identical to the real thing.'

'That's correct. I didn't know. No one did. And if an innocent person *had* died at his hands...'

Clare carried the teapot back to the kitchen table and sat down. She picked up her spoon and loaded it with granola.

'And that put a strain on your relationship with Tom?'

Clare chewed a mouthful then said, 'Bit more than that, actually.'

He waited.

'Tom, as you know, is a solicitor. Works for Jamieson Curr in Glasgow.'

Geoffrey nodded. 'Yeah, he mentioned it. Big offices just off George Square.'

'That's them. Well, the family of the dead boy engaged Jamieson Curr to represent them at the fatal accident enquiry.'

'Blimey.'

Clare shook her head, mouth full of cereal. 'I know.' She picked up the teapot and poured tea into a mug. 'Jamiesons have a good rep, you see, for defending the indefensible. It wasn't a surprising choice. Their clients have money and tend to get off on technicalities. This lad's family didn't have the money but it was high-profile enough to tempt them into pro bono work.'

Geoffrey sipped his coffee. 'But surely Tom wasn't involved? Conflict of interest.'

'That's just it,' Clare said. 'He hadn't been with them very long. I don't think they knew about Tom and me.'

'He didn't take it on? Surely?'

Clare shook her head. 'No, but they did offer it to him.'

'He turned it down?'

Clare put down her spoon. She was still full of chilli from the night before and somehow there was a lump in her throat that made it hard to swallow. 'Three days, Geoff. He thought about it for three days. He only told me once he'd decided.'

He stared at her. 'Bloody hell, Clare. Did you know he was considering it?'

'Oh yes. My sergeant's girlfriend was a receptionist at Jamiesons. She told him and he told me. I probably knew about it before Tom did. I also knew he said he'd think about it.'

'What the hell was there to think about?'

Clare stirred milk into her tea. 'Tom's a career man. It would have been a good case for him.'

'So you walked out?'

Benjy jumped up, putting his front paws on Clare's knee. 'He's hungry.'

Geoffrey put a hand on hers. 'He can wait a few more minutes.'

She squeezed his hand and smiled. 'No, actually. I stayed. Or rather Tom stayed – it was my flat, you see. But I think we both knew. Or I did, at least.' She removed her hand. 'I'd better feed the dog.' And she rose from the table. 'I was exonerated, of course. But I knew I had to get away. Change of job, change of scene. Tom tried to persuade me to stay, even came up to St Andrews to talk things over. But he was part of that old life and I didn't want him in the new one.'

'And now he's getting married.'

'Yes, he is. To *Gilly*.'

Geoffrey looked at her intently. 'Clare, how do you feel about that?'

She glanced down at Benjy, who was waiting obediently for her signal, and she nodded towards his bowl.
Benjy fell on his breakfast as though he hadn't seen food
for days.

Clare forced a smile. 'Oh it's fine, really. Just a bit of a
surprise.'

'Sure?'

'Sure.'

They ate on without speaking. Clare was grateful to
Benjy, whose noisy demolishing of his food broke the
awkward silence.

Geoffrey was the first to speak. 'About Gilly,' he said.
'She's a bit...'

'I know! I can't quite find the words either.'

'Think they're suited?'

'Probably. She's young, pretty, works at a private school
– she'll make an excellent solicitor's wife. And when she's
done that for a few years she'll bear him two beautiful
children who will grow up to be just like them.' A note
of bitterness had crept into Clare's voice. She heard it but
she couldn't help it. She rose and scooped the remains of
her breakfast into the bin then put the bowl in the sink.

'You and Tom – did you ever think you might marry?
I mean, before the shooting?'

'No,' she said. 'Or, at least, I didn't. I can't speak for
Tom.'

He seemed to be watching her. Waiting for something
more.

'I'd better have a quick shower,' Clare said. 'What will
you do with your day off?'

He was looking at her still, as though the subject of
Tom was unfinished. And then he smiled. 'I'm going to

look up an old chum. He's had a lot on recently but seems to have a bit more free time now.'

'In Dundee?'

'No – St Andrews. In fact, he said he'd met you.'

Clare eyed him. 'Who is it?'

'Nice chap. He taught me Fine Art at university, many moons ago.'

'Not...'

'Nicholas Stewart. He thought you might remember him.'

–

Clare drove into St Andrews, flicking between radio stations, trying to avoid news reports on Abi and Lisa's disappearance. It was now more than ninety hours since Abi had been taken. Almost twice as long as the doctor had said she might survive without digoxin. And, for the first time since Sunday, Clare allowed herself to consider the possibility that they might not find her alive. As she turned the car onto Largo Road, she wondered if Tony was right. Was it time to bring in someone else to run the search for Abi and Lisa? Was she, Clare, just not up to it?

The station car park was quiet when she arrived, save for a couple of reporters.

'As soon as there's any news we'll let you know,' she told them.

Inside the station she found little had come in overnight. She telephoned Rob, the DI from Dundee, for an update. He told her they had managed to find two neighbours who had identified Paul Sinclair and that they were still questioning his known associates.

'The popular view is Sinclair was running drugs for someone in the Dundee area,' he said.

'Any idea who?'

'No, but you have Amy Donovan there, yeah? I'd ask her.'

'What about his flat?' Clare asked.

'SOCO been up there all night. No evidence of a baby. They've cleared it for us to go in, if you want a look.'

Chris appeared shortly after Clare.

'No Sara?' she asked.

'She'll be in,' he said. 'Just trying to get some breakfast down.'

Clare nodded but made no further comment. Instead she said, 'Tony wants to bring in a DI from elsewhere. Says we're not moving fast enough.'

'Might help if he put in a hand's turn,' Chris said.

'Ach, he's better out of our hair. He is right about the lack of progress, though. We need to find that baby. Fancy another run out to see Kevin Mitchell?'

—

Wendy answered the door. 'Any news?'

Clare shook her head. 'How is he?'

'Not good,' Wendy said. 'Spends most of his time out in the shed.'

'What's he doing out there?'

'Not much that I can see. He seems to tidy a bit then he sits on a stool. Sometimes I take him out a cup of tea and he doesn't even look at me. Doctor's coming in every day though, just to keep an eye on him.'

Wendy led them into the kitchen and Clare looked out of the window towards the shed at the bottom of the garden. The door was ajar and she could see a figure moving about inside.

'Have you told him about the car?' Clare asked.

'I said it had been found in Dundee. He doesn't know about the two lads and the crash.'

'Did he react?'

'Not really. He's not thinking straight.'

'Any visitors?'

Wendy shook her head.

'Come on,' she said to Chris. 'Let's see what he's up to.'

Kevin barely glanced at them when they appeared at the shed door.

'How are you bearing up, Kevin?' Clare said.

He shook his head. 'Keeping busy. Suppose there's no sign of Abi?'

'Nothing yet,' Clare said. 'But no news is good news. It probably means she's being well cared for.'

'What about Lisa? Wendy said you've found her car.'

Clare shot a warning glance at Chris. She didn't want to tell Kevin about the crash until she'd spoken to the passenger at least, if not both lads. He gave the merest nod showing he understood. 'Not yet, Kevin. But we have a lot of officers out searching for both of them.'

Kevin returned to sorting through the contents of a cantilever toolbox.

Clare studied the shed, wondering how Kevin could occupy himself here for hours on end. Along one side, stout hooks had been bolted to the wall to hold an assortment of hand tools. At the far end was a lawnmower and what she thought was a strimmer. Something she would probably have to buy for the garden at Daisy Cottage.

There were bottles of plant food, weed killer and the usual gardening tools. Her eye was caught by a hook by the door. She hadn't noticed it on her last visit. It held a keyring with a single Yale key.

'What does this open?' she asked Kevin.

His brow creased. 'Not sure, to be honest.'

'Neighbour's house, maybe?' Chris suggested.

Kevin shrugged.

The key was shiny and looked new. 'Mind if I borrow it, Kevin?'

'Keep it if you like. I don't need it.'

Clare pocketed the key, then put a hand on Kevin's shoulder. 'Kevin, there's something I'd like to ask you about.'

He gazed at her, his face blank. 'Yeah?'

'You remember we said Lisa was seen taking a piece of paper from Abi's pram and reading it? When she discovered Abi was gone?'

'Yes,' he said, his voice hoarse. 'I remember.'

'Well, it seems Lisa told Ashley what was written on the paper.'

Kevin waited.

'It said "you were warned".'

Kevin's eyes widened. 'Warned? Warned about what?'

'That's just it, Kevin. We don't know. We were hoping you could help.'

Kevin shook his head. 'Doesn't make any sense. Who would write that? You sure Ashley wasn't out of her head when she said it? She's still on the drugs, no matter what she tells you.'

'I think she was telling the truth, Kevin. So I'll ask you again: were you and Lisa involved in anything you've not

266

told us about? It doesn't matter just now what it was. But if there was something, we need to know. And we need to know now.'

Kevin's eyes were swimming with tears now. 'You think this is our fault? That we've done something wrong and someone's punishing us for it?' He started to sob and Clare led him gently out of the shed and up the garden into the house.

When he had no tears left, he drew a grimy hand across his face. 'Sorry.'

'You've nothing to be sorry for,' Clare said. 'I'm sorry that we upset you. But we have to find out everything about you and Lisa in case it has a bearing on Abi's abduction.'

He looked at Clare, his eyes pink and his face blotchy. 'Honestly, Inspector, if I knew anything, do you not think I'd tell you?'

'I think you would, Kevin.'

Clare left Chris keeping an eye on Kevin and took Wendy into the hall to show her the key. 'Any idea what this could be for?'

Wendy took the key and weighed it in her hand. 'Nothing comes to mind. Leave it with me and I'll have a look round.'

Clare thanked her and she signalled to Chris that they were leaving.

'Poor bastard,' Chris said in the car. 'He's just about finished.'

As Clare started the engine a call came through. She handed her phone to Chris. 'Take that, will you?'

Chris spoke into the phone then hung up. 'Our car passenger's being released from hospital today. The uniforms up there are going to bring him in. Doctor's given the go-ahead for him to be interviewed.'

'Good. After speaking to Kevin, I'm just in the mood. I'm going to wipe the floor with the little scrote.'

As they drove back, Chris said, 'Where do you think Lisa is?'

Clare shook her head. 'Honestly, I've no idea. My head tells me Dundee somewhere, but I'm starting to wonder if she's still alive.'

'But why would she not be?'

'Take your pick. Guilt over Abi's abduction could lead her to suicide. She could easily be desperate enough. Or if she really has upset someone maybe they've got her too. Maybe right now she's being held against her will, somewhere, by the same folk who have Abi. Maybe she offered herself as a swap. I really don't know.' She pulled the car into the station car park, reversing into the last remaining space. 'Either way, it's a pretty grim lookout.'

Inside the station Elaine Roberts had arrived to meet with Sara to discuss her pregnancy. The other officers stared, wondering what Sara had done to deserve Elaine's attention. She cut a curious figure, the other staff dressed mostly in uniform or comfortable suits. Elaine's dress was dark red and plain but her shoes and accessories were considered and expensive. She was unwinding a Hermès scarf as Clare entered.

'Ah, Clare,' Elaine said in her usual syrupy tone. 'And how *are* you?'

'Very well, thanks, Elaine. Busy with this investigation.'

Elaine peered over her specs at Clare. 'Not too busy for a matter of officer welfare, I hope.'

Clare gave Elaine her best smile and led her to an interview room. Sara, who had arrived at work five minutes before, trailed in after them.

'PC Stapleton must not be required to do anything which will compromise her health or that of her unborn baby,' Elaine was saying.

'Yes, Elaine, I do know—'

'Equally, she must not be discriminated against on account of her gender or her pregnancy.'

Sara looked mortified by this unwanted attention. Clare gave her a surreptitious wink. Elaine began discussing dates and maternity pay with Sara, and Clare allowed her thoughts to wander. She had been focusing so much on Abi and Lisa that she'd paid little heed to who might have killed Paul Sinclair. They had found an address for him in Alderwood, north Dundee. That same housing estate again. Why did everything point to there? And was Susan Clancy involved? As far as Clare could tell, Susan didn't have the medical knowledge to steal the correct dosage of digoxin, but maybe she knew someone who did. Her thoughts went back to Paul Sinclair's house. SOCO hadn't found anything but they had been concentrating on finding a link to Abi. Maybe there was something else to be found there. Something that would fill in the gaps...

'And when Sara returns to duty...' Elaine was saying.

Clare rose suddenly. 'Elaine, I'm so sorry but there's something I need to do and it can't wait.'

Elaine's lips tightened. 'I hadn't finished.'

'Once you and Sara have agreed a course of action, just drop me an email, okay?'

Clare rose to leave and Sara shot her a look that said *Traitor*. Out in the front office she made a beeline for Chris, but Tony saw her first.

'Ah, Clare, remember I promised to bring you a shiny new DI?'

Clare's heart sank. He had done it. He was bringing someone else in over her head. 'Actually, Tony, I'm a bit—'

'DI Matt Fuller. He'll be here in an hour. Bring him up to speed, will you?'

'I just need to nip out.' She grabbed Chris by the arm and steered him towards the exit.

'Don't mess me about, Clare. Be back here before Matt arrives or I may forget I'm a gentleman,' Tony called after them.

Out in the car park, Chris said, 'What's the rush? Or are you just trying to get away from Elaine?'

Clare opened the car door and jumped in. 'Get on the phone to Dundee. I want to look round Paul Sinclair's house.'

—

The drizzle from the previous night had cleared and a watery sun was trying to break through. Clare drove as Chris tracked down the letting agency Paul Sinclair had rented from.

'They'll meet us there at eleven,' he said. 'Want to tell me what you're thinking?'

Clare was quiet for a moment as they drove past Railway Pizzas. Then she said, 'We think Paul was killed by whoever ordered Abi's abduction. But we've absolutely no idea who that person is. Maybe the answer lies in his

house. Maybe if we look round, something will jump out.'
She signalled left at Leuchars and headed for Dundee. 'Did
you see the list of possessions found on the body?'

Chris considered this. 'Can't remember really. No
money, I remember that much.'

'And no mobile phone.'

'That's not unusual. Most assault victims have their
phones stolen.'

'Paul Sinclair isn't most assault victims. And no one
mugs someone in the middle of an industrial estate then
lugs them into a high-sided skip.'

'That's true.'

'So if it wasn't a mugging, why take his phone?'

'Maybe it was a good one. Worth a few quid.'

Clare approached the roundabout and headed north
on the A92, towards the Tay Road Bridge. 'Could be. Or
maybe the killer didn't want us to find the phone...'

'Because his number would be on it,' Chris finished.
'Yeah, that makes sense.'

'But if we can find Sinclair's phone, or at least his
number...'

'The phone company will have a list of contacts.'

'Exactly.'

They fell silent for a few minutes, then Chris said,
'Thinking back to that footage in the pharmacy...'

'Yeah?'

'He didn't know what he was looking for. He was just
grabbing anything he could find. But the other one...'

'The one we think is a woman?'

'Yeah,' Chris said. 'She – if it is a she – was being
methodical, looking through the bottles. She knew what
she was doing.'

Clare glanced at him. 'Looking for digoxin. We know that.'

'But remember, it comes in three different strengths. This woman knew exactly what she wanted. Now how did she know that?'

'You're not thinking it's an inside job?'

'Someone from the pharmacy? Nah, I doubt it. The Dundee lot questioned the staff and there was no suggestion of anything like that. Besides, there's no one working there with long red hair. But I do think the woman knew her way round the drugs shelves.'

They were crossing the bridge now. Clare pulled the car off the bridge, passing the V&A Gallery. They fell silent as she drove on through the town. Then Clare said, 'We keep coming back to the same two questions: who hired Paul to take Abi, and why?'

'That note,' Chris said. 'Telling Lisa she'd been warned. Warned about what?'

Clare shook her head. 'The more I think about it, the more it looks as if Lisa Mitchell is involved in something dodgy.'

'Like what?'

Clare shook her head. 'I've no idea, but why is someone warning her? And, assuming she ignored these warnings, what could she be doing that's serious enough to make them take her baby?'

Chris frowned. 'Could be any number of things. Whatever she was doing, she's upset someone by doing it.'

'And I bet I know who.'

'Yeah?'

'Think, Chris! Who's just gone missing? Who were we trying to get hold of yesterday?'

Chris thumped the dashboard. 'Val bloody Docherty.'

'Exactly.'

They were nearing Alderwood now. Chris scrutinised the map on his phone. 'Take a left here,' he said. 'Then second right and – it should be just along here.'

Clare pulled the car up in front of the address the letting agent had given them. The houses were built in blocks, three storeys high, finished with battleship-grey harling. The walls were peppered with satellite dishes and some had new windows, suggesting the tenants had availed themselves of the Right to Buy scheme. The common close had a security panel with a keypad but there was no sign of anyone to let them in so she returned to her theory.

'Right, let's go with the idea that Lisa was involved in something illegal. If so, I reckon we have two possible scenarios.'

'Which are?'

'Either Lisa was working *for* Val and that's upset someone else, or she was encroaching on Val's territory and it's Val who's teaching her a lesson.'

Chris nodded slowly. 'And Val has conveniently disappeared.'

'Right.'

Chris sat back, running through Clare's theory.

'And,' she continued, 'there's that big house in Barnton.'

'What about it?'

'They're all big detached houses there. High hedges and the like. You could easily have a baby there and the neighbours would never know.'

'She's not there now, though, is she?' Chris pointed out. 'Did the neighbours not say she'd gone away for a few days?'

'Yeah, that's true. But maybe with Paul Sinclair's body being splashed all over the news she thought she ought to disappear.'

Chris sat.

'What do you think?' she asked.

'I think, either way, we need to get hold of Val Docherty.'

A car pulled up behind them.

'Looks like the letting agent,' Clare said, opening the car door. 'Come on. Let's see what we can find out about Paul Sinclair.'

—

The house was a mess of coffee cups, beer bottles and overflowing ashtrays. There was a film of dust on the TV and an odour from the bathroom that suggested it was long overdue a clean.

'He certainly won't get his deposit back, with this mess,' the agent said.

Chris surveyed the room. 'I'm not sure he'll be bothered about that now.'

Clare persuaded the agent to leave them the key. 'We'll return it when we're finished.'

The agent escaped, dusting down her coat as she went.

Chris surveyed the mess. 'Where do you want to start, Clare?'

'We're looking for anything that would help us find his mobile phone number.' Her eyes fell on a foil container sitting on the kitchen sink board. Spores of mould were forming on what appeared to be the congealed remains of a meal. 'See that?'

'I'd rather not, thanks.'

'I'd say that was our Mr Sinclair's last supper.' She put her nose closer to the container. 'Curry.'

She looked round the kitchen and then she saw it. A thin carrier bag bearing the logo of Spice and Rice Indian Restaurant. 'See if you can get an address for this place.'

Chris took out his phone and, after a minute or two, said, 'Looks like it's down Lochee Road. A couple of miles away.'

'Phone them and see if they deliver to Alderwood. If so, we want to know if they delivered to this address in the last few days. Go back a week if necessary.'

Clare's phone began to ring. She glanced at the display. Tony. 'I'm guessing Matt the Prat has arrived,' she said, muting the phone. 'I must be in a dead spot.' And she put the phone back in her pocket.

Seconds later, Chris was chatting to the owner of Spice and Rice. 'He's checking the address,' he said, as Clare worked her way through the rest of the house. He spoke into the phone again then started scribbling a number on his hand. 'Got it. Takeaway delivered on Saturday night about nine. I've got his mobile number here.'

'Great! Let's check the phone companies. If we can identify the network we can trace all the numbers he's called or texted.'

'And if one of them matches the number Lisa's been calling?'

'It could be his killer,' Clare said.

'Or Val Docherty, maybe.'

Clare said, 'Could be one and the same. Val could be our kidnapper and our killer.'

'You really think so?'

'God, Chris, I don't know. But if it isn't Val, then we're stuffed. I've honestly no idea who it could be.'

Chapter 25

Clare drove back to St Andrews, while Chris phoned round network providers. By the time they reached the station he had spoken to Paul Sinclair's phone company who promised him a list of numbers within the hour.

Clare removed the keys from the ignition and opened the door. 'Come on – let's see what Matt the Prat has to say for himself.'

Detective Inspector Matt Fuller was holding court in the incident room when Clare and Chris arrived back at the station. He seemed more like a football manager than a detective, dressed in suit trousers and a waistcoat, a narrow-striped tie knotted tightly at the neck. He was even wearing cufflinks, for God's sake.

'Ah, DI Mackay, I presume. I rather thought you'd be here to fill me in when I arrived.'

Clare held out a hand. 'Clare. And this is my DS, Chris West.'

Matt Fuller ignored her hand. 'The DCI tried to call you.'

Clare met his eye. 'Must have been in a dead spot. DS West and I were out on enquiries.'

'Then perhaps you'd be good enough to fill me in on your progress to date. I'll be heading up this enquiry, going forward.'

Clare groaned inwardly. Going forward! Why did anyone say that? 'With respect, Matt, this is my station and my case. I'm delighted to have an extra pair of hands but we're both DIs. I'm sure we can work on this together.'

Matt turned a curious eye on Clare. She wondered if he was unused to women standing up to him.

'I think you misunderstand the situation, Clare,' he said. 'DCI McAvettie has asked me to take over this case. I have agreed and I'd be grateful for your full co-operation.'

'Is that so?' Clare didn't flinch. 'Well, I'll speak to DCI McAvettie shortly but in the meantime, perhaps you'd like to hear our progress so far.'

The room was deathly silent. Clare smiled at Matt, who opened his mouth to speak. And then the front door opened and two uniformed officers appeared with the hit-and-run passenger, safely discharged from hospital.

'Where do you want him, boss?' one of them asked Clare.

'Interview Room One, please.' She smiled at Matt. 'Care to sit in?'

–

The lad was about eighteen, Clare thought. Nineteen at most. He sat slumped in the chair opposite Clare and Chris, his tattooed arms folded. Clare noted the plaster on his head and the bruises spreading out from it. His nose was cut over the bridge and his lips swollen.

'Are you sure you feel up to being questioned?' she asked.

He nodded. 'I just want it over and done with.'

'Now, you're entitled to legal—'

'I don't want a brief. Just get on with it.'

'What's your name?'

'Danny Edwards.'

'And your pal? The one who was driving?'

Danny's expression clouded at the mention of his friend. 'Liam Paton.'

'How is he?' Clare asked.

Danny shrugged. 'Dunno. Not good.'

'Can you tell us why you took the car?'

'Just a bit of fun, like.'

'And the keys? Where did you get them?'

Danny avoided her eye. 'Found them.'

Matt Fuller leaned across the table. 'Listen to me, son. You – are – in – deep – shit. A baby is missing and you're riding round town in the mother's car – the mother who is now also missing. So unless you come up with something that sounds even half plausible, I personally will see you go away for a very long stretch.'

Clare flashed Matt a look but he ignored her.

'I'm waiting.'

Danny looked at Clare and she gave a slight nod. He looked back at Matt. 'In a pub.'

'They were just lying around in a pub?' Matt said.

'Sort of.'

'Lying around in someone's pocket, am I right?'

Danny muttered something Clare didn't hear.

'What was that, Danny?' she asked.

'Aye,' he said. 'Jacket pocket.'

'Which pub was it?'

'Baxter Bothy. Up from the park.'

Clare glanced at Matt. 'I know it. Quite a big pub. Should have CCTV.'

'When was this?' asked Matt.

'Wednesday.'

'Time?'

''Bout twelve.'

'Midday?'

'Yeah.'

'You both there?'

'Yeah.'

Clare sat forward. 'So, Danny, you went to the Baxter Bothy with Liam about twelve o'clock on Wednesday. Did you buy a drink?'

He shook his head. 'Nah. No money.'

'So were you just looking for something to nick?'

Danny shrugged.

'Okay. Whether you were or you weren't, let's say you were in the pub and you saw the car keys. Where were they?'

'I don't know about this.' Danny shifted on his seat. 'I'm gonnae get my head kicked in.'

'Look, Danny,' Clare said, 'if we can find other evidence that ties these keys to whoever had them, we won't use your testimony. We'll only use your statement if we need it.'

'All right.' Danny cleared his throat. 'He was a big lad. Had a jacket. Nice leather one. You could smell it. Knew he had money.'

'Did you know him?'

'No, but you could tell he was a big player. Everyone got out of his way.'

'Would you know him again?' Matt asked.

Danny considered this. 'Maybe. Anyway, he takes off his jacket and hangs it on a hook. And he goes to the gents so I get talking to the barman while Liam checks his pockets. Then Liam heads for the door and I know he's got something. We get outside and he shows me the keys.'

'How did you know where the car was?'

'We didn't. We just wandered about, checking any Audis we passed. There were none in the streets near the pub so we crossed the park and there it was. Just outside the park gates on Bingham Terrace. Clicked the remote and we were in. It was only then we saw one of your lot get out of another car — he wasn't in uniform, like, but you can always tell. So Liam throws it into reverse and we're away.' He laughed. 'It was fuckin' ace. Cannae beat a car chase.'

'Danny,' Clare said, 'we'll get the CCTV from the pub. I'd like you to stay here while we fetch it. We need you to point out the man you stole the keys from. Okay?'

Danny settled himself back in his seat. 'Yeah, whatever. Not like I've anywhere to go. Can I have a coffee?'

Clare suspended the interview and the two DIs left Danny under Jim's supervision.

'I'll send my DS to download the CCTV footage,' she said to Matt.

'Quicker to take the lad and view it in situ,' he said.

Clare shook her head. 'No way. I'm not putting Danny in danger. If that bloke's there, he could remember Danny and Liam.'

'He's a thieving scrote. You're seriously bothered about him?'

'Like I say, I won't put him in danger. Thieving scrote he may be, but he's a material witness and I don't want him scared off. Or worse.' Clare signalled to Chris, who approached, one eye on Matt. 'Chris, can you get over to the Baxter Bothy and download their CCTV from between eleven and two on Wednesday morning, please? We need it back here as soon as, so our witness can identify the bloke he stole the Audi keys from.'

Chris grabbed his jacket. 'I'll phone ahead so they're ready for me.'

—

Sara was hovering, waiting to speak to Clare.

Matt regarded at her. 'And you are?'

'PC Sara Stapleton.' She looked from one to the other. 'I have the phone records for Paul Sinclair...'

Clare took the printout from Sara. 'Come on, Matt. Let's find a room. We can look at the phone records and I'll bring you up to speed.'

'Just if it's no trouble...'

—

Paul Sinclair's phone had hundreds of numbers, most of them stored without a name.

Clare leafed through the printouts. 'Typical dealer's phone.'

Sara had highlighted calls and texts from two days before Abi's abduction until Wednesday evening when it was either switched off or damaged. Clare scanned the list. There were outgoing calls and texts up to Monday evening but after that, all the calls were incoming. Maybe Sinclair was keeping his head down after the abduction.

She checked first for the number of the phone Lisa had hidden in her bathroom. It wasn't there. She took out her notepad and flicked over pages until she came to Ashley McCann's phone number. 'Let's check for this one.'

Again, there were no calls or texts between Paul and Ashley's phones.

'Dammit,' she said.

'You were looking for what?' Matt asked.

'A connection between Lisa Mitchell and Paul Sinclair.'

'Did you really think there would be?'

'No,' Clare admitted. 'But we're struggling to find a motive for Abi's abduction. And there must be a reason Lisa went AWOL on Tuesday night.' Clare continued poring over the list of numbers. 'Let's try Saturday night.'

They scanned the list together.

'This one.' Clare jabbed the printout with her finger. 'See, he's called it Saturday afternoon, Saturday night and Sunday morning at ten. Then another call on Monday morning. Too much of a coincidence. These calls must be to do with Abi's abduction. One call to say he's going to nick a pizza bike, the next one to say he's done it and then Sunday morning to say he's in position. As for Monday's call, who knows? Maybe asking for more money.' She stood. 'I'll get it checked out, although I suspect it'll be another burner phone.'

Matt rose. 'I'll go through the case file. Give me a shout when you're done.'

–

When Clare emerged from examining Paul Sinclair's phone records she found a message asking her to call one of the Dundee officers. Jenny, the Detective Sergeant, confirmed they could get nothing useful from Paul's known associates.

283

'I suspect they know more than they're letting on,' she said. 'But they're not talking. One of them did say Paul had mentioned treating himself to a couple of weeks in Spain. Like he was expecting to come into some money. But that's it.'

'And they won't say where he was getting the money?'

'Nope. A wall of silence. Someone's put the frighteners on them.'

Clare ended the call and sat thinking. She was more convinced than ever there was some connection between Paul and Lisa. That note, saying Lisa had been warned, then Lisa disappearing, probably the night before Paul was killed. Was it possible Paul wasn't killed by the person who now had Abi, but by Lisa? Was it Lisa who had traced him and followed him to that industrial estate? Maybe she had threatened him. Demanded he take her to Abi and, when he refused, she went for him. It sounded doubtful but Clare was convinced now that there was more to Lisa than they had first thought. But could someone of Lisa's size and build manhandle the likes of Paul Sinclair into a high-sided skip? Certainly not by herself.

The phone rang again. It was Neil Grant, the pathologist.

'Your body,' Neil said. 'Massive blood loss from five stab wounds, leading to heart failure. I'd put death at sometime between midday and midnight on Monday.'

'Wednesday, surely?' Clare said, before she could stop herself. 'His phone was still active right up to Wednesday.'

'Nope. It was Monday. Early hours of Tuesday at the very most. Absolutely no later.'

Clare thanked Neil and ended the call. That certainly let Lisa out of the frame for killing Paul. She and Kevin had been at home with officers stationed, inside and out, on Monday. Not that she'd seriously considered Lisa but, in the absence of any other suspects, Clare was getting desperate. Abi was still missing and Paul Sinclair now lay in a mortuary fridge, stabbed by someone who had carried on using his phone for the next two days. Was it Val Docherty? Or someone else? Clare's thoughts went back to Lisa. Why had she suddenly taken off on Wednesday night, and where the hell was she now?

Chapter 26

Clare contacted Diane at Tech Support to request a Stingray report on Paul Sinclair's mobile. 'Can you get me a full list of any masts he's pinged, please? I want to know where that phone's been since Saturday night.'

Diane said she'd get back to Clare within the hour.

While she was waiting, Chris returned with the CCTV footage from the pub.

'Let's look at it later,' she said. 'I want to see if Val Docherty's at her mother's house.'

'You think she might be?'

'Well, Lyall couldn't find any record of the house being sold and she's not at Barnton, so it's worth a shot. If she is involved in either Abi or Lisa's disappearance, she'll be laying low.'

They followed the same route out of St Andrews towards Dundee but came off the A92 before the Tay Road Bridge, dropping down into Newport-on-Tay. It was a small but bustling town, spread out along the banks of the River Tay, with a selection of shops collected in the centre.

As they drove into the village, under the high legs of the bridge, Chris squinted at the map Lyall had given them. 'Take a left up this hill.'

The house was in a narrow street with cars parked on either side.

'Best leave the car here,' Clare said. 'We can walk along and suss out the house without her hearing the engine.'

'If she's there.'

'Well, yes.'

They walked along the road, the pavement cluttered with blue dustbins awaiting the bin lorry.

'This is it.' Clare stopped at a low, wooden gate. Beyond the gate was a small garden laid out in slabs and gravel. There were blinds in the windows and the paint on the front door was peeling. There was another door on the gable end of the house. 'Must be divided. What's the number?'

Chris studied the printout again. 'Twenty-six.'

'Then it's this one at the front.' Clare looked at the windows. No sign of life. 'Let's check round the back first. Just in case.'

The windows at the back were tightly shut and it didn't look as if they were large enough to allow anyone to escape in a hurry.

'Certainly not someone of Big Val's size,' Chris said.

They walked noiselessly back to the front. Clare went to press the front doorbell when Chris grabbed her arm.

'It's a video bell,' he said. 'Press it and it'll take your photo. Probably send it to her phone. I wouldn't knock either, in case that triggers it.'

'Thanks, Chris.' She moved instead to a window, away from the door, and tapped on the glass. Then she put her ear to it and listened. There was no sound and no sign of life. She knocked again, louder this time. A window opened above them and a bleary-eyed head poked out.

'D'ye mind? I'm on the night shift.'

'Sorry to disturb you,' Clare said. 'We're looking for Val.'

'She's no' in,' the head said.

'Would you know where we could find her?' Chris asked.

'She'll be down the shops. Likely getting something for her dinner.'

Clare and Chris called their thanks and the head disappeared, slamming the window. They walked back down the path, stepping over the low, wooden gate and back out into the street. Clare lifted the lid on one of the blue dustbins. They hadn't been emptied yet and she had a good look inside the bins sitting near to Val's gate.

'No nappies or anything else for babies, as far as I can see,' she said.

'Long shot, anyway,' Chris said. 'From what I hear of Val, she's not the maternal type. If she has taken Abi, she'll have someone else looking after her.'

'Fair point,' Clare said. 'Come on – we can call back later.'

They walked back down the street. As they neared the car, a woman rounded the corner. She lumbered slowly up the road towards them, a plastic carrier bag dangling from one hand. Beneath a long leather coat, she wore a leopard-print blouse and a black skirt, straining at the waist. Judging by her leathery skin, she was another who was no stranger to a sunbed. Her blonde hair was dyed, the dark roots just starting to show, and her face heavily made-up. A pair of long, gold earrings swayed back and forth as she made her leisurely progress up the street.

She eyed Clare and Chris and made to walk past them.

'Excuse me,' Clare said, and the woman stopped. Clare noticed she was breathing hard.

'That hill,' the woman said, between breaths. 'Killer.'

'We're looking for Val Docherty,' Clare said, showing the woman her badge.

'Oh, are ye, now?'

'It's you, isn't it?' Clare said. 'You are Val Docherty, aren't you?'

The woman gave them the once-over. 'I'd love to stand and chat but I've a hot date with a bacon roll.'

'We need to speak to you on a matter of some urgency,' Clare said. 'We'll arrange to bring you back home once we're done. Chris here will even put your bacon in the fridge while we chat.'

'Will I be needing my solicitor?' Val asked.

'That's entirely up to you,' Clare said. 'But it's just an informal chat for now.'

'I think I'll call him, if it's all the same to you,' Val said, handing the carrier bag to Chris and taking out a gold Samsung.

—

Val entered the station at St Andrews as if she was at a red-carpet premiere. She removed her coat and handed it to a young constable. 'Here, sonny, get a hanger for that. And see you keep an eye on it.'

The officer shot a glance at Clare and took the coat without a word.

Val grinned when she saw Amy. 'Amy, doll. We meet again. Still thin as a rake, I see.'

Amy came across the room. 'Val. You know we've been looking for you?'

289

'Having a wee holiday. You should try it. You're looking tired, hen.'

'Sweet of you to care, Val,' Amy said, and turned away. 'I won't keep you. I'm sure these two have plenty of questions for you.'

Clare led Val into an interview room.

'Milk, two sugars,' Val said, settling herself down to await their questions.

Clare closed the door on her and gave Sara the shopping to stick in the fridge.

'There's a message from Diane at Tech Support,' Sara said, walking towards the small kitchen. 'She's emailed the Stingray information you wanted.'

Clare followed her over. 'Thanks, Sara.' She watched Sara for a moment then said, 'You look a bit brighter today. Feeling any better?'

Sara's hand went to her stomach. 'A bit, thanks boss. Not so nauseous.'

'That's good.' Clare was about to ask Sara how her meeting with Elaine had gone when she was called to the phone. It was Wendy.

'Funny thing, Clare,' Wendy said. 'Lisa's boss has just been in to speak to Kevin.'

'Sacha? What did she want?'

'It's a bit odd. She said she needed to get into Lisa's lock-up.'

'What lock-up?'

'That's what Kevin said. He knew nothing about it. So Sacha said that Lisa had an old garage somewhere in town. Something about it belonging to a neighbour who didn't want it any more.'

'Where?'

'No idea. Kevin doesn't know either. Sacha said she'd taken a delivery of new sunbeds but hadn't the room to store them, so Lisa said she'd look after them. Brought a van round and took them to her lock-up. And now Sacha needs the sunbeds. She was asking Kevin if he had the keys.'

Clare remembered the key she'd found hanging on a hook in the shed. The key she'd left with Wendy.

'Wendy…'

'Don't worry. I've still got the key. I told Sacha you had it and that I'd try to get it back as soon as I could.'

'Does Sacha have any idea where the lock-up might be?'

'No, but I got the impression it was quite close by. She recalls Lisa saying it was only a few minutes away in the car.'

Clare looked round the room and her eyes fell on the officer who had taken Val's coat. 'Wendy, I'll send a couple of guys over for the key and get them to start checking lock-ups in the town.'

–

Val's solicitor arrived soon after, dressed in a sharp suit and calf-coloured brogues. His hair was a little too long and his chin sharp. He looked round the station without enthusiasm and insisted on speaking to the officer in charge. He introduced himself to Clare as Dermot Callaghan then demanded to know why his client had been brought to the station. Clare explained they were hunting a missing mother and baby, and investigating a murder.

'I'm sure your client will be happy to assist,' she added.

She left Dermot and Val to chat for a few minutes and went to check if Diane had emailed over the Stingray report on Paul Sinclair's phone. The email was there and she read it twice, trying to make sense of it.

'Chris,' she called. 'Have a look at this.'

Chris came and stood behind her, squinting at the screen. 'But that doesn't make any sense. We found Paul Sinclair in a skip in the north of Dundee. According to the PM report he was killed and dumped there on Monday night. What the hell is his phone doing pinging a mast at Birkhill on Wednesday?'

Clare moved to a map on the wall. 'Where is Birkhill exactly?'

Chris traced his finger along the map. 'Here. Just north of Dundee. At least fifteen miles away.'

'But isn't that...'

'Templeton Woods, yeah. Just at the back of Birkhill.'

'Where those lads crashed the Audi?'

'Exactly.'

There was a silence. Then Clare broke it. 'Has that car been moved yet?'

'Not sure. Probably not.'

'Good. Get on the phone to Vehicle Recovery. Tell them not to touch the Audi. Get SOCO up there. I want every inch of that car checked. If I'm right, someone has put Paul Sinclair's phone in Lisa Mitchell's car and I want to know why.'

–

Matt Fuller insisted on joining Clare for her interview with Val and her solicitor.

'I think I'd like Amy in the room as well,' Clare said.

But Amy was less keen. 'I think she'll clam up if I'm there. Too afraid of giving anything away. I'd say give it a go yourselves and if you can't make anything of it, let me know and I'll come in.'

'Any suggestions?' Clare asked.

'My guess is that Val's in a turf war with someone in Dundee, and Lisa's been caught in the middle. If Val was moving her drugs operation into Fife and particularly up near Dundee, she's probably stepped on someone's toes.'

'Who are we talking about here?'

'All right.' Amy pulled Clare to one side. 'This is not for anyone else's ears, particularly Val's.'

'Okay.'

'We've been trying for months now to get something on a Dundee guy called Ronnie Tennant.'

Tennant! That name again. Clare racked her brains, trying to think where she had heard it.

'He's as slippery as hell,' Amy was saying. 'If you go blundering in, we'll lose him and we really do need to take him off the streets. He's pushing a ton of Class A and not just in Dundee.'

'You seriously think Val won't know that?' Clare said.

'She might. She might not. But if you give the game away, she could put the word out and we'll lose Ronnie.'

Clare looked over Amy's shoulder. Matt was signalling that Val and her solicitor were ready.

'Just don't mention Ronnie,' Amy said, her hand on Clare's arm.

Clare waved to Matt to indicate she was coming. 'No promises,' she said to Amy as she walked away. 'There's too much at stake.'

Dermot Callaghan was sitting bolt upright in a chair, fiddling with a fountain pen while Val lounged back in her seat. He began speaking almost as soon as Clare and Matt entered the room. 'My client has come here voluntarily, officers, but is at a loss to know how she can help.'

Clare began recording the interview with the usual preamble. Val confirmed her name and address and agreed that she had attended voluntarily. Clare cautioned Val and the interview began.

'How do you know Lisa Mitchell?' Clare asked.

'Lisa Mitchell?' Val crinkled her brow, raising her eyes to the ceiling, as if searching her memory. 'No, doesn't ring a bell.'

'Ashley McCann?'

Val looked blank.

'Let me refresh your memory. Ashley and you were jointly charged with drug offences a little over five years ago. Ashley was convicted but you were not.'

'Oh, is that her name? I'd forgotten.'

Clare pushed a photo of Abigail across the table. 'You've heard, no doubt, about this baby girl being abducted?'

Val's expression didn't change. 'Aye. Terrible. Parents must be frantic.'

'Know anything about it?' Matt Fuller asked.

Val regarded him with interest, the hint of a smile on her lips. 'No. Nothing.'

Clare decided to change tack. 'You live in Edinburgh. Barnton, isn't it?'

'What if I do?'

'It's a nice area,' Clare said. 'Expensive.'

Dermot leaned across the table. 'I fail to see the relevance.'

'Mind if I ask how you manage to afford a house like that, Val?'

Val smirked. 'You got a husband, love?'

Clare didn't respond.

'Choose well,' Val advised her. 'I did.'

'Where's your husband now, Val?'

Val suppressed a smile. 'As I'm sure you know, Detective Inspector, he met with an accident. Tragic. But the insurance paid out.'

'So you're not funding your lifestyle with illegal activities?'

Val laughed. 'My *lifestyle*? I'm eating bacon rolls, love.'

Dermot began tapping his pen on the table. 'May I ask, Inspector, what my client's financial situation has to do with a missing baby?'

Clare looked at the solicitor. 'Lisa Mitchell, the baby's mother, is the sister of one of your client's associates. We think it's possible Lisa may have been involved in some illegal activities. We were hoping your client could help us with that.'

'As you are doubtless aware,' Dermot said, 'my client has had an unblemished record for many years now and, frankly, she is offended at the implication of criminal activity.'

'Oh, was I being too subtle?' Clare said, before Matt could stop her. 'I rather meant to accuse your client.'

Matt Fuller rose. 'Excuse us a moment, please.'

He jerked his head towards the door and Clare followed him.

Once they were out of the room, Matt turned on her. 'And just what do you expect to gain by flinging accusations about? We've got nothing here and they know it.'

Clare was prevented from replying by Sara. 'Boss, phone...'

'Excuse me, Matt. I have to take this.'

Clare grabbed the phone. 'DI Mackay.'

'Inspector, it's Robbie here. I picked up the key from Wendy and we've got the garage.'

'Brilliant. You're sure it's the one? There should be a couple of sunbeds.'

'Oh, they're here all right. And that's not all.'

–

When Clare and Matt returned to the room, Dermot Callaghan had put away his fountain pen and Val was sitting forward in her seat.

'I believe my client has answered your questions and that she cannot be of further assistance,' Dermot said. 'I therefore suggest you arrange for someone to return Mrs Docherty to her home without delay.'

'With the bacon,' Val added.

Clare and Matt sat down and Clare restarted the tape.

'Did you hear me, Inspector?'

Clare said, 'Yes, Mr Callaghan,' her voice smooth. 'There's just one more thing. About half an hour ago, two of my officers opened a lock-up garage about a mile from here with a key taken from the house of Lisa and Kevin Mitchell, the parents of the missing baby.'

Val folded her arms. 'So?'

'Inside the garage they found a large number of packages which they believe may contain illegal substances, contrary to Section 5 of the Misuse of Drugs Act. The contents of the packages will be tested but I have also instructed a forensic team to go over them to obtain DNA samples.' She looked at Dermot, her eyes narrow. 'The prior connection between your client and the garage owner's sister gives me grounds to suspect your client may be involved. I would therefore like to invite your client to give us a sample of her DNA.' She smiled at Val. 'So we can rule you out of our enquiries.'

'Fuck off,' Val said. 'I'll do no such thing.'

Dermot turned to Clare and Matt. 'You heard my client, officers. She does not consent.'

'Then we'll arrest your client,' Matt said. 'Simple as that.'

Dermot glanced at Val. 'If we might have a few moments…'

–

Chris was waiting for them in the front office. 'The CCTV footage from the pub…'

'What about it?' Clare asked.

'Some pretty good images of the jacket owner. The guy the lads stole the Audi keys from.'

'Good work, Chris. Make sure Danny points him out from the footage first. Check we're talking about the same bloke. Then get a couple of the Dundee lads to see if they recognise him. If not, take some stills over to the pub and get the bar staff to give us a name.'

'Will do.'

'Oh, and Chris…'

'Yeah?'

'Not a word to Danny about the phone being in the car. Keep him in the interview room until we have something from SOCO. If he gets arsey, arrest him for taking and driving away – it'll buy us some time.'

–

If Val's demeanour was unchanged, Clare found Dermot's body language more conciliatory when she and Matt re-entered the room.

'My client struggles with her memory at times,' he began, wringing his hands. 'She thinks it's possible she met Ashley's sister on occasion and, well, I don't have to tell you officers how easy it is for DNA to pass from one person's clothing to another.'

Clare looked at him, unsmiling. What a weasel he was. 'Are you saying, Mr Callaghan, that your client has been in contact with the packages found in Lisa Mitchell's lock-up garage?'

'Oh no, Inspector. Nothing like that. Rather, if she was in Mrs Mitchell's company, it's possible some clothing fibres or even DNA could have been passed between them. I'm sure you understand what I mean.' He glanced at Val then smiled back at the two DIs, his lips thin.

Clare understood him all right. It was quite clear Val had something to hide. The question was would she trade it for information on Lisa and Abi's whereabouts? She turned from Dermot to Val. 'Val, do you know where Lisa Mitchell is?'

Val shook her head.

'And Abigail Mitchell? Do you know anything about her disappearance?'

Val's eyes narrowed. 'I wouldn't harm a wee baby. That's not my style. If I'd had a problem with Lisa, I'd have smacked her. Simple as.'

Looking at Val, Clare could believe it. She felt Val was unbending a little. If only she could decide how to play it.

'Val,' she began, her tone softer, 'has Lisa ever worked for you?'

Val began smoothing an imaginary crease from her skirt. Clare waited.

'She might have done bits and pieces. Not for a while, mind. And I'm not saying it was anything illegal.'

'Of course not. But you might have met her a few times?'

Val shrugged. 'Maybe.'

Matt shifted in his seat. Clare hoped he wasn't about to blow it. She went on before he could interrupt.

'So, if Lisa was doing one or two jobs for you,' she said, 'could that have upset other folk?'

Val looked Clare in the eye. 'I could see that might happen.'

'A name, Val.'

Val shook her head.

Clare could feel the frustration rising but she bit it back. She was so close now. 'Val, there's a wee baby out there somewhere, a baby that needs heart medication twice a day. And now her mum's missing too. Kevin Mitchell is frantic with worry. Please try and find it in your heart to help us. We're running out of time. If Abigail Mitchell dies…'

Even through the heavy make-up, Clare could see Val's face becoming pink.

'You don't understand,' she said. 'There's rules about these things.'

'Try explaining that to a tiny baby,' Clare said, her tone harsh. 'To hell with your rules.'

'I think, Inspector,' Dermot began, but Val waved this away. She moved closer to Clare. So close that Clare could see the open pores and broken capillaries around her nose, where her panstick make-up had worn off. She could see Val's eyes, the whites yellowed by years of drinking, and she could smell her breath, sour from the stale odour of cigarettes. She didn't flinch but held Val's gaze.

'You get your name,' Val said, 'I get a clean bill of health.'

Clare looked at Matt.

'We can't do that,' Matt said. 'It's way above our pay grade.'

Val sat back in her seat. 'Take it or leave it.'

–

Tony wasn't keen. 'It's bending the rules, Clare. You're asking me to ignore the fact that those drugs packages might have Val's DNA. They could be Class A, for all we know. And there's no guarantee the name she drops will lead us to Abi.'

'For the love of Christ, Tony, is it not a chance worth taking? Four days, that baby's been gone. Four days!'

'It's just, I can't be seen—'

'Your promotion. Right. We can't do anything that'll stand in the way of you getting the Super's post, can we?'

'I'll take the risk,' Matt said.

Clare looked at him. Was this the same Matt who Tony had brought in over her head? The Matt she had assumed was firmly in Tony's pocket? She might have to revise her opinion of him.

'I won't put a baby's life at risk,' Matt said. He looked at Tony, his expression stony. 'Go out on enquiries. Get something in your diary, anything that shows you weren't here to ask. Clare and I will take the decision in your absence.'

Tony gave Matt a wink. 'I knew I was right to bring you in, Matthew.'

They left Tony. Clare couldn't resist slamming the office door. 'He's such an arse. A complete waste of space.'

'Never mind him,' Matt said. 'Let's get Val talking.'

–

'Ashley gave Lisa a phone,' Val began. 'Poor lassie needed someone she could talk to. Someone who knew she was involved in stuff, ye know. Stuff she couldn't talk to you lads about.'

'So the number she was calling,' Clare said. 'That was you?'

Val avoided their eyes. 'Yeah, that was me. She called a few times a day. At first, I told her to keep calm. I'd put some feelers out, see what folk were saying.'

'And then?'

'Then she got desperate. Can't blame her, really. Wanted to know who'd done it. Who was warning her off.'

'Had there been other warnings?'

'Aye. A couple of notes shoved through the door the week before the wee lass was taken. A car driven at her one day. But I never thought they'd go this far.'

Clare waited.

'So Tuesday night, she calls again.' Val frowned at the memory. 'She sounded different. Harder, like. Said if I didn't tell her who was behind Abi's abduction she'd drop me in it.'

'What time did she call?'

''Bout half-seven. *EastEnders* was just coming on.'

'Okay. Go on.'

'Like I say, she was in a state. Said if I didn't tell her who it was, she'd go to you lads. Tell you things about our *arrangement*.'

Matt leaned forward. 'And did you tell her? Did you know who'd taken Abi?'

'I'd a pretty good idea. But listen, if it ever gets out it was me—'

'It won't,' Clare said. 'We just need the name.'

Val ran her tongue round her lips, moistening them. She swallowed. 'Tennant. Dundee fella called Ronnie Tennant.'

Chapter 27

Chris caught Clare as she left the interview room. 'We have a name for our man in the pub.'

'Let me guess: Ronnie Tennant?'

Chris gaped. 'How the hell did you know that?'

'Because between you, me and Matt, who is incidentally not a prat after all, Val Docherty's come up trumps.'

Out of the corner of Clare's eye she saw Val and Dermot emerge from the interview room. 'Now for God's sake go and get her shopping and get rid of her.'

—

Clare decided to have Sacha arrested, based on the haul found in the lock-up she had been seeking access to. 'I want Bronzalite tanning salon searched for traces of drugs. Pound to a penny that's where Lisa was selling it.'

'Should we wait for a warrant?' Chris said. 'Don't want the search to be deemed illegal.'

'Ideally, yes, I'd wait. But I think it's reasonable to assume they'll get rid of any drugs kept there if they get wind of our investigations.'

'Fair enough. Want SOCO in?'

Definitely. 'I want that place turned upside down. See what they can find.'

'Maybe better send a couple of uniforms with the SOCO team,' Chris said. 'In case there's any trouble.'

'Good idea, Chris. Ask SOCO to call in here on their way to Bronzalite. I'll have two officers waiting.'

Matt had already sent cars to Ronnie Tennant's house in Bingham Terrace, so Clare and Chris headed to the Baxter Bothy with photos of Ronnie, Danny and Liam. 'It's not that I don't believe Danny's story,' she said to Chris. 'But I want to be absolutely sure about them lifting the keys from Ronnie's pocket.'

–

Jackie had the look of someone who'd been a barman all his life. His manner was charmless and his forearms brawny, doubtless from years of hefting beer barrels. He moved around the mahogany-lined bar wiping tables with a cloth that looked as if he might have used it to wipe the floor. In response to their questions he said he had been working on Wednesday and confirmed that Ronnie Tennant was a regular.

'Was he in on Wednesday?' Clare asked. 'About lunchtime?'

'Aye. Usually is.'

'Can you remember how he was dressed?'

'The usual. Jeans, white T-shirt – wife beater kind of thing.'

Chris asked, 'Anything else, Jackie? A coat maybe?'

Jackie stopped wiping tables and thought for a moment. 'Think it was a leather jacket. Aye, it was. I remember cos he hung it on a hook at the end of the bar. Normally he keeps it on him, or at least on a chair beside him. But that day he hung it up. Like he was saying to the rest of the pub, "Look at me. Look what I can afford".'

Clare produced the photos of Danny and Liam. 'Seen these lads before?'

Jackie glanced at the photos. 'Aye, I remember those two. Hanging about like a bad smell.'

'Did they buy drinks?'

Jackie shook his head. 'I said to the boss they were likely sizing the place up. Wouldn't surprise me if we were broken into that night. But it didn't happen. Pair o' wee chancers, though.'

Jackie started walking between the tables, slapping down beer mats. 'If there's nothing else, then...'

'Just one more thing,' Clare said. 'When did you last see Ronnie Tennant?'

Jackie stopped to think. 'Oddly enough, I don't think I've seen him since yesterday. He's not been in today.'

Clare handed him a card. 'If he does come in, would you phone me please?'

Jackie made no reply and they left him to his beer mats.

As soon as they got outside, Chris said, 'Reckon he'll call us?'

'Not a hope.'

Back in the car, Clare was about to start the engine then she stopped. 'What he said – about Ronnie hanging up his jacket...'

'What about it?'

'Strike you as odd?'

'Not really.'

'Is it the kind of pub where you'd leave an expensive leather jacket on a hook?'

'Good point. And remember what Jackie said,' Chris went on. 'Normally, Ronnie looks after his jacket, but on Wednesday he left it on a hook. Now if you had the keys to Lisa Mitchell's car – the mother of a missing baby – would you leave them in a jacket pocket for anyone to nick?'

'You're thinking he set those two lads up?'

'Them, or any other chancers hanging around. It just so happened these lads were in the pub. A guy like Ronnie Tennant – he probably has a nose for thieving wee scumbags. What better way to get rid of a car?'

Chris exhaled. 'Clever. He leaves the keys dangling and the lads do the job for him.'

'Exactly. And their DNA is all over the Audi. So what I'd like to know is why was Lisa's car found parked near the Tennants' house in the first place, and how did Ronnie Tennant get his hands on the keys? And,' she said, turning the key in the ignition, 'where the hell is Lisa?'

Clare and Chris drove the short distance from the Baxter Bothy to Bingham Terrace where they found the officers Matt had stationed outside.

'No one at home,' one of them said. 'At least, they're not answering the door.'

'Neighbours?' Clare asked.

'One lot on holiday. The other lot said Mrs T's away at her sister's. They saw Ronnie earlier in the week but not since.'

'Any idea where the sister stays?'

'No, she didn't know.'

'Okay,' Clare said. 'I want two of you here at all times. Check if there's a back way out.'

'Already done. Houses behind, so he'd have to go over a pretty high wall.'

'All right. We may need to set up surveillance, but just try to keep a low profile for now.'

Chris drove back down towards the Tay Road Bridge while Clare phoned ahead. 'Get me everything you can on Ronald and Margo Tennant,' she told Sara. 'Address Bingham Terrace in Dundee.'

'Sure, boss,' Sara said. 'Oh, by the way, boss?'

'Yeah?'

'Call for you. A Susan Clancy. Said she needed to speak to you. She said it was urgent.'

'Got a number?'

Sara reeled the number off and Clare jotted it down on her hand.

'Pull over, Chris,' she said. 'I've a call to make.'

Chris drew the car into the side, bumping it up onto the pavement, and Clare dialled.

Susan was brief and to the point. 'I need to talk to you. But not at the flat.'

'Okay, Susan. We're in Dundee just now. Do you want to come to the station in Bell Street?'

'No way. You know the Technology Park? Just off the Kingsway – near Invergowrie?'

Clare squinted at the map on the satnav, moving the joystick around until she found the Technology Park. It was to the north-west of the city, close to the A90 dual carriageway. 'Yeah, got it.'

'Meet me there in ten minutes.'

–

Susan was waiting in a bus shelter as Clare and Chris approached. She peered in the car to make sure it was them, then climbed in the back.

'Susan,' Clare said, turning in her seat. 'Something wrong?'

'You're an Inspector, right? Detective Inspector?'

Clare said that she was.

'So you can make things happen?'

Clare wondered where Susan was going with this. 'Well, it depends...'

'I want you to get me a house. Somewhere away from here. Fife, maybe. And I want you to help me get Paige back.'

Clare blinked. 'You don't want much, do you? What makes you think I can do these things? I'm hardly the person to judge if you should have your daughter back. I doubt the court would even listen to me.'

But Susan wasn't to be put off. 'I saw you,' she said. 'When I showed you the house. You knew I meant what I said about being a good mum to Paige. You saw how I was.'

'That's true,' Clare conceded. 'I was impressed with what you've done in your flat. For what it's worth, I hope you get her back.'

'I want you to help me get her.'

'Susan, I don't see—'

'Listen.' Susan checked the rear window of the car then looked back at Clare. 'I want you to help me because, if you do that for me, I'll give you Ronnie Tennant. On a plate. I'll give you enough to put him away for years.'

-

Clare and Chris were driving down the Marketgait in Dundee, heading for the Tay Road Bridge, when her phone rang again.

It was Matt. 'Clare, I'm heading over to Dundee. Better get yourself up to Templeton Woods.'

'The Audi?' Clare said.

'Afraid so.'

Clare and Chris pulled on overshoes and stepped gingerly past the cordon. The Audi was a sorry sight, the front crumpled where it had hit a tree. The airbags which had inflated on impact now hung limply around the interior and the windows were obscured by condensation.

A SOCO officer approached Clare with a sealed plastic bag containing a mobile phone. 'Found it in the sunglasses compartment.'

Clare took the phone and thanked him. 'Can I see, please?'

The SOCO officer led her over to the back of the car. 'No touching, though. We're still taking swabs.'

They peered into the boot. Despite the condition of the car, the interior lights still worked. Clare knew what it contained before she looked. The stench was unmistakeable. She bent over the curled-up, bloodied body of Lisa Mitchell. Suddenly she turned and ran, through the cordon and into the trees. With one hand on a branch to support herself, she retched and vomited until there was nothing left to come up. She could hear the sound she made cutting through the quiet country air and she wondered if they were all listening – laughing, maybe.

Only there was nothing funny about the sight of Lisa Mitchell's body.

She stood, head bent for a minute or two then, when she felt the heaving subside, she raised her head and took some deep breaths. She walked, numb, towards her car and took out a bottle of water. Leaning against the car for support, she swilled and spat away the sour taste. Then she drew a hand across her face and walked slowly back to the edge of the cordon where the SOCO officer and Chris stood watching her.

'Boss?' Chris said, worry written all over his face.

'I'm fine.' She glanced at the SOCO officer. 'Sorry. Just that smell.'

He shook his head. 'It never gets any easier.'

Clare sighed. 'We'll have to let the husband know. How long until you'll have her back at the mortuary?'

The SOCO checked his watch. 'Probably teatime. Say six to be sure. But you might want to wait until they've tidied her up a bit. She's not a pretty sight.'

'Cause of death?'

'You should know better than to ask, Inspector.'

'Yeah, I know, but...'

'Well, judging by the blood loss, I'd guess she's been stabbed. But we won't know until the PM's been carried out. I'll get the office to phone as soon as she's presentable though, so you can have her identified.'

Matt drew up as Clare and Chris were heading back to the car. 'Do we know who it is?'

Clare sighed. 'Lisa Mitchell, our missing baby's mother.'

'Shit. Any sign of the baby in the car?'

'Nope.'

'Well that's something,' Matt said. 'Until we find a body, there's hope.'

'Except that Abi was taken to send a warning to Lisa. If there's no Lisa to warn, they've nothing to gain by keeping Abi alive.'

Chris looked at his watch. 'What do you want to do now, Clare?'

Clare's lips tightened. 'I'll tell you what we're going to do, Chris. We're going to sort Susan Clancy out and nail that bastard Ronnie Tennant. I'll see him behind bars if it's the last thing I do.'

—

They drove back in silence. They were across the river and into Fife before Chris spoke.

'There's something I don't get.'

'Yeah?'

'Paul Sinclair's phone. What was it doing in Lisa Mitchell's car?'

Clare glanced at him. 'I've been wondering that myself.'

'I mean, Paul died on Monday night. Now we know Lisa wasn't involved. She's had somebody with her every minute until she disappeared on Tuesday.'

Clare signalled left at the Forgan roundabout and took the road for St Andrews. 'It's Ronnie Tennant. Has to be. He had her car keys according to our joyrider.'

Chris shook his head. 'I can't think straight on this one. I mean, I get why Ronnie might have killed Paul: either Paul got greedy or Ronnie got scared.'

'Yeah, that sounds feasible.'

'But the phone. Why did Ronnie not just smash it? Or chuck it in the river. Why keep it?'

Clare stopped the car at a set of temporary traffic lights which had been erected just outside Leuchars. 'Maybe it has information Ronnie wanted.'

'You mean drug customers?'

'Yeah, could be.'

A beep from behind alerted Clare to the lights, which had gone green. She raised her hand in apology and pulled away.

'Still doesn't explain why we found it in Lisa Mitchell's car,' she said.

Chris began drumming his fingers on the dashboard.

Clare glowered at him.

'Helps me think,' he said. 'Right. Let's assume Paul Sinclair and Lisa Mitchell were both killed by Ronnie.'

'But why, Chris? Why would Ronnie kill Lisa? Abi is his bargaining chip. Why kill her mother? If he wanted Lisa out of the way it would have been a hell of a lot easier just to kill *her*. If that *was* his plan, why take Abi?'

'Give me a minute. I'm thinking it through.' Chris was silent again. Then he said, 'Right, try this: Ronnie kills Paul on Monday night, okay?'

'Yeah…'

'Then, on Tuesday, after the press conference, Lisa Mitchell phones Val who tells her she thinks Ronnie is the kidnapper.'

'Okay.' Clare saw what he was thinking. 'So Lisa heads out after Ronnie. Turns up at his house near the park, maybe shouting loud enough for the neighbours to hear. Ronnie tries to shut her up and there's a struggle. Ronnie kills her. Maybe he means to, maybe not. Either way, she's dead. So he waits until it's dark, then bundles her into the boot of her own car.'

'Hell of a risk,' Chris said. 'It's a residential street.'

'Yeah, but if he waited until the early hours there wouldn't be anyone about. Remember, most of the residents go out to work. They'd have been in bed, asleep.'

'Fair enough. But why put Paul's phone in the car?'

It was starting to rain again. Clare switched on the windscreen wipers and winced as they squeaked rhythmically. 'We keep coming back to that phone. It doesn't make any sense.'

Then Chris slapped the dashboard. 'Got it.'

'Go on.'

'Our two joyriders. If we're right in thinking Ronnie set them up, leaving the car keys where he knew they'd be nicked…'

'He'd reckon on us picking them up, hopefully while they still had Paul's phone on them,' Clare finished. 'Their DNA would be in the car and their prints on the phone. With Lisa's body in the boot, we'd charge them with the lot.'

Chris gave a low whistle. 'He's a cunning bastard.'

Clare's lips tightened. 'He is. But we have Susan Clancy now. And I reckon if anyone's a match for Ronnie Tennant, it's her.'

—

Clare, Matt and Amy gathered in Clare's office.

'What's this?' Tony said. 'A mothers' meeting?'

'Time to earn that promotion, Tony,' Clare said.

'Okay.' He looked at the three of them. 'What's going on?'

Clare related her interview with Val Docherty. 'The man we're after is Ronnie Tennant. House in Bingham Terrace in Dundee. According to what Amy's told us, he's the main supplier of drugs in the city. And beyond.'

'We've been after him for months,' Amy said. 'He's bad news and he's getting more powerful every day. Drugs is only the half of it and we have a real chance of nailing him now.' She looked at Clare, who took the cue.

'I think Ronnie Tennant is behind the kidnapping of Abigail Mitchell and probably the murders of Paul Sinclair and now Lisa Mitchell.'

Tony swore under his breath. 'You've found her?'

'Afraid so. In the boot of her own car.'

'Told the husband?'

'Not yet. That's next. But, before I do, I need you to start calling in favours.'

'Explain.'

Clare began telling him about Susan Clancy. 'She blames Ronnie Tennant for her own drug problems, for losing her daughter. Anyway, she's clean now...'

'So she says.'

'I believe her. Says she'll take a drug test. And she's offered to hand Ronnie to us. She says she knows where he keeps the drugs, where they're sold, who works for him. Enough for us to put him away.'

'It's her word against his, though,' Tony said. 'An ex-addict versus what you say is a powerful local guy with no previous.'

'She says she has photos of him with known pushers and, crucially, at the places where he keeps his stock.'

Amy said, 'Tony, this is the closest we've come to nailing him. We can't pass this up.'

'Okay,' Tony agreed. 'Bring her in and take a statement. Once we see what she has to say for herself, we'll pick him up.'

'It's a bit more complicated than that,' Clare said. 'She has certain conditions.'

'Oh, does she, now? Like what?'

'If she gives us Ronnie and his network of contacts, she'll be finished in Dundee. We'll need to get her out of Alderwood. She won't be safe. She'll need a new address. Now, for all we know, Ronnie has contacts in the housing department. So it has to be a private let. As low-key as possible.'

Tony shook his head. 'Far easier to stick a couple of uniforms outside her flat until we've picked up Ronnie and whoever else we can nail.'

'Too risky,' Clare said. 'She's currently fighting to have her little girl returned to her. Says she's clean and, having seen her flat and all the work she's put into it, I believe her. She wants us to help get her daughter back. So she needs out of Alderwood.'

'No way Social Work will give her the kid back if she's at risk of reprisals.'

'I know that,' Clare said. 'But if she knows as much as she claims, we can move her to somewhere she'll be safe and put the whole lot of them behind bars. Then she can start a new life in Fife with her daughter.'

Tony frowned. 'And she won't testify otherwise?'

'Nope.'

He pressed his hands together, quiet for a few minutes. 'It's a hell of a risk.'

'Right now, we don't have much else to go on. We need Susan's testimony.'

He nodded slowly.

Clare played her trump card. 'And it'll boost your promotion chances to no end if you can put away the likes of Ronnie Tennant.'

He rested his chin on his hands.

They waited.

Finally, he said, 'I must need my head examined. Go on, then. Tell Susan Whatshername I'll find her a place to stay.'

'And you'll speak to Social Work about her daughter?'

'One thing at a time, Clare. Let's get her a new flat and take a statement.'

Outside the office, Amy said, 'I'll call in some extra bodies from the drug squad. Once we have names we'll start picking them up. It's best if we can do them all at the same time.'

Chris said, 'Want me to come with you to see Kevin?'

Clare sighed. 'Yeah. But first, I'd better tell Susan to get her stuff packed. She's moving out.'

—

Kevin was out in the shed, as usual. Wendy saw Clare's expression.

'It's bad news, isn't it?'

'Yep.'

'Not Abi?' Wendy's hand went to her face.

'No. Lisa. We found her body in the boot of her own car. Possibly stabbed. But we won't know for a few hours yet.'

Wendy looked down the garden at Kevin. He seemed lost in a world of his own. 'Poor lad. Want me to call him in?'

316

'Let's phone his GP first. See if he can call round.'

—

Kevin looked more gaunt than ever. His eyes seemed to have sunk into his skull, dark shadows beneath them. He'd been wearing the same T-shirt for the past three days now and hadn't shaved. He seemed to have given up and Clare knew that what she had to tell him might finish him altogether. She led him into the sitting room and he followed her mechanically.

'Kevin,' she began, trying to keep her voice level. 'About two hours ago, the body of a young woman matching Lisa's description was found to the north of Dundee. I can't give you any more information at this stage but we do believe it to be Lisa.'

He stared at Clare. His mouth opened but nothing came out. He frowned, as though trying to process this, then said, 'But it can't be. She's only just gone. She'll be coming back.' He looked from Clare to Chris then back at Clare again. 'She'll be back.'

Clare tried again. 'I'm so sorry, Kevin. This must be a dreadful shock for you. We will need you to identify the body.'

'Don't call her that!' he said, his eyes flashing. 'She's not a *body*. She's Lisa. My wife. Abi's mum. Don't you call her that.'

Wendy moved to sit next to Kevin but he shrugged her off. 'Get away! I'm okay. Just leave me alone.' He rose and made to leave the room but Chris stood and gently led him back to the sofa.

'Kevin,' Chris said, 'please listen. We're working hard to find out what's happened to Lisa and we will find whoever is responsible. But for now, you have to stay strong. For Abi.'

Kevin turned to Chris, his eyes red-rimmed. 'Stay strong? That's all I've done, these last few days. I'm so tired of being strong.'

The doorbell sounded and Wendy went to admit Kevin's GP.

Clare rose. 'Kevin, we have urgent enquiries to carry out now, but Wendy will stay with you, and we'll be back to speak to you again in a few hours.'

Outside, Chris said, 'It doesn't get any easier, does it?'

Clare shook her head. 'Nope. Come on. Let's get back.'

—

The mood around the station was sombre. They were all acutely aware that, if Lisa was dead, the chances of finding Abi safe and well were slim. Clare heard the whispers and she saw the eyes on her. The looks that said they thought she should change tack. Start to face the reality that Abi Mitchell wasn't going to be found alive. She bore it for a couple of minutes then called them into the incident room, her hands shoved deep into her pockets so they wouldn't see them shaking. This time, there was no need to wait for the chatter to subside.

'I am aware,' she began, making an effort to keep her voice level, 'that there is some talk of a triple murder enquiry within these walls.' She looked round the room, meeting every eye. 'I want to make it absolutely clear that, unless we find clear evidence to the contrary, we continue to treat the Abigail Mitchell case as an abduction.' She paused then repeated, 'An abduction.'

A few faces continued to watch Clare. Others stared at the floor, at the whiteboard – anywhere, rather than meet her eye. 'As far as I'm concerned,' Clare went on, 'Abi Mitchell is alive until we know otherwise.' She scanned the room again. 'Everyone clear?'

There was a general muttering of 'Yes boss' and Clare left the room. She moved to the water cooler and poured herself a cup which she drank down in one go. Sara was back at her desk now, visibly upset. Clare reckoned it would be better to keep her busy.

'Any news?' she asked.

Sara blew her nose and tucked the tissue up her sleeve. She reached for a folder of printouts. 'Ronnie and Margo Tennant.' She handed it to Clare. 'It's all there. Car registrations, jobs, houses, the lot.'

Clare looked at it. There was a lot to trawl through. 'Anything of note?'

'Only this,' Sara said, fishing out one of the sheets. 'Margo Tennant. Worked as an A&E nurse until five years ago. She was caught stealing tramadol and diazepam from the pharmacy. Claimed she was dealing with personal problems and wasn't prosecuted. But she lost her job over it.'

'Margo Tennant's a nurse?' Clare said.

'Yep. Or she used to be.'

'Right. Get the word out to all stations. Margo and Ronnie Tennant wanted in connection with the disappearance of Abigail Mitchell and the murders of Paul Sinclair and Lisa Mitchell.'

'Want it on the news, boss?' Sara asked.

'No, I want a news blackout.' She turned to see Lyall, who was listening to the conversation. 'Not one word of this is to leave this room, Lyall. Understood?'

He nodded vigorously. 'Of course, Inspector. And if I can help...'

'Actually, you can, Lyall. I asked the DCI earlier today to try and find a two-bedroomed flat for rent. Somewhere in Fife. But the DCI – well, he gets distracted sometimes. Would you mind seeing what you can find? Private lets only and not silly money, either. Reasonable rent.'

'Anything to help, Inspector.' And he went to find a spare computer.

Lyall dealt with, Clare turned back to Sara. 'Can you also get the registration numbers for the Tennants' vehicles out to other forces and to traffic control rooms? See if any of them have pinged ANPR cameras in the past couple of days.'

Clare began leafing through the printouts. 'Sara, any photos of the Tennants?'

'Yeah. I've printed a couple off the internet. Nothing official. They've been interviewed a few times but never been charged with any offences.'

Clare put the folder down on the desk and spread out the pages. She retrieved the photo of Ronnie Tennant – quite clearly the man from the pub CCTV. And then she looked at Margo. Margo, who had red hair. The same red hair as the woman who had taken the digoxin from the pharmacy. They had to find her.

'If I find you,' Clare said to the photo, 'I find Abi.'

–

It was Matt who reminded Clare they still had Danny in an interview room.

'Dammit, I forgot him.'

'We can't release him,' Amy said. 'If it gets out that we're after Ronnie Tennant, God knows what'll happen out there. You'd better keep him here for his own safety.'

'I'll arrest him then,' Clare said. 'At least we'll be able to keep him a bit longer.'

'What if we don't find Ronnie in the next twenty-four hours?' Chris asked.

'Frankly, Chris, I'd rather not think about that.'

–

It was almost five o'clock when Clare received the go-ahead to bring Kevin across to Dundee to identify Lisa. They entered the viewing room, Kevin hanging back.

Clare guided him gently forward, her hand on his shoulder. 'Take all the time you need, Kevin. Just tell us when you're ready.'

He looked at the glass panel in front of him, then back at Clare. 'Is this it? I can't see her properly.'

'I'm sorry, Kevin. It has to be this way.'

He turned back to the glass. After a moment or two he said, 'Okay.'

Clare signalled to the attendant who lifted back the cover. She was relieved to see Lisa's face, although unnaturally white and waxy, was unmarked. The trauma that had befallen her remained hidden beneath the sheet.

She let Kevin look then, after a minute, said, 'Kevin, is this your wife, Lisa Mitchell?'

Kevin's head went forward until it rested on the glass. Clare saw silent tears falling onto the floor below.

'Kevin?'

Kevin stepped back and raised his head. He wiped his eyes with his sleeve and nodded.

'You're quite sure?' Clare asked again. 'This is Lisa?'

'Yes.' His voice was a whisper. 'That's my Lisa.'

As they left the room, Kevin said, 'When can I see her? Properly, I mean?'

'I can't give you a time, Kevin, but I'll do my very best.'

'What's Abi going to do without her mum?'

Abi. Missing for over a hundred hours now. As they walked back to the car, Clare wished she shared Kevin's faith that Abi would be found alive and well.

Chapter 28

To Clare's astonishment, Tony had found a flat for Susan Clancy.

'It's a block near the harbour. Scheduled for demolition in the next couple of years so the agents aren't keen to move too many new folk in.'

'I'm impressed, Tony,' Clare said. Then she saw Lyall out of the corner of her eye. 'Tell me the truth – did you find it all by yourself?'

'Of course I did.'

'You're a dreadful liar, DCI McAvettie. You owe Lyall a drink.'

'Ach, it's kept him busy.'

'When can she move in?'

He jangled a set of keys. 'Any time she likes.'

Clare took the keys and went into one of the interview rooms, closing the door. She took out her own mobile phone and dialled a number.

'Clare,' Geoffrey said. 'Lovely to hear your voice. How's things?'

'Oh, you know. It's a pretty grim case, Geoff. I'm phoning to ask a favour, actually.'

'Go on.'

'Doing anything tonight?'

Geoffrey was waiting by a white Luton van in one of the Dundee University car parks when Clare and Chris arrived in Chris's car. It was almost eight o'clock and the sun had set, casting a rosy glow in the sky to the west.

'You know I'll probably get the sack if they find out I'm using a university van, don't you?'

Clare squeezed his arm. 'I appreciate it, Geoff. Oh, Geoffrey, Chris; Chris, Geoffrey.'

The two men exchanged smiles, then Geoffrey unlocked the van and they all piled in. 'Tell me again where we're going?'

Clare gave him directions to Alderwood and within ten minutes they were pulling into Susan Clancy's street. She was waiting at the window and stepped back when she knew they had seen her.

'You two stay here,' Clare said to Chris and Geoff. 'And switch the lights off. We don't want to attract attention.'

She climbed the stairs to Susan's flat and tapped on the door. Susan opened it and Clare could see the hall was full of bags.

'All set?' she said.

Susan nodded.

'Okay, I want you to stay inside and out of sight until the last minute. I've two men with me and they'll carry your stuff out to the van. If anyone asks what they're doing, they know what to say. Once the van's loaded, you can come out, hood up, head down, and we'll get you away from here.'

'Cheers, Inspector. I really appreciate it.' Susan looked round her flat and shook her head. 'I worked so hard on this, ye know. But what's the point if Paige is growing up surrounded by the likes of Ronnie Tennant?'

'You're doing the right thing,' Clare told her. 'Now you stay here and I'll send the boys up.'

Clare waited with the van while Chris and Geoffrey carried out Susan's bits and pieces. She didn't have much furniture, apart from the cot and a couple of bookcases, but there were at least half a dozen black bags and as many boxes. A couple of lads sauntered up. Clare pulled her beanie hat down as far as it would go. She leaned against the side of the van and folded her arms.

'Hey missus,' one of the lads called. 'You doing a moonlight flit?'

'Fuck off,' Clare said in what she hoped would pass for a Dundee accent.

'Only askin',' the lad said. 'Keep yer wig on.'

Chris and Geoffrey came out carrying boxes and the lads stopped to watch, grinning.

'Beat it,' Chris growled, and the lads laughed and carried on up the road.

The other one called back, 'Shuda paid the bills, missus!'

The shouting had attracted some attention and a few figures appeared at windows.

'Are you nearly done?' Clare asked. 'We need to get out of here.'

'Yeah. One more trip,' Chris said.

Minutes later, the van was loaded and Clare beckoned Susan out. She climbed up, squeezing alongside the others on the bench seat, and Geoffrey roared away.

'Cheers for this,' Susan said, and he smiled in response.

'Like your Dundee accent,' Chris said to Clare.

'Better than yours.'

'You're both rubbish,' Susan said. 'I'll teach you…'

–

At the university car park, Geoffrey stopped to let Chris pick up his car.

'Follow us across,' Clare said, and Chris gave her a thumbs-up.

They waited while Chris started the engine then they were on their way once more, driving down towards the Tay Road Bridge.

'What's the flat like?' Susan asked, and Clare said that she'd not seen it herself. Susan made no reply to this. Then, as they crossed the bridge and entered Fife, she said, 'It's good of you — doing all this.'

'As long as you keep your side of the bargain,' Clare said.

Geoffrey glanced sideways at Clare but she didn't respond.

The street was quiet when they pulled up outside Susan's new home. Geoffrey bumped the van onto the pavement and Chris drew up behind. Clare produced the keys and she led Susan inside. The flat was basic and in need of decoration but it was clean. There were faded velvet curtains in the sitting room window, and Susan moved quickly to draw them closed. She walked through the rooms, examining them with a studied eye, issuing instructions to Chris and Geoffrey as they carried in her belongings.

'Cot on that wall, please,' she said, as she put two black bin bags in the foot of an old wardrobe.

'The furniture's basic,' Clare said, 'but once you get on your feet you might be able to pick up a few bits and pieces of your own. There's a great second-hand furniture warehouse just out of town. I think they even deliver.'

Susan turned to face Clare. 'Inspector, I'd sleep on bare boards if I had to. You've no idea what it means to me to get away from that place.'

Clare reached into her trouser pocket and took out a twenty-pound note. 'For bread and milk.'

Susan stared at the note and seemed about to refuse.

'Take it,' Clare urged her. 'If it bothers you, pay me back when you're earning.'

Susan closed her hand around the note. 'Thanks, Inspector. Appreciate it.'

'And now we'll leave you to sort things out. Sleep well, and I'll send someone across to pick you up tomorrow. But wait until you hear from me. Meantime, if anyone knocks on the door, don't answer it.' She looked at Susan intently. 'We need that statement.'

–

Outside, Chris said good night and reversed his car back down the narrow street. Clare watched him go then smiled at Geoffrey. 'Want to stay over at Daisy Cottage?'

He shook his head. 'I'd better get this van back tonight and you need to get to bed.'

'Of course. Geoff, thanks so much. I know it was an awful lot to ask.'

He put his arms round her and pulled her in. 'You've a good heart, Clare Mackay. That's why I love you.'

She held him to her and whispered, 'And I love you too, Geoffrey Dark. Very much.'

'Come on,' he said. 'I'll take you home and you can make me a cup of tea before I head back.'

Clare climbed back up into the van, empty now of Susan's possessions, and slammed the door. Geoffrey backed the van out of the street, more carefully than Chris had, and pulled away into the night.

Friday, 27 September

Chapter 29

Clare arrived on Friday morning hopeful there might have been some news overnight.

Jim had already spoken to the night shift. 'Nothing much, Clare, except that Ronnie Tennant's BMW pinged a camera heading over the bridge to Fife.'

'Ronnie's in Fife?'

'Looks like it. There's been nothing since he crossed the bridge so either he's taken the back roads, or he's in the area.'

Clare's thoughts went immediately to Susan Clancy. She took out her phone and sent a quick text.

> All ok?
> Will send a car in the next hour.
> Clare

Susan replied saying she was fine and would be ready for the car. Clare breathed a sigh of relief. There was no way Ronnie Tennant could know where Susan had moved to. Unless Lyall...

The door opened and the man himself entered.

'Lyall, a word, please.'

Lyall frowned. 'Have I done something wrong, Inspector?'

Clare took Lyall into an interview room. 'Sit.'

He did as he was told.

She studied his face. He seemed uneasy and shifted in his seat.

'Lyall, I trusted you with a job yesterday. To look for a flat. You remember?'

'Yes, I remember. Was the one I found not suitable? The DCI thought it was fine.'

'And it was. But Lyall, what I need to know is this: did you tell anyone about the flat? Anyone at home or any of your journalist friends?'

Lyall shook his head. 'Certainly not. Inspector, I have a privileged position here. I wouldn't dream of abusing it.'

Clare regarded him. 'I hope not. If any harm comes to the tenant of that flat because you let slip where she's living…'

Lyall looked close to tears now.

Clare relented. 'Okay, Lyall. Sorry, but I had to ask. Go and grab yourself a coffee.'

Clare sat in the interview room, thinking. She was as sure as she could be that Lyall was telling the truth. She honestly couldn't see him in the pocket of someone like Ronnie Tennant. So what was Ronnie doing in Fife? Was he going after Val? Or even Kevin? She moved to the door and motioned Jim to come into the room.

'Jim, I don't want a fuss about this, but I'd like a couple of lads each on Val Docherty's flat in Newport and Kevin Mitchell's house.' She reached for a scrap of paper and scribbled down Susan Clancy's new address. 'And I'd like two undercover cops watching this property round the clock. Anything remotely suspicious, I want to know immediately.'

Jim's eyes widened. 'Something up, Clare?'

'Ronnie Tennant, Jim. That's what.'

Chris appeared.

'Don't take off your jacket,' Clare told him. 'We're going to pick up Susan Clancy. I want her statement done and dusted.'

–

Clare sent Susan another text telling her she was on her way and not to come out of her flat until she saw Clare's car outside. Five minutes later, she was safely stowed in the back of the car, heading back to the station. When they arrived, Amy was there and Clare invited her to sit in on Susan's interview.

Clare went through the usual preamble and the interview began. She had asked Sara to assemble a set of photos of men around Ronnie's age to mix in with Ronnie's own photo.

Susan picked him out easily.

'That's him,' she said. 'Know him anywhere.'

She also picked out Margo from a selection of middle-aged women with red hair.

Clare asked her how she knew Ronnie.

'Everyone knows him. Everyone in Alderwood, anyway. Hangs about the pubs and shops. He owns a few houses there. Some folk had bought their council flats and run up huge debts with Ronnie. Borrowed money and couldn't afford the interest. So he took the houses. Signed over, all legal and that.'

'Does he collect the money personally?'

Susan shook her head. 'He has lads to do that for him. The one who took the baby, I saw him on the news. Paul Sinclair. He was one of Ronnie's boys. One of the many.'

'Give me names.' Clare wrote steadily as Susan reeled off the names of people who worked for Ronnie. And then she asked, 'Is Ronnie involved in any other illegal activities?'

'Yeah. Drugs. He brings them in and his lads sell them across the town.'

'Do you know where he keeps them?' Clare asked.

Susan nodded. 'In the flats he owns. Has the tenants scared shitless. If the police come round, it's their names on the lease and they're the ones who'll go to jail. He has a couple of shops too. The managers don't even know where he's stashed the drugs. But if the police search the place, it's the managers who'll take the rap for it.'

Amy leaned forward. 'Susan, how do you know all this?'

'I pay attention,' she said. 'I worked in one of Ronnie's pubs for a while. Ronnie and Margo – they don't allow staff to drink while they're working and I have sharp ears. Punters come in and they drink. They drink and they start to talk. And mostly it doesn't matter 'cause they're all drinking and talking. They forget about me. I'm invisible. I like it that way. But I hear stuff. And I remember it.'

Clare hesitated, wondering how to phrase her next question. 'Susan, I need to ask you about your daughter.'

Susan wouldn't meet Clare's eye. She began to fiddle with the cuff of her sweatshirt. 'Yeah?'

'Can you tell us why Paige was taken into care?'

Susan swallowed then cleared her throat. 'That was Ronnie.' Her voice was hoarse. 'Can I...?'

'Would you like a drink of water?'

'Please.'

Amy rose, returning a minute later with a plastic cup of water.

Susan took it and drank. Then she set the cup down and continued: 'It was when I was working in one of Ronnie's pubs. We had a lock-in one night. After hours. Used to happen quite often. Anyway, the drink was flowing and then Ronnie passed round some pills. Everyone else was taking them so I thought why not.' She raised her eyes and looked from Clare to Amy. 'If you've never done it, you can't imagine what it's like. The first time especially. Fucking brilliant. And so the next night he passed them out again. But after that he said I had to pay. Said he'd make it easy for me. He'd give me the pills and stop it out of my wages.' Susan lifted the cup and drank again. 'And then it became a habit. Pills, coke and eventually heroin. Then Ronnie – he said he didn't want me working there any more. So I went on benefits and he took that too. There was no money for Paige. The health visitor was calling, but I wouldn't let her in. Eventually, when they took her – well, I was past caring, wasn't I? I just wanted the drugs. She was better off without me.'

Clare looked at Susan. Her face was devoid of emotion. She had told this dreadful tale without shedding a tear. Was that what it did to you? Being controlled by a man like Ronnie Tennant?

'Are you still taking drugs, Susan?'

Susan shook her head. 'Nope. Clean six months now. No way would I go back to that life.' She moistened her lips. 'He tried, you know, Ronnie. Came round. Said he missed seeing me. Left me a little pack of pills. Goodwill gesture, he said.'

Clare felt the anger rising within her. Dealers like Ronnie, trading in human misery. She clenched her fists under the table.

Amy asked, 'What did you do with the pills, Susan?'

Susan looked her straight in the eye. 'I put them on the bookcase. Next to the telly. Two whole days I kept them. Wanted to see if I could do it, you see. I knew there was no point in me trying to get Paige back if I started on the drugs again. So I left them there, looking at them. I even picked them up. Put one to my mouth. And I could so easily have swallowed it. I'd have taken one and it would have been brilliant again. Like the first time. And I'd have been right back where Ronnie Tennant wanted me.'

She reached for the water again and drained the cup this time.

'After two days, I knew I'd never go back,' she said. 'So I flushed them down the loo. They were gone, and I was free. That afternoon I went out and bought paint for Paige's room.'

Clare put down her pen. She marvelled at the strength Susan had shown. Would she have been as strong in Susan's shoes? She wasn't sure.

She pushed back her chair and stood. 'Susan, I think we'll take a break. I'll get you a cup of tea.'

Susan nodded and sat back. Clare noticed Susan's hands were shaking and she left her to compose herself.

–

Jim was at the front desk.

'Any sign of Ronnie's car?' Clare asked.

Jim shook his head. 'Nothing yet. Tony's called in extra cars from all over Fife. They're combing the area now.'

'Good. I'll ask him to put descriptions and photos out to the media. If Susan's statement stacks up, we should have enough to nail Ronnie Tennant.'

Amy appeared at Clare's side with a cup of tea. 'Here you go.'

Clare took the cup with a nod of thanks.

'Clare…'

'Yes?'

'I'd like to get the ball rolling on what Susan's told us. Start searching those shops and houses.'

'Can it wait until we have Ronnie safely in custody?'

Amy frowned. 'It's tricky. If the word goes out that he's been picked up, evidence might end up down the toilet. Susan's info is great, as far as it goes, but it's only her word against his. We need the actual stuff to secure a conviction.'

'Don't forget the Moorov Doctrine,' Clare said.

Amy stared. 'The what?'

'Moorov v HM Advocate – 1930s, I think. If you have a series of offences, each with no corroborating witnesses, the similarity in character, circumstances and so on can mean they corroborate each other.'

Amy looked impressed. 'So if we have two or more tenants willing to stand up in court to say Ronnie stashes drugs in their homes, they corroborate each other? Even though they're different offences, witnessed by different people?'

'That's about the size of it.'

'How the hell did you know that, Clare?'

'Used to live with a solicitor,' Clare said. 'But that's another story.'

'The searches, though, Clare,' Amy said. 'I'd like to get cracking.'

Clare sipped her tea, weighing this. 'Okay. Go for it. But run it past Tony first, yeah?'

–

The station door opened. Clare looked up and her heart sank. Nicholas Stewart from the protest camp. When he saw Clare, he smiled. Much as Clare wanted to avoid him, she knew now that he was a friend of Geoffrey's.

'Mr Stewart. How can we help?'

'Ah, Inspector.' He took her hand and shook it warmly. 'It was so good to catch up with Geoff the other day. Such a talent.'

Clare wondered how she could get rid of him without seeming rude. She simply didn't have time for a protracted chat about Geoffrey's merits as a sculptor. 'Actually, Mr Stewart, you have caught us at a busy time...'

'Ah yes. That poor child. I heard on the news her mother was found dead. Such a dreadful thing. Indeed, that's why I've come.'

'Really?'

'Well, of course it may be nothing. But Zelda – you may not remember her but she's one of the ladies from the protest. She paints, you know. Anyway, I suppose you've heard we're vacating the field?'

Clare was surprised. 'I hadn't heard.'

'A court order, I'm afraid,' Nicholas said. 'We are a non-violent group so it's time to give it up.' He sighed then said, 'Hopefully we have made our point. The battle is lost, for now, but the fight goes on.'

Clare's eye went to her office door. She really needed to speak to Tony before Amy and her colleagues swung into action. She looked round for Sara. Maybe she could palm Nicholas Stewart off on her.

'…she pays to park it up for the winter, you see,' he was saying. 'And so she took it to her usual site. But she was later this year, what with the protest, you know.'

'Mr Stewart—'

'Oh, please, Inspector. It's so important.'

Clare sighed. 'Go on then. But I do have someone waiting for me.'

'Then I'll try to be succinct,' he said. 'Zelda takes her campervan every year to a site just outside Leuchars. She pays a nominal rent and leaves it there for the winter. Normally it's closed to occupants at this time of year but when she parked the van, she realised one of the other vans was still occupied. Zelda thought it was odd because the site doesn't have a view or anything like that. And certainly no toilets or showers. It's just a large piece of ground. She went and knocked on the door to say hello, but no one answered. She was sure they were in, but she thought maybe they didn't want to be disturbed. And then she heard it.'

'Heard what, Mr Stewart?'

'A baby. She heard a baby crying. Of course it's probably all quite innocent but—'

'Where is this site?' Clare said.

He fished in his pocket and withdrew a piece of paper. 'I've written down the address and directions. It's a bit off the beaten track.'

'Don't go anywhere.' Clare moved to the front desk where Sara was bent over some paperwork. 'Sara, can you get me that list of vehicles owned by the Tennants? Now. Run them through the computer and let me know if there's a campervan among them.'

Sara looked at Clare. 'You've not found them, have you?'

'Now, please, Sara,' Clare said. 'Not a minute to waste.'

While Sara checked the vehicles Clare went to speak to Tony. 'We may have found them. Sara's checking a vehicle registration for me now. If it turns out to be a campervan, I'll need every officer and vehicle you can lay your hands on.'

'Boss...' Sara pushed open the door. 'Got a match. Two-year-old Elddis motorhome.'

Chapter 30

Susan heard the commotion and came to the interview room door.

'I'm sorry, Susan,' Clare said, pulling on her jacket. 'We need to go out now.'

'Should I come back later?'

'No. Stay put. I want you here where you're safe.'

'Safe? You found them?'

'Just stay here. Please.' Clare waved Sara over. 'Sara, please stay here with Susan. I want to continue her interview in the afternoon but for now she's better off here.'

Lyall rose, but Clare waved him away. 'No, Lyall. This could be risky.'

'Oh, but...' he began, then he saw Clare's face.

'The three of you – stay here!' Clare said.

Tony spread an Ordnance Survey map out on a desk in the incident room. 'Where's this campsite?'

Clare peered at the map. 'It's not an actual campsite. Just a place to park up over the winter, so our protest man said.' She followed the directions Nicholas Stewart had written down and came to a large area at the end of a track. 'Here, I think.'

'Do we need to take your eco-warrior with us?' Tony asked.

Chris squinted at the map. 'It's okay, I know it. Dealers use it. I've tailed a few down that track.'

'Okay, then,' Tony said. 'Is there another way in?'

Chris jabbed the map with his finger. 'There's a sort of track here, leads to Tentsmuir Forest. If we block that off, we'll prevent them making a run for it.'

'I'd like aerial support on standby,' Clare said. 'If they give us the slip it'll mean we don't lose them.'

'Want the 'copter out now?' Tony asked.

Clare considered this. 'Can you get it to the old airbase at Leuchars? That shouldn't attract attention – it's still used for exercises. It'll be no more than a minute from the campervan park if we need it.'

They piled into cars and headed off towards Leuchars. As they approached the village, Matt and Amy drove on through Leuchars towards St Michael's Crossroads. Clare had told them to turn right at the crossroads towards Tayport, and follow signs for Tentsmuir. She was glad not to be driving that way herself, recalling a standoff at Mortaine Castle, just off that road, where she had come face-to-face with a gunman. Chris drove on through the narrow, winding streets in Leuchars village until the rows of old RAF houses gave onto fields. The landscape was flat at this point, with only Tentsmuir Forest between the fields and the River Eden.

Clare surveyed the forest up ahead. 'There's not much cover.'

'The camp's behind those trees,' Chris said, indicating the start of the forest. 'They'll only see us if they have someone on the lookout. And even if they do, Matt and Amy will have the other road covered.'

The radio crackled, then they heard Matt's voice saying they had left the main road and were now on the single-track road towards the campsite.

'Park the cars broadside so they can't make a run for it,' Clare said.

'Right-o.'

'Radio again when you're in position. Then we approach the van at the same time, from both sides.'

'Dammit,' Matt said. 'Farmer shifting a field of cows up the road. Going to be held up for a few minutes.'

Clare indicated to Chris to pull in and the cars behind her did likewise. 'Let us know when you're on your way again.'

They sat for a good five minutes, waiting to hear back from Matt. The road, being a dead end, was quiet with just the queue of police cars parked on the verge, waiting for the go-ahead. Clare glanced in the rear-view mirror and saw another car approaching, about half a mile back.

'Who the hell is this?' she said, but before she could check, Matt radioed to say they were moving again. Clare peered in the mirror but didn't recognise the car. It was hard to see at a distance but it was maybe a silver Nissan. She tried to remember if she knew anyone who drove one. She hoped fervently that it wasn't one of Ronnie Tennant's cars. She didn't want him with an exit route. Chris pulled away and the cars behind her followed suit. She craned her neck again to look behind, but the silver Nissan was too far away to see the occupants.

The track opened out onto a clearing with some trees ahead. 'It's just behind those trees,' Chris said.

Clare radioed that they were in position and Matt replied that they too were in place.

'All right, let's go.'

Clare, Chris and a dozen uniformed officers emerged from their cars and walked steadily towards the trees. To the left she could see Matt, Amy and their group heading in from the other end. She felt sick with nerves at what they might find in that campervan. What if it was the wrong van? Thirty officers, a helicopter on standby, all on a hunch of Zelda's. Who the hell was Zelda anyway?

She could see the van now, through the trees. There were a few other vans parked up, mostly with covers across the windscreens. But one had no cover. No lights on, but the lack of condensation on the windscreen gave Clare hope that it was occupied. She checked the number plate. It matched the one Sara found registered to Ronnie. Matt and Amy had officers lined up, forming a barrier across their track; Clare's group did likewise. She turned to check them and saw to her horror that the occupants of the silver Nissan were Lyall and Susan, and that Sara was speeding up behind them in a police car.

'What the hell...'

But Chris was already advancing on the van.

Clare glared at Susan and Lyall, waving them back, then followed Chris to the door of the van. Her heart was beating out of her chest now, her mouth as dry as a bone.

Chris rapped on the door of the van and they moved away, standing one on either side of it.

No answer.

He knocked again while a couple of uniforms circled the van, climbing up on the wheels to see in the windows.

Chris shook his head. 'Looks like no one's home.'

Clare turned to one of the officers who was carrying a crowbar. 'Open it.'

The officer moved forward and forced the crowbar between the door and the side panel. It gave with an ear-splitting creak and swung open. Clare was up the steps, eyes everywhere. She moved into the driver's cab while Chris checked the back.

'There's a baby here, all right,' he said, indicating a half-empty pack of nappies.

Clare was opening cupboards, checking under seats and was about to climb up into the roof space over the front seats when Chris spoke again.

'Clare...'

'Yeah?'

'This...'

She looked and saw that Chris had pulled on a pair of forensic gloves and that he now held a bottle in his hand. It was labelled *digoxin*.

A shout from outside alerted them and they jumped down the steps. A black BMW stood at the end of the track where it met the road. Vapour was coming out of the exhaust pipe and the passenger door hung open. A red-haired woman was running past the empty police cars towards the BMW, a bundle in her arms.

Clare's heart lurched.

Abi.

The woman was easily forty or fifty yards ahead and moving fast. The officers were in pursuit, some running for their cars, but it looked as if the woman would reach the BMW before they did.

'Stop her!' Clare's voice was strangled. But the woman was almost at the car.

The BMW revved and a cloud of smoke came out of the exhaust.

The figure came from nowhere.

'You bastard!'

Susan Clancy raced towards the woman.

And then another figure moving. In uniform this time. Sara.

Clare's instincts kicked in and she sprinted back up the track. Susan was gaining on the woman. The BMW revved its engine. Sara was gaining on Susan and Clare knew she had to stop them. And then the woman – Margo Tennant, surely – turned to face Susan. She held the bundle against her left shoulder.

Clare saw a flash of steel in Margo's right hand. Sara saw it too and she leapt on Susan, bringing her down, just short of Margo. But not short enough. Susan lay on the ground, only winded, but there was no mistaking the dark stain spreading from Sara's uniform.

Clare looked on in horror but she saw that Margo had turned back and was almost at the car. Shouting to Chris to tend to Sara, she sprinted as though her life depended on it. Her lungs were screaming for air, but she ran on. Margo was tiring but Clare knew she had only seconds to reach her. Amy was on her heels now and the pair leapt simultaneously for Margo. Clare went for her waist, yelling, 'The baby, Amy. Get the baby.'

The knife was still in Margo's hand, but Clare kicked her behind the knees; Margo buckled. Amy dashed the knife from her hand with a well-aimed fist and grabbed the bundle. Abi screamed and screamed and Clare's spirits rose.

She was alive. Abi was alive.

Margo struggled under Clare's knee, her wrists restrained. There was a roar and a screeching of tyres and the BMW sped away.

'Radio, Tony,' Clare yelled. 'We need the 'copter. Black BMW heading west. And get two ambulances here. Fast! Tell them, one adult with a lower abdominal stab wound and a baby with a heart condition.' She looked back at Margo, still face down on the ground. 'Margo Tennant, I am arresting you on suspicion of child abduction and attempted murder. You do not have to say anything but...'

Chris was bent over Sara, weeping. Matt pulled him off and ripped open Sara's clothes to reveal the wound. He pressed both hands down to stem the bleeding. 'Stay with me, Sara. Do you hear me? Stay with me.'

Having cautioned Margo and handed her over to a couple of officers, Clare bent beside Matt and talked to Sara.

'Sorry, boss,' Sara whispered.

'Shush,' Clare said. 'Don't try and talk. Just stay calm and breathe. The ambulance is on its way.'

'It's my fault,' Susan said, her face ashen. 'I made that journalist take me. She was in the loo – I heard her being sick – so I took my chance. I had to make sure you got them.'

Matt's hands were white with pressing down on Sara. Clare took over. She tried frantically to think of things to say, to keep Sara awake.

'We've got Abi,' she said. 'Can you hear her crying?'

Sara closed her eyes.

'Sara! Stay awake,' Clare said. 'Come on, you've got to stay awake now.'

A siren, distant at first, was coming nearer.

'Hear that?' Clare said. 'The ambulance is on its way. Soon have you sorted out.'

The radio crackled and Matt clicked to take the message.

'It's a result,' he said to Sara. 'They stopped the BMW. Ronnie Tennant made a run for it across a field, but they've got him.'

Sara's eyes fluttered.

'Good news, isn't it, Sara?' Clare said.

The siren came closer and Matt stood to wave the ambulance over. Within seconds the paramedics were at Sara's side, ripping open gel dressings which they applied to the wound. Clare stood back to let them do their work and found her legs were suddenly weak. She leaned against a fence post then saw Chris, his face creased with worry.

'Go with her,' she said, as the paramedics transferred Sara to a stretcher. 'I'll follow on when we've cleared up here.'

Chris gazed at her, seemingly incapable of speech. Having transferred Sara to the ambulance, one of the men helped Chris up the steps and put a blanket round his shoulders.

The second ambulance arrived and baby Abigail Mitchell, screaming at the top of her lungs, was handed over to a paramedic.

Clare took out her phone. Her hands were still damp, stained with Sara's blood. She wiped them on her trousers and dialled Wendy's number.

'We've found Abi,' she said when Wendy answered. 'Safe and sound. She's on her way to Ninewells A&E. Can you take Kevin over and I'll meet you there?' She heard the sound of Wendy running down the garden, calling to Kevin, and allowed herself a smile.

Clare's next call was to forensics. 'I've a campervan for you to go over for prints, DNA and possibly drugs. Can you ask your team to come over here as soon as they've finished at Bronzalite? I'll leave a couple of guys on-site until you get here.'

The cars were starting to leave now. Amy had bagged and tagged the knife and the Tennants were now both in custody. Sara and Abi were on their way to hospital and Clare suddenly didn't know what to do.

Matt came over. 'You okay?'

She nodded, not trusting herself to speak.

He gripped her arm. 'You got her. Abi. You got her, Clare.'

And suddenly, Clare burst into tears.

Chapter 31

Clare arrived at Ninewells and made her way to the A&E Department, flashing her badge to gain admittance to the main treatment area. She had seldom seen it busier as nurses walked briskly in and out of curtained bays, wheeling machines and calling to doctors. A trolley bearing an elderly man was wheeled past her and into a vacant bay, the curtains quickly pulled around him. At the nurses' station a male nurse was scrawling names on a whiteboard next to bay numbers. And, in the midst of all this activity, sat Chris, his hands wrapped round a mug of tea. His eyes were red-rimmed and his cheeks streaked with tears.

'How is she?' Clare asked, but Chris just shook his head.

'She's still in theatre,' a nurse said. 'We won't know until she comes out. But the surgeon didn't think her wound was life-threatening.'

Clare lowered her voice. 'Did you know she's pregnant?'

The nurse nodded. 'Chris told us. As I said, we'll know more when they've finished operating.'

Clare left Chris under the Charge Nurse's beady eye and went in search of Kevin and Wendy. The receptionist told her Abi had been taken to a paediatric admissions ward to be checked over and she gave Clare directions.

Wendy met her as she approached the ward. 'I'm heading off now, Clare,' she said. 'There's a duty cop down at either end of the corridor so I'm going home to catch up on my sleep.'

Clare gave her arm a squeeze. 'Wendy, you've been incredible. I can't thank you enough.'

'Just doing my job, Clare.' And with that, she headed down the corridor. Clare watched her go then pushed open the swing doors that led to the ward. In contrast to the busy A&E department, the paediatric ward was an oasis of calm. Instead of beds there were clear-sided incubators and cots, each surrounded by machines and monitors. Kevin was sitting at the side of a cot, his finger stroking Abi's hair. Clare stood and took her first proper look at Abigail Mitchell and found she was absolutely beautiful. She was lying gazing up at the ceiling, her legs kicking for all she was worth. She was hooked up to a heart monitor and a nurse was on the other side of the cot, writing on a chart.

'How is she?' Clare asked.

A smile spread across Kevin's face. It was the first time Clare had seen him look anything other than haunted. 'Doing well,' he said. 'They're keeping her in for a couple of days, just to get her medication regulated. But they say she's been well cared for. Suppose that's something.' He glanced at the nurse and lowered his voice. 'But Lisa… I can't take it in. Was she really selling drugs?'

'I'm afraid it looks that way,' said Clare. 'Did you never wonder, Kevin? You never suspected anything?'

He shook his head. 'Lisa always handled the money. She was better at it than me. She said the tanning salon was doing really well. She said Sacha was expanding. I didn't really think about it, the money. I just believed her.' He met Clare's eye. 'I've been such a fool. I knew nothing, Inspector, honestly.'

Clare patted his arm. 'I know that, Kevin.'

'And that's why they took Abi? And killed Lisa?'

The nurse moved away and Clare sat down. 'We may never know, Kevin. But from what we can see, it looks as if Lisa was caught in a turf war between two drug dealers. Abi was taken as a warning and when Lisa realised why she was taken, she went after them herself.'

'And – do you think they'd have given Abi back? If you hadn't found her?'

Clare nodded. 'Probably. My guess is they wanted to teach Lisa a lesson. At some point, Abi would have been left somewhere in a hospital. Here at Ninewells, probably. They'd have dumped her in a toilet or something like that and, once they were a few miles away, they'd have called the hospital to let them know. And Lisa – well, she'd have been so glad to have Abi back that she probably would have backed off.'

Kevin put his head in his hands. 'I still can't believe it. My Lisa, a drug dealer. It's – it's horrible.'

'I know. It's a lot to take in. But what's important at the moment is you and Abi. That's all you need to worry about for now.'

Kevin gazed down at Abi. 'I'll never let her out of my sight again. Never.'

Clare rose from her seat and patted his hand. 'I'll leave you now, Kevin. But Wendy and I will stay in touch. Meanwhile, you give Abi a hug from me.'

Downstairs, Clare found Chris waiting for her. 'She's out of theatre and the doctors say she'll be fine,' he said, his voice cracking. 'The knife missed her vital organs. Her intestines took most of the damage but nothing they couldn't patch up. She's sedated now but they say I can see her in an hour or so. She'll be in a few days but she's going to be fine, Clare.' He looked at her, his eyes bright with tears. 'And I thought...'

Clare gripped his arm. 'Don't go there, Chris. She's fine and that's the main thing.' She didn't know how to ask the next question. Chris saved her the trouble.

'They couldn't save the baby, Clare. The shock – the blood loss – it was all too much.' The tears began to flow again and he drew a hand across his eyes. 'It's funny, you know. I was pretty gutted when Sara told me – about the baby, I mean – and I've got to be honest, I questioned whether – well, you know.'

'Yeah. I know.'

Chris glanced at her, his face pink. 'And then, well, I sort of got used to the idea. And now it's too late, isn't it?' He shook his head again. 'It's like a punishment. For not wanting it, I mean.'

'Don't you dare say that!' Clare said. 'Margo Tennant tried to murder Susan Clancy and Sara was brave enough to stop it, putting her own life at risk. She's a real hero and whatever happened is Margo's fault. No one else's.'

'I suppose. The doctor did say there's no reason Sara can't try again...'

'Does she know?'

He looked away. 'No.' His voice was barely audible. 'I'll have to tell her once she's able to take it in, you know?'

'One step at a time, Chris,' Clare said. 'Come on, I'll buy you a coffee. Then maybe they'll let you in to see her.'

—

Lyall was sitting on a chair near the door, waiting for Clare when she finally returned to the station. He stood up as she entered. 'Inspector, how is the officer?'

Clare smiled. 'She's going to be fine, Lyall. They've operated to repair the damage caused by the knife. She'll be pretty sore for a few days and off work for weeks, but she will recover.'

He shook his head. 'I don't know what to say. I'm so sorry. I really am.'

Clare looked at him. He was near to tears. 'Lyall, you're not to blame. People like Susan Clancy – well, they can be very persuasive.'

Lyall flushed. 'She said she'd knock my fucking teeth out if I didn't take her in my car. I wasn't sure if she meant it, but she gripped my arm so tightly and pulled me out the door.'

Clare laughed at the picture Lyall painted. She could just imagine Susan terrifying him into taking her to the campsite. 'Listen, Lyall, if it hadn't been Sara it could have been any of my other officers. Margo Tennant and her kind have no scruples. Thankfully Sara will recover and Margo is under arrest.'

Lyall attempted a smile. 'Thank you, Inspector. I'll get out of your way. It's my last day here anyway. I think it's better if I just go.'

Clare's conscience began to prick her. 'Lyall, there's no rush. If you want to carry on writing up your findings, we've plenty of room now that the reinforcements are heading back to their own stations.'

His face lit up. 'Well, if you're sure, Inspector?'

'Very sure. And call me Clare. Everyone else does.'

—

Tony was in a bullish mood. 'That's what I call a result, Inspector. I knew you'd thank me for bringing in Amy and Matt.'

'A result? One of my officers almost died.'

'Yeah, but she didn't.'

'No, she didn't.'

He grinned. 'And we have the culprits under lock and key so it's a result!'

Clare decided there was little point in arguing. 'Have Amy and Matt gone?'

'Matt's away. Said he'd give you a call later on. Amy's taken a team to go through Ronnie Tennant's shops and flats. See if the occupants will talk, now that he's banged up. She seems to think she can stop Ronnie's associates taking over his dealing. And there's that stash found in Lisa Mitchell's lock-up. That's a whole load of gear off the streets.' He stood and looked out of the window. 'Oh yes, I think that'll go down nicely with the interview panel.' He turned back and grinned at Clare. 'Say hello to Superintendent McAvettie.'

Clare left him clearing his things out of her office. In the incident room the local cops were disconnecting laptops and collapsing desks to return to storage. The blinds were open and the room was bathed in autumn sunshine. She decided to leave them to it and went back out to the main office. Jim was behind the desk and she realised she hadn't asked about his wife for a few days. 'Fancy a cuppa, Jim?'

'Why not? I'm parched.'

They sat together, the first time Clare had sat down in what seemed like days. 'And how's Mary doing?'

'Oh, not so bad,' Jim said. 'She's hit a bit of a plateau now, mobility wise, but her speech is coming on. Sometimes I see her getting frustrated and the wrong word comes out, but she is improving, albeit slowly.'

'Jim, you'll never know how grateful I was that you came into work this week. You should really have been at home with Mary.'

Jim waved this away. 'It's nothing.'

'I can't imagine how I'd have managed without you here to keep things ticking over.' She lowered her voice. 'And keeping young Lyall occupied.'

Jim laughed. 'He's a good lad, really. A lot better than some of the press I've come across over the years. I just hope he doesn't write a warts-and-all exposé of his time here.'

'Frankly, Jim,' Clare said, 'I'm past caring. Let him do his worst!'

The front door opened and half a dozen reporters entered, clamouring for news.

'Inspector, is it true the baby's been found? Have you made an arrest? Was one of your officers injured?'

Clare glanced across at Lyall, tapping away at his computer. Then she walked over to the reporters. 'Ladies and gentlemen, if you would give me half an hour or so, my associate here will prepare a statement for you.'

Lyall beamed back. 'I'd be delighted... Clare.' He smiled at the reporters. 'Half an hour.'

'You've just made the lad's day,' Jim whispered.

Clare laughed.

Her phone rang. Chris. Suddenly, she felt nervous. Had Sara taken a turn for the worse?

'Clare,' he said. 'She's awake. They've propped her up in bed and she's high on morphine. She's blethering all sorts of nonsense. Says as soon as she gets out of bed she's gonna smack Margo Tennant right in the mouth.'

Clare laughed. 'Oh Chris, that's the best news I've heard all day. Thanks for telling me.'

'There is one thing, though, Clare,' Chris said, his tone more serious. 'Liam Paton...'

'The hit-and-run driver?'

'Yeah, that's him. The nurse just told me. They've called the family. The doctor's asking for permission to switch off his life support.'

Clare sighed. 'What a waste, Chris.'

'Yeah. Thought you'd want to know.'

Clare put down the phone and thought about Danny and Liam. Stupid, stupid boys. Liam's young life over; and now Danny would be up in court without his friend at his side. And all because Ronnie Tennant dangled the keys to an expensive car so someone else would take the rap for Lisa's murder. She rose and went to wash out her mug. It would give her enormous pleasure to charge the Tennants with murder, to say nothing of Abi's abduction. 'I'm going to throw the book at them,' she said to herself. She looked at the clock. Almost half-past four. She was tired out. As soon as she had checked the statement Lyall was drafting she would head back to Daisy Cottage. An early homecoming for Benjy. She'd put on her boots and take him for a tramp over the fields. It seemed ages since she'd spent any time with him.

And then, suddenly, it was all done. Lyall had delivered his statement proudly from the station steps, handing out copies to a bemused press pack. He bade them all farewell and told Clare to watch out for his article.

'Can you remind me again of that Chief Inspector's name?' he asked Clare, his pencil at the ready. 'Was it Tommy something?'

'That's right,' she said, unable to resist the chance to check Tony's overinflated ego. 'Tommy McVitie. Like the biscuits.'

He beamed at her. 'Ah yes, I remember now. Well, thank you, Clare.' He held out his hand. 'It's been quite a week. I'm so grateful for this opportunity.'

Clare watched him go with something approaching regret. He had been so willing to help. She thought she might actually miss having him around. She watched him drive off then, calling good night, walked out to her own car. But instead of driving straight home, she headed towards the town centre. There was something she had to do.

Twenty minutes later, Clare pulled up outside a small semi-detached house in a quiet street, near Hallow Hill in the south-west part of St Andrews. She took her purchase out of the car and walked up the short path to the front door.

Marjory Brown was surprised to see Clare. 'Inspector, how lovely to see you. Is there something wrong?'

Clare smiled. 'No, nothing wrong. I just wanted to give you this, for Devon, to say thanks for his assistance. He was so helpful and I remembered he liked pizza.'

She held out a pizza box and Marjory took it.

'Oh, how kind, Inspector. Won't you come in?'

'I won't, thank you,' Clare said. 'I'm just on my way home.'

Devon appeared at his mother's shoulder and peered round the door.

'I've brought you a pizza, Devon,' Clare said.

He frowned. 'Mushrooms?'

'No mushrooms.'

Devon's face lit up. 'I like pizza.'

'Me too, Devon. Me too.'

–

At Daisy Cottage, Clare stepped out of the car and, reaching into the back, brought out a second pizza box. She could hear an excited Benjy barking from inside and she put her key in the door. Instantly, she felt the heat. Stopping only to ruffle Benjy on the neck and to put the pizza box out of his reach, she walked through the house in amazement, feeling radiators and walking – yes, walking – on floorboards that had been missing for what seemed like weeks. A scribbled note from the plumber said he was finished, that it had been a real bastard of a job and he was sorry it had taken so long. Clare stood, leaning against a radiator, toasty warm, the freezing mornings and draughts from the missing floorboards all forgotten. She kicked off her shoes and padded through to the kitchen, Benjy at her heels. She opened the back door and he scampered out to the garden to pee.

While he was outside, Clare loaded a tray with a bottle of Chianti, a corkscrew and a large glass. She tipped the pizza (no mushrooms) onto a plate then opened the door to let Benjy back in.

She pulled over a coffee table and laid down the tray. Then she sat on the sofa and put her feet up. Benjy leapt up beside her and settled himself on her feet, watching hopefully as she ate pizza and sipped wine.

When she had eaten her fill, she set the tray down and picked up her phone. She dialled Geoffrey's number.

'Hello, you,' he said. 'How's work?'

'Very much improved,' she told him.

'I heard the baby's been found. All well?'

'The baby's fine. One of my officers is in hospital but we have the culprits under lock and key so I'm home with my feet up. And…'

'And?'

'I have heat!'

'No! Seriously? Well it's about bloody time.'

They chatted on companionably. For the first time since Sunday, Clare felt relaxed; the way she'd felt when they had been in France. Now that Abi was found, they would surely have more time together. Things would soon be back to normal. She stretched out on the sofa, tickling Benjy under the chin with her toes.

'I was thinking,' she said. 'Why don't you ask Nicola and Ollie here for dinner one night?'

'Really?'

'Yes, I'd love to have them over. Not the other pair, mind you. Just the two of them. Now that this case is mostly tied up.'

'Great. I'll call her and fix a date. Actually, Clare, there was something I wanted to ask you. Something I think you'll like. I'll come and see you tonight.'

All at once, Clare's stomach felt full of butterflies. Something he wanted to ask her. She rose from the sofa and carried her tray through to the kitchen, tidying away the pizza box and putting her plate and glass in the sink.

Something he wanted to ask her. Something he thought she would like.

And then she remembered Jude. Her sister who she had promised to phone. It felt like weeks ago, although it had only been a couple of days. She sank back down on the sofa and dialled.

'Jude,' she said when her sister answered. 'I'm so sorry I've not been in touch. Work's been shitty.'

Clare's sister sounded better than she had earlier in the week. 'Oh Clare, it must have been awful. I followed it on the news. I'm so glad the baby's all right, but that poor man. How will he cope?'

They chatted on for a few minutes, Clare trying to steer the conversation away from work. Finally, when her sister drew breath, Clare said, 'Jude, how are things? I mean, James…'

There was a sigh at the other end. 'I don't know. I really don't. I mean, nothing's changed. James is still as sweet as ever. Still doing all the things he should be, only now I'm watching him like a hawk. Trying to work out if he's – well, different. It's horrible, really. I seem to have lost the joy.'

Clare let her talk. Let her work through what she thought about James.

'The good news is that he's been referred to a specialist. We should have the appointment in a couple of weeks. So at least we'll get a proper diagnosis.'

The conversation ended with a loud wailing at the other end.

'I have to go,' Jude said. 'He's bumped his head.'

'Jude, I thought I might come through on Sunday.'

'Clare, that would be lovely. Oh, James! Your poor head. Clare, look, I'd better go. Speak soon. Love to Geoff.'

–

Clare sat back, the phone still in her hand, wondering. If James was autistic, what did that mean for his future? For all of them? She'd have to try and make more time for them. Let the job take a back seat and lift some of the load from Jude's shoulders. She looked round the room. Having the heating working made all the difference. It was starting to feel like home. Maybe she could have James to stay for a few days. Give Jude a break.

She rose from the sofa and began tidying the sitting room. It would be lovely for Geoff to come into a warm and inviting house, instead of the freezing barn it had been of late. Maybe she could cook something. But she was full of pizza now and dog-tired. She really couldn't be bothered. She went upstairs to her bedroom and sat at the dressing table. Possibly the first time she had done so without shivering. She clicked the switch above the mirror and peered at her face. The events of the past few days were clearly etched onto it, and she opened her make-up bag to try and make herself look presentable. Then she picked up a brush and pulled it through her hair. She wondered idly if she ought to grow it longer, maybe have a few highlights put in. She had more than a few silver hairs now, peppering the dark. Any more cases like Abi Mitchell and she'd be white-haired.

The doorbell rang. She switched off the lamp and ran downstairs to meet Geoffrey.

He entered, marvelling at the heat and the absence of holes in the floor. Then he took her in his arms and held her close. 'I'm so glad that case is over for you.'

Clare led him into the kitchen where she retrieved the Chianti and fresh glasses. 'Still a fair bit to do.' She poured the wine and handed him a glass. 'The couple we arrested are unlikely to plead guilty so we've a case to build, but it's looking hopeful. And we did catch them red-handed with the baby.'

Clare chattered on as Geoffrey sipped his wine. She knew she was talking too much but she was suddenly nervous. Then she found her courage.

'There was something you wanted to ask?' she said, taking another slug of wine to calm her nerves. She scanned him, his jacket. Was there a ring box concealed in there? Ridiculous, she thought. It was far too early in their relationship but, after Tom's visit, maybe love was in the air. It really did seem as if he was going to ask her…

His face lit up. 'I've been offered the most marvellous opportunity,' he said. 'It's a guest lecturing role in Boston. For a year, initially, possibly extending up to five. It depends partly on funding and partly on me. Have you been? It's the most wonderful city.'

'Boston?' Clare didn't know what else to say.

He took her hand in his. 'Clare, I wondered how would you feel about coming with me? The college I'll be working at has an International Law Department. You could maybe do some teaching? Choose your own topics. The Scottish Criminal System, that sort of thing. I'm sure I could swing it. Oh Clare, just think about it. What fun we'd have.'

Her mouth was dry and her cheeks felt hot. He wasn't asking her to marry him at all. He wanted her to give up her job, her cottage, to move three thousand miles away. She would be leaving Jude and James. Chris and Sara. Jim and his wife Mary, struggling with multiple problems since her stroke.

And to do what?

'I don't know how to teach,' she managed to say. 'I wouldn't know where to start.'

He laughed. 'It's easy. Honestly. I bet you do it every day at the police station. Training youngsters. You just don't know you're doing it.'

'But lesson plans and exams and things. Geoff, I haven't a clue.' A bark from the floor reminded her. 'And there's Benjy. What would happen to him?'

He laughed again. 'Clare, all these things can be managed. They're just trivial problems. If you really want to go, we'll make it happen. It's such a great opportunity. I mean, do you want to be stuck here for the rest of your life?'

His words stung. Stuck here? What did that mean? Clare loved St Andrews and she loved her job. She loved her sister, her nephew James and she loved her little dog Benjy so dearly. She had thought, too, that she loved Geoffrey. But now she was wondering if she even knew him at all. How could he have planned all this and Clare not even realise?

She stared him. He was smiling. Confident and relaxed. He was so sure of everything. So completely at ease with himself. Was there any room in his life for *her* plans? Or was she simply an adjunct to his?

'I thought…' she began, then stopped herself. She was embarrassed now. Mortified. How could she have thought he was going to ask her to marry him?

'What did you think?'

She shook her head. 'Doesn't matter.'

'What is it?'

'Geoff,' she said, 'I don't know. I'm – I'm not sure I can come.'

He blinked. 'Really? I mean, what's to keep you here?'

Clare looked at him for a minute. Then she said, 'If you don't know that, Geoff, I doubt I could explain it.'

And she rose from her seat, planted a kiss on his forehead and carried her wine glass into the kitchen.

Acknowledgments

I'm so grateful to the many friends who have kindly shared their knowledge and experience, in particular Ray Banks, Richard Renwick, Alan Rankin and my good friend Isabel. Any errors in the narrative are entirely mine.

As usual my family act patiently as sounding boards for ideas and plots, and they bear my endless questions with equanimity. To Iain, Stuart, Kenneth, Ally, Euan, Alicia and Peter, my grateful thanks – stand by for book three!

In Plain Sight is a work of fiction and, as such, I have taken some liberties with beautiful St Andrews and the surrounding area. Priory Marsh, McIntosh Water and NEFEW exist only in my head and, of course, in Clare's world. Similarly, I have created a version of Police Scotland its officers may not entirely recognise, but I hope they will balance this against DI Clare Mackay's excellent clear-up rate.

Finally, to my wonderful agent Hannah Weatherill of Northbank Talent Management and to my incredible editor at Canelo, Louise Cullen: I am so grateful to you both for your help and support, which both sustains and inspires me.

About the Author

A native of Dundee, Marion studied music with the Open University and worked for many years as a piano teacher and jobbing accompanist. A spell as a hotel lounge pianist provided rich fodder for her writing and she began experimenting with a variety of genres. Early success saw her winning first prize in the *Family Circle Magazine* short story for children national competition and she followed this up by writing short stories and articles for her local newspaper.

Life (and children) intervened and, for a few years, Marion's writing was put on hold. During this time, she worked as a college lecturer, plantswoman and candle-maker. But, as a keen reader of crime fiction, the lure of the genre was strong, and she began writing her debut crime novel. Now a full-time writer, Marion lives in North-east Fife, overlooking the River Tay. She can often be found working out plots for her novels while tussling with her jungle-like garden and walking her daughter's unruly but lovable dog.

Detective Clare Mackay

See Them Run
In Plain Sight
Lies to Tell